The Prodigal Sun is the first book in The Evergence Trilogy, which has become a phenomenon in science-fiction circles attracting widespread acclaim as well as bestseller status through ... This ... the author being commissioned to write a new trilogy of Star Wars novels in the New Jedi Order series.

THE AUTHORS

Sean Williams has written more than 50 short stories, two of these prize-winning and many nominated for awards. Metal Fatigue, his first full-length novel, won the Aurealis award for the best science-fiction novel and The Resurrected Man won the Ditmar Award, as did one of his anthologies. Aged just 33, he was honoured with the year 2000 Grand Award for Literature in his home state of South Australia.

Shane Dix has been writing since he was fifteen, mainly science-fiction. His story, Through the Water That Binds, won the 1991 Canberra SF Society's short story competition. It also featured in the Aphelion landmark science-fiction anthology, After Shocks. In addition to science-fiction, he has written masquerade stories, poetry and articles about the role of science-fiction in film and television. He is currently working with Sean Williams on a new science-fiction project.

EVERGENCE I
THE PRODIGAL SUN

Also by Sean Williams and Shane Dix

EVERGENCE II: THE DYING LIGHT
EVERGENCE III: THE DARK IMBALANCE

Also by Sean Williams and published by Swift

METAL FATIGUE

EVERGENCE I

THE PRODIGAL SUN

SEAN WILLIAMS & SHANE DIX

Published by Swift

An imprint of FPR-Books Ltd

First published in the UK 2001

1 3 5 7 9 8 6 4 2

Copyright © Sean Williams & Shane Dix 1999

The rights of Sean Williams and Shane Dix to be identified as the
authors of this work have been asserted by them in accordance with
the Copyright, Designs and Patents Act 1988

A catalogue record for this book is available from the British Library

ISBN 1–874082–34–0

Typeset at The Spartan Press Ltd,
Lymington, Hants
Printed in Great Britain by Omnia Books Ltd. Glasgow

Swift Publishers
PO Box 1436, Sheffield S17 3XP
e-mail: enquiries@fprbooks.com

For Peter McNamara, Patrick McNamara, Andrew Stunnell, Peter Stunnell and everyone involved in the Cogal project, without whom this book would not have been possible.

Violence can only be concealed by a lie, and the lie can only be maintained by violence. Any man who has once proclaimed violence as his method is inevitably forced to take the lie as his principle.

Alexander Solzhenitsyn

Darkness is looking back and saying: 'I have been deluded from the start; it has all been a mistake'.

Hubert van Zeller

Prologue

The pillow-shaped capsule tumbled end over end through the gulf between stars. Every point of its four-meter length showed evidence of age: its matte-grey surface was pitted from microimpacts; the molecules of its ablative shield were scarred by radiation; gravity waves from distant black holes spiraling inevitably to collision had warped it from true. Had it been noticed by any passing ship, it would have been ignored as flotsam, for after millennia of exploration and trade such drifting junk was common in the galaxy. It wouldn't even have been worth the effort required to destroy it.

Had it been noticed . . .

Junk it may have appeared to be, but it was far from that. A detailed analysis of the skin of the capsule would have revealed that nothing—not even radiation—penetrated deeper than five centimeters. It had retained its structural integrity despite the forces tugging at it. And, had its density been measured, the fact that it was hollow would have become immediately obvious.

As it tumbled through the void, sensors within monitored the frequency and intensity of incident radiation. It emitted nothing, yet analyzed in minute detail everything that fell upon it. Data was collated and processed. Three-dimensional maps were drawn, on which the course of the capsule—past and future—was plotted. Options were considered.

The capsule had passed through numerous governments and territories during its long journey: from the Giel, remote and aloof in the Perseus Arm, to the Bright Suzerains tucked hot and hardy close to the galactic core. There was hardly a solar system in the Milky Way that had not been colonized or explored at least once by the Human race in all its forms. The descendants of the apes who had once reached in wonder for the night sky now owned the stars. They were the sole heirs of a galaxy ripe for the taking.

Decisions were made.

Patient exploitation of the local magnetic field brought the capsule to the boundary between two nations: one an unwieldy alliance that had outlived its usefulness and was already dissolving under the weight of administration and ennui; the other a small but heated theocracy bursting like a boil from its parent's side. Stray emissions—some almost certainly decades out of date—carried reports of occasional conflict, harried officials, rising tension. . . . The capsule didn't care much for the details, just as long as there was friction, an ambient heat it could exploit. Who fought whom was irrelevant. There was only one Right and Wrong it cared to recall, for it was this duality the capsule existed to serve.

It was a seed looking for soil in which to germinate. A seed that had come a long way and waited a long, long time to bear fruit. A seed whose interior became increasingly active the more certain it was that the end of its journey was near. . . .

PART ONE:

MIDNIGHT

1

Morgan Roche was trapped, and she knew it. Trapped by orders, by circumstance, by the bracelet around her left wrist, and by the stare of the wide-shouldered, middle-aged man standing in front of the main viewscreen of the frigate *Midnight*.

"We have discussed this before," he said, frowning down at her from his elevated position. The captain's podium normally remained flush to the floor except during battle, but Proctor Klose preferred it at its full one-meter extension. Surrounded by the half-light of the bridge, with its flashing displays and blank-faced officers, he reminded Roche of a half-finished statue—so full of self-importance that, had she not been so frustrated, she would have found him laughable. "Has anything changed since then, Commander?"

"No, sir," she replied. "All I ask is that you reconsider your decision."

Klose shook his head. "Call me inflexible, if you like, but I see no reason to entertain the whims of my passengers."

"It's more than a *whim*, Captain," she snapped.

"No, Commander," said Klose, the ghost of a grin hovering at the corners of his mouth. "It is not. What you request is clearly outside your jurisdiction."

"Not necessarily." Her free hand betrayed the half-lie by adjusting the tight-fitting neck of her uniform, making her look nervous. When she realized what she was doing, she returned the hand to her side. The cord connecting the bracelet to the valise brushed against her leg as she straightened her posture, but she had learned long ago to ignore it.

"Without access to the relevant information," she said, "I am unable to determine where my jurisdiction lies in this matter. Perhaps if you would explain your reason for denying me access to the capsule, then I might understand."

Klose's frown deepened. "I am not required to explain anything to you, Commander. Need I remind you who is the commanding officer of this vessel?"

"No, sir." Roche gritted her teeth on an angry retort.

"Then I think that concludes our discussion." He turned to face the viewscreen.

Roche remained where she was, unwilling to let the matter rest—although she knew that technically he was in the right. But there was more than the life capsule and its contents at stake. There was a *principle*.

"Captain . . ."

Klose sighed. "Yes, Commander?"

"Forgive me for saying this, but your manner seems to indicate a resentment of my presence aboard this ship. I hope you have not allowed your feelings to cloud your judgment."

Klose faced her once again, his narrowed eyes displaying an indignation that told Roche her remark had hit home.

The captain of the *Midnight* outranked Roche, but *her* superior officer—and, therefore, her mission—outranked *his*. In the course of their voyage, the unassuming valise she carried had become a focus for every slight, real or imagined. That she carried it because of the cord and bracelet ensuring its permanent attachment to her person, rather than out of any real choice, he seemed to have forgotten. Orders were orders, and she had less choice than he did, if only in the short term. But the basic fact, the one the captain detested, remained: Klose was just a donkey for the courier on his back.

The situation might never have become a problem had it not been for the length of time available for circumstance to rub shoulders with resentment. In six weeks, the gentle but constant friction had generated enough heat to spark flame. The matter of the capsule and its mysterious occupant, although trivial in itself, was the catalyst of a much more significant reaction.

"On the contrary," replied the captain, responding to her comment with frosty politeness. "It is not I who has allowed emotions to interfere. Frankly, Commander, I would say that your curiosity has gotten the better of you."

"I'm an active field agent for COE Intelligence," she retorted. "It comes with the job."

"Nevertheless." Klose folded his arms. "The most intelligent thing for you to do right now is let the matter rest."

"With respect, sir—"

"Commander, the simple fact of the matter is that I am not permitted to allow you to place yourself in a situation that is potentially dangerous."

"I'm quite capable of looking after myself."

"I don't doubt that, Commander. But I think you underestimate the risk—"

"How can I underestimate him if I know nothing *about* him?"

"'Him'? You seem to have learned too much as it is."

She ignored this. "If you would simply let me view the science officer's report—"

"Which is classified."

"My security rating is as high as yours, Captain." It was higher, in fact, but she didn't press the fact. "At least give me the opportunity to use my position as I have been trained to do."

Klose sighed in resignation. "Very well, then. I will consider letting you view the report, but only after we have arrived at Sciacca's World and off-loaded our cargo. In the meantime, your mission—and mine—is best served by you returning to your quarters and remaining there."

"But—"

"Shields detecting microimpacts." The voice came from somewhere behind Roche, but Klose didn't take his eyes from hers to acknowledge it. "Captain, we are brushing the halo."

"Please, Commander," he said evenly, gesturing at the exit from the bridge. "Or will I have to have you removed?"

Roche fumed silently to herself. Klose's promises to "consider" or "review" the situation had proven worthless before, and she doubted that this time would be any different. But she had to admit that he did have a point. The *Midnight* was about to insert itself into orbit around one of the most hazardous destinations in the Commonwealth of Empires; he and his crew needed to concentrate on their work without distraction.

Refusing to concede defeat by speaking, she turned away from Klose and moved toward the exit. The door slid aside with a grind of metal on metal, but instead of stepping through, Roche stopped on the threshold and turned to watch the goings-on of the bridge. It was both a show of strength and a demonstration of her independence.

The main screen displayed an image of Sciacca's World. The grey-brown orb floated in the center of the screen, with the ring of densely packed moonlets that girdled the planet's equator glistening in the light from the system's primary. The occasional explosion flaring from some of the larger rocks made the miniature asteroid belt look deceptively attractive from the *Midnight*'s distance. Roche knew how dangerous it could be. Some of the moonlets were over ten kilometers in diameter; one slip near something that size would rip the *Midnight* in two.

Apart from the belt, what really struck her about the view was something that might have been lost on the average deep-space tourist. Few people outside military service would have noted the absence of orbital towers girding the planet; if they had, it was doubtful they would have understood the significance of the fact. To Roche, the planet appeared uninhabited, with nothing but a handful of navigation stations in orbit and the pocket asteroid belt to keep it company—like a reef holding all but the most determined at bay; a shoal around a desert island.

<They call it the Soul—not the *shoal*,> said a voice deep in her skull, intruding upon her subvocal thoughts. <The origins of the name are clouded, but one recurring folk myth from the planet's inhabitants asserts that the band of light—as the asteroid belt appears to those living on the planet—is composed of the souls of people who have died in captivity. The myth of transubstantiation from the mortal to the sublime is common to many repressed societies—but the image is still evocative, don't you think, Morgan?>

The voice fell silent. No one else on the bridge had heard it speak.

"You can go to hell too," Roche whispered, and walked out.

The Retriever Class Frigate *Midnight*, one of the few ships to survive the Ataman and Secession Wars, had been built around the 43rd-generation anchor drive common in the years '212 to '286 EN. Shaped like a fat sausage, with a shaft containing the drive mechanism running along its axis, she had five levels of concentric decking to house a 450-odd crew, two freight-locks and enough storage space to hold five independent fighters. Artificial gravity, produced as an aftereffect of the drive, had resulted in a sense of down being inward rather than outward as was the case on centrifugal ships. This feature also gave her a degree of maneuverability far superior than that of other ships of her day—which was one reason she endured both Ataman Wars relatively unscathed.

The centuries since, however, had left her behind, despite numerous remods and even complete refits in dry dock. Her drive systems had been replaced in '755 EN, upgrading her to 46th generation and full battle status. Her most recent overhaul had been after service as a supply vessel during the Secession War. In '837 EN, only weeks after the Terms of Revocation had been agreed between the Commonwealth of Empires and the newly independent Dato Bloc, she had received new viewscreens and E-shields but little in the way of either fundamental or cosmetic changes.

To Roche's eyes, as she left the bridge and headed through the cramped and dimly lit corridors to her quarters, the *Midnight* looked more like a museum piece than an active frigate. Doors clicked and hissed, elevators shuddered, manual systems still operated where in recent ships crude but efficient AIs had taken over. Current hyperspace technology in the COE—kept homogeneous by the nearby Eckandar Trade Axis and its links with the Commerce Artel—stood at 49th generation, three orders of magnitude more efficient and responsive than that propelling the ancient frigate. The discrepancy between the *Midnight* and other Armada vessels didn't surprise her, however; prison ships were renowned for being poorly outfitted, outdated relics fit for little more than so-called "cattle runs" and other routine jobs.

The uppermost level housed officers and command stations; levels two and three were the crew quarters. The lowest levels contained cells for the transportees heading to the penal colony on Sciacca's World. Roche's room—her own cell, as she thought of it—was the last on the first floor, sandwiched between the drive shielding and a water reclamation plant. Straining engines kept her awake during maneuvers, with bubbling pipes a constant counterpoint. She doubted that the room was used often, being too uncomfortable for either a regular officer or an important guest. As she was neither, it was her dubious honor to be its occupant.

The bulkhead leading to her section slid aside with a noise like tearing metal, jamming as it always did when it was only three-quarters opened. Set into the wall opposite the door was a security station inhabited by a single crewman. He saluted as she approached, recognizing her on sight, and she returned the gesture automatically. Behind him, a battered flatscreen followed the progress of the *Midnight*.

The view of Sciacca's World hadn't changed much. The *Midnight*'s contingent of fighters, standard escort for a prison ship, had adopted a defensive configuration for planetary approach.

Catching the direction of her glance, the crewman nodded. "Almost there," he said. "Not that we'll see much of it."

Roche felt compelled to respond, although her anger at Klose still burned. "We're not landing?"

"No, sir. We'll simply dock at Kanaga Station to off-load the cattle and to refuel." He shrugged. "No one goes down; no one comes up. That's the rules. No one escapes from this place."

"What about staffing changes?"

"Oh, DAOC sends a shuttle every year or so, independent of us. This is the fifth time I've been this way, and it's always the same. Occasionally we bring supplies to trade for service credit, but not this time. I wouldn't let it worry you though, sir," he added quickly, mistaking her dark expression for concern. "It's all very routine."

Roche nodded distantly—the last thing she needed at the moment was *more* routine—and continued on her way. The entrance to her room lay at the end of the corridor. Halfway there, the voice inside her head spoke again. She ignored it. It wouldn't do for the crewman to hear her talking to empty air. Rumors had spread as it was.

With a sigh of relief, she keyed the palmlock and opened the door to her room. Stale air gusted past her face as pressures equalized, indicating a faulty valve somewhere in the life-support system. Nothing serious; just an irritation. No doubt it was on a maintenance list somewhere, awaiting repair.

When the door slid shut behind her, she ran a hand across her close-cropped scalp and vented her frustration on the empty room.

"*Damn* him."

<Who?>

"Klose. Weren't you listening?"

The voice in her head chided her gently. <You know that I am unable to study information to which I have no direct access. Besides, it would be immoral to eavesdrop without your permission.>

Roche doubted both statements but kept her thoughts to herself, not wishing to encourage conversation. A short corridor led from the doorway to a small work space; the far end of her quarters housed a toilet, bathroom, and sleeping chamber. In cross section, the space was shaped like a narrow triangle with the door at its apex, its size dictated by the space available rather than by comfort or aesthetics.

Nowhere within it was there room for someone of her height to lie fully outstretched, let alone swing a cat.

The voice remained silent, perhaps considerate of her mood for a change. Before it could begin again, she walked to the work space and put the valise on the desk. The cuff was made of monofilament cord wrapped in black leather and ended in the bracelet that fitted around her left wrist tightly enough to prevent it slipping loose—or being removed by force—but not so tight that it caused her discomfort. Tiny contacts on its inner surface matched nodes on her skin, which in turn patched into a modified ulnar nerve leading up her forearm and into her spinal column, thus enabling data to flow in either direction. The voice in her head—intrusive, often unwelcome even though it was her only company—was not so much heard as insinuated directly in the aural centers of her brain.

Flipping open the valise's grey lid, she studied its interior with an emotion bordering on hatred.

"Oh, for an axe," she whispered out loud, although she had no need to.

<It wouldn't do any good, Morgan,> said the voice. <I am graded to withstand—>

"—a nuclear strike from one hundred meters." She nodded wearily. "I know, I know, but if it wasn't for you I wouldn't be in this mess. Can you understand how frustrating it is to be cooped up in here with nothing to do?"

<As a matter of fact, Morgan, I can.>

Roche bit her lip. Of course it understood. The AI's previous environment had been the massive information workshops of Trinity, the planet of its birth. There, protected by the system's neutral status, secretive craftspersons in the service of High Humanity produced the AIs of the COE—rare and precious mind-machines lovingly crafted by carefully guarded techniques. Few people were allowed onto the planet itself, and she had been no exception. As she'd waited in orbit for the envoy from the manufacturers to arrive, then for the *Midnight* to collect her on its way past the system, she had had almost a week to watch the world below, but had learned little. Only a handful of what might have been cities were visible above the smoky-orange surface of the planet; apart from a ring of five skyhooks circling the equator, there was little sign of advanced life. And yet . . .

Somehow she had been rendered unconscious prior to their arrival. She had no memory of the High Caste manufacturers—who they were, what they looked like, or how they behaved. There was just a blankness, after which she had woken in her singleship with the valise already strapped to her. The experience had been dreamlike, surreal—and frustrating. Such levels of secrecy were paranoid to an extreme—all for the sake of technology no mundane Human could understand anyway.

The valise's imitation cover fitted over an ebony rectangular box with a small keypad of touch points and recessed nodes along its top. The heart of the valise was a densely packed mass of complex microtechnology, crammed neatly into the small space available, both shielded and camouflaged by the shell of the briefcase itself. Molded in superhard composite along the inside of the lid was the AI's identification tag: JW111101000, one digit longer than usual. Without a name in the usual sense of the word to fall back on, Roche resorted as billions of people had before her to popular slang. In this case, the term "Black Box" was even more appropriate, given the shape of the AI's container.

"The sooner we're back in HQ, Box, the better."

<I agree, Morgan, although I feel no distress at our union; I am a burden upon you, not the other way around. If it makes you feel any better, it should take only another six weeks to reach Intelligence HQ.>

"*Only* six weeks . . ." She forced a short-lived smile. "If it wasn't for Klose being so pedantic, I'd probably enjoy the break from normal duties."

<I sense—>

"I don't want to talk about it." Swiveling the room's only chair to face the workstation and placing her left palm on the contact pad, she activated the console and called up the ship's outlet of the Information Dissemination Network. IDnet granted her access to all nonrestricted data, from the volume of processed foodstuff in the *Midnight*'s holds to current affairs on any of the worlds in the COE. Raw data coursed up her arm into the small processor at the base of her skull, where it was interpreted as visual and audio signals and routed to the implanted systems in her left eye and ear. Her implants were by no means the most sophisticated available—lacking three-dimensional clarity and line-of-sight commands—but set her above ninety percent of Armada employees. Such subtle means of communication were sometimes required of Intelligence operatives, so these basic implants were standard to all of her rank.

A virtual screen appeared over her field of vision, seeming to hang two meters from her, impossibly deep in the bulkhead. Skimming at random through the channels, she found a station devoted to general COE news and settled back to discover what the rest of the universe was up to. Try as she might, however, her mind kept returning to Klose and his reasons for denying her what she wanted, while the patient, steady voice of IDnet murmured into her ear, an incessant counterpoint to her thoughts.

// in the wake of crippling solar flares, which destroyed asteroid mining facilities and a hydrogen purification plant in orbit around the system's innermost gas giant. Ede Prime's Presiding Minister today released a statement exonerating two members of her advisory staff who yesterday committed ritual suicide, after it was revealed that the Eckandar Trade Axis has been conclusively linked to corruption within a local chapter of the Commerce Artel //

Ship and captain: for better or for worse, their destinies and characters were intertwined. The post of ship command, contrary to popular opinion, offered not liberation but a lifetime of snaillike confinement. With a prison strapped to his or her back, unable to shrug free even for a moment, every captain had the power to travel vast distances but in reality no more freedom than any of the convicts on Sciacca's World.

Few deep-space commands led to promotion, at least in the COE Armada; captains quickly learned that the chance of achieving advancement via success in battle was slim, as battles themselves were rare and usually fatal to those involved, and most missions were more concerned with distribution of resources across that region of the galaxy than the expansion of the COE—the Commonwealth of Empires, which had ceased expanding entirely some centuries ago and indeed had, upon the secession of the Dato Bloc, begun to shrink. If they failed to die in space, captains inevitably retired to one of the bleak Space Command planets (whose very architecture mirrored deep-space engineering) and spent their remaining days reminiscing about imagined glories. Meanwhile their ships, unfaithful lovers at best, flew on, piloted by younger versions of themselves who were no less doomed than their predecessors. Doomed to a life of confinement, first in their ships and later in retirement or death.

In a very real sense, then, Proctor Klose *was* the *Midnight*, but only for a little while. Jealous of his small command, he would resist any attempt to undermine it. And therein lay the problem.

Roche didn't want to take over. She just wanted something to do. Armada training had prepared her for a wide range of combat scenarios, not months of being cooped up on a worn-out frigate acting as nursemaid for an artificial mind. She knew she should be patient, and perhaps even grateful for the undemanding task, but it wasn't in her nature to sit still for long. She wanted to move, to act, to investigate.

// shock discovery of remains in the Greater Vexisen Republic dating the emergence of Pristine Humanity into the wider galaxy fifty thousand years earlier than the previous best estimate. Renowned xenoarchaeologist Linegar Rufo, nominal overseer of the excavation, was not available for comment, but acting overseer Dev Bogasi commented that "This find represents the most exciting development in the field for over five hundred years. I'm not saying we've found the ultimate source of the Human race, but we're well on the way. The further back we push the envelope—and we're up to half a million years, now—the closer we're coming to a pure genetic strain. Give us another discovery of this magnitude and I predict we'll be able to narrow our field of search to a handful of //

Feeling the tension knotting her muscles, Roche shifted in her seat and unbuttoned the tight collar of her uniform. Brooding on it wasn't going to do her any good, and talking was better than doing nothing. The Box wasn't the confidant she would have chosen, but she had no choice. It was either that or go stir crazy.

"To be fair, Box," she said, picking up the conversation where she had ended it earlier, "it's partly my fault. You remember that derelict we picked up seven days ago?"

<I do recall it in the daysheets.>

"Well, I've been hearing rumors among the crew—"

An all-stations announcement interrupted her, warning the crew and transportees alike of imminent deceleration. The *Midnight* had come out of the anchor point at the edge of the system seven days earlier; this final maneuver would bring the frigate into an inclined polar orbit around the planet, dipping through the belt of moonlets once every two hours. Within moments of the announcement, the engines groaned through the bulkheads of Roche's room, and a wave of rattles and clatters shivered through the ship.

<You were saying, Morgan?>

"Hang on." She adjusted the workstation to bring up a view of the planet, overlaying IDnet. "It's nothing, really. The derelict was a life-support capsule with one man inside."

<Alive?>

"Apparently. No one knows where he's from, though, which makes me curious. The other eight capsules we picked up coming here all contained survivors ejected from the wreckage of the *Courtesan*, the passenger cruiser that broke up near Furioso. But this one . . . They don't recognize him. I asked Klose if I could interview the man, but he told me to mind my own business." She shrugged. "That's it, I guess."

She didn't mention the other snippets of gossip she'd heard: that the capsule had been drifting through space far longer than usual before being detected by the *Midnight*, and that its design was anything but orthodox.

<Your curiosity is understandable, Morgan,> said the Box. <And commendable.>

The AI's overt praise surprised her. "It is?"

<Of course. The man in the capsule might be anyone. He might even be a threat to your mission, a saboteur posing as a castaway to cover his true intentions.>

"That doesn't seem likely."

<Nevertheless, it is a possibility. The capsule might contain a bomb, or some sort of communication device. Or a virus. I am, after all, an information-retrieval device—albeit one of spectacular sophistication.>

"Not forgetting modesty," Roche cut in.

The Box ignored her. <The point is, Morgan, that the plan may not be to destroy me, but to corrupt my function.>

Roche rubbed her chin thoughtfully. She hadn't considered this possibility before. The *Midnight* had been chosen as the vehicle to carry the Box because its route to Intelligence HQ was circuitous, not the direct route one might expect for such an important cargo. If the man in the capsule was a spy, all he had to do was ascertain that the Box was definitely aboard *this* ship, instead of one of the many decoy ships, and notify his superiors.

It was barely plausible, certainly not likely.

And it didn't make sense, not if the capsule was older than the plans to ferry the Box to Intelligence HQ. Still, it would be an interesting point to raise when she and Klose were next at loggerheads.

// until the vector has been isolated and the outbreak contained, all scheduled traffic in- and out-system—including that for the purpose of trade and Armada activity—is either severely restricted or canceled indefinitely. Anyone attempting to break the blockade will be in violation of the Commonwealth of Empires Security Act and liable to face the severest penalty, by order of Chief Liaison Officer for the COE Armada, Burne Absenger. Repeat: Palasian System has been declared a no-go zone as a result of a Class Three Medical Emergency //

The *Midnight*'s engines roared again, swinging its ponderous bulk around to the correct attitude for polar insertion.

"So this is the way you spend your time, Box. Is there

anything that could go wrong that you *haven't* thought about?"

<Of course there isn't. The datapool of this ship is too small to provide stimulating conversation, and I am hesitant to intrude upon you any more than I already do. I am therefore left with one means of amusement: to explore possible situations and prepare contingency plans.>

"Such as?"

Before it could answer, a red light flashed in the virtual screen, indicating a deviation from the mission plan. She returned her attention to the view of the planet and its attendant asteroid belt—"the Soul," she reminded herself. The halo of moonlets had grown in size dramatically; individual motes of light now stood out against the indistinct glow of dust and pebbles. Nothing seemed immediately out of the ordinary, so she superimposed a navigation overlay across the view. Multicolored lines defined the vectors and mass of the largest rocks, while bold green angles indicated the *Midnight*'s orbital approach. The latter should have been clear of all obstacles larger than the frigate's shields could handle, but it wasn't.

Four red circles—ships, judging by their mass and velocity—occupied the exact center of the *Midnight*'s path.

"That's strange," Roche mused, more to herself than to her artificial companion. "The corridor should be clear by now."

<I agree,> replied the Box. <I am monitoring this development through the bridge log. The ships moved into this orbit fifteen minutes ago and have not made any attempt to alter their course since then.>

"Any ident?"

<Surface scan indicates ore freighters from the Eckandar Trade Axis, although their size suggests otherwise.> The Box hesitated for the briefest of moments, as though scanning data. <Captain Klose has received a communication from the commanding officer of the largest ship. It is this woman's opinion that she has right of way in this corridor, and that the *Midnight* should adjust its course to compensate. We will overtake the nearest vessel in approximately

fifteen minutes. A course correction is required shortly. Captain Klose has denied her request.>

"Typical." Roche could well imagine the *Midnight*'s captain fuming at the woman's impudence. All maneuvers by the Armada were booked well in advance; there was no question that Klose was in the right. That didn't mean, of course, that he couldn't do the courteous thing and oblige her, but it wasn't in his nature to deviate from the regulations one iota. Not for COE Intelligence, as Roche knew well, and especially not for a civilian.

<A compromise has been reached,> announced the Box shortly. <The captain of the freighter will instruct her ships to spread their formation. The *Midnight* will pass between the three smaller vessels without need for course correction in—fourteen minutes and seventeen seconds.>

"*Between* the freighters?" Roche frowned, concerned.

<Although unorthodox, the maneuver has been authorized by Kanaga Station traffic control.>

"That's not what worries me. What if they're freebooters? We'll be at a disadvantage should one of them take a shot at us. It goes against everything I learned in Tactics."

<It would seem that Captain Klose does not share your concern.> Something in the Box's tone suggested that it was playing devil's advocate, rather than honestly defending the captain.

"Captain Klose is—" *A fool*, she had been about to say, but thought better of it. He had traveled this route many times, after all, and knew its dangers better than she. A course correction would cost them energy and delay their docking at Kanaga Station. Why *should* he give way, when he was so obviously in the right? Besides, fears of freebooting and other forms of treachery seemed naive even to her.

"—just doing his job, I guess," she concluded with a sigh, and settled back into the chair to watch the approach. The red circles on the navigation display drifted apart, widening like a mouth to swallow the *Midnight*. Although she was no longer protesting, she was unable to quell the flutter in her stomach.

• • •

// continuing hostilities forced intervention on the behalf of the Commerce Artel. The long-running dispute between the Hierocratic Kingdom of Shurdu and the Pan-Rationalist Alliance of neighboring Zanshin flared into open warfare two months ago, following racist comments made by Hierocrat Kaatje Lene in response to a plea for peace from his opposite number, Provost Hemi Felucca. The exacerbation of inter-Caste tensions as a result of these comments has been cited by concerned observers as a major contributing factor to the current situation. Some have even suggested that the comments were made deliberately, in order to incite war. Exactly why the Hierocrat would do such a thing remains a mystery at this time, although some delegates have not ruled out interference from an unknown third party keen to see war between the two nations.

Meanwhile, on a more cheerful note, an explanation has come from High Human Interventionist, the Crescend, regarding a garbled transmission received from the homeworld of the Jaaf Caste—which, it turns out, has successfully Transcended to the status of High Human, not been annihilated by the nova of their primary star as was first thought. Concerned friends and business associates can contact //

A brisk rap at her door startled her from both the view and IDnet's incessant patter. She stood automatically and straightened her uniform. The moment her hand left the contact pad without canceling her link to IDnet, an inactive screen mounted in the wall above the workstation flickered to life, continuing the display of the *Midnight*'s approach.

"Who is it?" she called into the intercom.

"To be honest, I was hoping you might be able to help me answer that question."

Her hand hovered over the switch that would open the door. The voice had been male, deep and articulate, but the statement itself suggested anything but conviction. "If this is some sort of joke—?"

"I assure you it's not." There was a moment's pause before the man on the other side of the door spoke again. "Look, my name is Adoni Cane, but that's about all I can tell you. Everything else is just—" Another pause. "Please, I need to speak to you."

Roche removed her hand from the switch and checked the name in the ship's datapool; it didn't register. Although she was no rigid stickler for standard military procedure, as Klose was, there were some broad guidelines she simply wouldn't break. Admitting a mysterious visitor at her door in the middle of a potentially dangerous maneuver while on a priority mission was one of them.

"I'm sorry," she said. "I'm going to need a positive ident before I let you in. Come back later, when we've docked, and maybe we can discuss it."

Symbolically turning her back on the door, she switched off the intercom.

With a hiss, the door slid open behind her. Roche's left hand was instantly on the cover of the valise, slamming it closed, while her right reached across the narrow work space for her service pistol. The grip slid smoothly into place as she snap-turned to face the intruder.

Her breath caught in her throat.

His skin was very dark, almost chocolate-brown, and he was tall, a full half-head taller even than herself, with strong shoulders, a wide chest, and powerful hips and upper legs. He was dressed in a simple grey shipsuit, and its narrow fit accentuated the impression of power. He reminded Roche of an oversized Surin war-dancer—exuding a rare physical presence that went beyond simple strength—except that he appeared to be completely hairless. And looked like a Pristine Human, not an Exotic.

The smooth dome of his skull was lit by the overhead door-light as he took a step forward into the room. The flow of muscle beneath his shipsuit was powerful, oddly graceful, and potentially very dangerous.

Roche reacted with alarm. "Hold it right there," she barked, gesturing with the pistol.

"I don't understand," he said, raising his hands placatingly. "Why did you let me in if—"

"*Me* let you in? I told you to go away. The door was locked."

Despite the pistol trained on him, his eyes betrayed not the slightest hint of fear.

"I didn't open it." He glanced over his shoulder at the door, which remained open, then back to her. "If you want me to leave—"

"No, wait." She grasped the handle of the valise and lifted it off the desk. "I want to know what you're doing here."

He lowered his hands slightly and took another step inside. The door slid shut behind him. "I was told to see you."

"See *me*? Who told you this?"

He shrugged. "Somebody spoke to me through the security intercom in my cell. He told me that when the doors opened I was to come here to you, to these quarters. He gave me directions, but no name." His face, when the light caught it, displayed a genuine puzzlement. "I'm sorry I can't be any more specific than that."

"You said you were in a cell," said Roche, keeping the pistol trained upon him. "What happened to the guards? Didn't they try to stop you?"

"I suppose they should have. But when the door opened, there was no one there."

Suspicion made Roche apply slightly more pressure upon the trigger. "Conveniently allowing your escape."

His eyes dropped to the muzzle of the pistol; when they met her own a second later, he was smiling. "If 'escape' is the appropriate word. After all, no one ever told me why I was locked up in the first place."

"You're not a transportee?" she asked, although something about his manner had already convinced her of that. He didn't seem like a petty criminal: too self-possessed, perhaps, or too confident. And despite the absurdity of his tale, he didn't seem to be lying. Roche's curiosity began to outweigh her sense of caution.

"I don't know what I am," he said. "All I know is that I awoke a week ago and have been confined to a cell ever since. I have no memories of a time before that. All I have is my name." He shrugged. "I was told that you would be able to help me."

"*Help* you? In what way?"

He offered his hands, palms up, to demonstrate that he had no answer to that question either. If she wanted answers, she would have to deduce them herself from what scant information he had to offer.

Roche swallowed her frustration with difficulty, kicked the chair to him, and indicated for him to sit. Keeping the pistol trained carefully on his chest, she retreated to the far corner of the room to think.

Adoni Cane. If he wasn't a transportee, then he could have been a passenger, but then why didn't his name register in the datapool? He *had* to be lying. But why? She could ask the Box to investigate the mysterious message that had led Cane to her; it would have been recorded by security monitors, if it existed at all. And if it didn't—

Her hand instinctively tightened on the valise as she realized the stranger's intentions. Before she could express her concerns to the Box, the AI's voice cut across her train of thought:

<Morgan, that freighter has just—>

She blinked and subvocalized: <Not now. Listen—>

<I strongly suggest that you check the monitor, Morgan.>

Roche swung her gaze to the screen. It showed an overhead view of the *Midnight*'s bridge, from cameras mounted above the access locks at the rear of the chamber, and took in most if not all of the hemispherical sweep of workstations.

Klose was standing on the podium, his first officer, Terrison, with him; both were studying the forward displays. There was a superficial impression of calm about the scene that belied the tension in their stances. Roche could tell at a glance that they and the other personnel on the bridge were operating under unusual pressure. Something had gone wrong.

As she watched, Janek, the tactician, turned from her station to face Klose and Terrison.

"Ident confirmed," the tactician said. "Dato warships. Four of them."

Roche slipped her hand onto the contact pad to overlay the navigation display in one corner of the screen, hardly believing what she was hearing. *Dato* ships? From where? The Dato Bloc had no business this side of the border.

A moment's glance showed her what had happened: the three Eckandi "freighters" had deactivated their sophisticated camouflage systems, revealing the truth beneath. A dreadnought and three raiders, plus at least a dozen tiny fighters, swooping free of the dreadnought even as she watched.

// *disturbance within the sector under Olmahoi control has both puzzled and concerned COE observers. Reaves in neighboring systems have reported surges in epsense* //

Roche irritably killed IDnet and swore softly to herself. Cane leaned closer; out of the corner of her eye she saw him echo her frown.

"Trouble?" he asked.

"You might say that." Mindful that her pistol no longer covered him, she waved him back. "We've just cruised straight into an ambush."

"Is there conflict between your people and the owners of these ships?"

"Are you serious?" She saw no indication of irony in his composed features. She had never met anyone who wasn't at least vaguely aware of the political realities of the region. "How long have you been imprisoned here?"

"Seven days, as I said."

"This really isn't turning into a very good day for me," she said, shaking her head. Then, returning to the screen before her, she added, "Officially the Commonwealth of Empires and the Dato Bloc are at peace." She focused her attention on the ships on the screen. "But I get the impression that this isn't official business."

"Could it be a mistake?"

She glanced down at the valise. "Unlikely."

The Dato ships had assumed a tight arrowhead formation and were powering up their drives to meet the incoming frigate. Alert strips above the door to her room flashed to amber simultaneously with the light in the tank. A sterile voice announced an order for provisional battle stations.

"Four against one," mused Cane, studying the formation intently. "Not insuperable odds. Why hasn't the captain—" He stopped in mid-sentence and glanced at Roche quizzically, as though suddenly remembering her presence. "You're an officer. Why aren't *you* on the bridge?"

"I'm just a guest, noncombat." She turned to study him in return. If the impending battle concerned him, he didn't show it. Even his voice echoed the easy strength and confidence of his physique. "What were you about to say? Do you know something about this?"

"Nothing." Klose's voice had taken Cane's attention back to the screen, and Roche followed it at once.

"Any communication?" the captain had asked.

"None, sir." The officer glanced up from his console. "They are not responding to our signals."

"Janek: ETA?"

"Three minutes, sir," replied the tactician without looking up. Then she leaned in close to her console. "Sir, that dreadnought—"

"What about it?"

"It's not a dreadnought. Configuration reads way off." She leaned in close again. "It could be the ship we've heard rumors about—the new Marauder."

Roche studied the image forming on the screen. The ship *did* look different: a large dolioform drive facility connected to seven pointed nacelles by a complicated web of what looked like threads but were probably access tubes and girders made small by distance. Streamlined mouths at either end of the drive flashed red as the ship maneuvered; smaller spiracles on five of the nacelles were inactive but open, obviously weapon bays or fighter launchers ready for action. The ship looked like nothing Roche had seen before, but she could tell just by its appearance—an ominous cross between a spider and shark—that it was designed for speed and resilience in battle.

"Broadcast full battle alert," announced Klose, his voice booming. "Seal the bridge and all compartments! Prepare for defensive maneuvers!"

"Too late," mumbled Cane. "Much too late."

"What is?"

"The captain should have attacked the moment he saw them."

"Not Klose." She grimaced bitterly. "He'd never risk a diplomatic incident on the off chance there'd been some sort of misunderstanding."

"What do you think?" The approaching Dato ships glinted in Cane's eyes. "Does this look like a misunderstanding to you?"

"They haven't attacked us—"

"But they will," Cane interjected calmly. "And if the captain waits any longer—"

A groan from the bulkheads interrupted him. The view in the telemetry display shifted suddenly as the *Midnight*'s engines kicked into life, thrusting the ship along a different course. Life support dampened the violent shift in momentum, leaving a lingering sense of disorientation in its wake.

Roche blinked and shook her head. Cane seemed entirely unaffected, although she realized with alarm that he was standing much closer than he had been before. If he had wanted to overpower her, he could have done so easily during the maneuver. The fact that he hadn't did not reassure her. That she had let him get that close in the first place—

Another disturbance rolled through the ship, more violent than the previous one. Cane's hand came down on her shoulder. She brushed it aside with the hand holding the pistol before realizing that he was only steadying her.

He raised an eyebrow at her confusion, then turned back to the screen.

Klose had sent the *Midnight* angling along a path heading below the approaching triangle of Dato ships, demonstrating an initial reluctance to engage but without placing the ship in too vulnerable a position. The frigate's contingent of five fighters peeled away to draw fire. Instantly, the arrowhead formation dissolved, with the Marauder swooping to intercept the *Midnight* and the three raiders at the rear peeling to either side and below to pen the COE frigate in a potential cross fire.

The *Midnight* turned again, to port, disturbing the deadly symmetry of the pattern. The Marauder followed while the raiders jockeyed for new positions.

Klose ordered the raising of hyperspace disrupters and E-shields. The *Midnight*'s armory targeted and tracked the Dato ships, awaiting the order to fire.

Roche's hands gripped the valise tightly. Cane's observations had been acute: she did want to be on the bridge, instead of watching the action impotently from her room; and Klose had indeed waited too long to act. Her heart beat faster; she was reluctant to take her eyes off the screen for fear she would miss the crucial moment.

When it came, however, it surprised her. The Dato raider to starboard of *Midnight* was the first to fire—not the Marauder. A salvo of flicker-bombs, dropping in and out of hyperspace with intermittent flashes of light, lashed toward the green dot at the center of the telemetry screen. Fast in its wake came a wave of A-P fire.

The first of the missiles struck the aft disrupters, making the ship shudder. Roche flinched automatically.

"Lucky," said Cane, as Klose finally ordered the firing of the *Midnight*'s laser and A-P cannon. The power in Roche's room flickered at the same time as spears of light darted across the telemetry screen in the direction of the dots representing the Dato ships. "If the trailing ship had fired first, a missile could have passed through the afterwash shields and blown the engines."

"So why didn't it?"

"I would have thought that was obvious," he said. "They don't intend to destroy us." He glanced at her and the valise in turn. "There's something aboard the *Midnight* they want."

She ignored the unspoken implication. On the screen, the battle was proceeding rapidly. The lights flickered again, followed by wave after wave of subtle nausea as the *Midnight* weaved for position. Two of the fighters vanished as they engaged the Dato; outnumbered by ten to one, the *Midnight*'s contingent would not last long.

The Marauder, however, had not fired once. Under combined fire from the three raiders—two were easily a match for the aged frigate—the tiny singleship fighters were little more than target practice. A steady stream of missiles battered the *Midnight*'s disrupters and E-shields, gradually weakening them. It was only a matter of time before the shields failed entirely, leaving the frigate open to direct assault—or a boarding party.

Klose was no master tactician, but Roche doubted she could do any better herself. Besides, she had other priorities to consider.

The lights went out entirely for a split-second, then returned in emergency red. A tang of smoke filtered into the room, and the pit of her stomach rolled disturbingly. The last COE fighter fell with a flare of light. On the screen, the Dato raiders swooped nearer, harrowing the beleaguered frigate.

Roche came to a decision.

"Okay," she said, swinging the valise into a more accessible position. Cane watched curiously from his position nearby, and she reverted to subvocals. <Box, we're in trouble, aren't we?>

<It would seem so. The *Midnight* is experiencing gravity fluctuations, which means the disrupters are failing. Quite soon now the shields will collapse entirely and we will be boarded—unless Captain Klose orders a self-destruct.>

<Klose won't do that,> she said. <He'd rather be killed than commit suicide.>

<Be that as it may. We probably only have a short time in which to act. Should Klose either surrender or otherwise allow the ship to be boarded, that would be tantamount to handing me over to the Dato Bloc, in direct contradiction of his orders—which are, of course, to prevent my capture at any cost. He should therefore allow the ship to be destroyed in the hope that the wreckage of the *Midnight* will conceal my remains. Fortunately, due to my structural resilience, I will not be harmed.>

<Great,> said Roche dryly. <But what about *me*?>

<Patience, Morgan. Remember your own orders.>

<I *know* my orders, Box,> she snapped impatiently. Then, more calmly, she added, <Look, is there any way out of this?>

<Would I waste time like this if there wasn't?>

<I don't know. *Would* you?>

<Perhaps, if things were totally hopeless.> The Box seemed almost to be enjoying her discomfort. <I suppose I

might attempt to take your mind off the situation. However, it is not. The solution, clearly, is to evacuate the ship.>

On the screen, one of the Dato raiders loomed, partially occluding the image of Sciacca's World.

<A great plan, Box. Any ideas *how*?>

<In one of *Midnight*'s landers would seem our best option.>

<But the launch controls are locked from the bridge.>

<With your approval I can override the locks.>

<Do it.> She glanced at the screen as more missiles barraged the Frigate's struggling defenses. <Just do whatever it takes to get us out of here.>

<Very well.> The Box fell silent, then returned a moment later, sounding faintly surprised. <It would seem that somebody else has thought along the same lines. The doors to Lander Bay Three are already open, and all approaches to it have been sealed off—except from the lower levels. The bay is two sectors away. I have opened the corridors between here and there.> After a further pause of a few seconds, the voice spoke again inside Roche's head: <Haste at this juncture would be prudent, Morgan.>

"Right." She stood to leave, the valise gripped tightly in her hand. Cane, forgotten during her exchange with the Box, startled her as she turned to face the door.

"You're leaving?"

She hesitated briefly. "I'm sorry," she said. "I have no choice."

<Take him with you, Morgan.> The Box's words broke across her thoughts like the voice of a guilty conscience.

"What? *Why*?" Startled by the Box's request, she spoke aloud. Cane frowned, but didn't speak.

<Remember your dispute with Captain Klose?>

"What about it?"

<The man standing before you is the subject of that dispute.>

"He is? How do you know that?"

<His name does not appear in the ship's log. Ergo, he was not on board when we left Ivy Green Station. Ergo, he must have been in the last life capsule we salvaged.>

"I—" She stopped. It made sense—but explained nothing. If that was so, why was he *here*?

Confusion wrinkled Cane's brow. Roche belatedly realized that she'd been talking to the Box out loud, rather than by subvocalizing. What he made of her side of the conversation, she couldn't even guess.

Torn between her mission, curiosity, and basic Human compassion, she tried to decide what to do with him. If she left him behind, he would surely be captured by the Dato Bloc—at best—and she would never learn who he was, nor why Klose had not wanted her to see him. On the other hand, she knew too little about him to risk him coming along; having a total stranger in tow at a time such as this could prove a threat to her mission.

<I remind you, Morgan, that time is not what you might call an ally at this point.>

"Okay, okay." Cane's stare hadn't faded, and she returned it with one of equal intensity. "My name is Commander Roche of COE Intelligence," she said quickly, collecting as she did a handful of magazine charges for her pistol and slipping them into her belt. "I'm going to try to escape in one of the landers. You can tag along, but only on the understanding that I give the orders. Clear?"

"I understand." His smile was slight but genuine. "And I agree."

"Good. Because should you so much as cross me once, I swear I'll shoot you."

"That won't be necessary."

She wrapped the belt loosely about her waist and keyed the door with her palm. "Okay, then let's move it."

The ship lurched as they stepped out into the corridor. Roche swayed, steadying herself with the walls. Ahead of her, Cane hardly missed a step. For the second time she shrugged away his helping hand.

"That way," she said, gesturing with the pistol.

Nodding, he obeyed, and Roche followed a pace behind. His steady pace displayed no concern at the gun at his back, and neither did he stop to question her plans. That sudden— and unreciprocated—trust bothered her more than anything else about him. Whoever he was, he seemed quite content to place his fate in her hands. Perhaps, she thought, the only alternative open to him was worse than mere imprisonment by the Dato.

<You had better be right about this, Box.>

The Box might have chuckled softly at that, but she couldn't be certain.

<Aren't I always?>

2

Lander Bay Three was one of two on the officers' deck, situated at the fore of the *Midnight*. Due to the frigate's unusual configuration, the ceiling of the uppermost decks comprised the outer shell of the hull; Roche's quarters, being the last on the officers' deck, were near the midway point. To reach the lander bay, she and Cane had to follow one of the main access corridors along half the length of the ship—but at least they were not required to change levels.

The security station at the end of her corridor was empty, the crewman who had occupied it earlier obviously performing battle duties elsewhere. The main access corridor was likewise unoccupied. The occasional rolling boom echoed along its length as Dato weapons exploded near the hull of the frigate. Perhaps it was Roche's imagination, but the explosions seemed to grow louder, and more frequent, as the minutes passed. If so, the disruption shields were failing, allowing the blink-bombs to jump out of hyperspace and explode a little closer to the frigate every time. It was only a matter of time before one snuck through entirely and detonated deep in the heart of the ship. Although small enough to defeat the constraints that normally prevented matter from slow-jumping in a gravity well, just one contained sufficient explosive to cripple a vessel.

Gravity fluctuations kept their pace to a steady jog; any faster risked a fall, especially with the weight of the valise to upset her balance. Cane matched her stride easily, moving with the powerful grace of a trained athlete. The occasional lurch of the floor didn't even break his stride, and it was he who occasionally lent her a hand, never the other way around. Not bad, she thought, for someone who had just emerged from a life-support coma.

By the time they reached the end of the corridor, smoke had begun to filter in—a slowly thickening blue haze coming from somewhere beyond the abandoned security point. She watched it carefully as they neared it, assessing the inflow. Her first impressions were correct: the buildup was gradual, probably isolated to the local ventilation system, and not a serious problem—yet.

Roche turned left at the end of the corridor, away from the source of the smoke. A series of doglegs led to EVA control, a large self-contained chamber onto which the two lander bays opened.

<Lander Three has been breached,> the Box said as they took the first corner. <Whoever we are following has beaten us to it.>

<How many can the landers hold?>

<Full complement is five, although four is optimal.>

<What about Lander Two?>

There was a momentary hesitation as the AI assessed the available data. <The smoke you saw earlier is coming from burning insulation, caused by an overheating E-shield generator. The source of the fire is dangerously close to Lander Two, suggesting that the vessel may be damaged, or soon will be.>

<How long do we have?>

<That depends on Captain Klose. The disrupters are close to failing.>

<Not long, then. Certainly not enough time to try another bay. We'll have to make do with what we've got.> Turning to Cane, she explained the situation. "We need that lander. If

whoever's got there ahead of us amounts to more than three people, we may have to fight for it."

Cane nodded calmly. The idea of combat didn't appear to faze him in any way. "Understood, Commander. You'll have my full support."

"Good." Although she halfheartedly listened for accent or anomalies of syntax, there were none. He spoke with the sort of generalized Standard that one heard all over the galaxy. "Not far now."

They rounded the last corner slowly. Roche was up front, her pistol at the ready. The all-purpose magazine clipped in the long barrel allowed her a number of diverse selections; before turning the corner, she set it for scatter.

EVA control was empty. The outer airlock to Lander Three stood open. Beyond the airlock was the lander bay— a round antechamber roughly three times the size of her room—then a steep ramp that curved upward to the lander, doubling back on itself once along the way. The manual controls for the outer airlock were next to the entrance to the ramp. Roche inched forward through the airlock, into the bay. It too was empty, so she kept moving.

Cane's hand gripped her forearm, bringing her to a sudden halt only meters from the ramp. Instinctively she tried to pull the arm free, but found she could not.

"What?" she hissed, uneasy in his firm grip.

His gaze was fixed on the open doorway, and for the first time she noticed that his head was cocked slightly. He was listening to sounds coming from within the lander.

"Someone's coming," he said. "Down the ramp."

"Are you sure?" She could hear nothing.

Instead of answering, he pulled her away from the entrance to the lander, back into EVA control. Moments later, the sound of soft footsteps padded toward them.

Cane let go of her arm and put his mouth close to her ear. "Only one. I'll draw that one's fire while you shoot from here. Can you do that?"

"Of course I can," she said with some annoyance, although whether that annoyance came from his questioning her ability or from his suddenly taking charge of the situation, she wasn't sure. "But you're putting rather a lot of faith in your speed, aren't you?"

"No," he said, the faint trace of a grin splitting his dark features. "I'm putting it in your ability to hit them before they hit me."

She opened her mouth to voice her doubts, but got no further. An explosion shook the ship, the shock wave slamming through the bulkheads and snapping her head back into the wall. Cane maintained his balance and caught her with astonishing ease, held her until she regained her footing.

The tang of smoke in the air thickened almost immediately, and the lights dimmed.

<That was primary life-support,> said the Box. <The disrupters are failing. E-shields are down to five percent.>

As though he had heard the Box's words, Cane let her go and inched sideways to the entrance of the bay. "We haven't got time to play it safe, Commander," he whispered back to her. "We have to go in now, while they're still reeling from that explosion."

Raising the pistol to her chest, she nodded once. Cane immediately leapt through the door with a speed and agility she would not have believed possible—so fast that her own movements seemed belated and slow in comparison.

Following the small of his back with her eyes and swiveling her entire body to face the airlock, she covered the interior of the bay with one sweep, gun held at shoulder height in her right hand.

The first thing she saw was the light: the flash of blue laser fire from somewhere to her left, slicing through the air toward Cane's back. Only his speed saved him, kept him ahead of the beam.

Then she was through the door herself, the Box tucked up against her rib cage, cushioned from the Armada-trained roll that she executed with a sureness her instructors would have been proud of. All the time her eyes were focused left, her free hand and the pistol clear of the floor, tilted toward the expected target—

—a thin figure in a grey transportee uniform, definitely an Exotic Caste, Eckandi perhaps, with white hair, a gaunt face, and an industrial laser held in a double-handed grip,

*arms swinging to follow Cane's progress across the open
bay floor, the trigger held tightly down, blue light arcing
lethally toward Cane's retreating back—*

Roche's scatter-fire took the transportee full in the chest.
The man crumpled where he stood, then fell forward onto
his face. The blue beam flickered out, but not before scoring
an ugly black line across the floor of the bay, terminating in
a rough interrogative just short of Roche's toes.

Cane's momentum carried him up the ramp and out of
sight into the lander, his feet soundless on the metal deck.
Roche lingered for a moment to ensure that the transportee
had not been unduly harmed. An Eckandi prisoner on a COE
ship was rare enough to be treated delicately under any circumstance. The elderly man—perhaps over a century in age,
middle-aged, but not infirm—had fallen awkwardly onto his
side. His respiration was even, if a little slow, and his stac-
cato pulse regular. Although no expert in Exotic physiognomy, she suspected he would recover before long.

With a grunt, she rose to her feet and went to run up the
ramp to see what Cane was up to. Barely had she taken a
step when something dark and cold thrust itself into her
mind.

She stopped in her tracks, reeling with panic and confusion as the force squeezed her entire brain in an invisible
psychic fist, sending a retching wave of sickness and self-
hatred deep into her gut, where it blossomed into a bitter
flower of bile.

The muscles in her hand relaxed involuntarily, and the
gun clattered to the floor.

A reave.

She wasn't sure if she spoke the words or thought them.
The mental intrusion had caught Roche unaware, not allowing her to employ the epsense resistance techniques she had
been taught at Military College. She slipped to her knees,
clutching first at her stomach, then her head, wanting desperately for the intrusion to cease. This was different from
anything she had ever experienced before—much more intense.

Her vision greyed, became cluttered with images that
confused her: the inside of the lander, and huddled within its

shadows the reave—a Surin, not more than fifteen years old by the sheen of her fur. She was small of stature and, cowering, looked deceptively vulnerable. And frightened, Roche noted through her own suffocating anxiety. The girl was terribly frightened. Which perhaps explained the intensity of the intrusion.

And her face—

A narrow, stained bandage wrapped about the girl's head hid her eyes from view. Fully developed reaves "borrowed" the eyes and ears of the people around them rather than using their own senses, and communicated purely by thought. Roche sucked air sharply in sudden revulsion as she recalled that some fundamentalist factions of the Surin Agora actually *forced* their latent psychics to do so by a mutilation ceremony that accompanied the completion of their training. It was either that or go mad from sensory deprivation. This Surin girl, Roche guessed, was eyeless behind the bandage—probably declawed and a deaf-mute as well.

Despite her own discomfort, Roche couldn't help but feel pity for the girl. The ritual mutilation usually occurred in the very last stages of the transition from latent talent to full fledged epsense adept—a process that often took decades. Yet the Surin in the lander was less than half Roche's age. Power at such a price had to be a dubious gift.

"You're reading my mind," said a familiar voice, disconcertingly nearby. It belonged to the reave's primary subject. *Cane*, Roche realized. The voice belonged to Cane!

<Stay back.> The reave's words reached Roche's mind as thoughts rather than sound. She could feel the creeping tendrils of the Surin girl deep within herself, holding her at bay, their very presence aching dully. Yet the will that had so incapacitated her hardly seemed to be affecting Cane.

"Why?" he said, taking a step closer, his eyes—and thus Roche's—fixed upon the girl. "You have no reason to be afraid of me. I have no wish to harm you."

<What about Veden? You killed Veden!>

Roche winced as the Surin's grief twisted at her mind.

"Your friend fired upon us first. My companion was merely defending herself." Roche felt the reave's tentacles tighten a little at that, searching for the truth, as Cane took another step forward. "Listen to me; we haven't much time. We need this ship to escape. If we can just work—"

<No! Stay back or I'll—> The Surin hesitated, and Roche realized that, despite the clarity of mind generally required to enable epsense transfer, the reave was close to panic. <If you come any closer, I'll kill your friend!>

Roche hissed through her teeth as the pain increased. She swore she wouldn't scream, no matter how bad the pain. Half-formed words blossomed in her throat, but were stifled by the reave.

She's bluffing! she wanted to scream. Reaves rarely killed someone they were riding. The personal consequences were too great.

Cane either suspected this or simply didn't care what happened to Roche. Taking another step forward, he came within arm's reach of the Surin, who turned her face away.

<I can't read you.> Roche sensed fear and timidity in the girl's words.

The view of the cockpit vanished as the reave switched from Cane's point of view to Roche's. The lander bay was filled with dense smoke, billowing through the airlock leading to EVA control. The fire had either worsened dramatically or spread to the corridor outside. Through the pain in her head, she could hear klaxons wailing.

The reave's voice superimposed itself over everything— pervasive and irresistible: <Can you pilot the lander?>

Cane's response was prompt and without concern: "No."

Roche felt the pain in her head increase once more, slicing through her thoughts as though it were a red-hot scalpel.

<Morgan Roche.> The tone was cut with panic and confusion. <That case you carry—why do you believe that it can fly the lander?>

Roche clenched her mouth shut, using every iota of Armada training to resist replying.

Even as she struggled, a series of small explosions, quite near, rumbled through the hull. Then, with a sudden high-pitched screaming noise, the smoke began to fly away from her back down the corridor.

The pressure from the reave suddenly vanished, and full control of her body returned. Gasping, she fell forward onto the deck, scrabbling for the pistol. Her muscles felt spastic, jerky, as she struggled to her feet and staggered for the air-lock controls. She thumped the SEAL prompts in quick succession, hoping that her training would overcome the fogginess in her head.

The outer door slammed shut. The sound of klaxons diminished.

<Morgan,> said the Box, <we have very little time. Klose has surrendered to the Dato Bloc.>

Fighting the haze, she tried to concentrate. "He's *what*?"

<He has given permission for one of the raiders to dock. It may be a ruse, of course. Either way—>

"I understand." Blinking to clear her vision, she stumbled for the ramp and the lander. Cane met her halfway, raised his arms in mock surrender as her pistol swung at him. Then he smiled. The calm with which he did that, his ability to instantly relax once a moment of tension passed, disturbed her. It was more than control. It was almost inhuman.

His resistance to epsense was no less remarkable. Armada cadets received a basic training in mental defense, but no one she knew of, least of all herself, had the degree of control necessary to resist a reave as he had—and she hadn't—without actually being an epsense adept as well.

"Hull's punctured," she said with a calmness she didn't feel. "Not far away. The airlock is sealed. We're here to stay."

"Understood." He steadied her with a hand on her arm, then continued down the ramp. Moments later he returned with the semiconscious Eckandi draped over his shoulder. "The mind-rider will need him when she regains consciousness," he explained in response to her sharp look.

"Mind—? Oh, the reave." The outdated term threw her for a moment. He was making sense, though; the Surin would need someone to give her sensory input, preferably neither her nor Cane. "What did you do to her?"

"Nothing serious. She will awaken shortly."

Roche wasn't sure how she felt about that, and couldn't fight the sensation that she was being backed into a corner: first Cane, and now two others. Her mission was in enough jeopardy without complicating things further. But without saying anything, she hurried the short distance to the lander itself. When Cane had ducked through the inner airlock, she keyed it closed and made sure the seals were tight.

A short companionway led to the cockpit and its standard, if slightly out of date, hemispherical layout: five acceleration couches, centrally placed in rows of two and three; main controls located ahead of the front row; pilot's position right and backup to the left, auxiliary systems away to either side and rear. There were no viewports this far forward; heat shields covered the nose completely.

Roche dropped into the pilot's couch, made the fundamental adjustments to suit her physique, and placed the valise on her knees. "Out of curiosity, Box, *can* you fly this thing?"

<Of course, Morgan. Its interface is simple and will respond to my commands.>

"Good." She turned in her seat to see what Cane was up to. He had strapped the Eckandi into the chair in the center of the rear row and lifted the Surin from where she lay on the floor. The girl, limp and even smaller than Roche had guessed, went into the seat on the far side of the cockpit from Roche. "We have a reave on board, Box."

<I know—>

"If she wakes up and takes me over, you have my permission to fly the ship on your own. I don't want us stuck in limbo again waiting for her to decide whether or not she should trust us."

<A sensible precaution, Morgan.>

Cane strapped himself into the copilot's seat next to her, and Roche belatedly realized that she had been talking aloud.

"The briefcase," he said. "It's some sort of computer, isn't it?"

"Yes." She cursed the slip. "It's going to fly us out of here in—how long, Box?"

<Shortly.> The Box paused. <The *Midnight*'s fuel reserve will self-destruct at any moment.>

"What? Klose gave the order to scuttle the ship?"

Before the Box could reply, Roche had to grasp at the armrests as the frigate's gravity stabilizers failed completely.

"Shouldn't we be launching, then?" If the stabilizers had gone, the main energy pile wouldn't be far behind. And if the Box was right about Klose's order to free the antimatter reserve—

She was suddenly aware of perspiration beading her forehead.

<A little decorum, Morgan,> the voice lilted in her ear. <We have almost a full minute left to us.>

Roche forced herself to stay calm. "To hell with decorum, Box. Would you just get us out of here?"

<Morgan, must I explain the obvious? If we launch immediately, we will be picked up at once by Dato fighters— an easy target for their gunnery. There is a high probability they will take us for unimportant crew attempting to abandon ship, not the valued personnel we most certainly are, and destroy the lander. Do you agree?>

"Yes. So?"

<The magnetic bottle containing the antimatter reserve will fail in twenty seconds.>

"Box!" It was an exclamation of disbelief, nothing more. She had passed beyond panic.

<Outer door sequence employed. Stay calm, Morgan. Put colloquially: by the time they react to the opening of the outer doors, the ship will be history.>

"Just don't cut it too fine—"

<Ignition sequence commenced, Morgan. Take position.>

"Brace yourself!" Roche shouted to Cane, remembering that she alone could hear the voice in her ear. "We're launching!"

<Three seconds,> intoned the Box. <Launch.>

Riding a wave of energy as mighty as that on the surface of a small sun, the lander ejected itself into space. Roche closed her eyes against the sudden pressure, and put her fate into the Box's hands.

3

DBMP *Ana Vereine*
'954.10.30 EN
0765

From his coffin in life support, Captain Uri Kajic viewed the assault on the *Midnight* via his ship's various external sensors with interest.

The battlefield was complex. At its heart, the angry speck that represented the COE frigate spun like a primitive atom in primordial soup. A ring of Dato fighters harried this defensive position, swooping closer with every pass, supported by the greater might of the three raiders and, further back still, the Marauder itself: the *Ana Vereine*.

Occasional stray bolts spun free from the intense web of destruction woven by the raiders about the blazing frigate. Some were deflected from the *Midnight*'s remaining shields; others might have originated from the frigate itself. Although most dissipated harmlessly, the potential remained for an unlucky mishap. The narrow channel through Sciacca's World's asteroid field had been mapped in advance and was updated every millisecond by the Marauder's battle computers—but every new, unplanned explosion altered the orbits of nearby asteroids and increased the risk of collision.

When the *Midnight*'s antimatter reserve suddenly spilled

free of its containment and annihilated the ordinary matter surrounding it, that risk increased tenfold.

"Pull the fighters back!" Kajic ordered, sending the command hurtling down electromagnetic paths to the bridge in the Marauder's primary nacelle, where his holographic image appeared a moment later. "Prepare for impact!"

His second in command, Atalia Makaev, turned away to relay the order. The expanding bubble of energy reached the *Ana Vereine*, making it shudder. Kajic's image flickered slightly with the energy surge, but otherwise remained steadfast. The officers on the bridge gripped their stations as the disturbance washed over them, steadying themselves against the lurching motion. When it eased, and the ship's g-field restabilized, the normal bustle resumed.

"Report!" Kajic was unable to suppress his impatience. If the ship had been holed, he would have known immediately, but there were thousands of smaller ailments that might slip by unnoticed. The inevitable lag between his orders and their enactment was never as irritating as it was in battle.

"Telemetry reports—" The ship shuddered again as the shields sustained another impact, draining power. Makaev waited for her superior's image to reconfigure itself properly before continuing. Not that it was necessary—Kajic could receive the information with or without the presence of his hologram—but it was considered polite. "Telemetry reports that the *Midnight* has broken into seven substantial fragments." She paused again, adjusting the communication bud in her left ear. "Their trajectories have been noted and extrapolated."

"Damage to the raiders?" Although Kajic's primary concern was the *Ana Vereine*, the information available to him showed an alarming void where moments earlier a dozen fighters had been.

"*Paladin* has sustained minor damage. *Lansquenet* reports no incident. Awaiting word from Captain Hage regarding *Galloglass*."

Kajic sighed, folding his simulated hands behind his back—using body language consciously, as just another means of communication of the many in his repertoire—and did his best to radiate calm. On the bridge's main screen, the

brilliant fireball that had once been the COEA *Midnight*
boiled away into space, leaving a shower of particles and radioactive dust in its wake. The larger fragments that telemetry had noted were ringed in warning red to aid navigation:
bull's-eyes where perhaps gravestones should have been.

Kajic knew from intelligence reports that every COE
frigate carried a crew of two hundred and fifty, each with
families scattered throughout the Commonwealth of Empires; some of these people might conceivably have had ties
with the Dato Bloc, no matter how distant. The *Midnight*
had also been carrying a score of transportees. . . .

Gone, all of them, in a single blinding explosion as the
Midnight's pile went critical.

Gone also—and more important—was his hope of exe-
cuting his mission smoothly and without error.

"Captain?"

Atalia Makaev regarded him with a steely expression. It
always felt to Kajic as though she were looking into his soul,
seeing all of his personal doubts, searching out his weaknesses.

"Yes, Atalia?" he said.

"We have regained contact with Captain Hage. Communications are currently restricted to coherent transmissions.
Galloglass's main communications nexus was overloaded
by neutrino flux at the peak of the explosion."

He nodded. "As would be expected, given the *Galloglass*'s close proximity to the *Midnight*. It was ready to dock
the moment the frigate's shields fell."

"With all due respect, sir," said Makaev. "The self-
destruction of the *Midnight* should have been anticipated."

Kajic noted her thin, almost imperceptible smile with
some irritation. "It was not a consideration," he said. "There
was nothing within Captain Klose's professional or personal
profiles to suggest that he would take such drastic action."

"Nevertheless, Captain," said Makaev, "he did self-
destruct."

Kajic hesitated, fixing his stare squarely upon her for almost a full minute. He had his doubts about her true role
aboard the ship, and how that role related to his own, but this
wasn't the time to let suspicion interfere with duty.

"Bring us back to yellow alert," he said eventually. "Stabilize our orbits and commence repairs. I want all fighters returned to the *Ana Vereine*. We must be ready to leave at a moment's notice."

"Yes, sir."

"What of the target? Has a sighting been confirmed?"

"Debris scanning is under way."

He returned his attention to the data flowing from the sensors. "Replay the destruct sequence. Bring reserve computers on-line to plot the dispersal pattern and extend scan accordingly. It has to be out there somewhere," he said. "I want it found."

"Sir." Makaev's left arm snapped a salute; then she turned away.

On the main screen the fiery death of the *Midnight* returned to haunt him. He could have accessed the data directly, but for the moment he preferred the luxury of viewing the information from a distance, allowing him a more . . . *Human* perspective.

The outcome of the battle had indeed taken him by surprise. A protracted engagement had always been a possibility; on that point the tacticians agreed, and Kajic had prepared himself for Dato Bloc losses—but not for this. Not for the complete annihilation of the frigate and all its contents.

detain or disable COEA Midnight

His orders, hardwired into his circuitry, sprang into his thoughts unbidden. With his mission suffering such a spectacular setback, he was not surprised that they had. They were intended as a prompt, to surface with any doubt or uncertainty over the success of his mission.

capture and return Commander Roche and AI JW111101000

They continued—and would keep doing so until his thoughts were once again focused upon his mission, and all reservations concerning its success were dispelled.

priority gold-one

He shrugged aside the mental prompts and concentrated upon the recent battle:

Operationally, the strategy had been a simple one, and

had been well executed. With the DBMP *Lansquenet*, *Galloglass*, and *Paladin* in support, the *Ana Vereine* had translated with extreme precision to the coordinates provided. The *Midnight* had been exactly where the Espionage Corps had reckoned it would be—too far in-system to make a run for the nearest anchor point, and foolishly vulnerable in Sciacca's World's orbital ring. Decelerating, outflanked, and outgunned, the *Midnight* had, ultimately, no choice other than surrender—or so reason would have had it.

The destruction of an Armada frigate in COE space, by its own hand or not, unplanned or not, had all the makings of a major diplomatic incident. A high cost, even if the mission ultimately proved to be successful—which was still by no means certain.

While the bridge bustled around him, Kajic accessed Klose's files and restudied the captain's profile. Klose's service record, stolen by Espionage Corps spies from COE Armada databanks, was long and unremarkable. CEO of an old frigate, normally given unimportant duties, Klose had been marked as a conservative living off remembered glories, full of hubris, disrespectful of the "new breed" of well-educated military administrators, stubborn and authoritarian—much like the Commonwealth he served. The possibility that Klose had also been unstable was something Kajic had not considered—had no *reason* to consider. There was nothing in the man's records to warrant it.

Klose had taken his own orders—to prevent the Dato Bloc from capturing the AI—to the absolute extreme. He had done so knowingly, choosing death before surrender, and had taken his crew with him, regardless of what their individual choices might have been.

Unexpected, yes. But if Kajic had not counted on Proctor Klose's reaction, then the opposite was also true: Klose could not have anticipated Kajic's own response to the situation. He had no intention of letting the destruction of the *Midnight* prevent him from fulfilling his mission. Nor would he permit any interference from the prison planet itself to stop him. Nothing was going to get in the way. Not even his often debilitating fear of failure.

priority gold-one

He forced the fear down, away from the surface. If there was one thing Kajic was, it was focused on the mission.

His orders had been explicit, and ranked in order of priority. These three priorities had been stamped into the fine mesh of bio-implants infiltrating the tissues of his living brain to ensure that there could be no possibility of misunderstanding their significance. No matter how omnipotent he felt at times—with his mind roving the labyrinthine networks of the *Ana Vereine*—priorities A to C were a constant reminder of his limitations, of just how much he owed the machines in his coffin.

Life. Senses. Command. Duty:

(A) capture the AI;

(B) capture Roche;

(C) perform (A) and (B) with as much stealth and speed as possible.

Focused.

"Atalia?"

His second returned instantly to his side, as though proximity to his image actually meant something. Microphones and cameras scattered throughout the Marauder provided him with the ability to communicate with anyone, anywhere, at any time he wished. She, of all the people on board, should have known that. Had she forgotten this, he wondered, or was it a deliberate action?

But then, he reminded himself, this was one of the many things the experiment was designed to test. Was effective command dependent on genuine physical presence, or could it be simulated? Could a simulation breed resentment, even fear, among those it was supposed to deal with most effectively?

"Sir?" Makaev's voice was as controlled as it always was.

"Dispatch shuttles to examine the larger pieces in situ."

She frowned. "If we do that, sir, we will be unable to leave until the shuttles have returned."

He manufactured a glower and turned its full force on her. "Are you questioning my orders?"

"Of course not, sir, but—"

"Then see that they are carried out immediately."

Makaev turned away and relayed the order to a subordinate while Kajic watched the *Midnight* explode an uncounted time and let the anger percolate through him.

He would not allow this temporary setback to get on top of him. He would not allow himself to doubt that he was capable of fulfilling the expectations of those who had designed him. He would not, *could* not, afford to fail.

It was just a matter of time.

4

COEA Lander _M-3_
'954.10.30 EN
0775

Roche slammed back into the couch, the valise crushing her rib cage and forcing the air from her lungs. The roar of the thrusters threatened to split her eardrums. She wanted to turn her head to check on the others, but the acceleration would not allow her.

Thrust increased twofold for an instant, accompanied by a thunderous rattling on the hull. The lander slewed violently, as though flying through atmospheric turbulence.

<What's happening, Box?> Her mental voice was faint beneath the noise.

<We're riding the _Midnight_'s shock wave, Morgan. I apologize for the bumpy ride, but it cannot be avoided.>

She forced herself to relax as much as she could, letting her abnormally heavy body roll with the vibrations and trying not to worry about damage to the lander's hull. It was out of her hands entirely now. All she could do was hope that the Box knew what it was doing.

<Applying lateral thrust to alter our course.> The voice of the AI was no different from normal, as though riding the envelope of a thermonuclear explosion was all in a day's

work. <The Dato do not seem to have noticed our launch, obviously confused by the general debris around us. However, to avoid the increasing likelihood of thruster detection, I am cutting the main burn—now.>

Roche felt herself lift from the couch, her body pressing momentarily against the sudden tautness of the restraints. The rattling on the hull continued for a while before fading into silence. The occasional *tap-tap* of smaller thrusters came through the hull, changing the attitude of the lander slightly and making her stomach roll. A few minutes later she was weightless.

Her mind was heavy, however, with the knowledge of the carnage they had left behind.

<I have set a course for Sciacca's World,> said the Box. <Our orbit is highly elliptical, first taking us away from the planet and then back to perihelion at the edge of the atmosphere. We will exit the Soul in approximately ten minutes. Reentry will be in approximately nine hours.>

Roche forced herself to think about the future. <How long to perihelion?>

<Six hours. A slow trip, I know, Morgan, but this way we continue the pretense of debris.>

She nodded. It was a sensible strategy, given the situation: with no anchor or slow-jump drive and only a small amount of fuel, their possible destinations were limited to Kanaga Station in orbit or Port Parvati on the surface. Their decision would depend on the Dato and the movements of the Marauder. <Could be worse, I suppose.>

<Indeed. The pretense might have been reality.>

Roche loosened her restraint harness and massaged her aching muscles. The Box was right: had the *Midnight* exploded a minute sooner, they wouldn't have made it. <So what now?>

<Nothing. Rest, perhaps, if you feel the need to. I can handle the lander. Apart from monitoring the Dato, there is little to do.>

"Except find a few answers, perhaps," she muttered as she swung herself free of the chair, hooking the fingers of one hand around a grip to stabilize herself in the zero-g.

Cane watched unblinkingly from his seat at the copilot's station as she swiveled in midair to face him.

"We survived," he said. His natural smile reflected his calm disposition. Their abrupt departure didn't appear to have affected him in any way. "Whoever it was that spoke to me in my cell was right: you have been able to help me."

"So it would seem." She sensed no dissembling in his face and posture—and his gratitude seemed genuine—but she still couldn't afford to trust him. She knew too little to turn her back on him just yet.

She moved over to check on the Eckandi and the Surin, her movements within the cramped lander awkward and clumsy. A quick look confirmed her suspicions.

"Good. They won't wake for a while." She returned to her own couch and looked across at Cane. "I think it's time we talked."

"Whatever you want, Commander."

"How much do you actually remember?"

"I told you: I woke up a few days ago on the ship with no memory beyond my name. Since then, apart from a few visits from the ship's science officer, I've been left alone."

"Do you know that you were picked up in a life-support capsule?"

"I was told that much, but little else."

"They didn't tell you how long you'd been drifting?"

"I did overhear something to the effect that it might have been a while," he said. "But nothing was officially mentioned."

"I don't suppose you happened to 'overhear' anything else, did you?"

"Little. Why?"

"Because the science officer's report was destroyed with the *Midnight*." Along with any records of the conversation that had led him to her, she added to herself, rubbing a hand across tired eyes. The rush of adrenaline she had experienced over the last few hours had left her feeling more than a little exhausted. "Your recollections are all we have left to go on, I'm afraid."

Cane raised an eyebrow. "Well, I know I was picked up near an anchor point leading here. Not by chance, either: the

Midnight apparently detected a distress signal. Where the signal came from, however, is a mystery; the capsule had no transmitter, and the signal vanished once they picked up the capsule on scan." He shrugged. "I can't explain it, and neither could the science officer."

Roche nodded, absorbing the information. "What else?"

"Not much. He wanted to know more about the way the capsule worked. I gather it contained a lot of equipment not normally required for any sort of emergency coma."

"Such as?"

"Biofeedback systems, I believe, but I really don't know." He shook his head. "I have no memory at all of any time before the capsule. If there was any."

Roche frowned. "What do you mean by that?"

"Nothing." A smile touched his lips but was gone a moment later. "It sometimes feels as though I was born inside the capsule."

"If you were, then you've grown up quick; you can talk, think, and move like an adult." And a very adept one at that, she thought to herself. She could see his potential in the way he held himself: constantly primed, ready to act, and yet, paradoxically, always at ease with his situation. The way he had carried himself in the lander bay had been more than impressive. An army of soldiers like Cane would be hard to stop. "Perhaps you were a combat soldier?"

"Maybe," he said, but without conviction.

A groan from behind them made them both turn. Roche instinctively reached for her pistol, then saw it was the old Eckandi, struggling in his chair. He was little more than semiconscious, and she noted with approval that Cane had locked the harness tight—something she should have done herself. Still, she kept the pistol ready. If the Surin had been a reave, who knew what the Eckandi—the Surin had called him "Veden," she recalled—would be.

Veden shook his head, opened his eyes. Taking in the interior of the lander with one quick glance, he turned to face Roche and Cane.

"Where—?" His voice was thin and accented faintly, but clear. His wide-pupiled eyes were startled, flitting between Roche and Cane, their movement beneath the fine milky film that was peculiar to the Eckandar Caste causing Roche some discomfort. "Where am I?"

"On the lander," Roche replied. "Heading for Sciacca's World."

"The *Midnight*?" Without waiting for a reply he turned to the unconscious Surin strapped into the seat beside him. "Maii?" He made to move, then realized that he too was restrained. "What have you done to her?"

Roche watched with interest the concern on the Eckandi's face. "She'll be okay."

"You know she's a reave?" Roche nodded; Veden shook his head. "I can't even begin to imagine how you managed to get past her."

Nor can I, Roche admitted to herself, but said: "We surprised you in the lander bay. Do you remember that?"

"I remember you shot me." Thin but distinct muscles tightened around the Eckandi's eyes. "I remember that much."

"You fired upon us first," said Cane.

"What else was I supposed to do? We had to get out of there. The ship was about to blow."

"How could you have known that?" Using a hand-grip, Roche pulled herself forward slightly. "And how did you escape from your cell?"

"Maii—" He hesitated, glancing again at the Surin. "She was monitoring the guards when the Dato hit. She got one of them to open the cell and let us go. It's considerably easier to manipulate people when they are panicked or confused, you see, so the attack on the *Midnight* was fortuitous in a way." He shifted beneath his restraints. "After that it was a simple matter of getting to the lander bay. I've flown landers like this all my life; launching wouldn't have been a problem." He seemed about to say something further, but decided against it and fell silent.

"Sounds a bit too easy," said Roche doubtfully. "If it was that simple to escape, then why didn't you do it sooner? I mean, surely there would have been other times in other systems when the guards were vulnerable. Why wait until we're at Sciacca's World?"

"That's none of your business." His milky glare fixed on

Roche for a few seconds before he turned away and faced Cane. "Who's *he*, anyway?"

Cane met Veden's unexpected hostility with a broad grin, the lights from the lander's displays flashing in his steady eyes. "That would appear to be none of *your* business," he said.

Veden's gaze returned to Roche. "He's working under-cover for the Armada—for COE Intelligence—is that it? I don't remember seeing him in the brig." Roche ignored the question. "Whoever he is, he moves like one of those damned jarapines from Proebis-12."

<Morgan.> The Box's voice sounded in her mind.

<Yes, Box?> She was careful to subvocalize in front of the Eckandi.

<There is an Eckandi named Makil Veden listed on the *Midnight*'s freight transcript.>

<What was his charge?>

<Code violation and gross misconduct. Apparently he trod quite heavily on someone's toes—someone in the Commerce Artel, I would guess, given that he used to work for them. Death sentence commuted to transportation.>

<Any mention of the Surin?>

<Conspirator. Same charges.>

<Thanks, Box.> She returned her attention to Veden, regarding the Eckandi silently for a few moments before speaking. "So," she said, "was it fraud, or outright rob-bery?"

His eyes widened. "I don't know what you mean."

"The code violation. You must be more stupid than you look to mess with the Commerce Artel."

"If you say so, Commander." He dismissed her accusa-tion with a flick of his head. If he was surprised by her knowledge of his history, he showed no sign of it. There was more than just a hint of contempt in his crooked smile. "Who am I to question an Armada officer?"

Their eyes locked for thirty seconds or so before he fi-nally looked away, his smile fading beneath a sigh. "At least we're alive," he said, closing his eyes and lying back into the chair. "That's all that matters right now."

"For you, maybe," Roche muttered. "What matters to me

is that I'm stuck with you for at least another five hours."
She watched the Eckandi closely for a reaction, but there
was none. With the typical arrogance of his Caste, he had
decided to terminate the conversation. For all intents and
purposes, he had totally closed himself off, and Roche knew
that further questioning would be useless for the time being.
Maybe, she hoped, things would change when the Surin
awoke.

To Cane she said: "I'm going to check out the lander, see
what we've got in the way of supplies. Can I rely on you to
keep an eye on him?"

Cane nodded. "Of course."

"If the reave tries anything when she wakes, knock her
out again." The words elicited no response from the supine
Eckandi. "We're some way from safety, and I don't want
anything else to go wrong."

"Understood." He folded his arms as she left the cockpit.
When she returned five minutes later to check on him, he
hadn't moved a muscle. *A perfect sentry*, she thought. Almost too good, in fact.

<Box?>

<Yes, Morgan.>

<Watch him via the cabin monitors. If he makes the
slightest move, let me know.>

<You're a trusting soul, aren't you?>

She didn't smile as she returned to the storeroom. "That's
a luxury I can't afford at the moment," she said, more to herself than to the Box.

Four hours later, a voice roused her from a deep slumber she
couldn't remember entering:

<Wakey-wakey, Morgan.>

Her head jerked up, and the sudden movement sent her
drifting across the room. More by chance than anything else,
she managed to catch hold of a stanchion and bring herself
to a halt. A rush of panic subsided when her eyes adjusted to
the dim light of her surroundings and she realized where she
was: the lander's storeroom. She had come in to check on
what equipment was available to them, but the low lights
coupled with her exhaustion had seduced her into sleep.

Not, however, before she had ascertained how little in the way of supplies they actually had: two medical kits, three basic communicators, six survival suits, and enough food to last them two days—five if rationed severely. The only weapons on board were Veden's laser and her own pistol.

<Morgan.> The voice was sterner this time, cutting through her tired thoughts.

Roche rubbed her eyes, shook her head. "Yes, Box," she said. "I'm awake. How long have I been out?"

<Too long. I would have let you sleep longer, but there has been a development.>

"Oh? What?"

<The Surin has regained consciousness.>

She shook her head one last time to clear it of the residue of sleep, then pushed herself toward the door. It slid aside with a hiss, and she slipped out into the narrow accessway. The only other room in the lander, a privacy and waste cubicle opposite the storeroom, was sealed, occupied. Sparing it but a glance, she brushed past it and into the cockpit.

Cane had moved to a position by the main entrance. The Surin lay with her back to Roche, still strapped into the central couch. The only movement as she entered the room came from Cane's eyes, which glanced at her before returning to the reave.

<I can detect peripheral vision also.> The reave's voice echoed deep in Roche's head, although the statement was intended for Cane. It was a strange and intimate kind of intrusion—almost a rape—and felt as though someone was using her brain to think their own thoughts. It was very different from the Box's clear input, and Roche detested it. <I admire your perseverance,> continued the Surin. <But I knew Roche was awake the moment she did. I could have taken her then, if I'd wanted to. Doesn't that mean anything to you? That I didn't?>

Roche watched from the other side of the cockpit as Cane kept his eyes still. Nothing was spoken aloud, but a conversation took place nonetheless.

<I'm trying to tell you that you can trust me!> The Surin's tone was desperate. She was clearly uncomfortable in her restraints. <I know I can't hurt *you*. But, Roche—Yes,

I am aware of what would happen if I tried. I'm just saying that I *could*. Why don't you *believe* me?>

Roche cleared her throat pointedly. "Where's Veden?" The couch next to the Surin was empty.

<He's in the privacy cabin,> replied the reave. <And stop thinking of me as just a Surin. My name is Maii.>

Roche forced herself to reply civilly. "Thank you," she said, "Maii."

<You don't trust me, do you?>

"Should I?"

<You tell her, Cane.>

"She's telling the truth." Cane finally wrenched his eyes away from the Surin's. "He's locked in the cubicle. The couch was too uncomfortable for an old man to be confined to for such a long period of time."

Roche nodded. It seemed reasonable, she supposed. "What about you two?"

Cane shrugged noncommittally.

<He's trying to resist me,> explained the Surin. <He doesn't like me using his eyes, and keeps them focused on my face to stop me seeing anything. But it isn't working.> Roche sensed amusement as the girl added: <It's okay now, Cane. You can relax. I'm not using them anymore.>

Roche suppressed a shudder, and barely caught herself from using her training to keep the girl out of her head, if she could at all. There was no point. If the reave noticed her revulsion, she didn't mention it.

"Maii, I want you to tell me about Veden. Who is he, and what were you doing with him?"

<Cane can answer that,> said the girl. <I've already told him.>

Roche turned to Cane, who shrugged. "She says they're not really transportees—or rather, they are, but not criminals."

"That doesn't make sense."

<I know, but that's all I can say.> The Surin's narrow tongue licked at the fine hair around her black lips. <You'll have to ask Veden.>

"I did," said Cane.

Roche's eyes flicked from Maii to Cane. "And what did he say?"

"Nothing."

"I didn't think he would." Roche moved around the cockpit and came up beside the girl's couch. "Is he using you against your will?"

Something rippled gently through Roche's mind—Maii was chuckling. <I'm not a *slave*, if that's what you're suggesting. Veden wouldn't dream of doing anything like that.>

"No, I meant . . ." She shook her head. "You know what I meant."

The girl looked annoyed for an instant, the flash of emotion the first true vitality Roche had seen in the Surin's face. <I don't know *everything* about you. Just the surface thoughts; the obvious details. I could read deeper, of course, if you'd let me.>

"That didn't stop you before," said Roche. "Back in the lander bay." The experience was still vivid in her mind.

<You caught me by surprise. One moment Veden was going to seal the airlock, and the next he'd been knocked out. I panicked.> The girl looked genuinely sad for a moment. <Contrary to popular belief, Commander, we epsense adepts do have some moral standards.>

Roche snorted. "Yeah, they just aren't very high."

<That isn't fair,> said the Surin. <You make it sound as though what happened back on the *Midnight* is something I enjoy doing. But I don't. It happens to be very draining.>

"Not to mention immoral."

<And a pistol isn't?>

Roche mentally conceded the point, and wondered if she was being more than a little paranoid. She was imagining dark motives behind everything the reave said and did—sophisticated deceits that only an adult would be capable of. The ritually blinded Surin, for all her psychic talents, was still little more than a child. Petulant sometimes, perhaps even vicious, but a child nonetheless.

What the Surin had been doing in the company of Makil Veden remained a concern, however. To Roche, the long-faced and grey-skinned Eckandi made an odd figure beside the tawny Surin, with her wide jaws and lightly fuzzed complexion. Obviously their relationship went back a lot farther than the *Midnight*, perhaps even as far as the Surin's birth. Certainly Maii seemed to regard Veden in a respectful light; maybe the Eckandi had adopted her as his surrogate daughter.

"You're very young," said Roche. "Far younger than any other reave I've met."

Maii's face closed instantly. <I developed young. Let's leave it at that, okay?>

"Hey, I was just—"

<I'm sorry to interrupt, Morgan.>

Roche turned away from the Surin. <What is it, Box?>

<Good and bad news, I'm afraid.>

She groaned inwardly. <Let's have it.>

<First: despite my precautions, we have been located. The undamaged raider has changed course to pursue us. They clearly intend a leapfrog maneuver—overtaking us and launching interceptors before we reach perihelion—which seems sensible under the circumstances.>

<Okay.> She braced herself against the nearest couch. <The good news?>

<That was it.>

<Come on, Box. This is no time for—>

<I am being completely serious, Morgan. Relatively speaking, that *was* the good news: they haven't decided to destroy us outright. The bad news is that the local authority in orbit around Sciacca's World has made no move to avenge the destruction of the *Midnight*. Furthermore, I have detected coded transmissions between the Dato Marauder and Kanaga Station.>

Roche frowned, trying to comprehend what the Box was implying. <The Dato wouldn't take over a COE Communications Base, would they? That'd be tantamount to a declaration of war.>

<You misunderstand me, Morgan. Ask yourself why these transmissions are coded in the first place.>

Even as the Box posed the question, the answer had formed in her own mind. <Because neither party wants what they have to say to go public. A strictly private exchange.>

<Precisely. Now consider: four ships from the Dato Bloc

attacked and destroyed an Armada frigate within a planetary system under the nominal control—or at least the scrutiny—of the Commonwealth. How could they hope to execute such an attack and get away with it, camouflaged or not? The repercussions would be severe.>

<I don't like the sound of this, Box.>

<It is decidedly unpleasant. I have recorded the times each transmission took place; you may need the detail later. For now, it is sufficient that you know that the command on Kanaga Station is, to some degree at least, corrupt.>

<Dato sympathizers?>

<It is unlikely to be anything so moral. Just corrupt. The attack on the *Midnight* was no incident of opportunity; it was carefully planned in advance, using information gathered even higher—from the very top of the COE Armada. A high-priced deal was struck with those in power here around Sciacca's World in order to facilitate it. It is also likely that an even more generous deal is being negotiated to ensure our recapture.>

<So it *is* you they're after?>

<Both of us, it seems, or else they would have destroyed the lander immediately upon sighting it. Negotiations will currently be determining the true extent of our value to your opposite numbers in the Dato Bloc Espionage Corps. I would guess the ultimate figure will be exceedingly high.>

<That's something, I guess.> Roche tugged herself forward to the lander's array of instrumentation and the pilot's couch. The feel of cushions against her back was somehow reassuring. <So, let me guess what happens next. Either we dock at Kanaga Station and are handed over to the Dato—for a tidy sum and no questions asked—or we go into the atmosphere and take our chances on the ground. We have no way of knowing how Port Parvati figures in this, but we know that it'll cost the Dato considerably more to land a search party, or pay for one to be sent after us. Either way, going to ground is our best option.>

<An essentially accurate summary.>

<Then do it. Take us down. Try to put us down at Port Parvati's landing field, or nearby. They'll have communica-

tors there. At the very least we'll be able to let HQ know what happened.>

<As you wish.> The Box paused for a moment, then added, almost as an afterthought: <I suggest you get everybody into the acceleration couches. In order to take the Dato raider by surprise, I will have to use maximum thrust.>

<Right.>

Roche sat up and looked around. Cane was studying her closely.

"From the look on your face," he said quietly, "I take it we're in trouble."

"We are. Get yourself strapped in. No, wait—we need to wake Veden."

Cane stepped from the room to get the Eckandi. At least with him nearby, Roche thought, the Surin would no longer need her senses, or those of Cane.

A couple of minutes later, when Cane had returned with Veden, Roche turned and addressed everyone. "The Dato are on to us, but there's a chance we can outrun them. We'll be thrusting at max, so make sure your harnesses are firm. Let me know when you're set."

Cane dropped into his couch and fastened the harness with all the speed and surety of a veteran. He smiled reassuringly at Roche but said nothing. She didn't respond. Veden swung himself into the couch next to Maii and sealed himself in.

<We're fine,> said Maii a moment later.

"Okay here," Cane added.

Roche locked the clasps around her own chest and midriff and let the couch enfold her.

<When you're ready, Box.>

Immediately the thrusters crushed them back into the couches. Roche felt the air empty from her lungs, and struggled against the acceleration to refill them. Purple spots floated in her eyes as blood drained from her retinae. She wondered briefly how Veden was managing; he was an aging man, surely not up to such strain. If the burn continued for too long, he might exhaust himself, be in danger of asphyxiating—

Her thoughts were interrupted when she felt the Surin's

mind-touch come and go. She glanced up to the monitors above her and had the Box display a view of the others. Maii's face was turned up, her breathing strong and even. She at least was having no difficulties. Veden also seemed to be breathing steadily, which surprised Roche. His eyes were closed, almost as if he were asleep. He was handling the burn with considerable ease.

Then Roche realized why: Maii had taken over his autonomous systems. The girl was regulating his breathing and heart rate in sympathy with her own. Veden was in a state far deeper than sleep; he had given himself over completely to the reave.

The degree of the invasion was abominable, but Roche knew that the acceleration would be life-threatening for Veden if Maii had not been controlling him. And she had checked on Roche in passing—to make sure that she hadn't required similar assistance.

Roche shuddered. It made her skin crawl just thinking about it.

She withdrew into herself, concentrated on riding out the burn. She thought about asking the Box how long it planned to stay at max, but decided it was better not to know. She cleared her mind and focused inward upon her body, riding the stress rather than fighting it.

Even so, the burn seemed to last forever. When the pressure suddenly lapsed, there came in its place a sensation of relative weightlessness, but Roche knew from experience how false the feeling was. The Box was still holding the lander at somewhere between two and three gees. Although the lander's instruments had come to life—now that the pretense of dereliction was over—her eyes wouldn't focus properly.

<What's the situation, Box?>

The Box's voice was annoyingly free of strain. <It would appear that the opposition lacks a decisive strategist. The raider moved to overlap us, but declined to drop its interceptor craft. They seem reluctant to maneuver so deep within the Soul—probably because of the threat of damage to hull integrity posed by the ever-present dust—and so have

opted to allow us to land. The safer but more expensive option.>

<So why are we still accelerating?>

<To put it colloquially, Morgan: I do not wish to tip our hand too soon. We have an advantage in that the opposition does not know that I know about their communications with Kanaga Station, and I intend to keep that advantage as long as possible. My strategy is to continue to give the appearance of a pursued vessel. This means a hot descent to Port Parvati—which will, unfortunately, be uncomfortable.> The Box hesitated before continuing: <I believe the time has come, Morgan, to abandon our heretofore one-on-one communication status.>

Roche didn't answer immediately. One-on-one was a basic security precaution prescribed by her superiors in COE Intelligence. Technically, she could not countermand it.

<Why?> she asked, instinctively suspicious.

<I am simply suggesting that we open an internal com channel so that I will be able to communicate directly with everybody in the lander. If I am to make decisions based on constantly changing random factors, then critical information will have to be available to everybody. A successful outcome may depend on the swiftness of our response to an unforeseen emergency.>

Roche felt weary. The move made good sense, and the Box could open the channel itself if it really wanted to. But to go against a direct order . . .

With difficulty, she reached for the pilot's console, selected an internal com channel, and flicked it open. "Okay, Box. You've got what you want. The stage is yours."

<Thank you,> the Box lilted. <Internal com will not come through your implant.> Even as Roche heard the voice in her ear, it delivered a separate message over the newly opened channel.

"The thrusters are about to be cut," it said loudly, employing more than enough volume to gain attention over the background noise of the burn.

Roche glanced at Cane, then at the others. Cane's eyebrows had risen sharply when the voice of the Box broke the relative silence of the cabin, but he quickly regained his composure. Veden looked completely relaxed, his eyes focused somewhere ahead of him. He gave no indication that he was even listening.

"We will be entering the atmosphere of Sciacca's World within minutes," the Box went on, sounding more like a tour guide than the present arbiter of their destinies. "It will be a hot and bumpy descent. Further maneuvers will be necessary once we're able to deploy our glide foils, so please remain in your harnesses. I will inform you when it is safe to release them."

<I hope your little black box knows what it's doing.> Maii's tone was sharp. AIs, Roche remembered, were regularly used to counteract reaves, unable as the latter were to read electronic thoughts.

"It knows," Roche said aloud, but with an uncertainty that mirrored the Surin's own feelings. Then the burn died, and suddenly they were weightless again.

She looked toward Cane, found him watching her impassively. "That was the Box?" he asked.

"Yes."

"Interesting," he said thoughtfully. "It sounds very . . . Human."

Something struck the hull of the lander with a short but decisive bang, and Roche jumped in her seat. "Box?"

<Particulate debris,> replied the AI, in her ears only. <Nothing to be greatly concerned about. At our velocity, small impacts are inevitable.>

<The hull will hold?>

<It is being damaged but, yes, it will hold.>

<How long until we hit atmosphere?>

<Not long. The burn changed our orbit significantly. Using the velocity we already possessed as a result of the downward leg of our ellipse, I have directed the lander into a near-vertical descent. Our trajectory will change in approximately five minutes to soften the impact with the upper atmosphere.>

Roche closed her eyes and tried to relax, hard though it was with the lander hurtling straight down into an unknown situation. Two minutes passed, then three, and no one in the cockpit made a sound. Then:

<Slight change of plans, Morgan.>

<What's happened?>

<Port Parvati has launched a squadron of fighters to intercept us before we land.>

She groaned. <So they're involved as well.>

<It would seem so. We can't rely on them for assistance, in any case. That forces us to reassess our intentions. I suggest we continue along our current course, to present the illusion of surrender, then peel away from the landing field at the last possible moment.>

<Peel away to where?>

<That, Morgan, is something I do not yet know.>

Roche blinked. She had never heard the Box admit anything but omniscience before. <But you will, right? When the time comes?>

<Let us say that I will go with what seems the best option at the time.>

Roche could hardly believe what she was hearing. She knew that independent Boxes could be unpredictable—unlike their rigidly controlled, and therefore less flexible, counterparts in the COE Armada—but they simply didn't *say* things like that.

<At the risk of sounding critical,> she said, with a growing disquiet, <your strategy seems to be constructed of and entirely dependent on random factors.>

<Yes, Morgan. Exciting, is it not?>

The thrusters burned again, bringing the lander into a less steep descent.

"Not the word I would have used," she said quietly. Then, shouting over the noise to the others in the cockpit: "We can't afford to trust anyone on the ground. The government here is corrupt. If we fall into their hands, they'll turn us over to the Dato Bloc. The Box's strategy is to let them think we're coming straight in—that we know none of this. We'll change course as late as possible and look for other hands to fall into. Everyone happy with that?"

On the monitors she saw Cane cock an eyebrow and give the faintest of shrugs. At the same time she heard Maii mind-whisper: <Too bad if we're not.> Roche saw Veden grin at this.

Roche could appreciate the irony of his situation. The Dato were after Roche and the Box, not the transportees. Perhaps Veden had expected to be turned over to the authorities in Port Parvati as soon as the lander made planetfall. Had that indeed been Roche's intention—and she'd had very little time to consider her plans for him and the Surin—then the discovery of treachery on the planet rendered it unlikely. From Veden's point of view, as long as he pleaded ignorance, the betrayal of Port Parvati's wardens was good news, not bad.

Accordingly, it was Veden who spoke next:

"Your Box should know that outlaw forces are currently operating on Sciacca's World."

"I hear you, Veden," the Box said through the com. "Elaborate, please."

"There's a group operating in the mountainous area to the north of Port Parvati. They may be able to assist us."

"I have relief maps on file. Can you provide coordinates?"

"They're a mobile group. That's how they survive."

"Then your information has little value." A viewtank winked into life on the pilot's display, showing an expanded view of Sciacca's World. The main continental mass zoomed close; Port Parvati was in the center of a large but relatively featureless desert with a forbidding range of mountains to the immediate north. A cursor traced a wide arc along the southernmost peaks. "We must assume that our hypothetical allies exist somewhere in this region. The range known as Behzad's Wall offers sufficient cover not too far from the port for any number of resistance operations."

"Take us along the spine of the range, then," said Veden. "There's a plateau containing an old strip mine and an abandoned town. Land us as close us possible to that location. They'll find us, if they want to."

"Understood."

Both the Box and Veden fell silent. Roche turned to look at the old man. "Just who are these people?"

"Commander, you belong to COE Intelligence. As such,

you're the last person I should discuss this information with."

Roche felt mounting exasperation. "But if the Port Parvati authorities are corrupt, then COE Intelligence needs to be informed. If your friends have formed some sort of resistance, then they should be making every attempt to communicate with us. We can help them."

Veden frowned. "COE Intelligence is an arm of the Commonwealth, just as the Enforcers in Port Parvati are. Why should one arm act against another?"

Roche stared at him, unable to believe that her government could be so distrusted. But Veden went on before she could protest.

"Anyway, they are not my friends. They are merely clients. I was coming here to do a job. Why they have done or not done certain things is not my concern."

"But you're a transportee," Roche said. "How could you—?" She stopped in mid-sentence. There could be only one answer, the one Maii had provided earlier.

Veden confirmed it. "As a transportee, I could be moved here without arousing suspicion. All I needed was a conviction and a life sentence."

Easy, Roche thought, although not without skepticism. "You're being well paid for this, I take it?"

"Perhaps."

"To do what, exactly?"

"That, Commander, is a matter safeguarded by professional confidentiality. I'm in business, after all, not an agent of COE Intelligence."

"I—uh!" The lander suddenly shifted, jolting Roche violently against her harness. She saw Veden's face twist in pain, felt Maii's desperation as she quickly tried to regain control over the old man's autonomous systems. "Box! What the hell is going on?"

"We are about to strike the ionosphere." The Box's voice came loudly over the com. "Most of our reentry velocity will be shed by aerobraking, during which time I will maintain a standard approach to Port Parvati. At the last moment, however, we will overfly the landing area and proceed north at roughly treetop level. Somewhere in the mountains I shall attempt to simulate a crash."

"'Attempt' . . . ?" Roche gaped. Landing in a gravity well was the most difficult maneuver a pilot could be asked to perform; she knew it would be all too easy to *genuinely* crash, no matter what the Box's intentions were.

But the Box had obviously anticipated her misgivings. In her ear only, it said: <This is the best strategy, Morgan. If we appear to perish, they might lose interest in us. Trust me on this, please. It is the only option open to us at this time.>

Over the com, the Box continued its spiel. "I will attempt to land as close to Veden's target as possible. Once down, there will be very little time to get clear before the engines overload."

"How long exactly?" said Roche.

"That I cannot predict. It depends on the severity of damage sustained as a result of the impact. Regardless, a hasty departure will certainly be in order."

"Will we have time to gather supplies?"

"Perhaps. We will have to see what happens."

The retros ceased their noisy burn. A few seconds of weightless glide followed; then the atmosphere touched the hull, feather-light at first but with a steadily increasing force. The lander began to bump and slew, the series of jolts gradually building in violence. As friction tore at the pockmarked nose of the vessel, the temperature inside the cockpit began to rise, and Roche began to feel decidedly uncomfortable.

In her ear, the Box's emotionless voice whispered: <The fighters from Port Parvati are tracking us. They are also attempting to communicate. I am ignoring them, of course. Thus far, they have made no overtly hostile moves. It could be that they are present simply to ensure that we head for the landing field.>

The lurching descent continued, and the temperature continued to rise. Roche heard a mental curse from Maii, but the girl sounded in control—which meant that Veden was all right also. And she knew that Cane would be coping as easily as he seemed to cope with everything else.

She tried to push the mounting heat aside, but her mind

refused to settle. There were too many unknowns swirling about her: Veden with his connections to whatever waited on the surface, Maii's connection with him and her ability to know anything and everything Roche herself knew, and a Box that was trying its best to cook them all.

Not quite. Just when she felt she could stand it no longer, the temperature began to fall again. The wild ride was finally easing.

"Box?"

"Extending glide foils in thirty seconds. Lining up on the landing area."

The cabin jolted again as the airfoils extended and the lander began to maneuver in clear air. Moments later, the ride became relatively smooth.

"Accelerating again in twelve seconds," the Box announced. "Brace yourselves."

Roche counted down the seconds, clutched the arms of the couch tightly to steady herself, but was slapped back into the cushions anyway. The lander slewed violently to the left, and the wild ride began afresh.

In her car: <I'm making it look as if we've lost control. We'll put down near this end of the range, just as soon as I get us into radio shadow.>

Over the com: "Hard landing in approximately one minute. The cargo doors will be open. Be ready to disembark. Try to put as much distance as possible between yourselves and the lander. That or some large objects."

And again in her ear: <It's going to be rough, so don't worry about supplies. Just up and run.>

<You're one hell of a strategist, Box.>

<Don't knock it, Morgan. We're still in the game.>

"Twenty seconds to impact," it said over the com.

Roche braced herself yet again. The lander swayed extravagantly, but she noticed that the vertical component of the glide remained smooth. The Box had full control. Still, she was glad there was no viewing portal. Better not to see what was happening outside.

Then came a frightening few seconds of silence—no slewing, no whining of the airfoils, just waiting for impact. She didn't know what was worse.

<Hold onto me, Morgan,> the Box said to her.

Then they hit.

Roche was thrown against her harness with such force that it felt as if the couch would tear loose from its mountings. A long, terrible scream of ripping metal shrieked through the cabin; smoke suddenly filled the air. Anything not secured ricocheted around the cockpit.

Something clipped the side of Roche's skull, making her head ring. She closed her eyes and tried not to scream.

Cane called out something, but his words were lost in the noise.

The lander bounced once, twice, then careened violently to the right. Another lurch—this time upward, giving the impression that the craft was about to tip end over end. Sparks and blue flame erupted about them as the control panels and monitors exploded simultaneously. A series of small slews and lurches, a long dull grinding noise—

Then nothing but smoke.

"Evacuate immediately," the Box said into the ringing silence. Roche wasn't sure whether it was in her ear or over the com, but she needed no further prompting.

"Okay," she gasped, slipping the clasps on her harness. "Let's get out of here."

Cane reached across her and freed her rear clasps. Before she could move, he was doing the same for a badly dazed Veden. Roche couldn't help but marvel at him. He had been out of his harness almost instantly; with no sense of undue rush, he was moving faster than she could manage with all her Armada training.

"Help him out of here," she ordered as Veden stumbled, disoriented. Cane put an arm around the Eckandi's shoulders and guided him to the airlock.

Roche tucked the Box under her left arm, slid off the couch, and helped Maii to her feet. The Surin shrugged her hand away; the smoke in the air made her cough, but otherwise she was unharmed.

<I can walk,> Maii whispered in her mind. <Just point me in the right direction.>

Roche smiled to herself. "That way," she said, and started the girl forward. "Just keep moving. I won't be far behind."

Cane and Veden had already vanished. It was hard to tell through the thickening smoke exactly where she was. Something exploded with a *crump* beyond a bulkhead, showering her with sparks and temporarily blinding her. She had to rely on her hands to guide her along. At the storeroom, she stopped and tried the door.

"How long, Box?"

<Sixty seconds. I told you—>

"I know, I know. But we *need* those supplies."

The door to the storeroom had jammed shut, the frame warped by the impact. She kicked it open and stumbled through. The smoke was thicker in the tiny room, and the heat more oppressive. More sparks showered in a stream from one corner, burning her exposed skin. She clutched randomly at containers and, gagging upon the suffocating fumes, quickly thrust them into a plastic sack.

<Thirty seconds.>

"Okay," she said, coughing. "I hear you." Shrugging the half-empty sack over a shoulder, she hastened out of the room and through the cockpit. Halfway to the airlock, her foot tangled in a strip of burning insulation, making her stumble. Barely had she regained her feet when she felt strong hands clutch at her shoulders.

"Roche!" Cane's voice bellowed in her ear, straining to be heard over the rising rumble from the depleted fuel tanks. "Come on!"

Unable to reply, Roche let herself be hauled through the lander. As they crossed the lip of the airlock, her legs gave out entirely, sending her tumbling forward. As one, she and Cane fell down the steep egress ramp and onto rocky ground.

Maii was at their side immediately, pulling Cane to his feet. Roche had landed heavily beneath him, with the Box crushed up against her ribs. She had a bad feeling that one or more of them was broken. She reached for Maii's hand and heard Cane shout from somewhere above them: "I'll carry her! You get clear!"

Roche's head was swimming now. She was aware of Cane standing over her, and of his powerful arms dragging her upright. Pain shot across her chest as he lifted her onto his shoulders.

"*The sack*," she tried to say. If he replied, she didn't hear.

The pain increased when he started to run, but she fought against unconsciousness as long as she could. A loud explosion slapped the world behind her, and a flash of heat seared one side of her face—and then, finally, she blacked out.

PART TWO:

HOUGHTON'S CROSS

5

DBMP *Ana Vereine*
'954.10.30 EN
1225

Down through the complex matrix of information that represented the Dato Marauder, *Ana Vereine*, the soul of Captain Uri Kajic flew like an electric bird of prey—
feeling
—the hull humming with energy, singing like vibrating glass—
seeing
—sensors alive with light and radiation, feeding a constant stream of tactical and telemetry data directly to his nervous system—
tasting
—the drive mix: potent and powerful, exactly the right texture of elements at exactly the right temperature—
hearing
—the babble of voices chanting an epiphany to the process that was war and the great metal beasts that served its purpose—
dreaming
—of a faceless woman whose very presence threatened his existence in some vague, unstated manner.

While the remains of his body lay in its fluid-filled coffin, attended by patient machines, the various networks and subroutines implanted in the tissues of his brain ticked over without rest. From spinal column to cerebrum, every ganglion of his nervous system had been rewired to interface with some aspect of the ship. As a result, only part of his mind slept while the remainder continued its perpetual chores of monitoring the ship's activities.

His previous life—before the slow-jump accident and the operation—had been completely forgotten. Erased by surgery. The wire net lacing his plastic skull caught any ghosts long before they could disturb his thoughts, waking or unconscious. On every level of his being, he was the captain of the *Ana Vereine*—capable, efficient, and, above all, loyal. His dreams were always of the ship, his new body, and his mission; the never-ending flow of information from the *Ana Vereine* rarely allowed him anything else. Most filtered through his subconscious without ever requiring further attention, although occasionally certain elements of a dream would catch his interest and linger longer than normal.

Such as this threatening, faceless woman. . . .

He had no doubts that the dream was a warning, and that the woman was his second in command, Atalia Makaev. Since the beginning of the mission she had been undermining his leadership at every opportunity. Not overtly—that would constitute treason—but certainly subtly. It was in the things she said, the *way* she said them, and the manner in which she looked at him. Everything was a threat to his authority.

He had been designed and rebuilt to *lead*. Any challenge to that was a challenge to the very core of his being.

A soft but insistent alarm purred through his coffin, distracting him from his reverie. The image of the woman faded almost immediately, although he was unable to free himself of the apprehension that the dream had brought.

Focusing his thoughts on the specific rather than the general, Kajic glanced at the message. Makaev, with an uncanny sense of timing, had summoned him.

His sensory input jumped from sensors scattered across

the ship to the two task-specific cameras mounted on the bridge command dais. They swung to focus on the position Makaev usually occupied, but found it empty. Belatedly studying the summons in detail, he discovered her in the command module, a small niche used for privacy at the rear of the bridge.

Changing his position took less will than the blink of an eyelid. His hologram faded from the bridge and reappeared in the module, where Makaev stood watching him with her hands folded behind her back, her lips parted in a slight and narrow smile.

"News, sir." Her voice was brisk and businesslike, a sharp contrast to the way his brain presently felt. The hormone delivery systems of his life support needed tuning again, he guessed. He nodded, gesturing for her to continue.

"Our mole in DAOC flight control reports that the shuttle has crash-landed in a region to the north of Port Parvati, under cover of mountains."

He stared at her, momentarily disoriented.

priority gold-one

"*What* shuttle?" He quickly accessed the relevant data that had collected in his "memory" banks during his artificial slumber, waiting for him to find the opportunity to review it. There was nothing Makaev could tell him that wasn't already there, but a lesson in respect and humility wouldn't hurt the woman.

She inclined her head with an expression that approximated genuine bafflement. "I'm sorry, sir. I assumed you were observing—"

"You don't *assume* anything, Commander," he snapped, scowling. "I have been resting for the last three hours, and therefore disconnected from virtually all data input."

"I had no idea—"

He interrupted her again. "Don't play the fool with me, Commander."

"Sir, I swear . . ." She faltered. Then, more surely: "All information regarding your bodily needs and/or states of mind is restricted, and no inferior officer may access your network without reasonable cause. Given the nature of this mission, the only acceptable cause would be that your actions had somehow threatened its success. Anything else would be regarded as mutiny." She added, "Sir."

Kajic studied her carefully. The expression on her face was one of concern, but he was suspicious of what lay underneath—of what intentions her thoughts kept hidden.

"I'm aware of the regulations, Commander," he said distractedly. "Nevertheless, there is a back door in my life-support program. I found it in the mainframe two days ago." He hesitated before voicing his suspicions. "*Someone* has been monitoring me."

The crease in her brow was slight and forced. "A back door? But who—? I mean, *why* would there be such a thing?"

"To spy on me, of course. To make sure I behave." His image leaned closer to Makaev. "And please, Commander, if you must play the fool, then do it with more conviction."

Makaev's back straightened, and she met the stare of the hologram evenly and without flinching. "I have no knowledge of what you speak, sir," she said. "Clearly the leak must have been placed there before we left Jralevsky Minor."

Kajic allowed himself a wry grin. "Clearly."

"Whoever is behind it must be somehow involved in the design of your program itself."

"Or somebody opposed to it." He shrugged. "One of the conservatives, perhaps."

Kajic, although he had been deep in the surgical process at the time, was aware of the controversy the Andermahr Experiment had caused. While extremes of genetic modification remained illegal, the Ethnarch's Military Presidium still had a keen interest in bettering its troops. The long-dead Ataman Ana Vereine—after whom the Marauder was named, and who had begun the research centuries ago—had desired captains who were as much a part of their ships as was the anchor drive, an integral, reliable system rather than a merely flesh-and-blood addition to it.

Kajic was the first prototype of a radical new technique, one that had the potential to transform the Ethnarch's Military Presidium into an unopposable force across the region. Naturally, there would be resistance to the idea. Those sympathetic to the cause of coexistence, and those who believed the process itself to be an immoral perversion of the "natural" Pristine state, would be eager to see the project fail.

"I'm still being tested," he said, almost to himself. Despite all the implants, and his three unalterable priorities—which, even now, throbbed in his mind like guilt—he still wasn't completely trusted.

And if he failed to complete the mission—and thereby failed the test—what would happen to him? Would he be excised from the ship and thrown out with the scraps? Of what possible use would a man such as he be—one flayed and twisted, unable even to live without the aid of expensive machines?

capture AI and Roche with as much stealth as possible

Priority C stabbed at his thoughts like a physical pain, an ache in his left temple. In this, at least, he had failed—and whoever was watching him knew it too.

But the mission wasn't lost yet. Priorities A and B remained to be fulfilled. If he could only do so quickly enough, he could salvage his honor.

Focus, he told himself, dispensing with his doubts. *Focus.*

Makaev hadn't moved during the split second it took him to think the situation through. She denied knowing about the back door. Perhaps it was true, although he doubted it. She may not have been directly involved, but she must surely have been aware of the monitoring taking place.

He sighed. "We can discuss this later. For now, though, tell me about this shuttle."

"It seems that it escaped the destruction of the COE frigate under cover of the debris," she explained, her face carefully deadpan. "The *Paladin* moved to intercept, but it managed to evade them."

"You said it crashed," said Kajic. "Were there any survivors?"

"Unknown at this stage, but unlikely. The explosion was detectable from orbit."

Kajic mulled this over. "Any progress yet in the wreckage of the frigate?"

Makaev shook her head. "The dispersal pattern of the

fragments has been thoroughly mapped and studied—twice—but our scanners and probes have failed to locate the AI."

"So it must have been in the shuttle."

"That conclusion seems obvious, sir."

Kajic glanced sharply at his second in command, but her face was still stonily blank.

"Has the wreckage of the shuttle been investigated?" he asked.

"Not yet. A search party is on its way as we speak. The authorities at Port Parvati assure me that no detail will escape their attention."

"Have you told them what we're looking for?"

"Of course not, sir. They are simply to study the wreckage and convey the data to us."

"At considerable expense, no doubt." The Port Parvati wardens were voracious—and if there was one thing Kajic hated, it was fighting a war with money—but there was no other option. His future, if not his life, might well depend on their help.

Kajic's instincts continued to nag at him. He felt that he was in danger of letting success slip through his fingers unless he acted decisively.

at all costs

If the AI wasn't in the wreckage of the *Midnight*, then it must have escaped in the shuttle. The Espionage Corps had, however, reported that in its present form the AI wasn't able to move itself. Its escape must therefore have been facilitated by someone else. And as it was also known to be secure-cuffed to the wrist of a COE Intelligence agent . . .

"Instruct them to expand the search," he said. "Tell them we are looking for survivors."

"Sir?"

"We have underestimated our opponent, Atalia."

"Opponent?" Atalia Makaev could not conceal her bemusement. "Sir, we *have* no opponent. The *Midnight* and the shuttle which escaped from it were totally destroyed. It is just a matter of searching through the wreckage and retrieving the AI."

"I'll wager that the AI will not be found."

Makaev frowned. "Sir, may I ask what you are basing this assumption on? Have you access to information I have not been privy to?" There was a hint of mockery in her voice.

"Call it a gut feeling," said Kajic. Then, seeing his second in command's expression of disbelief, he added, "Inform the search party that we are looking for a Commander Morgan Roche, and have her image relayed down to them."

"The AI's courier?"

"We have unwittingly locked horns with a formidable enemy, Atalia." He nodded thoughtfully as something else occurred to him. "And I think we have found the cause of the *Midnight*'s destruction."

"But, sir," said Makaev, annoyance flaring in her eyes, her voice. "Proctor Klose was the only one who could have—"

"That is what we are meant to believe, Commander. In the same way we were meant to believe that nothing could have survived the destruction of the frigate; and in the same way we are now meant to believe that there are no survivors from the shuttle. But all the while we search that wreckage, the further away she gets." He set his gaze firmly upon her. "Commander, I want the search for survivors extended immediately. Roche must not elude us!"

"Sir." Makaev straightened her posture and snapped a salute. Nevertheless, Kajic detected cynicism in her tone. "I will convey your request to Warden Delcasalle. If there are any survivors, they will be found."

"Indeed they will, Commander. And this time you *will* keep me informed."

"Yes, sir." Makaev turned away as Kajic's image faded. While the bridge staff attended to their duties, he retired to his usual pattern of overall monitoring, letting his thoughts surf the vast sea of data crashing mercilessly on the sands of his mind.

Roche was the key. He had been a fool not to have seen it earlier. He hadn't misjudged Klose at all; his assessment of the man had been sound. It was Roche he had underestimated; her personal files had deceived him. Yet his subconscious mind had suspected, and had tried to warn him with the image of the faceless enemy. Had he analyzed the hunch in more detail, he might have been prepared.

At least now the problem was isolated, and all he had to do was focus his attention upon it. The Intelligence officer would not outwit him again. Not now . . .

Leaving the running of the ship in the hands of his junior officers, he opened the mission portfolio and began to study his adversary in more detail. And as the information filtered through his mainframe, he found something akin to admiration for the woman who momentarily distracted him.

priority gold-one

The prompt was sharp and burning. He cast aside the unwanted emotion and continued with his research.

6

Sciacca's World
Behzad's Wall
'954.10.30 EN
1650

All her life, Morgan Roche had enjoyed working with machines. Left without parents at an early age, she had been raised in an orphanage on Ascensio run by the planet's social welfare AIs. The orphanage's environment was one in which her social skills lagged (although contact with other children and adults was not rare—the orphanage understood the need for the Human interaction that a biochip could not provide, and so stays with a host family were frequent), but her proficiency with AIs soared.

By the age of eight she was entertaining herself by devising ways to circumvent the programming of her tutors; by the age of ten she had been so successful in this venture that she knew the inner logic of the AIs better than the programmers themselves. Every foible, inconsistency, and subtle glitch was committed to memory along with her basic education, which she absorbed by default.

At seventeen she left the orphanage to seek employment, although with Ascensio in the shadow of a local recession there were few jobs to offer someone whose expertise lay in artificial intelligence. By circumstance rather than choice, she was drawn toward the Armada (the preferable alternative to poverty or prostitution). Within a year of being out on her own she had applied for and taken the entrance exam; a further three years saw her inducted into the COE Intelligence training course.

The course itself was held on the second moon of Bodh Gaya, and it was here that she received her first neural implants and was thus exposed to the glowing web data that surrounded each and every being in the Commonwealth of Empires. To access this epiphany of information, all she had to do was touch a contact with the fake skin of her palm, and her mind would receive unimaginable tracts of data, fed directly into her cortex by the most sophisticated technology available in the Commonwealth of Empires.

Lessons were conducted from her quarters in the Intelligence dormitories, plugged directly into the vast virtual reality that comprised the college's mind-pool. She had no way of knowing if the minds she conversed with—her teachers and fellow students—were Human or artificial. Even those she suspected to possess manufactured origins were of a sort far superior to the lowly educators she had sabotaged in her childhood. Yet still she attempted to fathom them: probing their weaknesses, assaying their strengths, all the while allowing them to guide her in the ways of COE Intelligence.

Along the way she learned something of the history of the Commonwealth itself, and of the wider galaxy surrounding it: of the way Humanity had speciated following its colonization of the stars, from the High Humans, who had transcended their biological origins and existed in isolation from the mundane Castes (themselves divided into Exotic and Pristine categories), to the Low, who eked out primitive, animal-like lives on unnoticed worlds; of the immense number of empires that had risen and fallen down the millennia, waxing and waning like tides, many of them forgotten; of the lesser—although still extensive—number of such empires currently in existence, in varying degrees of torpidity. There was so much about Humanity to learn, both past and present, and the first thing she had learned was that one could *never* know it all. Perhaps only the High Humans could even hope to come close, but few mundanes ever had the chance to ask them.

On completion of the Intelligence course, Roche was assigned to the Quyrend System to work as a passive agent with a team of scientists repairing a major COE information network. It was there that she learned the basic rule of AI science: that no truly intelligent mind had yet been created to equal in every way that of a mundane Human. Minds equivalent to animals had been built, and it was these that fueled all of the AIs currently in service. Empowered by vast resources of information, they might have seemed equal or even superior to a Pristine Human, but they lacked the sophistication of thought, the degree of creativity, that every individual possessed. The quest for true artificial intelligence, she learned, had floundered centuries earlier, confounded by some unfathomable failure of design and theory that no amount of thought could remedy.

It came as no surprise to learn, five years later, after ten missions in as many solar systems, that the quest for true AI had been all but abandoned. The adept minds of COE Intelligence adequately filled the gaps machines could not. Yet rumors persisted: somewhere in the galaxy, perhaps even in the COE itself, work was continuing apace on a new theory, one that would render every early model of Box instantly obsolete. The ramifications of such a rumor, if it was true, were enormous, but it was dismissed by all in authority, including—and especially—the invisible rulers of Trinity, where all Boxes were made. Only the High Humans could build such a thing, and if they did it was doubtful that they would ever allow it to be released into the hands of a mundane government.

On the anniversary of her twelfth year of service in Intelligence, Roche received word of a new mission. The head of COE Intelligence, Auberon Chase, had requested her specifically. She was to travel alone to Trinity to collect a Box commissioned by the Armada and return it to COE Intelligence HQ. The AI had been designed to meet certain demanding specifications, and was thus highly expensive, yet it would receive no special escort. It would instead travel with her along a route remarkable only for its apparent randomness. Twelve other ships would leave Trinity at the same time, however, each carrying an Intelligence field agent, thus confusing any attempt to follow her and her ward. Such extreme measures to ensure secrecy made her curious, of course, but she knew better than to pry. She knew her place. Morgan Roche's service had been diligent and faithful, though not particularly distinguished. If she could complete this mission successfully, then she imagined she would earn another promotion; if she were to rock the boat, on the other hand, she might find herself off the mission entirely, or relegated to one of the dummy ships, headed nowhere. Whether the Box was the first of a new generation of super-Boxes or nothing more than a device to decode the transmissions of the Dato Bloc, she would be better off not knowing. At the very least, she would have plenty of time to converse with this Box. Who knew what she might learn in the process?

Two months on the *Midnight*, however, with little more than this Box for company, had been nearly enough to make her doubt even the most basic tenet of her short life. One machine at least, it seemed, she simply couldn't fathom—no matter how she tried. And neither, as a result, could she bring herself to like it. . . .

<Morgan.>

The voice was gentle but insistent, drifting through her thoughts, her dream. There had been shouting and panic and running—but she hadn't been able to move properly, hadn't been able to get clear of the explosion.

And pain. There had been a lot of pain.

<Wake up, Morgan.>

The voice continued to whisper through her half-sleep, compelling her to leave the dream behind.

With some effort, her eyelids flickered open. She squinted as the light from the yellow-hued sky stabbed at her eyes, dispelling some of her confusion, and what she had mistaken for a dream quickly adjusted itself and became a memory. Only the pain remained; in her shoulder, across her back, down one side of her face.

<Wake up now, Morgan,> the Box said, persisting.

Then another sound, this time the snarl of engines, ripped the quiet around her. Above, through a tangle of dead, petrified branches, she saw a flyer bank sharply, turning a tight figure eight before continuing back the way it had come.

As the whine of its engines faded into the distance, two voices sounded simultaneously in her head:

<Welcome back on-line, Morgan.>

And: <Do you think they saw us?>

The figure of Maii unfolded from the narrow crack in the rock face. Cane was beside her, staring in the direction in which the flyer had disappeared.

"Without a doubt." Roche recognized Veden's voice. "And even if they didn't, it's only a matter of time."

"Perhaps," said Cane. His head was cocked, as if listening to the fading engines.

"What's going on?" The words felt awkward in Roche's dry mouth. She tried to stand but found herself unable to move her left arm.

Cane glanced down at her, the thin suggestion of a smile creasing his otherwise composed features. He reached out and helped her to her feet. Waves of agony shot from her shoulder along her arm, making her dizzy for a moment. Cane's strong hands held her firm until he was sure she had her balance.

"You okay?" he asked.

Roche noted that her arm had been strapped firmly to her side using strips of cloth from Cane's uniform. "Dislocated?" she asked.

Cane nodded. "You'll be all right."

Roche quickly checked around her and saw they had taken refuge in a long and shallow ravine. Maii was slumped against a boulder, the slight movements of her head synchronized with Veden crouching a meter away. He was scowling at Roche and Cane.

"We should be going before they come back," he said.

Roche turned to Cane. "I take it our plan didn't work?"

Cane shook his head grimly. "A couple of flyers appeared on the scene not long after we bandaged you up. They've been scouting the area ever since, so our progress has been a little slow."

"Do you know where they're from?" said Roche.

"No idea," replied Cane. "But whoever they are, they seem to be heading back toward the wreck of the lander."

"So you say," Veden hissed, rising to his feet.

Roche ignored him. "Let's have a proper look," she said, gesturing upward. "We can't see a thing from down here."

"Good idea," said Cane.

Veden turned away. "We're wasting *time*," he muttered, just loud enough to be heard.

Cane clambered up a relatively shallow section of the wall, then leaned back to give Roche a hand. With difficulty she followed him, the valise scraping against the rock face as she went. The biofilaments lacing the skin of Roche's suit were fueled by sunlight, and chilled perceptibly at the sudden exertion, but the air on her face and right hand seemed only hotter in comparison, and as dry as a furnace. The earth beneath her fingertips, completely devoid of life, crumbled into dust. It smelled of ancient spices mixed with gunpowder.

When they reached the surface of the stony plain, they crouched behind a rock outcrop to peer at their surroundings. With no suggestion of Maii's presence in her mind, Roche realized that the girl must be using Cane's senses to view the scene.

The ravine in which they had taken refuge snaked across the orange lava plain, a jagged crack three meters wide and ten deep leading upward into the foothills; not a dry riverbed, but a fracture resulting from gentle seismic expansion, the only such fracture—and therefore the only true cover—for many kilometers. Farther ahead, shadowing the horizon like bulky storm clouds, lay a range of mountains. Behind them, back the way they had come, a tower of smoke rose against the backdrop of a pink-brown sky: the wreckage of the lander, still burning. A glint of light at the base of the tower of smoke might have been the flyer, although at this distance Roche could only guess.

With pursuit so close at hand, she could understand Veden's sense of urgency, but she was grateful at the same time for the opportunity to get her bearings. Unlike the others, she'd had no opportunity to view the world upon which they had crash-landed.

The sky directly above was a uniform sand-yellow, deepening to pink toward the horizon. Running the length of the sky was a faint, white streak that Roche had first assumed to be a cloud, but was, she now realized, the planet's belt of moonlets—the Soul. The rising sun hung low in the horizon, at the base of the Soul, its light a dull orange tinged with green. Away to her left, a large cloud mass was gathering.

The axial tilt of Sciacca's World was large enough for pronounced seasons, she knew. During winter or summer, the sun appeared at either side of the Soul—above or below, depending on the observer's latitude. At other times it would be partially occluded by the orbital debris. The Soul, therefore, indicated the direction of the planet's rotation, and the displacement of the sun to either above or below geographical north or south.

With this as a rough guide, but without knowing the season, she guessed that the ravine headed roughly northeast.

Roche turned to Cane. "That flyer," she said. "Did you get a look at its insignia?"

He nodded. "A circle, with a green cross on a white background."

"Not Armada or Dato Bloc, then." Roche frowned. "Still, whoever they are, they seem pretty eager to find us." Looking back to the wreckage of the lander, she added, "Box?"

<Yes, Morgan?>

"Anything you can tell me about this place that might give us an idea of who we're dealing with?"

<As you may know,> it said in a patient, lecturing tone, <it possesses a turbulent history—owing mainly to the fact that Sciacca's World lies close to Dato Bloc territory. In '112 EN, before the Commonwealth reached this far, the original Dominion colony was razed by Olmahoi retribution units under the orders of the Dato Bloc, then known as the Ataman Theocracy. This incident triggered the Ghost War, even though the Theocracy never laid claim to the system. Not until '293 EN, during the First Ataman War, was the Hutton-Luu System captured by the Ataman Theocracy and Sciacca's World annexed. In '442 EN, during the Second

Ataman War, when the Theocracy finally submitted to the Commonwealth, the COE took control and the planet changed hands again. Despite, or perhaps because of, its strategic location, the COE leaders of the time chose not to house an Intelligence base upon it, opting instead for a small penal colony overseen by the Armada; it is possible that they might have intended it as a beachhead for covert operations into the Dato Bloc, although whether they did or not is un-recorded. In '474 EN, when the extensive mineral deposits of the Soul were discovered, a private contractor—OPUS—applied for mining rights to the system. The rights were granted, clearing the way for OPUS to begin surveying.>

"If there is a point to all of this," said Roche, "then I wish you'd get to it."

<Morgan, the presence of the penal colony on the planet could not be ignored by OPUS. They recognized cheap labor when they saw it. By the time OPUS folded and Dirt & Other Commodities Inc.—DAOC—assumed control of the operation, the previous Armada command had been re-placed by a system of private overseers and hired security. Today, only a token Enforcement and Armada contingent re-mains, divided between orbit and Port Parvati. DAOC is the main socioeconomic force on the planet which—"

Roche interrupted. "So you're saying that the flyer was a DAOC Enforcement vessel?"

<Yes, Morgan.>

"You're sure?"

<The ship did bear the DAOC insignia.>

Roche's tired sigh was lost to a flurry of scalding wind that skittered off across the plain, raising a cloud of orange dust in its wake. "And you couldn't have just *told* me that?"

<Morgan, survival in any culture depends principally upon having an understanding *of* that culture.>

Roche shook her head. "Is there anything else you can tell me that might be relevant to us here and now?"

<Little, I'm afraid. I have been cut off from my usual sources of information. Before the lander crashed, however, I did record an aerial view of the region. If we are to head for the village Veden indicated, then I recommend a course

due north, into the foothills. I estimate our distance to be roughly thirty-five kilometers—>

"They definitely landed at the wreck." Cane's words distracted Roche from the voice in her head. She faced him again, saw him squinting into the distance. "I can make out their downdraft swirling the smoke."

"You can *see* that?" Once again Roche was amazed at his abilities. She was beginning to wonder if there was anything he couldn't do better than she. "I don't suppose you can make out how many there are of them, can you?" she added wryly.

The humor seemed lost on Cane. "No. I'd need some binoculars to discern anything more at this distance."

She leapt on the word instantly: "Binoculars? You remember using them before the capsule?"

His eyes met hers evenly. "No. But I know what they are."

"Just like you knew how to splint my arm?"

"That was Veden's doing." Cane shrugged. "I merely assisted him."

Roche sighed. If he was lying about how much he remembered, then she could trap him—unless, of course, he was better at lying, too. In the hours she had known him, he had demonstrated nothing but trustworthiness in her presence—and had, in fact, saved her life once already. She wasn't sure whether that bothered her more or less than if he hadn't.

<Veden is growing impatient,> said Maii. <He says he'll leave without you if you delay much longer.>

"Tell him we're on our way." Roche mentally prepared herself for the descent into the ravine. Her shoulder ached right down to the bone, the pain reaching from her neck to the tips of her fingers. The secure-cuffing around her wrist had left yellow-black bruises where she had hit the ground after the explosion of the lander, but the Box looked little the worse for wear. Its outer casing had been scarred quite badly from the explosion, but was otherwise intact. The handle still slotted into her hand perfectly, even though she was unable to bear its weight with her left arm.

As she clambered back down the slope into the ravine,

she took one last look around at the surface of Sciacca's World. An arid moonscape, plus an atmosphere. Not a pleasant place to live by any means. But for its mineral content, it would probably never have been settled in the first place.

She failed to see why anyone would *want* to come here. . . .

Veden and Maii were waiting for them at the bottom of the ravine. Barely had they regained their wind before the Eckandi headed off up the ragged slope, toward the foothills.

Roche took a deep breath and followed. Cane stayed with her, considerate of her weakness rather than of his own strength. She had no doubt that he could outperform the Eckandi easily, in both speed and endurance.

"Has he said anything?" she asked him, not loud enough for the other two to hear.

"About what?"

"About why he's here."

Cane shook his head. "No, but he is impatient to get to wherever it is he wants to go. That much is obvious."

"Patently." She spat a mixture of saliva and dust into the rocks. The spittle was stained red. "But why? What does he expect to find here?"

Cane shrugged. "Exercise?"

<Hope.> Maii's silent voice was barely audible above Roche's own thoughts.

Roche glanced ahead. The set of the Surin's narrow shoulders told her that the message had been intended for her alone.

"On a prison planet?" Roche mumbled to herself.

Cane turned to her. "What did you say?"

"Nothing," she said, and kept on walking.

The day darkened, paradoxically, as the sun rode higher into the sky. Once, the flyer passed overhead again, but this time didn't turn immediately back. Her mind was fogged by exhaustion, and she could only vaguely guess that their intentions were to intensify their search by looking farther from the wreckage. Not that it mattered. With the wind lifting the dust the way it was, in another hour or so the people in the flyer were going to have a visibility factor of about zero.

To while away the time, and to distract herself from the constant pain, she tried to talk to the Box. Something more substantial—even access to a basic medical database, accessible by the contact pad in her quarters—would have been preferable, but the Box was all she had. It could add little to what she had already learned from Cane: that the lander had exploded shortly after landing, as planned; that Maii and Veden had made it to shelter in time, but that she and Cane had taken a touch of heat-flash, in addition to Roche's dislocated shoulder and bruised ribs; that she had been carried on Cane's back away from the burning wreckage like a sack of potatoes; that Cane hadn't wanted to move her at all until she had regained consciousness and had agreed to do so only after Veden had threatened to leave them behind.

Among the supplies Roche had managed to rescue from the lander were a sack containing five survival suits and two basic ration packs. There was no medical kit, no painkillers to numb the aching, and as their trek continued her discomfort worsened. Despite her Armada biofeedback training, it was all she could do to keep her eyes focused on the ground ahead. Only when the Box finally complained that she had asked the same question three times in five minutes did she stop talking altogether and concentrate solely on walking.

Then, as the sun reached a position corresponding to late afternoon, she could take it no longer.

"Stop," she gasped, clutching at Cane for support as she staggered to halt. Pain from her shoulder and ribs made her head spin. Only with difficulty did she fight nausea back down. "I have to rest."

"No," Veden spat, his tone a whiplash of irritation. "We must keep moving until nightfall."

"I can't. Please. Just five minutes. That's all I ask."

"No." Without looking back, Veden kept walking.

Roche was unable to prevent the collapse of her thigh muscles. Cane made sure she was stable and went to follow the Eckandi.

"Let him go, Cane." That she had to raise her voice to be

heard made her realize just how much the wind had risen in the last hour.

"We should stick together," asserted Cane. "Separated, we will be more vulnerable."

"If he wants to risk an ambush, let him." Roche felt only contempt for the old Eckandi, but the overriding emotion was one of despair at her own fading strength. It would come as something of a relief, she noted with alarm, to be captured. At least the wait, and the walk, would be over.

She shook her head firmly, denying the thoughts. Yes, the *Midnight* had been destroyed with all hands; yes, she was trapped on an unfamiliar planet, being pursued by a hostile security force; and yes, she was in a great deal of pain—but that was no reason to give in. Her passage into COE Intelligence had taught her that hard work and sheer determination could take a great deal of the edge off fate's sometimes cruel sting.

But the feeling wouldn't dissipate, no matter how she tried.

Biting down on the sense of hopelessness, she forced herself to smile up at Cane. "We'll catch up. You'll see. They'll stop when night falls, and—"

"Wait." Cane's head cocked; his eyes darted along the edges of the ravine.

Roche glanced upward, startled. The sky had grown dark without warning. As she watched, it darkened even further to a deep ochre mottled with grey. Small sprays of dirt leapt from one wall of the ravine to the other, occasionally showering down on them.

Then she heard it: a rumble, distant at first but growing louder with every second. The low-frequency sound reminded her of a heavy-armor tank, or an unusually large ground-effect vehicle.

"What is it?"

Cane shook his head. "I don't know, but I don't like it."

Roche's despair abruptly deepened, and she found herself fighting an overwhelming urge to cry. She cursed herself. She had never experienced anything quite like this before. Why was she feeling it now? Her entire body trembled with the intensity of the emotion.

She reached out to steady herself on the nearest wall, but

withdrew the hand as a tiny spark arced from her fingertips to the stone.

"What—?"

Suddenly, Cane took her by her good arm and flattened her against the wall of the ravine. "Cover your face!" he hissed, his voice nearly drowned under the now-deafening sound.

She stared at him, too surprised to move. When she failed to obey him immediately, he reached behind her head for the hood of her survival suit. Tugging it over her face, he did the same with his own, holding the edges closed with one hand. Only his eyes stared at her, unblinking and frighteningly rational.

"What the—?"

"Close your eyes," he shouted. "Now!"

Roche blinked, delayed a second longer than he. At that moment, something roared across the top of the ravine—a dark, swirling mass of dust traveling at an awesome speed. The air in the ravine, sucked by the low pressure of the front, exploded upward. The turbulence created a partial vacuum, which in turn rolled a layer of dense air at the bottom of the front down into the ravine, instantly filling it with swirling clouds of choking dust.

Roche gasped, then coughed, doubling up into Cane's wind-shadow. Her one good hand flew to her face in a belated attempt to seal her nose. Her ears rang with the sound of tortured, screaming air. Only Cane's hand on her back prevented her from toppling forward. Even as she struggled to breathe, she finally understood what was happening:

A dust storm had struck them, one more violent than any she had previously encountered. That explained her sudden mood swing and the spark of static electricity: the charge in the air, rolling ahead of the storm, pervading everything.

After half a minute of the onslaught, Cane knelt beside her to bring his mouth close to her head.

"The front will be the most turbulent!" he shouted. "If we can hold on for a moment longer, it should ease slightly!"

She wanted to yell back—*How do you know*?—but her throat only rasped, irritated by dust and dry air. She concentrated on holding herself still, waiting for the tumult to release her.

Then, over the howling wind, came the reave's voice:
<Roche! Cane!>

Roche opened her eyes, and was instantly stung by a thousand particles of dust. There was no denying the urgency in the voice. But—how did one reply to a reave?

"What's wrong?" she shouted back.

She was unsure whether the Surin had heard her call, but a reply came nonetheless: <They're here! I—we—need help!>

"*Who* are here?"

"Listen!" Cane had his head cocked again. "Gunshots."

This time even Roche could hear the discharge of weapons over the storm. "We have to help them," she said, trying in vain to climb to her feet.

"No." He pressed her back. "I'll go." He opened his suit and slipped her pistol and Veden's makeshift laser from the pockets of his transportee uniform. Handing her the pistol, he glanced around him, eyes narrowed to slits. In the darkness of the storm, little could be seen but swirling, dust-filled air. The mouth of the ravine showed as a faint lightening in the air above them. Apart from that, Roche was blind.

"Could be Veden's friends," Cane said. "But then again—"

"Better safe than sorry."

"Exactly. Stay here." With one smooth movement he ducked away from her and was swallowed by the storm. Roche leaned back against the wall of the ravine, clutching the pistol to her chest while protecting her eyes as best she could.

Moments later, a sharp rattle of projectile weapons issued from farther up the ravine. Voices followed, shouting in confusion. With the sounds came the realization that she was hearing more clearly; the fury of the storm front had indeed abated slightly.

Maii said nothing more, however, and Roche couldn't stand aside when help might be needed. The wind allowed her to reach a standing position; from there, with the hand holding the pistol on the ravine wall, keeping her upright, she made her way cautiously across the ragged rock face.

Another round of shouting and gunshots broke the silence, followed by the sharp hiss of an energy weapon discharging through the atmosphere. Then the muffled thump of impact. She flinched instinctively but continued forward.

The voices ceased in the wake of the explosion, but the exchange of gunfire continued in ragged bursts. Roche pressed on as fast as she could, but the ravine seemed endless. Her breath burned in her chest as though her rib cage was on fire.

Then, almost before she realized it, she stumbled into a shallow section of the ravine. The rock walls stood barely chest-high, with open ground to either side. The wind was stronger here, and the dust more dense. A projectile whined past her, sent rock fragments flying a meter from her shoulder. She dropped instantly to a crouch and leveled the pistol in the direction from which she felt the weapon had been discharged.

Even as she did so, a man in a green uniform dropped into the ravine barely two meters farther on. He obviously hadn't seen her from above, hidden as she was by the swirling dust. The moment his feet touched rock, however, his pistol swung to target her. Roche fired instinctively, taking him squarely in the chest. He looked momentarily surprised; then his eyes rolled back and he toppled sideways to the ground.

Roche didn't move, frozen to the spot. In the wake of her surprise and the sudden movement, her ribs sang like a saw dragged across a wire, sending pain in waves through her chest. Her breath came in short gasps.

A pebble dropped on her head, and she rolled forward, twisted, and fired behind her. A second man, also in the green uniform, tumbled into the ravine, the back of his head black and smoking. Her own shot had missed. Someone else, outside the ravine, had been more accurate.

<You all right, Roche?> Maii's soundless voice filled her head.

The body of the second officer twitched once where it had fallen, then lay still. Roche formed the word <Okay> in her mind and tried her best to hold it steady for the reave to find.

<I sense no one else near you at the moment,> continued the Surin. <But stay down just in case.>

"What happened?"

<They took us by surprise.>

"Enforcers?"

<Yes, from Port Parvati. They were in the ravine, heading down from the foothills. Veden and I were arguing when the sandstorm hit. There was a cave, and we all headed there for shelter at the same time. I think we surprised them as much as they surprised us, but they had weapons and we didn't. If Cane hadn't come when he did—> Roche sensed something akin to a shrug touch her mind. <We're armed now, if that means anything.>

Roche stayed put as the Surin drifted off into silence. She doubted whether she'd be able to move anyway, even if she wanted to. In dust this dense, sight gave little advantage. She wondered how it would feel to be Maii, a hunter aiming for the very eyes that helped her see. . . .

If Maii caught the thought, she made no comment.

Roche heard a couple more shots, another thump of energy discharge, and a single strangled cry. Then the wind picked up again, reducing her world to a meter-wide circle with her in the center. Even with her eyelids half-closed, the dust forced her to blink. Effectively blinded and deaf, she huddled close to the wall of the ravine and waited. Small bolts of lightning, triggered by the charge in the air, crackled into the soil around the ravine, stabbing the darkness with an eerie light.

A hand reached out of the maelstrom to take her by the arm, and she raised the gun to strike it away. Someone shouted her name over the wind, but whatever other words followed were instantly swept away. The hand was large and strong, and she couldn't fight it off. With immense relief, she recognized the plastic of a survival suit above the wrist and guessed it to be Cane, although the rest of him was erased by the storm.

He dragged her to her feet and farther along the ravine. A

flash of energy briefly lit the gloom, arcing over her shoulder and exploding harmlessly into rock.

Maii's voice rose out of the racket.

<We have to move. They know this weather better than we do. There's no way for us to tell how long the storm will last.>

Silence, then: <Agreed. We don't have any choice. The other two Enforcers only have to wait us out. Follow the ravine as before, try to put some distance between us and them before the storm breaks. We'll see—>

The reave's voice broke off suddenly. Roche glanced at Cane in alarm, but his face remained hidden. As though he too was alarmed, he urged her to move faster. The best she could manage was a quick shuffle, through the sand gathering at the bottom of the ravine, with her lack of sight and the constant buffeting of the wind constantly upsetting her balance, but she hurried as well as she could.

Again the energy weapon flashed, this time from farther away. Barely had she thought that they might be able to escape when something brushed against her, and a shadowy shape reached for her out of the dust. She flinched away, but not quickly enough to escape a pair of enormous, grasping hands. One seized her wrist; the other took her about the face, stifling her shout of alarm. She tried to raise the pistol, but the hand on her wrist twisted it savagely, sending agony burning through her shoulders.

When the hands tried to drag her away, however, they met the resistance of Cane's strength. She endured a brief, painful, tug-of-war between the two; then the unknown pair of hands fell away. The shape moved around her to confront Cane, and she thought she could hear voices shouting over the wind. Then, clearly silhouetted against a brief bolt of lightning, she saw a gun raised and pointed at Cane's head, aimed by a shambling bipedal figure at least as tall as Cane himself, and far broader.

Cane glanced at Roche, then nodded. Feeling his hand loosen, she clutched at him, trying to keep him close, but a cloud of dust erupted around them, and Roche suddenly lost sight of him. She called out in panic and tried to go back, but the large hands of her captor held her firm, dragging her away into the fury of the storm.

7

Darkness and silence wrapped themselves around Roche as the wind abruptly fell away. Startled by the sudden absence of noise, she stumbled. The strong hands of her captor roughly righted her.

"This way," he said, guiding her forward. His voice was coarse, almost guttural, and clearly Exotic. His Caste eluded her for a moment, until she caught a whiff of him. Mbatan, definitely. No other Caste possessed that distinctive bitter smell. A soft flare illuminated their surroundings a moment later and confirmed her suspicions. He was as solid as a bear beneath a brown, stained coverall, with a shaggy mane of hair and limbs like tree trunks.

In the Mbata common tongue, Roche asked the huge figure where he was taking her. He laughed, turning to face her in the dim light. The sound was a throaty bark, testimony to non-Pristine physiognomy.

"I don't speak Bantu." His voice was thickly accented, although intelligible nonetheless. "Not anymore." The blue-green light from the chemical flare flickered over the Mbatan's heavily bearded and tanned face, catching now and then in the weathered lines that covered his features. "My name is Emmerik," he said.

"You're a convict?" Cane's voice, coming from near Roche's shoulder, made her jump.

If Emmerik took offense at the question, he didn't show it. Instead, he grinned widely, revealing a complete, if slightly yellow, set of teeth. "Time for talk later. This way."

Again he guided Roche forward. The light revealed that they were traveling through a rough tunnel carved from ancient lava, barely high enough for Roche but broad enough to allow her and the Mbatan to walk side by side. The stone was a uniform, dirty orange, except for the occasional vein of dark grey. As the tunnel wound its jagged way underground, she noticed scars in the rock, suggesting that it had been carved by shaped explosives and with the bare minimum of finesse. A rush job.

"You were following us?" She began it as an accusation but ended it as a question.

"We expected the Eckandi and Surin in the next shipment. When the shuttle crashed, Haid sent me to investigate. I recognized Veden from the file we had on him—but you I wasn't so sure about." He shrugged mightily, all the muscles in his back and shoulders rippling. "No offense. It wasn't until the Enforcers moved in on you that I was fairly certain you were working with the Eckandi and not against him."

"So why take so long to help us?" Cane's voice was smooth in the cool quiet of the cave, but Roche thought she detected a hint of annoyance underlying his words. "We were struggling out there, in case you didn't notice."

"I felt it would be best to wait for the cover of the storm before acting. They come in waves on Sciacca. The one that just hit us was the second of a tri-rage. I knew it had to hit soon—as did the Enforcement—so I just kept my distance until it did."

"And this?" said Roche, indicating the tunnel they were walking along. "This is the base of the resistance?"

Roche had suspected they had been captured by the covert movement Veden had mentioned, and when Emmerik failed to deny it, she knew she was right.

"No. We just use these tunnels and the ravine for recon, mainly. If we need to get to the port unseen, and so on."

"Is that where we're going? Port Parvati?"

"Not yet." The Mbatan gestured for her to continue walking, but said nothing more.

The tunnel continued for five hundred meters or so farther, dipping downward at one point, until it opened onto a slightly larger chamber.

Veden looked up as they entered, his cold eyes glittering in the unnatural light. "What did you do to her?" he asked Emmerik, his tone harshly accusing. The Surin lay in a fetal position on the rough stone floor at his feet.

"Xarodine." The burly Mbatan ushered Roche and Cane into the chamber ahead of him. "If she'd squawked at the wrong moment, the Enforcers would have known where to find her."

"She has more control than that!" Veden barely kept his rage in check. "She's not some fledgling talent you'd buy for a copek at a local—"

"I couldn't take that chance," said Emmerik calmly over Veden's outrage. He slipped a filthy hand into his coverall and removed the dart gun that had administered the dose. "Besides, it'll wear off in a few hours—then we'll get to see exactly what she can and cannot do."

Roche, studying the curled form of the Surin, felt suddenly sorry for her. Xarodine inhibited the epsense ability. The girl was, as a result, cut off from her senses, trapped in her own skull like any other blind deaf-mute.

"You." Emmerik handed Roche a tablet with a flask of water. "Take this."

"Why?" She eyed it suspiciously. "What is it?"

"Painkiller. We need you fit if we're going to make the hills by nightfall."

Veden's glare doubled in intensity. "She's not with us. Nor is he."

Emmerik glanced from the Eckandi to Cane, but there was no suspicion in his expression. "If I'm not mistaken, he saved your life back there."

"She's with COE Intelligence," he said. "And he's with her."

"Regardless. The Enforcers fired at her too."

"I don't care," said Veden. "They're not *with* us."

"I'll keep that in mind next time you need help," said Roche.

Veden stared, the half-light highlighting the anger on his face. "I don't need the help of the Armada!"

"We could have left you on the *Midnight* to fry, and you know it."

"Hey!" Emmerik cut Veden's response off before the Eckandi had a chance to speak. "I don't give a damn *who* she's with. What happens to her is up to Haid, okay?" When he was certain that neither Roche nor Veden would continue the argument, Emmerik turned away and shrugged into an old, well-used backpack. "I leave in five minutes. Whoever wants to come with me can. Whoever doesn't can stay." The Mbatan's eyes settled on Roche again. "And if you don't want that tablet, give it back. Medical supplies aren't easily come by on Sciacca."

Roche placed the tablet in her mouth, wincing at the bitter taste. She quickly washed it down with water from the flask, which tasted of dirt and left an oily residue on her tongue.

"I'm with you," she said, handing back the flask. "Not that I have much choice."

"Too right, lady." The Mbatan came close to a smile. "You wouldn't last a day out there in your condition—even with your friend."

"What about Maii?" Veden interrupted brusquely.

"You can lead her." The Mbatan smiled, teeth glinting in the eerie chemical light. "Think she'll trust you?"

Veden turned to help the girl to her feet. Maii's hands fluttered for a moment over the Eckandi's face and hair, then became still. She allowed herself to be led across the room with her hand clutched tightly in his. Roche noted, however, that there was more desperation in the clasp than affection.

"Good." Emmerik nodded. "We'll move in a line with me in the middle. You," he said to Cane, "go first, then you." Roche nodded. "Then the others. And I'll have your weapons before we go, thanks."

Cane hesitated for a moment, then handed over the laser.

Roche did likewise with the pistol. Veden produced a stolen Enforcement rifle from under his robes. All three vanished into the voluminous folds of the Mbatan's pack.

"Good." Emmerik swept the chamber with the flare to ensure that nothing had been overlooked, then gestured down the corridor. "Let's go."

<What do you think, Box?> Roche subvocalized as she walked along the dark and dank tunnels.

<It would be optimistic to believe we have been saved, Morgan,> replied the AI, <but pessimistic to succumb to despair.>

Roche nodded to herself, remembering the wave of gloom that had almost overwhelmed her earlier. The emotion had been accentuated by the ions presaging the dust storm, she knew, but that knowledge did little to console her. <Do you have anything in your datapool about the rebel movement on Sciacca's World?>

<No, but given the violent history of the planet, I'm not surprised it exists.>

<Nothing on what their aims might be?>

<One can only wonder. Given that the planet is a prison, liberation seems unlikely. The same with vengeance: even if the complete resources of the local Enforcement arm were turned over to them, they would possess little more than they already do. The only ships here are intrasystem vessels, with no ftl capability.>

<Apart from the Dato.>

<Yes, but surely that is a possibility too remote even to consider?>

Roche shrugged and sighed. They had been walking rapidly for almost half an hour without once leaving the underground tunnel. The painkiller Emmerik had given her had dulled her shoulder to a mere ache without numbing her mind as well. And, with little to distract her, she found herself slightly bored—despite her uncertain circumstances.

Cane's voice suddenly broke the quiet, his words resounding along the tunnel down which they walked. "Those people who attacked us," he said over his shoulder. Roche could tell he was talking past her to the Mbatan. "There were six of them, right?"

"That's right," said Emmerik. "Standard recon team."

"And we took out four."

"The Surin one, your friend one, and you two," the Mbatan confirmed. "You fight well in the dust, for an off-worlder. For anyone, to be honest. Where were you trained?"

"That leaves two," said Cane, ignoring the question.

Emmerik grunted a laugh. "Yes," he said. "That leaves two. If we're lucky, they'll believe you staggered off into the storm and died."

"And if we're not?" put in Roche.

"They'll have this area swarming with Enforcers."

"Will they find the tunnel?"

"Probably." Emmerik scratched his beard, the rustle of fingertips on hair clearly audible over the dull echoes of their footsteps. "But I don't believe that will happen. Most likely they'll just send another recon team to quarter the area."

"And then?"

"That depends on how badly they want you, doesn't it?" he said. "And why. What did you do? Blow up the ship?"

"No. We were ambushed by the Dato Bloc."

"Dato? Here?" Emmerik couldn't keep the surprise from his voice. "Well, well. That *is* interesting."

Silence fell for a moment. Roche could almost hear the Mbatan's mind turning, until Veden spoke up.

"She's carrying something they want. An AI. It's strapped to her back."

"They must want it badly to raid the Commonwealth."

"Obviously," said Veden.

"Maybe they'll even be prepared to pay for it," ventured Emmerik.

"A great deal, I'd imagine," said the Eckandi.

"Yes." The Mbatan's voice changed to mimic the Eckandi's suggestive tone. "And all we'd have to do is sell her out, right? Hand her over like some low-grade ore in exchange for a few credits?"

Veden fell silent.

"I don't like you much, Makil Veden," said Emmerik, "no matter what Haid says you can do for us. Remember that. I don't care what she is or what she's carrying; it's what she did that counts. On Sciacca's World, a life saved is worth something."

"My name is Roche, Emmerik. Morgan Roche. Not 'she.'"

Emmerik ignored her. "Do you hear me, Veden?"

"I hear." The Eckandi's voice was low and dangerous. "But I will raise the matter with Haid when we arrive. The reality of your situation makes sentiment meaningless. Perhaps he will see things differently."

"You obviously don't know him very well." The Mbatan's heavy palm descended onto Roche's shoulder. She couldn't tell whether the gesture was meant to reassure her, but she knew it wasn't threatening. "If the AI Roche carries is so valuable, then we may be able to use it to our advantage."

She said nothing, let the moment bury his words. Pledging herself and the Box to Emmerik's cause seemed premature, no matter how much she owed him.

"I will freely offer any assistance I can give," said Cane.

Roche frowned in the dark, surprised by Cane's words.

The Mbatan laughed. "That I expected. You are clearly a man of action: a trained soldier for certain, someone who recognizes debts of honor." He paused for a few steps. "I suspect that I can trust you, wherever you are from."

"My origins are unknown," said Cane. "Even to me."

"An unknown soldier, eh?" Emmerik shrugged, the fabric of his coverall shifting noisily over his large frame. "Then it must be a natural ability." His hand fell away from Roche's shoulder as he added, "Quiet now. The exit is nearby."

A few meters farther, and Emmerik called the party to a halt. He lit another chemical flare, and the weird light revealed that they had stopped in a chamber similar to the one they had left earlier. This time the tunnel did not continue on the other side. Instead, a rope ladder dangled from a gnarled cavity in the ceiling.

"I'll go first," said Emmerik, "to open the hatch and make sure the area is secure. Wait here."

The Mbatan swung his bulky form up the ladder with surprising speed. The mica in the rock wall flickered under the light from his flare as he ascended into the shadows. Moments later, a shaft of muddy light spilled through the hole, followed by the sound of wind and a shower of fine dust. Roche waited patiently, idly flexing the muscles of her right arm and wondering how she was going to climb the ladder one-handed.

Emmerik returned, his pack gone and his dirty teeth cutting a wide grin through his beard. "All's clear," he said. "You, soldier, go first." Cane nodded. "I'll bring the reave. Veden will follow me. Then I'll come back for you, Commander."

The rope ladder danced as Cane began his graceful ascent, his movements as nimble and surefooted as any Surin child Roche had seen. Emmerik reached out for Maii, who immediately retreated from his alien scent.

"Don't be afraid, little one." Emmerik's voice was gentle and soothing as he tried to ease his arms about the Surin's shoulders.

The girl shied away even farther.

"She can't hear you," said Roche. She reached out to touch the Surin's arm, to offer reassurance. Much to her surprise, the girl clutched at her hand with both of hers and held it tight.

"At least *she* trusts you," observed the Mbatan. "But that doesn't help us. You can't carry her."

"I know. Just give me a moment." Roche soothed the girl, stroking the fine hair of her cheeks and ears, feeling the grainy texture of the skin beneath it. Slowly Maii quietened, nestling into Roche as a small child might to its mother. When the girl was completely relaxed, Roche let Emmerik come closer and place his enormous arms in a clumsy embrace around her own. Then she slowly slipped aside.

The Surin stiffened for a moment, then seemed to accept the situation. With barely a grunt of effort, Emmerik slung her across his back. She clutched him tightly, looking like a rag doll tossed over the shoulder of a giant child.

"I won't be long," said the Mbatan. Tossing the chemical flare to her, he began the steady, careful climb up the ladder. The rope, although it stretched slightly, didn't break under their combined weight.

Shortly afterward, Emmerik called back down for Veden to follow. He did so, facing Roche briefly in the fading light of the flare. For a second she felt he was about to say something, but in the end he simply fixed her with a cold glare and scurried up the ladder.

Watching after him, she suddenly found herself smiling at the Eckandi's enmity toward her. His reluctance to have her and Cane along was understandable: after all, Enforcement was after *her*, not him. DAOC might not even be aware that he had escaped the *Midnight*. If he could get rid of her, he would be free to do whatever he had come to Sciacca's World to do. If, however, he stayed with her, the chances increased that he would be captured.

She could follow Veden's logic, but she didn't like it. Emmerik's uncomplicated way of thinking mirrored her own. She and Cane had saved the Eckandi's life twice now; that should have counted for something. But the Eckandar Trade Axis was renowned for its pragmatism in both business and life. The borders of its trading empire were far-flung, and its influence, in concert with the Commerce Artel, all-pervasive. Sharklike, the members of the Eckandar Caste had little room for sentiment or other emotions that she took for granted. In order to win his support, she would have to demonstrate her material worth to him: she had to prove that she offered more than her presence risked.

The answer to that, she suspected, lay in Veden's mission. Whatever that was.

A quiet murmur of voices broke the silence and her train of thought. She listened to them for a few minutes, following the rise and fall of inflection rather than the words themselves, which were mostly inaudible. They seemed to be arguing about something. Maybe Veden was trying to convince Emmerik to leave her behind again.

No. The voices were coming from behind her, from the tunnel, not from above.

She immediately smothered the chemical flare and

moved away from the dull cone of radiance into the security of the shadows. The light from above was relatively dim, not bright enough to travel too far along the tunnel, but still a concern.

She fought the urge to warn Emmerik and the others, knowing that her voice would carry to whoever approached as surely as theirs had carried to her.

The voices grew louder: a woman talking into a radio, the static-dampened responses not reaching Roche clearly. There was no way of telling exactly how many approached, or how close they were. The echoes of voice and, faintly, footsteps might have traveled hundreds of meters through the stone tunnel or not very far at all.

As she watched, a faint glimmer of light appeared in the depths of the tunnel: an electric torch tracing their path in the dirt.

The movement of the ladder in the dim light startled her momentarily; she glanced up and saw Emmerik descending from the hole. When his night-sensitive eyes saw her in the shadows, he opened his mouth to say something, but Roche was quick to raise a hand and gesture him to silence. When she had his attention, she pointed along the tunnel.

He instantly realized what she meant. "Quick," he said softly, reaching out with his arm. "No time for a harness. Put your arm about my neck."

She did so, and Emmerik grunted with effort as he straightened, lifting her off the ground. Closing her eyes, she concentrated on holding onto his coverall as he slowly climbed upward. The ladder strained under their weight but held nonetheless. Awkwardly, they moved up and out of the cavern, swaying slowly from side to side as Emmerik constantly shifted his balance.

"How many?" Emmerik whispered as they slipped through the narrow opening and into the confined space that led to the surface.

"Too far away to tell," said Roche. The calm of his voice surprised her. "But I think at least two—maybe the two from the ambush. They were talking to someone on a radio."

"Great," Emmerik muttered.

The footsteps from below grew steadily louder; the opening above them seemed impossibly distant.

The Mbatan fumbled a handhold and grunted under his breath. Roche gasped as they swung for a second from his other hand, until he regained his grip and took another step upward.

"Almost there . . ." His tone reflected her own doubts.

The voices from the tunnel took on an urgent note as the Enforcers came near enough to make out the dancing base of the ladder. The sturdy Mbatan began to move faster, muscles bunching in his back as he moved his hands from rung to rung. His lungs wheezed with the effort.

Then the ladder shook violently as one of the Enforcers grabbed the lowest rung and began to pull, shouting for them to halt. The extra load proved too much for the already straining material. With a stomach-wrenching lurch, one of the ropes snapped, sending Emmerik and Roche swinging into the stone wall of the chimney. Her hand bit into the Mbatan's neck as she fought to hold on. Dizziness swept her senses; pain flared through her injured shoulder. Flashing lights and shouting voices broke her concentration.

Her hand slipped at the same moment Cane reached down from above and grabbed the Mbatan's right hand. Emmerik grabbed her with his left and held as she scrambled to regain her grip.

Above her, the glare from another flare.

"Veden!" she called out as he threw it into the shaft, then felt it deflect off the valise strapped to her back. She glanced down to see it drop, its light illuminating the shaft as it fell. Below she could make out two figures scattering for cover.

Cane hauled on Emmerik's arm, pulling them upward, while the Mbatan's feet dug into the walls of the chimney. Clear of the opening, Cane dropped the Mbatan and Roche onto the dry, hard ground. In a single, smooth motion he moved back over the hole, reached in, and snapped the remaining strands of rope.

Three bursts of energy fire sounded from below; Roche watched in awe as Cane easily avoided the bolts that hissed from the opening, arcing harmlessly toward the sky. Then, with no sense of urgency, he was at her side, helping her to her feet and guiding her up a slope of tumbled rocks where Veden and Maii waited.

Raised voices issued from the shaft, and a quick patter of gunfire. Roche looked back to see Emmerik raise a device no larger than his fist and hurl it into the mouth of the shaft.

The gunfire ceased abruptly. A moment later, a muffled *crump* lifted the earth beneath them and sent a cloud of dust shooting out of the hole in the ground.

"And then there were none," said Emmerik without smiling. He grasped Roche's arm, indicating for her to move.

"If others heard the explosion . . ." Veden began.

"I know," Emmerik said. "We must hurry."

The Mbatan led them up a rough slope into a narrow valley between two low foothills. The ground was littered with grey stones, a rough shale that had flaked from the hills over thousands of seasons. The sandstorm had dissipated, but still the air was murky with dust; an erratic wind tugged and squeezed it into a series of small twisters that slid across the landscape before dissolving again into the larger mass.

Ahead, looming over them like the end of the world, were the mountains. The sun had almost set behind them, and the sky had deepened to the color of blood, darkened by the last tatters of the storm. The yellow-silver arc of the Soul bisected the sky like an enormous bow, taut with strain, its bright glow visible through the clouds.

They ran until the sun set, with Emmerik constantly casting glances behind them and at the sky, expecting pursuit to appear at any moment. When, as darkness fell, the distinctive buzz saw of a flyer broke the twilight, he tugged them under an overhanging shelf of rock, where they hid from view.

Roche took the opportunity to catch her breath, nursing her bruised ribs. The painkiller had worn off, and every mouthful of air burned through her throat and chest. Fighting her pride, she asked Emmerik for another painkiller, which he freely gave.

"We'll have to stay here for the night," said the Mbatan gloomily. His breathing was labored, as though he had found the run more wearying than he was prepared to admit. After quaffing from the flask, he passed it around for the others. "They'll be sweeping the area with infrared from now on, so it would be best if we just stayed put."

Roche dealt with the pain as best she could and forced herself to talk. "The survival suit," she wheezed to Cane, who stood nearby. He seemed none the worse for the exertion, perhaps even healthier than he had been before—more *alive*. ". . . I brought five . . . out of the lander?"

"That's right. Maii has the other, in one of the pockets of her own."

"Good." She turned to Emmerik.

"I'm too big," he said, understanding what she was about to suggest.

"Doesn't matter," said Cane. "It'll block IR. Any cover will help, just as long as we can keep on moving."

"That's right," added Roche. "As much as I'd like to rest . . . I don't think we can afford to."

He nodded. Veden calmed Maii while Cane rummaged through the Surin's pockets for the suit. The one-piece garment unfolded from a parcel scarcely larger than her hand. Roche showed the Mbatan how to activate the chameleon circuits and moisture reclaimer. The processor in the belt would do the rest. IR opacity was standard in all Armada survival suits; the heat would be absorbed to hold the desert chill at bay through the night.

Emmerik managed to get his arms into the elastic fabric, but had no luck with his legs. The rest of the suit, where it couldn't be tied into place, flapped from his body like an overcoat.

"Better than nothing," he said, the gruffness of his voice offset by the look of gratitude he directed at Roche. Leaning out from the overhang, he listened for a moment. "They've moved on, and so should we. The others will be waiting for us at the Cross."

"The Cross?" asked Cane.

"Houghton's Cross is the town we're heading for," said Emmerik. "And if we can get there by dawn, then we'll be able to rest."

"How far?" asked Cane.

"Four hours' walk, at a steady pace."

"Night here is how long?"

"This time of year, about eleven hours."

"Okay," said Cane. "Morgan? Are you sure you're up to it?"

Roche glanced at Cane. This was the first time he had used her first name; she supposed he had earned the right. "I'll manage," she said, "once this painkiller takes effect."

Cane smiled. "And maybe we can rustle up something to eat on the way. Anything edible in these hills, Emmerik?"

The Mbatan smiled. "Depends what you regard as edible," he said. "We should be able to find some vintu buds, and choss roots are closer to the surface at night. If you're really lucky we may be able to find some rapeworm-infected animal. It's a parasite indigenous to Sciacca. It paralyzes the host and injects the eggs into the animal's gut. Two weeks later, the young emerge. If you get the larvae on about the eight or ninth day, the meat can be quite delicious. . . ."

Roche listened with only half an ear as she performed brief stretching exercises to ease her aching muscles. Feeling confined under the shelf of rock, she stepped out to look at the stars. Despite a fine haze of lingering dust, it was a beautiful sight.

The sun, although it had set, was still shining on the Soul. At the eastern horizon, the band of moonlets twinkled a dull silver; above her, it brightened considerably, colored by the coppery light that filtered through the thin lens of the planet's atmosphere; to the west, it was brighter still, catching the full, unrefracted light of the sun. Occasionally, one of the larger moonlets would reflect the light, making it twinkle. Otherwise the belt was a solid band—a long, glowing cloud on fire with the colors of sunset.

She didn't hear the conversation behind her cease, or the Mbatan move to her shoulder, until his voice boomed in her ear. "Heartwarming, isn't it?"

She started slightly, then nodded. "Yes, very." When she turned to look at him, his face was beaming with an emotion almost like pride: pleased both by the sight and by her appreciation of it. "Small compensation, though, for being condemned here forever."

"Perhaps." The Mbatan returned her gaze steadily, and she wondered what crime he had committed to warrant transportation. Murder, perhaps; he'd certainly disposed of the two Enforcers in the tunnel easily enough. Yet he seemed so trustworthy, so at peace with himself, that she found it hard to imagine him committing a crime of passion. Maybe he had learned temperance, not achieved it naturally.

As though reading her mind, he said, "I was born here, you know."

Roche stared at him. "But you—I assumed—"

"My parents were transportees. I was conceived illegally, and should have been shipped back to Vasos when I came of age. Of course, I was an outcast by birth, and couldn't return, even if I wanted to." He shrugged his huge shoulders. "Regardless, I wouldn't have let them take me. *This* is my home." He paused again before saying, "I suppose it's hard for you to understand that anyone could feel genuine affection for a prison planet."

"Well, yes," she said slowly. She did find it difficult to believe, even though the proof was standing before her. "Are there many like you?"

"A few. We tend to stick together, away from the port, although we have our differences. You'll meet them soon enough."

"I'll look forward to it."

"Will you? I hope so. We need allies desperately."

She shivered then, catching herself by surprise. Night had fallen rapidly, and the temperature with it. Her survival suit's heating system had not yet responded to the change.

Emmerik noticed the small movement and nodded. "We should be going." He turned back to the others. "Veden, are you and Maii ready to move?"

"Almost," replied the Eckandi, opening his eyes as though stirring from a deep sleep. Rising to his feet, he stretched his legs experimentally and rubbed his hands. "Give me a moment."

<I am ready too.> The reave's words whispered through Roche's thoughts. Her voice might have belonged to the wind, it was so faint, but it was definitely there.

"How long have you been . . . ?" Roche stopped, unsure how to phrase the question.

<Long enough to take a look around.> The Surin smiled and turned to the Mbatan. <You have loving eyes, Emmerik.>

The burly man nodded awkwardly. "Thank you. I hope you will forgive me for the way I mistreated you."

<If I hadn't, you would already be dead.>

The Mbatan grinned, although the tone underlying her words was ominous. "I can believe it. Veden has warned me that you're not to be underestimated."

<I can do everything I am here to do, and more besides. You'll find me a worthy ally—and a formidable enemy.>

"Then here's to the former." Emmerik slapped his hands together. "And to our journey. We still have far to travel before we can resolve our differences. I think we should get moving."

<Agreed,> the Surin purred, then fell silent with her hands clasped behind her back, waiting.

"So let's go," Cane said. "Do you want me to lead the way again, Emmerik?"

The Mbatan shook his head. "No, I'll lead. You can take the rear, or wherever you feel most useful. I'll leave it up to you. Just keep your eyes and ears peeled. They won't be far away." He glanced at the ring of faces surrounding him. "That goes for all of you."

"Understood. Whether we like this or not," Roche said, deliberately catching Veden's steely eye, "we're in it together."

The night deepened with unnerving speed. The only light came from the Soul and its constantly changing colors. The last dregs of the dust storm gusted through the valleys and ravines of the foothills like short-lived ghosts, robbing warmth and occasionally blinding them. Roche quickly learned to anticipate their arrival, as Emmerik did, by the distinctive whistle each gust made, and bunched closer to the others to prevent losing them.

Conversation was hesitant, confined mainly to Emmerik's infrequent lectures on the vagaries of the weather. Dust storms had been known to last for days at this time of the year. Although the foothills were catchments, with a rudimentary vegetation and a small amount of insect life, the moisture-stealing wind made life difficult even for the hardiest of species.

Roche listened to him with half an ear, expending the remainder of her concentration on her surroundings. Occasionally flyers buzzed overhead, scanning the area, and a couple of times she even noticed the distant flicker of lights lower in the hills. Enforcers, Emmerik had told them, searching for evidence of their passage. Pursuit was never far behind, it seemed, and constantly at the forefront of her mind. She swore to herself, and to her distant superiors, that she would not let herself be captured.

That she was trapped on a prison planet many light-years from her destination with, as yet, no concrete plan to reach a communicator didn't deter her. There had to be some way left to complete her mission. The Box was too important to be allowed to fall into Dato hands.

The others, with the possible exception of Cane, seemed to share her tight-lipped determination. Veden kept to himself, his expression stony and unapproachable. Maii walked with a stubborn independence, as though the time spent severed from her secondhand senses had humiliated her and left her needing to prove her abilities. Emmerik plodded steadily onward with the sure footing of someone who knew his way well.

Cane just walked, silent and pensive, taking in everything around him.

After an hour or so, the foothills steepened into a mountainside with paths that doglegged through crevasses and gullies. Roche's side and shoulder began to ache again, but she didn't allow herself the luxury of complaint. She simply bit down on the pain and kept walking.

Then, after three hours, a warning from Maii:

<I can sense them.> The reave's words were cut with urgency. <Nearby.>

"How near?" asked Emmerik, keeping his voice low.

<Near enough to sense,> Maii replied. <Maybe five hundred meters. In this terrain, I cannot be more accurate.>

"Very well." The Mbatan scanned their surroundings. "Over there—in that small niche. We'll rest there."

They did so, squeezing awkwardly into the narrow split in

the rock. Something crawled across Roche's hand, but had disappeared by the time she reached down to brush it away.

"Wait here," Emmerik said when they were settled. "I'll go look around." Cane followed him out of the niche, moving, Roche noted, with all the soundless grace of the silver dust-moths she had chased as a child on Ascensio.

Roche leaned into the rock and breathed deeply, cautiously, feeling the pain in her ribs but thinking through it, trying to negate it by willpower alone. Years of advanced medicine had undermined her basic survival training, however; the twinge in her bones refused to fade. At home, or on almost any other civilized planet in the galaxy, relief would have been moments away under the care of an automated medkit. She was slowly learning that, on Sciacca's World, access to such fundamental medical treatment would have been a luxury.

She wondered how Emmerik could stand it.

<He knows nothing else,> said the Surin suddenly. <This is the life he leads, and has led all his life. His fight is not simply against authority.>

Roche glanced at the Surin's blindfolded, unreadable face. She found it ironic that one who could appear so closed, so isolated from the viewpoint of others, could have such intimate access to her thoughts.

<Would you like to see me?> asked the reave unexpectedly. <As I truly am?>

"No, I—"

<Why not? Do you hate me that much?>

Roche gritted her teeth. She knew it was nothing more than her personal aversion to epsense that had made her react badly to the Surin, nothing to do with the girl herself.

<You know nothing about me,> said Maii. <But you knew as little when you helped me before, when Emmerik tried to carry me. How can you damn me now for something over which I have no control?>

"Because you *do* have control. It's not like any other sense. And I—I guess I find the power unnerving."

<No.> The Surin moved closer in the confined space. <You're afraid I'll expose you—reveal your weaknesses and Pristine frailties. Everything that your uniform hides.>

"You're wrong—"

<About what? Your fear or your self?>

Before she could answer, Maii had entered her mind and filled it with images:

A Surin woman with pendulous breasts bent over her, touching her, pleasing her, in a town called Erojen on an outpost far from the heart of the Surin domain, where outriders and social outcasts came for shelter, where those on the edge of society sought succor, where the normal could find what the rest of the Caste rejected—where anything that had a price could be bought. Yet somehow, in the squalor and perjury, was a strange dignity, a perverse pride, and dreams too, of betterment, profit, and sometimes, revenge . . .

. . . a place of passion, of vivid memories . . .

. . . a Surin adult taking her hand and leading her from her mother, her tears staining the front of her white smock, the world seeming so large and awful everywhere she looked, through ten kilometers in a jeep to the sanctuary, then the soft snick of the lock to her room sealing her in . . .

. . . in the hospital . . .

. . . learning to use the implants, with their gentle, cajoling voices, learning to avoid the discipline if she somehow got it wrong, learning to know what the doctor wanted in advance and what the treatment involved (if not what it meant), learning not to be afraid (or at least bottling it up where no one else would see it, where not even she could feel it, unless she wanted to), learning to forget what she had been, to concentrate on the now . . .

. . . feeling the sharp sting of the needle, feeling the voice of the doctor vibrating in the electric tingle of the implant (rather than hearing it pounding on her now-sensitive ears), feeling darkness creep over her from her toes up, feeling nothing in the end but an echo of the fear, and then feeling nothing at all for a very, very long (and yet somehow timeless) single moment . . .

. . . then . . . awakening to nothing.

Her higher senses—visual and aural, not the primal, animal senses of touch, taste, and smell—were gone, as was her ability to talk. The implant could still communicate with her, but it did so reluctantly, to quell her overwhelming panic, and then only via the bones in her skull, tapping out words of instruction and guidance into the outer layers of her brain itself. It monitored her every neuron, testing, probing, rearranging, rebuilding, using the tissues that had once belonged to her severed senses to rebuild a new sense, a new ability, one that (it said) would make her more valuable than anyone else on the planet.

She was the first successful outcome of a new procedure, one that could replicate in months what years of training could only hope to achieve. A procedure that was both illegal and immoral—in that it could only succeed when applied to children in their prepubescent years—but one that had the potential to increase her worth by millions after one simple operation.

All this, and more, she learned from the doctor in the spectacular moment her mind first opened—when, effortlessly, she reached into him with an invisible hand, searching, feeling, sensing, and leaving nothing but a burned-out ruin in her wake.

She was a reave. And she had been *made* that way.

It took time—and practice—to come to terms with this wondrous new ability of hers. And in a way it was perhaps fortunate for her that of every ten subjects she practiced upon, nine of them died. Had the doctor lived, and the process been completely successful, who knew what might have happened to her, to whom she might have been sold?

Even as her control improved—and she came to realize that the years of training endured by naturally occurring psychics were not necessary so much to develop the power, but to control it when it finally appeared—she understood that they would never use the process again. Not only had much of the theory gone with the doctor, but the risks were too great—the risk of creating a monster, of creating a failure, of being caught. Of creating another *her*, whom they would have to get rid of somehow, without her realizing it.

So she escaped. And entered the real world. And came to realize that what she had was even less of a gift than she had thought.

It wasn't sight—not sight as she had once known it, but an impression of sight, sight with all the baggage. Someone saw a knife and thought of a lost lover; buildings evoked memories of people long dead, of past events that had no relevance to her, the observer. Sounds were even worse, bringing unwanted impressions of voices, songs, screams, and sighs. Her world was secondhand, passing through the filters of other peoples' minds and emerging tainted rather than purified. She began to lose her own voice in the relentless ambience of echoes, overwhelmed by a world full of other peoples' thoughts.

But she maintained, grew bolder, traveled . . .

. . . received guidance from a bonded reave on Fal-Soma, many light-years from home . . .

. . . worked . . .

. . . and . . .

. . . returned with no thoughts left for herself. Not for a long while. All she saw—through her own eyes, her own sense of touch—was the orange-grey shelf of rock before her and the grit of dust on her fingertips.

Roche. Not Maii, the child sold, the experimental subject, the wanderer—the young Surin woman sitting opposite her, her mind elsewhere, far away and unreadable—whom she *had been* for an instant. Not Maii, not anymore.

All Roche felt was herself.

When Emmerik returned, he was pale-faced behind his beard. Cane followed, as soft and as silent as the Mbatan's shadow, yet full of the same vitality Roche had glimpsed earlier.

"Did you find them?" asked Veden.

Emmerik glanced at Cane and did not reply immediately.

"We found them," said Emmerik softly.

"And?" Veden prompted.

<I can no longer sense them,> Maii said. <At all.>

"We should keep moving," said the Mbatan, shifting his pack awkwardly, impatiently. "More could be following, and the Cross isn't far away now."

"Good." Veden was on his feet before Emmerik had finished speaking. "We've wasted enough time for one night."

In a wordless silence broken only by the crunch of their footfalls, they filed out of the niche and headed up the path.

8

The wind picked up as they crested the ridge of the mountains and rose above the dense layers of the storm. From the ridge, illuminated by the Soul, a wide plateau stretched below them: a deep bowl ringed by cliffs, perhaps an ancient, collapsed volcanic crater, with a small town in its center, too far away and too low in the dust to be seen clearly. The uppermost levels of two thin towers connected to each other by walkways were the only obvious detail.

"Houghton's Cross," said Emmerik, speaking for the first time in almost an hour.

"*That's* where we're headed?" Although he hadn't said so, Roche could tell that the town was dead, and had been for many years.

"Yes. The others are waiting for us there."

"'Haid'?" The name had been mentioned a couple of times earlier, in a context suggesting leadership or at least some sort of coordinating role. If Roche was ever going to find help getting off the planet, she guessed that he was the person she needed to talk to.

"Maybe. Depends what's happening in the port." The

burly Mbatan shifted his pack into a more comfortable position. "We'll talk when we arrive. Let's keep moving."

They descended along a thin path barely wide enough for one person. An avalanche of dust falling through a dip in the ridge enveloped them, reducing their line of sight to the back of the person in front, but at the same time effectively hiding them from the eyes of anyone in the area. If the air within the crater was as gloomy as it appeared to be, they would be invisible to Enforcers standing on the ridge.

Roche walked grimly onward, the pain somehow keeping her focused on who she was and what she was doing. The straps holding the Box to her back were like whips in slow motion, digging into her bruised and battered shoulders with each step she took. The valise itself had been attached to her for so long that it was starting to feel like an extra limb—and a useless, hindering limb at that, dragging as it did behind her. In a way it seemed more of an inconvenience than her strapped left arm, yet without it she doubted she would ever feel complete again.

That thought depressed her more than any merely physical pain. That, and the still-ringing echoes of Maii's life.

The floor of the crater was relatively flat and composed of a loose, grey dirt. Although the soil here seemed as parched as that of the neighboring foothills, hardy weeds grew from it, clinging to the ground in a desperate embrace against the severe winds. They crossed an unused road at one point, then a wide, flat area that might once have been a landing strip. An abandoned machine—an ore carrier—loomed out of the gloom, rusted and hulking, left to the elements centuries ago and now barely recognizable. Dust had sanded its paint and windshield back to bare metal, which itself was scored and pitted. A ragged hole in one side offered a mute explanation for the neglect, although Roche was unable to tell if the hole had been caused by an internal malfunction or external interference.

Closer to the town, the crater floor undulated in a series of low dunes, possibly a forestalled attempt at irrigation. Something glinting in the dirt at the bottom of one of the trenches caught Roche's eye, and she stopped to pick it up.

It was a silver coin, heavy in her palm, with a bold "U" on one side. She didn't recognize the denomination.

<Underground currency,> said the Box. <Early Ataman Theocracy.>

<Here?>

<No need to be concerned, Morgan. Such coins have been out of circulation for over seven hundred years; this one was no doubt left by an early colonist. Furthermore, being a penal colony, Sciacca's World has no official economy, and therefore no use for money.>

"Except to deal with outsiders," she muttered.

<Who are unable to come here anyway.>

Roche glanced at Veden, whose back was receding up the slope of the trench. <No money at all?>

<DAOC trades for credit with the Pan-Human Finance Trust. The transportees work to gain what comforts they can, with benefits such as health care and rations accrued by points. Officially, there is no commerce between parties on the surface, with no economic medium to enable it.>

<And unofficially?>

<We have no way of knowing that until we see it at work—although the existence of this coin, here, could be taken as suggestive.>

<That's what I think.> Roche dropped the coin into the dirt and hurried to catch up with the others, suspicious yet again of the Eckandi's motives. If the rebels on Sciacca's World had no current means of paying Veden for his services, what did he hope to gain from coming here?

Emmerik glanced back at her as she approached. "Don't wander," he said. "We're almost there."

Made curious by the forbidding tone in his voice, Roche obeyed but kept her eyes peeled. Another road crossed their path, and Emmerik turned to follow it. The brown, stony surface was cracked and split in places, and puddles of sand had collected in the cracks, making footing treacherous. The ever-present dust allowed them to see no more than six meters in any direction; even via infrared, the world was dim and featureless. Roche wondered how Emmerik could tell their position relative to the town.

Then, rising out of the haze, shapes appeared lining the

road and spreading off into the distance: a field of posts, perhaps, barely a meter high, or the trunks of long-dead shrubs, stripped of their branches. Roche couldn't tell exactly what they were, except that there were a lot of them. The wind moaned eerily through them, making the hair on the back of her neck rise.

She approached the edge of the road to look closer at one of the objects. Through the haze of dirt, she recognized the dull sheen of blackened metal and the sweep of a stock, sight, and barrel. It was a weapon, buried barrel-first in the dirt.

<Mbatan high-frequency microwave combat rifle,> said Box. <A very old model.>

She crouched down to study it more closely. She hadn't seen a HFM peace gun outside the Armada Museum, but the distinctive line of the trigger guard, designed for digits larger than her own, confirmed that the Box was right at least about the Caste that had built it. <There must be hundreds of them.> She reached out a hand to touch it.

"Roche!" Emmerik's warning snapped at her.

She glanced guiltily upward. An indistinct figure was moving toward her through the gloom from deeper in the field, a vaguely Human shape wrapped in rags, hissing menacingly. She jerked upright, reaching automatically for her empty holster.

The figure stopped in its tracks and stared at her. Two more approached out of the dust, and stood on either side of the first. She stared back, mystified, waiting for them to make a move. It was only when Emmerik's gently restraining hand came down on her shoulder that she realized they would approach no closer while she stayed away from the rifle.

"Leave them alone," Emmerik said from behind her. "We have no right to interfere with them, and what belongs to them."

"Who are they?"

"Caretakers." Emmerik's hand, now on her good arm, led her away from the edge of the road. "They preserve the killing fields."

"The guns?" she said.

"No," said Emmerik firmly. "This is neither the time nor the place to discuss what happened here, Roche."

Roche opened her mouth to speak, but Emmerik was already moving off down the road, into the dust. She followed slowly after him, her attention caught by the three ghostly figures disappearing once again into the gloom. The movements of one of them disturbed her a little. With each step it took, its garments moved in such a way as to suggest that it had more than one right arm.

When the three figures completely vanished into the haze, Roche hurried her pace to catch up with Emmerik.

"How many?" she asked, coming to his side. "The guns, I mean."

Emmerik kept his attention on the road ahead. "Not now, I said."

"*When*, then?" she snapped. "I'm sick of not knowing anything."

"When we meet the others."

"You keep saying that." Roche fought to control her anger, but she could still hear the snap in her voice.

"Not far now," he said, adjusting his dust-specs. "The town's just a little further on."

The field of rifles petered out after a hundred meters. Moments later, a large shape appeared through the dust, glowing with the remnants of the day's heat: a wall, natural for the first five meters, then artificial above. Exactly how high it rose above the floor of the crater, Roche couldn't tell, but it showed no sign of ending at the limits of her infrared vision. She supposed that the builders had situated the wall, and the city within, on the central peak of the ancient impact crater to thereby gain the strategic advantage that would give the town. Higher than the crater floor, it was well placed to repel ground attacks—the unbroken expanse of the floor itself gave little cover for an attacking army—and the ring of mountains was far enough away to reduce the accuracy of sniping.

The road came to a halt at the base of a gentle ramp, which led to a wide pair of sliding doors set into the natural base of the wall. The doors were firmly shut, and looked as though they weighed tons. A sign on the door proclaimed a brief message in letters almost too faint to read, in a script Roche recognized but could not decipher.

<'Ul-æmato,'> read the Box. <Dominion alphabet, circa twenty-fifth century EN.>

<What does it mean?>

<'Founder's Rock.'>

<Could be the name of the town, before the Ataman Theocracy took over.>

<One would assume so.>

<Does it appear in your datapool?>

<Briefly.> The Box paused, as though scanning its extensive memory. <The Hutton-Luu System was the first of many fought over by the Ataman Theocracy and the Dominion during the Ghost War, as I said earlier. The city of Ul-æmato was a target during this period. Beyond that, I can tell you little.>

Roche absorbed this information while Emmerik approached the massive doors. <Olmahoi greyboots, Mbatan peace guns, Theocracy coins, Dominion ruins . . .>

<And a Commonwealth of Empires penal colony,> chimed the Box.

Roche nodded. <This place has seen a lot in its time.>

<It is steeped in death.> Maii's words intruded, suddenly, upon their silent conversation.

Roche glanced at the Surin, who had spoken even less than Emmerik since their brief break in the mountains. The girl shivered deep in her survival suit—which had turned a deep, gloomy grey, mirroring both the night and Maii's mood.

<What do you mean by that?> asked Roche.

<I can sense echoes of the people who live nearby,> said the reave. <They do not enter the city itself. They remember suffering and terrible pain—and they believe it to be inhabited by the shelaigh.> Maii read Roche's confusion and answered the question that had arisen in her thoughts: <Spirits, ghosts, qacina, jezu . . . >The explanation ceased the moment Roche's confusion cleared.

<Can you read anything more about them?>

<No. Their minds are confused, vague. Sickened.>

Roche felt a slight chill at the reave's words. Not sick, but *sickened*. By something.

A deep, bone-jarring rumble distracted her. She looked up in time to see the mighty doors slide open a meter, then crash to a halt. Emmerik slid his bulk through the crack and gestured that they should follow. Cane did so first, sniffing at the air before entering the darkness. Veden and Maii went next, leaving Roche alone in the chill night air. If it was a trap, she reasoned, better to face it with the others than alone.

Darkness overwhelmed her as she slipped through the narrow space—a deep black broken only by the faint heat profiles of those ahead of her. Echoes told her that the passage was slightly wider than the doors, and barely as high. She was reminded of their earlier journey through the tunnel leading from the ravine. This passage seemed more oppressive despite its greater width—perhaps because it was designed to be lit, and was not.

Several minutes passed before anything changed. Veden grunted with surprise, and Roche tensed. Then she realized that his heat image was rising, as were those of Emmerik, Maii, and Cane. A second later, she too hit the ramp and began to climb. The passage had been designed to accommodate wheeled vehicles, not pedestrians, for the slope was steep and the walls lacked handholds. She maintained her balance carefully, conscious that if she slipped she might not be able to arrest a slide back to the bottom with only one arm to stop her.

The ramp leveled out after twenty paces, and reached another set of doors. Emmerik again approached them, and manipulated the controls of what could only be a magnetic lock, although one of ancient design. Roche felt the tingle in her implants as powerful fields shifted to a new configuration and the heavy barrier slid aside.

They stepped out of the tunnel into a square on the edge of the town.

The pearly sheen of the Soul, diffused though it was by the dust-laden air, seemed bright in comparison to the interior of the tunnel. Roche glanced behind her, and realized that their journey had taken them only as far as the inner edge of the wall, the base of which must therefore have been nearly thirty meters thick. Its top was studded with ramps and walkways, and sturdier emplacements where weapons might once have peered over the wall at the crater below. Every fixture seemed perfectly designed, intended to last centuries—as it seemed they already had. Roche could only admire the builders of the wall, and the military function it performed so well.

The square split traffic from the tunnel into five wide roadways that diverged as they led deeper into the town. The buildings were uniformly squat and solid, with rounded corners and domed roofs—an architecture common to Dominion military emplacements. Apart from the efforts of wind and time, not one of the buildings appeared damaged in any way. Every door was open, and the few windows were utterly black. In the absence of wind, the square seemed unnaturally still.

Raising her eyes from the buildings before her, she saw the two large towers at the heart of the city: the only buildings higher than two stories. From this close—less than two kilometers—they were far more impressive. The shorter stood at least one hundred meters high; its taller twin might have reached one hundred and twenty, although dust hazed its upper limits. They stood roughly ten meters apart with a tracery of scaffolding connecting the two, as though they had been undergoing repair when the town had been abandoned.

No, Roche reminded herself, not abandoned. Emmerik intended to meet someone here.

"Which way?" prompted Cane, gesturing at the five roads.

"Second from the left." The Mbatan's voice was muted, muffled by an emotion Roche could not read. "Please stick to the road and don't disturb anything. I'll follow in a moment."

"Are we in danger?" Cane studied the darkened doorways with suspicion.

"No." Emmerik shook his head. "It's not that."

Roche suddenly guessed what was bothering the Mbatan. Studying the silent streets more closely, she could see the way sand had gathered in every crevice, untouched for decades, perhaps centuries; the very air tasted pure, despite the tang of dust, untainted by the outside world. It was as though the whole town had been sealed in memoriam to whatever in its past had killed it. The town was a shrine, and they were violating it simply with their presence.

Again she swallowed her curiosity and forced herself to walk, eager to reach the end of their long journey. The others followed her lead, heading slowly along the road with their footsteps echoing off the stubborn buildings. Cane took the rear, his keen gaze studying the shadows for movement. Roche looked also, but from training rather than suspicion; in those deserted streets she didn't expect to find life of *any* kind. Still, the absence of Emmerik's steady steps among theirs made the procession seem somewhat unnatural, even tense. And the fact that he had their weapons only made her feel more uneasy.

Roche trod onward, refusing to look behind her. There were other ways to find out what was going on.

"What's he doing, Maii?" she asked, once they were out of earshot.

<I don't know.> There was a hint of resignation in the reave's tone. <He has a very effective epsense shield.>

"Can you sense anybody else? The people he's supposed to be meeting, for example?"

<Faintly. They are not far away.> She hesitated for a few moments. <They seem to be waiting. Perhaps they noticed the doors opening.>

Roche sighed. <Box? Do you have a map of this place?>

<Only an aerial reconnaissance photo.> The display in Roche's left eye flickered and superimposed a grainy picture over the dimly lit street: a high-altitude, low-res scan of the city. A bright dot of light moved across the image. <This is the street we are following. Note that it doglegs shortly before we reach the central square.>

Roche looked ahead, trying to locate the corner but failing. <How far?>

<Perhaps a kilometer, maybe more.> The image zoomed closer, became even grainier. <Note also that the scaffolding around the towers appears to be missing.>

<You can see that? I can't see any such thing.>

<Well, it's missing, although I am unable to explain why.>

<So the picture was obviously taken before it went up.>

<I had realized that, Morgan.> Did she detect indignation in the AI's tone? <The question is: what purpose does it serve now that did not require servicing earlier?>

<I don't know.>

<Quite.> The Box fell silent for a moment, and the image in her eye disappeared. <Speculation is useless in the absence of data.>

<Not really. We could at least form a hypothesis to test later, when we do have the data.>

<Better to have no hypothesis at all, than an incorrect one.>

<Perhaps.> Roche withdrew into herself, rubbing her aching shoulder through the survival suit and makeshift bandages. The road seemed endless, and the night deeper and colder than ever. Her survival suit, and those of her companions, had turned a deep charcoal black. But for the faint heat signatures, they would have been totally invisible. "Damn him," she muttered. "He could have at least left us some water."

They reached the dogleg fifteen minutes later. Roche studied it cautiously before sending Cane ahead. The blind corner would be the perfect place for an ambush, and she wasn't prepared to risk anything in this place. The lanky figure of her only Pristine companion strode confidently across the open space until he disappeared from sight. Roche found herself holding her breath until he appeared again, waving an "all clear." Tenuous though her connection to him was, right now, in this town, she felt she would be lost without his presence. It wasn't an emotional issue, but one that any realist would admit to. In her weakened state, she needed someone strong to rely on. And if she was wrong to place her trust in him, then . . .

Not that she had any choice. She was vulnerable, cut off from the support structures that usually surrounded her. She had to take what she could get, and learn to live without the rest.

As they approached the heart of the abandoned town, the towers loomed higher than ever. The scaffolding became clearer, although its purpose remained a mystery. Wires and thin poles tangled like an abstract sculpture across the gap between the towers; the faint light from the Soul touching various sections gave it the appearance of a giant spider's web. Roche strained her eyes to see more clearly: could she see something, a tiny speck, in the center of the web, or was that just her imagination?

The road turned once more before reaching the central square, which occupied the space between the towers. The curve was gentle, hardly threatening, but Roche's nervousness increased with every step along it.

"I don't like this," she said. "I feel like we're walking into a trap."

"Don't be stupid," said Veden, his grey eyes glinting in the darkness. "They know who I am."

"Still . . ."

<It has become very quiet.> Maii's words cut across Roche's unfinished sentence. <I don't like it either.>

"There are two people ahead," said Cane.

Roche stopped in mid-stride. "Where?"

"In the square."

She squinted into the gloom. "I can't see them."

"I can just make out the shapes of their arms and legs," said Cane, his eyes narrowed. "Only just, but they are definitely there."

<Ask him what color, Morgan,> said the Box.

"What color, Cane?"

"A very deep purple, around the edges. Like silhouettes."

<They are shielded, then. He is detecting high-frequency interference where the fields are narrowest.>

<Are you saying he can see in ultraviolet?> Roche couldn't contain her disbelief.

<It is the only possibility. You yourself can see nothing in either visible or infrared, so therefore—>

<Okay, okay.> Roche fought to concentrate. Should they separate, or move in en masse and risk being cornered?

<I detect no ill intent,> said the reave.

"You can read them?"

<Now, yes. They were closed before. Their camouflage shields are simply precautionary, to prevent them being seen from the city walls or from the air. They await Veden.>

"Should we keep going?"

<We are in no danger,> said Maii, <from them.>

Roche noted the qualifying phrase, and nodded. "Okay. But keep an eye out. Or whatever." She wished Emmerik were back with them; at least then they would have somebody to speak on their behalf. It was unlikely that Veden would.

They continued onward, closer to the square. As they approached, the shields fell away from the pair, revealing a short man and a tall woman, both dressed in black. Beyond the dropping of the shields, neither made any move.

Roche walked until she was within ten meters of the pair, then stopped. Cane did likewise, as did Maii. Veden hesitated, then continued walking.

"Makil Veden?" said the man, his voice booming into the silence.

"Yes," replied the Eckandi. "I am he."

The man and the woman moved simultaneously, drawing heavy weapons from beneath their tunics and directing them at the Eckandi. "Come no closer."

Veden stopped immediately, with his hands half-raised in an automatic gesture of surrender. "What—?"

"Take another step and we will execute you for the crimes your Caste has committed against us."

<They don't mean it,> gasped the reave, her voice urgent. <It's a distraction. They're trying to—>

Cane moved. From a standing start to a rapid sprint, he ran for the shadows cloaking the square. Roche gaped, startled by the swiftness of his response; his legs almost seemed to blur in the darkness. The woman spun to follow him. Chattering gunfire chased his heels, too late to catch him. He disappeared into an open doorway, reappeared an instant later through an alleyway, then disappeared again.

Roche automatically extrapolated his path. He was circling the square, not running away. Stunned by his sheer speed, she could only watch, frozen.

The man and woman turned to face her and Maii.

"Put your hands on your head," said a voice from behind them. "Lie facedown on the ground and do not try to resist."

Roche spun to face the familiar voice. Six more people had appeared from the shadows with rifles in their hands. One of them was Emmerik.

"Do it," he spat, gesturing with the rifle. "Now!"

Roche obeyed, clumsily lowering herself to her knees, then lying flat on the road with the cold stone against her cheek.

"We'll kill her!" Emmerik shouted, his voice echoing through the empty square. The words chilled her less than the tone of his voice. The Mbatan's eyes searched the shadows, desperate for any sign of the fugitive.

Something moved on the far side of the square, and the woman's rifle turned to face it.

"I mean it," Emmerik said, less loudly than before. The rifle clicked at her back: a projectile weapon, she absently noted; lethal at such close range. "I swear."

<They want *you*, Cane,> said Maii, her mental voice stabbing the night. <Just you. They won't hurt Roche if you come out. They *will* hurt her if you don't.>

Emmerik nodded. "She's telling the truth. Too many people have died here for another to make a difference."

Silence answered him, heavy with potential violence.

Then a shadow moved, and Cane stepped into view. His hands hung clenched at his sides. His expression was one of anger, tightly reined.

"Down." Emmerik gestured with the rifle.

With his eyes focused on the Mbatan, Cane obeyed. A rifle butt, held by the woman, jammed into the back of his neck as her companion fixed his hands and feet in carbon-steel cuffs. Cane made no sound at all as he was bound, although Roche could see the rage boiling inside him, waiting for a chance to escape. But with the gun at his neck, he had no opportunity to break free.

When he was securely bound, rough hands lifted Roche upright. She gasped, staring in confusion at the Mbatan.

"What the hell—?"

"We had to do it," he said, his eyes pleading for her to believe him.

"But he swore to help you," she hissed. "He deserves better than this."

"He's too dangerous, too unpredictable," the Mbatan said. "You saw how fast he moved. Until he tells us who or what he is, he stays like this. I'm sorry."

Roche glanced at Cane, prostrate on the ground, then at Maii and Veden. The Eckandi was looking smugly superior now that the object of the trap had been revealed: not Veden himself, or even Roche and the Box, but Cane alone.

Roche turned away, feeling frustration bubbling within her like a ball of superheated water. She couldn't bear to look at him, potentially the most powerful fighter she had ever met betrayed by a handful of low-life rebels.

"What about honesty?" she snapped back. "Integrity? Trust?"

"Look up," said one woman standing close behind her.

"What?" said Roche.

"Look up," the woman repeated. "Between the towers."

Roche did so, and was gratified to hear Veden echo her own involuntary gasp of revulsion.

Suspended by the scaffolding between the two towers, crucified horizontally by wires and impaled upon iron spars, hung the mummified body of a naked Eckandi male.

"Blind trust on Sciacca can often prove expensive," said Emmerik, and gestured with the rifle that she should walk ahead of him to join the others.

9

"Newcomers to our planet usually mean trouble." The woman brushed strands of black hair from her narrow face. Roche had heard Emmerik address her as "Neva," although she hadn't been formally introduced. "It's an unfortunate fact of life," she added.

Roche glanced inquiringly at Neva from where she sat, but the woman averted her face and busied herself at one of the tables. Emmerik crouched nearby with a gun in his lap, his attention fixed on Cane sitting against the wall opposite Roche. Through the only doorway leading into the room, Roche could make out Veden and Maii discussing business with a half dozen other rebels, their conversation kept carefully out of earshot.

If the woman's remark had been an overture to an explanation, it seemed Roche would have to wait a little longer for the rest.

They had been brought to the shorter of the two towers, which obviously served as an impromptu base for the rebels in the town. The room they were in was slightly run-down and thick with dust; around them were scattered ten camp beds, a number of the crude projectile weapons she had seen earlier, a small cache of food and water, and a dozen or so unmarked containers. The only light in the room came from a battered fuel-cell heater in the corner; the only window was currently shielded by a carbon-mat, presumably to prevent their heat from being detected at night.

Neva came to Roche's side to tend her injuries, gently peeling back the survival suit to take a closer look. Roche winced as her bruised muscles submitted to the woman's examination.

"I think you're being a little harsh on us," said Roche. "I never wanted to be here in the first place—and if the only way to leave is by helping you, then that's what I'll do."

Neva grinned wryly. "Whether you want to or not." She slipped a ration-stick into Roche's mouth. The stick burst upon chewing and became a thick, sweet gel. "The transportees don't want to be here either, remember."

Roche nodded in appreciation for the food, but couldn't bring herself to offer her gratitude. The rebels may have helped her so far, but she was still decidedly wary of their motives.

"Well," she said, "this *is* a penal planet—"

"That's not the half of it." Neva roughly unstrapped the Box from her back. "If you think *we're* being harsh, then you don't know the meaning of the word."

"Not now," Emmerik interrupted. "She needs rest, not a lecture."

"Be quiet, Emmerik," said the woman evenly. It was clear to Roche from Neva's tone that her rank in the rebels was higher than that of the Mbatan. "She wants to know who we are. She *needs* to if she expects us to help her."

"And if you expect us to help you." Roche smiled, but the light from the heater reflected in the woman's eyes was cold. That she wanted to talk, though, was obvious. "Why don't you tell me what happened?"

"What happened was the Ghost War," Neva said, settling back onto her haunches and continuing to work on Roche's injured shoulder. "Prior to then, this was a comfortable planet, with forests and lakes and fields of grain. And rivers."

"It's hard to imagine."

Neva's fingers dug deep into Roche's shoulder, making her wince with pain. *Be quiet* was the obvious message.

"A strike on a Dominion installation in the Soul changed—*ruined*—everything," the woman went on. "There was massive destruction. Three large moonlets fell from orbit. Killed millions, smashed the ecosphere. A few small cities survived, such as this one, but the moonlets— along with the quakes and volcanic activity that followed— left virtually nothing else standing. The Ataman Theocracy didn't even bother to hang around to mop up the survivors. Bigger wars to attend to, perhaps. I don't know. History doesn't supply an explanation. And it doesn't matter. The old world was gone."

Neva's fingers stopped working, and for a few moments she remained very still, staring off over Roche's injured shoulder. Roche made no attempt to prompt her, but glanced over to where Cane sat huddled beneath a cowl of shadows, attentive as always. His eyes were fixed upon her, but she suspected he would be listening to every word that Neva or Emmerik said.

Then Neva's fingers began to move again, and with them her labored account of Ul-æmato's history. "For the survivors, life went on. They adapted to the new environment: the deserts, the sandstorms, the predators. Sciacca's World was still home to a couple of million people, and I guess they believed they could tame it again. They became a harder breed, tougher than their ancestors. A more resilient type of Pristine altogether, although not a new Caste.

"The First Ataman War came and went. Officially, from then on, we were part of the Theocracy, but they had no substantial presence, so it didn't mean much to people here. Only during the Second Ataman War did things change. The Commonwealth of Empires took the system, and they invaded in force. But we were stronger on the ground, and we held a number of small territories in the hills and mountains free from the invading forces."

"Such as Houghton's Cross?" Roche said, noting Neva's unconscious switch from "they" to "we."

"It wasn't called Houghton's Cross back then," said

Neva. "It was called Ul-æmato, and it became the capital of this region." She shrugged. "And although the Commonwealth occasionally conducted raids in the hope of destabilizing the Dominion population, the two nations coexisted in relative peace for quite a while."

"It was around then that the penal colony was founded," put in Emmerik. "To mine the Soul, and the places on the shattered crust where minerals had come to the surface."

Neva nodded once more. "The Theocracy, when it destroyed the planet, ignored that resource, just as its soldiers ignored the Human suffering they left behind."

She paused, concentrating for a moment on Roche's shoulder. Then: "Port Parvati was rebuilt—along with the installations in the Soul—and the entire project was turned over to OPUS, a mining consortium. The planet became a business venture, and the board of directors wouldn't tolerate competition or interference from unruly neighbors. Ul-æmato became *competition*."

Neva began to rub salve into Roche's shoulder. It burned and stung, but she didn't interrupt the woman's narrative with complaint.

"Then DAOC, another mining company, took over the administration of the planet. Its prospectors exhausted low-lying deposits and decided they wanted the hills. They mounted a full-scale military campaign against Sciacca's people. There are ruins all through these mountains where DAOC troops—mercenaries, most of them—razed entire communities to the ground, leaving nothing but rubble and ashes in their wake. Yet, despite being outgunned in almost every way, the defenses of Ul-æmato held while other towns fell around it. The fight went on for weeks, until Ul-æmato was teeming with injured and frightened refugees.

"Food and water were scarce. DAOC had destroyed irrigation and mist-collection plants. The siege of the city was in its seventh week when a lucky strike crippled one of only two fusion generators in the area. It all seemed hopeless until a gunrunner approached the defenders from out-system with a large supply of weapons."

Neva paused to tie a bandage in place. "Word must have spread, and I guess it was only a matter of time before somebody tried to profit from the situation. But any chance of improving the odds had to be considered seriously. DAOC was well armed, whereas Ul-æmato was relying on technology centuries out of date. The Mbatan rifles, nearly five thousand in all, were high-frequency microwave weapons—designed to disable electronic equipment rather than to kill. They would be effective against the battle armor of the attacking troops. They were cheap, efficient, and honorable, and the gunrunner agreed to sell the weapons on credit."

"Credit?" said Roche. "What sort of illegal—?"

Neva raised a hand to silence her. "He agreed to supply the weapons in exchange for a substantial down payment in underground currency. The deal was signed. With the weapons, the troops of Ul-æmato went into battle.

"And they did well, taking first one and then another DAOC squadron by surprise and forcing them back. As the squadrons retreated, Ul-æmato's territory expanded to something like its original size. Anything with powered systems could not enter this area, or the peace guns would disable them, and the Ul-æmato fighters were so well trained at more primitive methods of combat—having practiced them for generations—that DAOC was reluctant to send troops in unarmored. Orbital bombardment was ruled out, because that method of fighting would be frowned upon by the interstellar community. For the first time in several months, it seemed that DAOC would have to capitulate and allow the original owners of the planet their small territory."

Having finished ministering to Roche's shoulder—as well as changing her makeshift bandages—Neva strapped the injured arm into a more comfortable position, leaving the valise free. She sat back upon the gritty floor, facing Roche.

"Then, for no obvious reason, Ul-æmato's troops began to weaken. A tiredness afflicted them: a terrible malaise that sapped both strength and will. It caused bleeding, skin damage, and occasional loss of hair; in the long term, it led to death. No physical cause could be found. The popular theory was that a biological agent had been unleashed by DAOC to quash the town's resistance.

"The strange thing about it, though, was that the disease

only affected those who fought in battle, never noncombatants. And as the battle continued, the weakened fighters were replaced by others, who in turn fell to the mysterious illness. Lacking an advanced medical center, the colonists had no means of determining the illness's cause until it was far too late. And even then, it was only by chance. By that time, nearly three quarters of the town had fallen prey to the disease."

"The rifles," said Cane softly.

Neva nodded. "One of the town's elders, a woman named Madra Hazeal, returned from the front with one of the Mbatan peace guns. Its batteries were dead, and she intended to recharge them the following day. Legend has it that, feeling tired and sick with the disease, she retired to bed and absently left the weapon near a tub of water. Somehow the weapon slipped and fell into the water and remained immersed for a number of hours. When she retrieved it the following morning, she discovered something very peculiar: despite the chill of the desert night, the water in the tub was distinctly warm."

"Beta decay," said Roche, echoing the voice of the Box in her skull.

Neva nodded again. "The rifles were radioactive—so contaminated that only a few doses resulted in debilitating sickness. The gunrunner had deliberately sold them, knowing the harm they would do. This left the people of Ulæmato in a bind: continuing the defense of the town with the weapons meant slow death by radiation sickness, while surrender meant that they would be invaded." She lowered her eyes to the floor. "So the town fell to DAOC without a fight, killed by the rifles that had almost liberated it."

Roche waited for her to continue, but Emmerik picked up the tale.

"Shortly after taking the town," he said, "the DAOC troops learned what had happened. Naturally, they were appalled. Along with orbital bombardment, the use of radiation weapons was forbidden. Breaking the Warfare Protocol carried a heavy penalty. If conciliatory measures were not taken immediately to demonstrate their innocence, word would spread that the DAOC troops had planted the weapons themselves."

"So," Cane guessed, "as a gesture of goodwill, DAOC allowed the few remaining survivors to keep the town?"

Neva glanced back to him in the shadows. "Yes," she said. "Although they took the mountains around it, the security forces vowed to leave the town and its inhabitants alone." Again she faced Roche. "In the weeks remaining to them, the dying townsfolk buried the dead in a ring around the town, using the poisoned rifles as gravestones."

Roche remembered the endless field of rifles pointing at the sky, and shivered. "And the gunrunner?" she asked.

Emmerik snorted. "You've seen what happened to him," he said.

Roche nodded slowly. "The Eckandi."

"Lazaro Houghton," said Neva, her voice cold, "was eventually captured by the Dominion with the help of the COE—in a further gesture of goodwill. After his trial, he was sent to Sciacca's World as a convict. He only lasted a year before the inhabitants hunted him down and meted out their own justice."

"Thus 'Houghton's Cross,' " muttered Cane.

"That's right." Emmerik stared at him in the half-light, the glow from the heater catching his intense expression. "Only a handful of children survived the radiation sickness, but DAOC's promise still holds. They won't attack us here. The Cross, the old city, has become a symbol of everything we strive for: justice for past wrongs, freedom to live as we wish—"

"And it's safe," said Cane, cutting through the Mbatan's rhetoric with hard-edged pragmatism.

"That too." Emmerik glanced at Neva, and Roche noted the look that passed between them. "We do not seek a bloodbath, and we are not interested in leaving the planet. Our cause does not belong with the convicts, or the wardens. We were born here, all of us. This is where we want to live, in peace, for the rest of our lives. In order to do so, we will attempt diplomacy, but not open rebellion."

"Except as a last resort," added Neva. "Our reluctance to trust off-worlders is ingrained, you see. Sciacca's World has been betrayed at various times by the Ataman Theocracy, the Dato Bloc, the Commonwealth of Empires, and even by the Dominion, who abandoned it to its fate eight hundred years ago. Any treaty would be regarded as suspect until proved by time."

"Patience is what we should be embracing, Neva," said the Mbatan wearily, as though they had had this disagreement many times. "There has been enough death here."

"But not enough, it seems, to convince the wardens to agree to our terms." Neva returned her attention to Roche. "Haid seeks a hearing with the High Equity Court of the COE to discuss our claim of sovereignty. To do this we need a hyperspace communicator. But our requests to use the MiCom facilities at the landing field have been denied, and Warden Delcasalle refuses to negotiate."

"So you fight," said Roche, finally feeling that she understood the nature of the rebels. The why of their actions, if not the how.

"No, we *resist*." Emmerik leaned forward to accentuate the word. "We will never give up hope of finding a peaceful solution."

"Even if it means using a stranded Armada officer as a bargaining point?"

"Perhaps," said Neva. "It might come to that."

"But it won't." Emmerik gave the woman a warning look. "We have other plans, plans that don't involve betrayal."

"But do they involve Veden?" said Roche.

Neva glanced at Emmerik, and the Mbatan looked away. "It's important that you understand us," said the woman, "to enable you to decide where you stand. But until you make that decision, we will tell you nothing more."

Roche took the hint, although she was more curious than ever about how Veden intended to help. She looked into the adjacent room to see what Veden was doing, but the Eckandi and Maii, along with the other rebels, had gone.

Until you make that decision . . . Neva's sentiment bothered her. Although she could sympathize with the rebels' plight, she wasn't sure she should take a stand at all. It wasn't her job to get involved—unless that was the only way she could get off-world.

Roche lay back on the bed that Neva had prepared for her and closed her eyes. <What do you think, Box?>

<Intriguing,> said the familiar voice deep inside her head.

<But are they telling us the whole story?>

<Possibly not. Certainly there are a number of aspects that the official records do not corroborate, although that could be because the records I have were compiled by the Commonwealth of Empires and would certainly be biased, if what Neva says is true. We have no reason to disbelieve her. Her explanation does match the evidence we have gathered so far: the coin, the weapons, the town itself.>

<But where does Veden fit into it all?>

<Obviously they hope he will enable them to reach their goal. Perhaps he can talk reason to Warden Delcasalle; the Eckandi are renowned negotiators, after all. Or perhaps they intend to use Maii's epsense ability to force the warden into making the decision the rebels desire. There are a number of possibilities, none of which seems any more likely than the others at this time.> The Box paused for a moment, as though considering the situation. <When I said 'intriguing,' Morgan, I was actually referring to the curious way in which our needs almost exactly match theirs. We need access to communications, and so do they. The only difference is that we want to leave the planet, whereas they intend to stay.>

Roche tried to find a comfortable position. <And they're welcome to it.>

<I know you are tired, Morgan, but try to concentrate for just a few more minutes: the rebels have been attempting to get what they want for many years, and have failed thus far. Without Veden, we all lose. And that makes us—meaning you and me and Adoni Cane—dangerously vulnerable.>

Roche absorbed this disquieting thought in silence. Her fate rested in the Eckandi's hands: if he chose not to help the rebels because of her involvement, then she could hardly blame them for turning her in. What did she have to offer them in return for their help? All she had done so far was bring the Dato with her into the system, and increased Enforcement's presence in the mountain range—neither of which was likely to sit well with the rebels.

<At least all is not yet lost,> said the Box.

<Why's that?> she asked, beginning to feel the tug of sleep.

<You still have me.>

In defiance of sheer physical exhaustion, her mind wouldn't let her rest. She lay for two hours on the camp mattress—staring at the orange, unflickering glow the heater cast across the ceiling, and thinking about everything Neva had said—before finally giving in to restlessness.

The atmosphere of the room was thick and heavy with sleep. The floor was carpeted with a dense, aging fabric that might once have been a vibrant red, although the years had faded it to a musty brown. Roche tried to imagine the room filled with people—dignitaries, diplomats, soldiers, partisans—but failed. The town's oppressive stillness had penetrated every building, every room, robbing it of even ghosts of memory.

No one stirred as she climbed out of the bunk and donned her survival suit. Cane's eyes were open, but he neither moved nor made a sound to disturb the others. Grasping the valise by its handle, she eased out of the room and into the hallway, where she waited a moment, listening. Still no sounds of alarm. When she felt certain she would not be followed, she swiftly and silently retraced the steps that had led to the room from the street below.

The wind had picked up in the hours she had been sheltered. It blustered around the base of the tower, snatching at her cropped scalp and stealing her warmth. Not yet certain where she was headed, she put down the valise for a moment to tug the hood of her suit over her head. As she did so, she happened to glance upward and glimpsed the Eckandi gunrunner, Lazaro Houghton, his twisted body silhouetted against the Soul.

She shivered, picked up the valise, and walked away, heading into the darkness of the city.

How long it took her to reach the town's outer wall she had no way of knowing, but when she arrived, the eastern span of the Soul had grown perceptibly brighter. Dawn was approaching. Randomly choosing a walkway, she climbed the network of ladders and platforms up the inside of the wall until she stood on its lip, thereby gaining an unobstructed view of both the town behind her and the crater around it. The wind moaned incessantly, seeking to tug her from her ancient perch. She gripped a brass rail with her one good hand and watched patiently, her mind empty of all thought, as the orange sun rose over the horizon.

Below her, still in shadow but growing more distinct with every second, was the field of graves encircling the town— rifle after rifle in an endless procession. So many graves, she thought. So much—

"You are restless," said a voice from behind her.

She turned, startled. It was Emmerik. She let herself relax. "Yes."

"Everyone has a still point, a focus, a place where one can find peace." Emmerik tipped his head to the sunrise, at the stain of blood spreading over the crater lip. "Mine is here. Houghton's Cross at dawn."

"You didn't follow me here, then?"

"Oh, I followed you. I was watching the tower from across the street. When you left, I chose not to stop you, thinking you might be headed here. Hoping." The burly Mbatan sighed deeply, the deep crinkles in the thick skin of his face smoothing slightly. "A moment of stillness is all I desire of every day. It's a shame you can't partake fully of it."

Roche turned back to the sunrise. "I have such a place also, but it's far away from here."

"Further than I can imagine, most likely. I have never traveled through space, even to a place so near as the Soul. Leaving my planet seems impossible, sometimes, although I hope to one day."

"How?"

"That will be up to Haid to tell you. It is not my place to discuss such matters."

"But Veden is essential to your plan?" Roche asked, and noted the contempt in her tone.

Emmerik heard it also, and smiled. "Don't let him worry you so."

"*Worry* me . . . ?" She stopped and sighed. "I guess he does a little. I can't help thinking that he will betray us to Enforcement the first opportunity he gets."

"He is simply afraid," said Emmerik.

"Afraid of what?"

"Of what you represent."

Roche studied the Mbatan's bearded face closely. "What about you? Are you afraid? Do I frighten you?"

Emmerik laughed, the thick sound rolling out across a sudden gust of wind. "No," he said. "You don't frighten me." He paused. "Your companion, however—Cane—he chills me to the bone."

"Why?"

Emmerik shook his head and folded his beefy arms against the wind. "When we halted in the mountain pass last night, while you and Maii and Veden waited in the rocks, Cane and I found a recon team up on the far side of the rift. They were waiting for us to come up. We'd doubled back another way and come on them from behind. They were scanning the path with infrared, waiting for us to appear."

"An ambush."

He nodded. "They were armed. We couldn't wait for them to lose interest and move elsewhere. We needed to get past them, and they had to be dealt with swiftly, but there were six of them and only two of us. I could see no easy way to approach them, or to overpower them without raising an alarm. I turned to Cane to suggest we return to your hiding place, but he wasn't there." Emmerik winced as the memory returned to him. "They didn't see him coming, or hear him. It was . . . unbelievable. I've never seen anyone move so fast. He killed them with his bare hands, soundlessly and efficiently. One of them, the last, had time to gasp for mercy, but Cane simply reached out and snapped his neck." Emmerik gestured with his right hand, imitating Cane's killing blow.

His eyes stayed on Roche. "What *is* he, Commander?"

"I don't know," she said, and recognized the doubt in his expression. "It's the truth. I wish I *did* know something more about him, but—" She looked out across the expanse of impromptu headstones. "You can always ask Maii if you don't believe me."

"I have. She says only that he is good at what he does, as are all of you, in your own ways."

"And that's all we can ever hope to be," she replied. "To fight ourselves is pointless. We must use what we have to the best of our ability and do as we see fit."

"And that includes killing in cold blood?"

"No!" She faced him angrily. He was twisting her words. "That's not what I mean. You can't blame Cane for what he did. They were the enemy. Given the chance, they would have done the same to us."

Emmerik didn't speak for several seconds. "I don't blame him," he said at last. "But if he ever turned against us—"

"He won't," Roche cut in quickly, although even as she spoke she could feel her own reservations. They were slight, but they were there. "He promised to support us," she said with more resolve. "And he will. I'm sure of it. I don't know much about him but I do know he is honorable. You yourself said that much."

Emmerik gestured to the makeshift graves below. "Needless killing is never honorable, Commander."

"That at least I can agree with," Roche said. "Perhaps we only disagree on our definition of 'need.' . . ."

Together they fell into silence, watching the dawn tighten its grip on the world. The sky lightened to its familiar yellow-red, and the radiance of the Soul dimmed in comparison. The only blemish was a dark shadow looming over the crater's northern wall. Moving perceptibly, it seemed to creep over the lip, spilling into the bowl of stone to flood the town. Its speed surprised her. Although she had experienced once before the terrible power of a dust storm, she still had trouble comprehending the sheer ferocity of the front. The turbulent shock wave riding at the fore of an atmospheric war.

"Fodder for the Soul," said Emmerik, following her gaze. He caught the look of confusion on Roche's face and smiled. "It's something we say when a particularly bad storm is about to hit. Sort of a presage of doom. You see, some people believe that the Soul is made up—"

"—of the spirits of those that have died here," finished Roche.

Admiration flashed briefly in his eyes. "Exactly," he said. "Anyway, one myth has it that these storms are the hands of a god collecting spirits to illuminate the Soul." He glanced up at the sky. "Somebody invariably dies whenever one hits, so maybe there's some truth in it."

Roche stiffened. "If it is a god, then it's working with DAOC." She pointed in the direction of what else she had seen, hovering at the edge of the cloud. "Look!"

A tiny speck of light flickered as clouds of dust rolled around it. An instant later, it disappeared entirely, tossed by the unpredictable currents that had briefly brought it into view.

There was only one thing it could be: a flyer attempting to use the front as cover for an approach to the town.

"Quickly!" Emmerik gripped her good arm and dragged her away from the wall. "We have to warn the others!"

They climbed down from the top of the wall and started running through the empty streets of the city. The moaning of the storm was distant at first, but growing rapidly louder. Beneath it, Roche imagined she could hear the nasal buzzing of the flyer, swooping toward the city to catch them unaware.

"Do you think they saw us?"

"Undoubtedly," replied the Mbatan without breaking stride. His heavy legs pounded the pavement relentlessly, and it was all she could do to keep up. "But they knew we were here anyway, otherwise they wouldn't have come."

"It couldn't be a routine patrol?"

"No." Emmerik slowed his pace as they rounded the final corner. The looming shadow of the storm spread across the sky ahead of them, beyond the two towers and their grisly mascot. The day—not even half an hour old—began to darken. Again Roche felt the numbing despair that had crippled her the previous day, but this time she was ready for it and therefore able to resist it. Lightning flashed in the brown cloud with increasing frequency, as though the elements understood their predicament and actively encouraged a sense of emergency. "Flying a storm front is dangerous," Emmerik gasped. "Not to be undertaken lightly. Only a lunatic or a soldier would attempt to approach the town this way."

"I thought you said they wouldn't attack."

"They never have before. Perhaps that's why they're using this method of approach: to hide from eyes other than ours."

Even as he said this, a siren like the bellow of a dying animal sounded in the distance, seeming to come from all directions at once. Emmerik stumbled to a halt, listening, as the ululating cry resounded eerily across the town.

"They must have noticed it too," he said. "Good. Perhaps now we have a chance."

"Who—?" Roche used the pause to catch her breath. It seemed that she had been gasping ever since setting foot on the planet, and she wondered if the thin atmosphere was entirely to blame. "Who's making that noise?"

"The keepers of the city," Emmerik replied.

Roche remembered the strangely robed figures who had confronted her the previous night, when she had reached out to touch one of the cemetery-rifles. "The keepers? You mean the descendants of the Dominion colonists?"

"They have guarded the city for over five hundred years," he said. Then, with a wry smile, added: "They are also responsible for the rumors of it being haunted. If it is attacked, they will defend it."

"But they won't enter the city, you said."

"Not normally, and perhaps not on this occasion either. At the very least, they will repel a ground assault, should one be attempted." The Mbatan grabbed her arm again and dragged her forward. The first of the rebels had appeared in the foyer of the tower, summoned by the wail of the siren. "Come on."

Neva, still slightly sleep-fogged, led the evacuation from the tower, followed by Veden and Maii. Two rebels escorted Cane with pistols at the ready. Catching sight of Emmerik, Neva hailed him loudly, with words that belied her obvious relief at seeing him.

"I leave you on duty, and look what happens. You unlucky bastard."

Emmerik gestured helplessly at the storm. The massive clouds had almost reached the northern wall of the city. The wind had picked up to the point where its noise made speech difficult. Briefly, he explained the situation to Nèva while Roche went to check on Cane.

"The underground, then," Neva said when Emmerik had finished. "That's our only hope."

"Let's pray there's enough time."

"But not too much."

"Aye." Emmerik grinned slightly. "It's cramped enough down there without Enforcement teams getting in the way."

Cane's ankle shackles had been removed, but his hands remained firmly pinned behind his back. The muscles of his shoulders flexed restlessly, as though he could sense the coming battle and yearned to be free. His face, however, betrayed none of this tension; his smile was casual, relaxed, when Roche approached.

"You're okay?"

A thin smile broke his easy expression. "Fine."

"Did you sleep?"

"No. I didn't need to."

She studied his face. He showed no sign of fatigue, despite everything they had done in the previous day. She reached out a hand to touch his shoulder, and a bright spark of static electricity snapped between them.

"We don't have long," Neva said.

Roche raised her head. The storm was on the far side of the tower, but she could feel its rumble in the air and through the soles of her feet. The sky had darkened to the color of dried blood.

As she stared, a flyer swooped around the towers, flying low over the buildings, scanning the area. The high-pitched scream of its motors was barely audible over the noise of the storm. It dipped its nose suddenly, swooped even lower, and dropped a handful of objects into the town: armored Enforcers, drifting on jets of gas onto the streets.

Neva gestured for them to move. As one, they began to run.

At that moment, the storm front hit. A solid wall of dust struck the tower and was bisected, each half curving around the circular wall to strike Roche and the rebels from opposite sides. All was instantly confusion, with opposing gusts of wind meeting and forming a giddying vortex around them.

Someone grabbed Roche's arm and tugged her along. She let herself be led, confident that the rebels knew where they were going and that the dust would hinder DAOC as much as it would them.

The imposing shadow of the Mbatan drifted closer, and he pressed something into her stomach. Shifting the valise to her injured arm, she grabbed at the object and felt the grip of a pistol enter her hand. The stocky projectile weapon was primitive, but she was grateful to have it nonetheless. At least she wouldn't be totally defenseless.

Neva led them along one of the arterial routes away from the towers, heading roughly east. After half a kilometer their route switched to narrower streets and alleyways, winding circuitously between empty buildings. Skull-like, empty doorways and windows gaped fleetingly at them as they passed, glimpsed and then gone in an instant, swallowed by the thick, choking dust.

Roche stumbled in a clogged gutter and lost her grip on the valise. The thin cord tangled, causing her to trip and wrench her shoulder. The pain was blinding, and she hardly felt Emmerik's hands lifting her to her feet, pressing the valise to her chest, and helping her along once again. The fall cost them seconds, during which time the others had disappeared from sight.

"It's okay!" Emmerik bellowed into her ear, his mouth only centimeters away. "I know the way!"

With her eyes protected by the dust-specs that Emmerik had pressed upon her, Roche peered into the thick dust and frowned. She could barely make out Emmerik, and he was standing right there beside her. "How . . . ?"

He couldn't have heard her half-muttered word, but he must have read her expression of bewilderment. "Trust me!" he shouted, and quickly moved on.

Roche stumbled along with him, grateful for the

Mbatan's guiding hand on her shoulder. Together they rounded another corner, then another, and finally caught sight of a figure struggling through the wind.

Roche sighed with relief, despite Emmerik's assurance that he knew where he was going—until she realized that the figure approaching out of the gloom was wearing full ceramic battle armor and carried a cocked percussion rifle in both hands.

She instinctively ducked to one side and dragged the startled Mbatan with her behind a nearby pillar. The domed helmet of the Enforcer, its visor a deep nonreflective black, turned to scan the area around it. She tensed as the impassive gaze swept over their hiding place, then relaxed as it drifted past.

The suit's gloves tightened on the rifle's handgrip, and the Enforcer continued onward, heading away from them.

"Too close!" she shouted to Emmerik.

"Worse than that!" The Mbatan pointed in the direction the guard had headed. "We have to go that way!"

"The others—?"

"I'm afraid so!" Emmerik turned. "We'll have to get around the Enforcer somehow, to warn them!"

He lumbered off with Roche firmly in tow, heading down another route. The path they followed was even more elaborate, avoiding as it did any connection whatsoever with the road along which the Enforcer and the rebels had traveled. Roche kept her eyes peeled for other Enforcers searching the town, looking for them.

So intent was she on this task that she automatically ducked when a voice spoke into her ear:

<The Siegl-K powered combat armor was discontinued in '895 EN. Surprising to see a working model.>

Her internal voice wanted to shout, as her actual vocal cords needed to, but she resisted the impulse. <This is hardly the time—>

<The Armada must have sold them to DAOC on the cheap, decades ago,> returned the Box, <instead of mothballing them. Half of their systems will therefore be inactive, or removed.>

<Just armor?>

\<Basic body-maintenance and power-assist, no sophisti-cated weapons or—\>

An explosion ahead cut the Box off in mid-sentence, fol-lowed by the high-pitched scream of a low-flying vehicle arcing over their heads and away. The muted thud of per-cussion rifles pierced the aural veil of the storm and made the Mbatan's hand grip her arm even more tightly.

Abandoning stealth, he led her along a wide thoroughfare to the source of the noises. Shadowy figures crossed their path—more bulky armor, crunching heavily across the road—but quickly disappeared. Swerving to his right, Em-merik ducked through a narrow alleyway with Roche in tow. At its end, a small courtyard exploded into light as an energy weapon discharged into a wall, splintering the dust-laden air with a short-lived corona of sparks.

They stumbled to a halt and began to retreat. Out of the gloom, before either of them could dodge, an Enforcer ap-peared. The suit had lost its balance, and seemed more to fall into them than attack, knocking Roche to the ground. Em-merik kicked its left leg out from beneath it, dodged a flail-ing arm and fired two shots through the matte glass of the visor.

The Enforcer twitched, and the powered armor magnified the motion into a body-racking spasm. One heavy boot caught the Mbatan on the hip and sent him sprawling. Roche fired wildly at the thrashing figure, not caring where she hit. Sparks and spatters of blood issued from the smashed visor until finally the massive body fell still.

Roche clambered to her feet and helped the Mbatan do the same. As he rose, Emmerik grabbed the fallen Enforcer's percussion weapon. Shadows moved at the edge of the square, and this time she dodged quickly enough to avoid another armored figure as it staggered by, firing its percus-sion rifle in random, furious bursts.

A second figure danced out of the gloom, catching the armor square in the chest with one firmly planted foot, em-ploying both balance and strength to tip it over its center of gravity. Roche and Emmerik fired as it fell. Black explo-sions flared on the armor's ceramic exoskeleton, stitching a ragged path from groin to throat, until something shorted in the power-assist mechanisms and the armor became still, locking its inhabitant in a coffinlike embrace.

Cane, who had delivered the overbalancing blow, nodded appreciatively at the Mbatan, then turned to go.

"Wait!" Roche called him back, then turned to Emmerik. "Free his hands!"

The Mbatan hesitated for an instant, obviously weighing the ease with which Cane, even with his hands shackled, had overpowered two Enforcers in full combat armor.

"Emmerik!" Roche shouted. "We *need* him!"

With a faint and uncertain shrug, Emmerik placed the muzzle of the rifle against Cane's outstretched wrists and severed the mesh chain with a single shot.

Cane smiled his gratitude at both of them. Then, leaving the second percussion rifle for Roche, he dashed off into the gloom with Roche and Emmerik vainly trying to keep up.

The sharp whiplash of projectile fire became increasingly loud as they ran, interspersed with shouts for help and cries of anger. Then, more ominous still, another sound rose above that of the wind: a deep, bone-tingling rumble that seemed to come from no particular direction. As it grew in volume, the smoke and dust around them began to agitate from side to side—not swirling as it normally did through the streets and openings in the buildings, but vibrating in confined circles. The sharp smell of ozone was almost over-powering.

A pair of Enforcers darted through the oscillating clouds, boots crunching as they came. Emmerik and Roche separated as the Enforcers' percussion rifles swiveled and spat at them. Returning fire, they ducked and weaved around the pair, using their small advantage of mobility over the suits' inertia. The Enforcers followed swiftly, however—the whine and clank of power-assist an atonal accompaniment to their every movement. The short hairs on Roche's scalp stiffened as a bolt narrowly missed her. She rolled to one side with the valise clutched to her chest, wishing she'd had time to strap it to her back, out of the way. Firing over her shoulder, she weaved across the courtyard as though heading for an inviting doorway, then ducked into an alley at the last moment. Running furiously, not knowing or caring where she was headed, she concentrated solely on putting distance between herself and the Enforcer, hoping to lose herself in the dust.

Pursued by the whirring armor, she burst out the far end of the alleyway and ran headlong into another person. Limbs tangled as she fell skidding to the ground. She scrambled to her hands and knees, feeling in the dust for the fallen rifle, while the person she had collided with fought for breath nearby.

The crunch of heavy boot treads arrived at the end of the alley at exactly the same moment that the bone-tingling rumble reached a peak. With a strange sensation—as though every item of clothing on her body had suddenly inflated—the dust around her vanished.

Blinking in the suddenly clear air, she looked up.

Hovering not twenty meters directly above her, all black carbon fiber and armored struts, was a troop carrier—slightly smaller than a salvage craft and shaped like a flat-bottomed bullet. The concave panels of the field-effect generators that striped its underside looked like ribs on the belly of some deep-sea beast.

The troop carrier was using its field-effect to clear the dust.

"Roche?" Emmerik's distant shout distracted her from the sight hanging above her. Blinking, she turned away, and belatedly realized that the footsteps of the Enforcer following her had ceased.

The armored figure stood at the entrance to the alley, not five meters from her, its rifle already rising. Her own rifle lay just out of arm's reach, too far away for a desperate lunge, and the nearest cover was farther away still. The Enforcer would shoot before she reached either. Yet she didn't feel any fear, just a vague anger for the undignified manner in which she was about to die: on her knees in a dusty square of some forgotten town on a backwater planet.

The black eye of the Enforcer's rifle stared at her for what seemed an excruciatingly long time before the Surin's words whispered in her thoughts:

<Hurry! I can't hold him forever.>

Roche gaped first at the motionless Enforcer, and then at

the girl sprawled out on the ground next to her, into whom she had just stumbled.

She reached for her rifle and trained it on the Enforcer. "I owe you one, Maii," she said, preparing to fire.

<Morgan, wait!> protested the Box, before she could fire. <Don't shoot!>

Her finger froze on the trigger. <Why the hell not?>

<We can use the suit.>

The eye of the Enforcer's rifle began to waver. <If you think I'm getting into that thing—>

<We need a glove,> insisted the Box. <Along with its command nexus.>

<Roche?>

<Hang on, Maii.> She looked around. They were too exposed in the courtyard. Under heavy fire from below, the troop carrier had drifted, and the turbulent edge of the clear space was drawing closer—but the heavy tread of other Enforcers was too close for comfort, and the threat of fire from above was still very real. As she watched, two gun emplacements on the underside of the carrier began to swivel, targeting the source of attack below. <Can you walk him?>

The Surin nodded. <Yes, but not far. It's difficult.>

<Okay. Let's just get under cover.> She glanced around. <That building, over there. Is that too far away?>

The Surin shook her head, and the petrified Enforcer took one hesitant step forward, then another. The three of them reached the building's vacant doorway just as the storm reclaimed the area. As the howling wind descended, Roche thought she heard the Mbatan calling for her again.

<Tell Emmerik where we are,> she said to Maii. <We'll wait for him here.>

The Surin thought for a moment, then said: <He has met Veden and the others. They are trying to disable the troop carrier. He will be here as soon as he can.>

<Good.> Roche faced the Enforcer. "Now, Box, what did you have in mind?"

<Unseal the helmet. The clasps are hidden at the seal in the small of the back.>

Roche felt for the concealed tabs, found them, and pulled until they clicked. With a hiss, the helmet unsealed and fell forward, revealing the shaved head of a female Enforcer, her eyes staring vacantly. Roche raised the butt of her rifle and brought it down on the back of the Enforcer's skull, knocking her unconscious.

The suit shuddered but stayed upright, held immobile by emergency overrides.

<Now what?>

<Reach into the neck ring. There's a stud about five centimeters down, in the center. Push it.>

Roche did so, and the ceramic armor parted along invisible lines like a three-dimensional jigsaw puzzle. The slabs of armor lifted outward a centimeter, then remained in that position, awaiting her next move. The air inside stank of sweat and fear, and aging rubber seals.

With Maii's help, Roche managed to wrestle the limp Enforcer out of the suit's intimate embrace through a sliding panel in the back. The interior was black and uninviting, a nest of glistening cables and contacts with holes for limbs to pass through.

<Each glove will have a palm-link,> said the Box. <We need to get your left hand down the sleeve.>

Roche eyed the interior with distaste, but she had little choice. Slipping her left arm out of the bandages, wincing every time she moved her shoulder, she stepped into the suit. Maii slung the briefcase across her back, out of the way, and stepped back.

The moment her left hand made contact with the palm-link, the armor came to life.

<Wait!> She struggled to control the suit as it sealed around her. <I can't walk out of here like this. I'll be shot by the rebels!>

<Relax, Morgan,> said the Box. <Simply remove the helmet.>

<But the controls—>

<I can handle them, and display them via your implant.>

Roche shrugged herself into a more comfortable position and felt the armor imitate the motion. Reaching up with her gloved right hand, she ripped the helmet from its hinge on the chest-plate and threw it aside.

Taking an experimental step forward, she felt the seductive strength of the power-assist echo through her limbs. She hadn't used combat armor more than a couple of times in her career, but the old moves came back to her with ease. Although mindful not to shift her left arm more than was absolutely necessary, she began to feel confident for the first time in days.

<Okay, Box. We're in business. Where do we go?>

<Nowhere, unless you feel the need. Emmerik and the others have identified the problem succinctly: apart from the thirty to forty Enforcers on the ground, the main threat is from above. We could evade the Enforcers without the carrier clearing the air. I will attempt to neutralize that threat via the suit's command nexus.>

<Okay, you do that. In the meantime, Maii and I are going to help the others.> She swiveled to face the Surin. <Lead the way.>

Together they left the building and headed out into the storm. The Surin called out directions, using mental images of the town to find her way and her epsense abilities to target Enforcers through the dust. Four armored suits fell to Roche's percussion rifle before word of the rogue spread through the Enforcement communication network. Then the uneven rumble of the troop carrier began to grow louder again, and the dust agitated more violently than ever, stirred by the field-effects of the craft above. Maii led her away from danger, deeper into the cloud.

<We make a good team,> said the Surin at one point, and Roche, too caught up in combat to really think about what she was saying, could only agree.

They passed Cane moments later. His nimble form appeared out of the gloom, poised to strike her, but he realized who she was in time. He relaxed, made a gesture that might have been a salute but one Roche didn't recognize, and stepped back. He had acquired both a percussion rifle and a bloody gash across his forehead. His manner, although outwardly relaxed, was urgent.

"There are too many of them!" He had to shout to be heard over the sound of the troop carrier. "The others are holed up not far from here, and the big ship is on its way."

"What weapons do they have?"

"A handful of rifles. I've tried to pass on the ones I've come across, but . . ." He shrugged. "It hasn't been easy, and the charges on the ones they have won't last forever."

Roche imagined Cane flitting through the dust like a demon, reaching out of the gloom to snatch rifles from the hands of the Enforcers, then vanishing again. His major problem, as had been Roche's, was locating the others. It was all very well to have found weapons, but no use at all if he couldn't distribute them.

"Okay," she said, intending to ask him to lead the way, but getting no farther than that.

The vision through her left eye suddenly shifted, becoming clear. She blinked furiously, then realized that the Box was feeding her an external image taken from above the storm, or from a clear space within it. It showed the city not far below, moving slowly past. Armored Enforcers darted from building to building through the streets, converging on an area just inside the clear space.

With a jolt of surprise, she realized that the view was taken from one of the turret guns on the troop carrier itself.

An auxiliary view showed the airspace above the city. To her shock she saw not one flyer but five, circling the area like birds of prey, waiting for an opportunity to move in.

Furious sparks of light reached upward out of the clouds toward the troop carrier from a low building at the edge of a small courtyard. This, she assumed, was the work of the rebels. As she watched, her aerial view swiveled to focus on the building, and zoomed in to aim.

"The others are in trouble," she said, blinking the view aside for a moment to focus on the world around her. "The troop carrier's arrived. We have to hurry."

Cane nodded and moved off. "Follow me."

Roche lumbered after him, grateful for the power-assist enabling her to keep up. Maii sprinted behind, barely maintaining the pace.

<Veden's still with them,> mind-whispered the Surin. <If he is harmed, I'll never forgive them—or myself.>

<Don't worry,> said Roche, although she had little reassurance to offer in the face of such superior firepower. <We'll make it in time.>

The dust swirled around them, and the omnipresent rumble of the troop carrier reached a mind-numbing peak. Suddenly, and without warning, the three of them burst into clear air. Two Enforcers stood between them and the building, firing burst after burst at the roof where the others were hidden. Roche tackled one from behind while Cane tipped the other off balance. A third appeared from around the corner of a building, but Maii was quick to act and kept the Enforcer frozen until Cane could bring his weapon to bear.

Gasping, Roche looked around and up. The troop carrier had descended to a point not ten meters above the building. Turrets pumped powerful bolts of energy into the stone walls, sending short-lived blossoms of rock into the air. Sporadic fire lashed up at it from windows and smashed walls, as the rebels tried to fight back—but the superior weaponry of the troop carrier forced the defenders back under cover an instant later.

Behind her, two flyers swooped low over the city to lend the troop carrier support. They too concentrated their fire on the building.

Roche took one step forward, not certain what she was going to do but knowing she had to try something. Before she could fire a single shot, the Box suddenly whispered in triumph:

<Success, Morgan.>

Seconds later the troop carrier stopped firing and banked to the left, turning away from the building. Its turrets swiveled wildly, searching the earth below and the sky above. Lances of energy speared the air, striking a handful of locations in the city. Two higher bolts connected with the nearest of the two flyers, sending it spinning out of control. The high-tech arrowhead dipped low, bucked for control, then clipped an ancient building. With a shriek of engines, it crashed out of sight and exploded in a crimson and yellow fireball.

Roche watched, stunned. <Box? Are you doing this?>

<I have infiltrated the AI controlling the vessel via the command nexus of this suit, and have overridden the commands of the pilot. The troop carrier is now under my control.>

The battle below halted for a moment at the sudden reversal. Soon, though, the rebels took advantage of what must have been to them a mysterious turn of events. Firing at the Enforcers below, they began to clear the area for their escape. Likewise the underbelly turrets of the troop carrier picked out individual Enforcers, striking them from above.

Within moments, the Enforcers retaliated. The four remaining flyers swooped low to blast the treacherous troop carrier, while individual Enforcers fired from shelter underneath. The carrier was too bulky to successfully dodge the concentrated fire; only its heavy armor prevented it from being destroyed immediately. First one and then another of its underbelly turrets exploded, but not before a second flyer had been downed and perhaps ten more Enforcers shot from above.

With a bone-wrenching lurch, it ducked away, and the storm rushed into the area once more.

<They're leaving the building!> Maii cried. <I've told them what's going on—they say to meet us by the south gate.>

Roche looked around. <Do they say which way to go?>

<No need. I've constructed a map from their minds. I'll show you the way.> The lithe Surin danced off through the dust. Cane and Roche followed, the latter observing the continuing battle for control of the sky through the implant in her left eye.

Under heavy fire from the remaining flyers, the troop carrier spun in a lazy arc above the town. Its starboard flank was ablaze, and deep craters pitted its armored surface. Two of its gun turrets still functioned, however, and with these it managed to down another flyer. The heavy crunch of impact and subsequent explosion were nearly enough to make Roche stumble. The two remaining flyers darted away, then returned a moment later. Furious bolts lashed at the troop carrier's damaged flank, making it shudder. The steady rumble of its engines began to waver.

"It's going to blow!" Roche watched breathlessly as the troop carrier banked sharply to starboard, its injured side seeming to drag it down from the sky. Its remaining firepower surged at the most distant flyer, damaging it. The last one darted closer, preying on the hulk's damaged state. The rumble of the field-effect became a whine, and the troop carrier began to slow. Drifting in a sluggish circle, it passed over the area where the rebels were fleeing. The distinct dots of the dozen remaining Enforcers appeared out of the dust, doggedly pursuing the rebels. At that moment, Roche guessed what the Box was going to do and dragged the others to cover.

<Warn Veden!> Her message to the Surin was steeped in urgency. <Tell him to keep them moving as fast as they can!>

The last flyer dipped dangerously close to the troop carrier, strafing its bulk with concentrated fire. Suddenly the carrier banked again, this time swinging sharply around its center of gravity to bring its nose in line with the flyer's trajectory. With a flash of flame, the two collided, and the rumble of engines ceased altogether. Roche's view through the carrier began to fade, but not before she glimpsed the milling Enforcers rising up at her, slowly at first, but with increasing speed.

"Down!" She leapt for an open doorway, dragging Maii after her. Cane was a step ahead of them, rolling for safety within the stone walls.

With an earthshaking bellow of tortured metal, the crippled troop carrier crashed nose-first into the town. Its stricken power plant instantly exploded, enveloping everything around it in a ball of fiery heat. The shock wave flattened buildings, killed the Enforcers nearby despite their combat armor, and expanded at the speed of sound through the streets toward the building where Roche and the others had taken shelter.

The wall collapsed, and would have crushed Roche's legs but for her stolen suit. Fragments of molten metal and glowing stone rained down on the rubble. For an instant, everything was white, even through her closed eyelids. Then something else, an uncomfortable mix of panic and grief, washed through her, causing her to shudder.

<Veden? Veden!>

Roche wanted to bury her head in her hands as the cries intensified, but her position in the armor didn't allow her any movement. All she could do was lie there, pinned to the ground, screaming as Maii's hysterical anger burned ferociously, relentlessly, in her mind.

    <No!>

PART THREE:

PORT PARVATI

10

In the wake of the transmission from Port Parvati, a deathly silence fell.

On the main screen, a satellite view of the mountain range known as Behzad's Wall replayed the explosion of the troop carrier in slow motion. The brilliant flash of light was followed by a billowing bubble of dust and superheated air, rising upward and obscuring the town. When it had passed, the storm once again enfolded the region. Like a blanket cast from the sky, the dust smothered the fires and enveloped the damage as though nothing had ever changed the eternal stillness of the doomed city.

"Summarize the report," Kajic said to Atalia Makaev, when the video had finished. His hologram did not turn to face her.

"It would appear that—"

"In as few words as possible, if you please." He kept his tone carefully controlled and even.

Makaev swallowed. "They have escaped, sir."

"Succinctly put, Atalia." Kajic killed the main screen and

faced his second in command. "I can only be grateful that your analysis of the situation is not correct."

Makaev frowned. "Sir, the warden's report is quite clear." She paused, obviously conscious that her remarks bordered on the insubordinate. "Evidence recovered from the wreckage of the lander has established that there were at least four people on board—two Pristines, an Eckandi, and possibly one Surin—yet the search team has found no traces of their bodies. The battle we have just witnessed, along with the disappearance of the recon team, strongly suggests that surface intransigents—"

"Nevertheless" —Kajic's smooth voice washed smoothly over hers—"the fugitives have *not* escaped."

"Sir?"

"They remain on Sciacca's World, do they not?" The question did not require a response, nor did Kajic wait for one. "Commander Roche is obviously aware that the wardens are unsympathetic to her cause, or else she would have surrendered herself to the port upon planetfall. She must therefore know that she is unable to leave the planet by official means, and has thus allied herself with the local underground in order to escape." Kajic smiled. "All we have to do is ensure that she cannot."

"Naturally, but—"

"To that end," he continued, "you will place the *Ana Vereine* in a geosynchronous orbit directly above Port Parvati. Any craft attempting to reach orbit from the landing field will be boarded and searched." He hesitated before adding, "Or destroyed in transit."

"But sir, this directly contravenes the—"

"Regardless." Kajic's image wavered slightly.

priority gold-one

"Nothing will leave Sciacca's World without our permission until the AI and the commander are in our hands. Is this clear, Atalia?" Again there was no expectation of a response, and again Makaev did not offer one. The straightening of her posture alone conveyed her understanding. "You will arrange this with Warden Delcasalle," Kajic said, "within the hour."

"The cost will be enormous," she protested.

Kajic's smile widened. "Cost is meaningless when the stakes are this high," he said. "Make sure the warden is aware of this. Let him know that I am prepared to raze the surface of Sciacca's World to slag and sift through the ruins to find that AI." He shrugged. "It is practically indestructible, after all. And this method would certainly save us a good deal of time and effort—not to mention money." Kajic's image froze momentarily, the only movement being the flicker of its light. Then: "When you have convinced him, dispatch one of our own teams to assist his incompetents in their search."

"Yes, sir. I shall lead it myself."

"No. Send Major Gyori. I prefer you here, where I can keep an eye on you."

Makaev winced slightly—which gave him some gratification—but she kept her eyes fixed upon Kajic. "As you wish, sir."

"Good. See to it immediately, then join me in the command module. I wish to speak with you privately."

Kajic let his hologram dissipate and his mind retreat from the bridge with a feeling of immense relief. The energy required to maintain a semblance of confident control had been enormous. His thoughts were in turmoil, his confidence was only an act—and these were facts he wished to keep carefully to himself, not parade in front of the bridge crew. But anyone with access to the back door in his mainframe could browse through his most intimate details at will.

With half a mind he followed the activities of his senior officers as they prepared the ship for reorientation and thrust. His virtual senses reported the firing of attitude jets and the priming of the reaction drive. The slowly changing orientation of the stars kept him occupied for several seconds. The sight was peaceful, and reminded him of his true purpose.

Where had he failed? His ship ran well; not one major system had been compromised on this, the *Ana Vereine*'s maiden voyage. And with the superior ability he possessed to study crew as well as ship, he had suffered none of the minor dissensions many new captains endured on their first command. Ship, crew, and captain were all in perfect working order, a unified system operating under his command.

Yet, to his dismay, there *was* evidence that he had failed, and it was mounting steadily. . . .

Priority C (stealth) had already been broken, and now, after the day's events, priority B had followed. Despite his denial, Roche *had* escaped from the ambush and was roaming free somewhere on the planet. She was the only person within easy reach who might be able to explain the operation and purpose of the AI, but the chances of her being captured alive were diminishing by the second, and his desperation to meet the last priority increased proportionately. If he failed at this mission, regardless how he had performed every other aspect of his mission, his command, and therefore his life, *would* be terminated. He had no doubts about that. To the Ethnarch's Military Presidium, there was only success or failure; there was nothing in between.

Priority A was all he had left to hope for now.

capture the AI

Destroying the planet to find it wasn't really an option, as far as he was concerned. Even his mission wasn't worth risking all-out war with the COE Armada, which would retaliate regardless of Port Parvati's inherent corruption. But he had no choice: whatever he did, it would *work*. He would achieve his goal and satisfy the orders written into his mind, branded onto his thoughts. What other choice did he have?

His priorities were like steel bars enclosing his free will: contemplating even the slightest deviation caused him severe mental pain. He could not disobey his superiors in the Military Presidium even to save his own life. And, to make matters worse, he would not want to. No matter how he might rationalize the alternatives, he would sacrifice his own life to meet his orders, if the situation demanded it. Where might once have been written "Do what thou wilt," now it read "*Obey* . . ."

Some minutes passed before Makaev came to meet him. When she did, he projected his image into an armchair and assumed a relaxed disposition.

"I received your message," he said without preamble. The memo had arrived just moments before the data from the warden of Port Parvati, leaving him little time to ponder it. The timing had seemed a little too unlucky, which only made him all the more anxious. "A full report, please."

"Yes, sir." Makaev remained at attention, standing with her arms at her sides in the center of the room. If what he suspected was true, she hid it well. "During your last rest period, as you instructed, I ordered a technician to examine your life support."

"And?"

She leaned over the desk to key a wall-screen. Complex schematics appeared, an endless series of lines and junctures scrolling from top to bottom. "The system matches the diagnostics in the *Ana Vereine*'s mainframe exactly, with only one exception. At the base of your brain-stem interface, there is this." The display zoomed in on one particular point, where a knot of biocircuits converged; highlighted in bold red was a denser clump, not unlike the network of fibers surrounding a dreibon root.

"The back door?" Kajic prompted.

"No, sir," said Makaev. "At least the technician doesn't believe so. The device is quite ingenious. It will lie dormant and not interfere with the overall system until it receives a coded command from an outside source." Makaev paused, her eyes suddenly restless. "Upon receiving that command, it will immediately sever all communication between your brain stem and the ship's mainframe."

"A kill-switch?" said Kajic.

"That appears to be its purpose," said Makaev. "Yes, sir."

"But who would dare sabotage a warship in such a way?" His ship—his very being—had been compromised!

"With respect, sir," Makaev said, "it is not sabotage. Although the device does not appear on the circuit diagrams we have access to, it is not an afterthought." Again she paused. "It's an integral aspect of the life support's design."

"Integral? What are you saying? That it cannot be removed without damaging the system?"

"No, sir. I'm saying that it's *supposed* to be there."

Kajic used every sense at his disposal to assure himself that she was being honest. All the data concurred: she was telling the truth. A truth that he feared, that brought his mind to a halt.

"Why?" he finally managed.

"I can hazard a guess, sir," said his second in command, then waited for him to indicate that she should continue. He did so irritably. "It makes sense, sir, if you examine the 'how' of it first. The plans for your life support were approved by the Presidium itself. If such a device was deliberately included, then the decision to do so could have come from nowhere else. As to the 'why,' well, we must remember that you are a prototype, one that has never been field-tested in genuine combat before. Who could anticipate what might happen, or how you would respond to the pressures of battle? The kill-switch must be a safeguard against command instability. Were you to become unstable at a critical moment—and I am not suggesting that you have, or will—your actions could cripple the ship. The kill-switch could then come into play, freeing the command systems for another officer to employ."

Kajic mulled it over. Yes, it made sense, and it mirrored almost exactly his first thoughts on the matter. Makaev put the case well. Too well for Kajic's liking. If she was lying, then her only fault was that she was too convincing.

"So where does the command signal come from?" he asked, following the argument to its conclusion. "And who decides whether to send the command or not?"

"One would assume, sir, that a high-ranking officer would enact that decision. Perhaps not the person who would actually assume control of the ship," she added quickly, "but someone at least who knows the truth and is in the correct position to act upon it."

"Which could be anyone from the bridge crew," he said. "Or even life support. Anyone, in fact, with access to the back door. He—or she—need not necessarily be high-ranking, either."

She nodded. "That is true."

"Nevertheless," said Kajic, "regardless who actually *gave* the order, it would be you who would assume command of the *Ana Vereine*." *Of my ship*. His unblinking image locked eyes with her, daring her to look away. *Of me*.

She nodded. "Yes, sir. It would seem that I am the most likely candidate."

"So tell me, Atalia," he said coldly, "*are* you the betrayer? Are you the one waiting for the first opportunity to strike me down?"

"If I said I wasn't, would you believe me?"

Kajic smiled, finding some pleasure in the confrontation. "I might," he said. "But I still wouldn't entirely *trust* you." He broke the locked gaze, letting his smile dissipate as he glanced again at the circuit diagram. "Perhaps I shouldn't even ask."

"Perhaps." She squared her shoulders and took a deep breath. "The only way to be sure is to watch every member of the senior crew as they go about their duties. Try to find the one who is acting suspiciously."

"That might work," he said. "But I am just like any other Pristine: I can only think one thing at a time; I am limited to one single point of view. And—"

priority gold-one

"And I have more important things to contemplate at the moment than my own personal survival."

She absorbed this in silence—perhaps with relief—and he watched her closely while she did so. How true his words were: the data he required might have been at his fingertips, but he had neither the ability nor the freedom to study it. He could feel the priorities bending his thoughts subtly back to his mission. Even now, at such a moment, he was unable to take concrete steps to save his own life. To remove or to interfere with the deadly mechanism would be to disobey the Ethnarch's Military Presidium itself.

"Atalia," he said after a moment. "This conversation will be kept between ourselves. We will continue our mission as though nothing has changed." What else *can* I do? he asked himself. The fact that the Presidium didn't fully trust him— had never trusted him—could not be allowed to interfere with his duty. Otherwise it would become a self-fulfilling prophecy—which was, perhaps, exactly what Makaev intended by telling him about the kill-switch, if she truly was the betrayer at his side. She could just as easily have lied about it to protect herself. Instead, she had thrown him off balance by sowing the seeds of distrust in his mind. . . .

"I agree, sir," she said, killing the display before them. "When we have recovered the AI and completed our mission, perhaps then we can discuss the matter in more detail."

Yes, he thought to himself, and in the meantime I have my neck on the line. The slightest mistake and—

"Atalia?"

"Sir?"

"Please reinforce with Major Gyori that our orders are to capture both the AI and its courier. I want those orders obeyed to the letter. I want Commander Roche taken *alive*." That way, he hoped, he might be able to improve his position with his superiors when the *Ana Vereine* returned from the mission.

"Yes, sir." Makaev snapped a salute and turned to leave.

"And one more thing," he said. She stopped and faced his shimmering image once again. "The investigation was to be conducted discreetly. The technician that you used—?"

"Has already been . . . transferred, sir," she said. "No one will ever know the truth."

Again Kajic studied her minutely, searching for the slightest sign of deception—and this time he thought he detected something. A tiny smile played across her lips, seeming to add silently but more evocatively than speech one single word:

Unless . . .

Kajic ignored it; better for her to think him a fool than to allow his fear to weaken his position further. "Good. You may return to your duties."

"Thank you, sir." She turned away for the final time and left the command module.

11

The orange sun rose above the horizon, casting brownish dawn-light over Port Parvati. Dull shafts crawled over the already bustling cityscape, here touching foodsellers arranging their produce in preparation for the day's business, there catching artisans dusting their wares. The light crept with casual sureness into dusty streets and garbage-strewn alleys, melting pockets of shadow that had gathered in the night and waking the few remaining curb-sleepers that had yet to join the growing throng.

Even at this early hour, business was brisk. The sound of complaining machinery was nearly drowned by a rising hubbub of bargaining and arguments. And over that, the constant arrhythmic chug of the truck that carried Roche and her party through the streets.

At first, Roche watched the proceedings going on around her with indifference. Then, as they moved through the streets and various marketplaces, she found herself succumbing to a profound melancholy—one she saw reflected in the faces of the people bustling around their truck.

If Port Parvati had been a city on any other planet, Roche

thought, it would have been demolished years ago: flattened, pulped, and turned into artificial topsoil fit for treading on and little more.

There was also an unpleasant smell about the place—something other than the stench of sewage occasionally spilling from the inadequate drain system, or that of rotting food rising from the dirty market stalls. The air was thick with it, lingering through all the streets they passed along, strong enough even to penetrate the fumes issuing from the methane-fueled engine of their vehicle. It was with some revulsion that Roche suddenly realized what that smell was: disease.

"Destroyed," Roche muttered to herself, "*and* burned."

Emmerik leaned forward from his place on the flatbed to speak. "What was that?" He raised his voice to be heard above the noise of the truck.

Roche shook her head. "How much further?"

"About five minutes." The Mbatan raised a hand to shield his eyes from the sun and turned to bang on the cab of the truck. The truck suddenly veered down a narrow alleyway. Emmerik cursed aloud, steadying Roche. The abrupt turn unbalanced her before the armor's built-in overrides could react. The truck's suspension had needed an overhaul about twenty years ago, Roche thought; now, suspension was the least of its worries.

When their trajectory steadied, Roche turned her attention once more to the goings-on beyond the truck. This particular section of the city they were passing through appeared dirtier and more cluttered than other parts. The streets were certainly narrower and grimier, the dwellings often low and shabby. Wide and jutting verandahs shaded dark interiors from which dirty faces glanced briefly as they passed. Others paused upon the flimsy walkways that now and then arced between buildings, their solemn expressions enhancing the already growing melancholy that Roche was feeling.

Most of the people, she noted, were Pristine—but not all. The penal colony held all manner of nonviolent criminals, from habitual thieves to industrial conspirators, from Olmahoi to Hurn. Yet all looked the same beneath the universal garments of cheap robes and wide-brimmed hats, as dictated by environment and limited resources rather than fashion. Roche herself had donned similar garb to cover the combat armor. From a distance, she hoped, she would pass as a skinny Mbatan.

She ran her hands over the coarse and threadbare garment and frowned. "How the hell can people live like this?"

Despite the noise, Emmerik seemed to have heard her. "Ninety percent of the population lives here, Commander," he said. "But it's not as if we have any choice. There just isn't anywhere else."

<This is true, Morgan.> The Box's voice was clear beneath all the noise from the street. <With the planet's population of convicts and Enforcement staff, Port Parvati remains the capital and sole large settlement. Apart from the ruins of places like Houghton's Cross, there is nowhere else for them to go.>

<Couldn't they build—?>

<Yes, although the question of whether the inhabitants *want* to better their planet or not becomes an issue. The fact is, the authorities prefer it this way. It is easier to maintain order. The greater the number of towns, the more difficult security becomes.>

Roche nodded to herself, leaning away from Emmerik. Indeed, as she watched the crowd milling through the dusty streets, she realized that security was lighter than she had expected—and feared. Only infrequently did an Enforcement patrol serve to remind her that this was a supervised penal base, not one of the poorer COE planets.

Waving a hand to ward off the stench of a herd of vat-bred cattle, she looked back to Emmerik. Even his eyes seemed slightly more moist than usual in the high air of the city.

"Is all of Port Parvati like this?" she said.

He shook his head. "These are just the outskirts. Like any other city, we have varying standards."

The truck lurched again as it took another sharp corner. This time Roche was prepared, and the suit kept her balanced. When their motion had steadied somewhat, she glanced under the makeshift canopy tied over the truck's flatbed. The stretcher hadn't been disturbed by the sudden turn, and the Eckandi's face expressed no more distress than it had at any stage of their journey so far. Strapped to the Mbatan's back through the old mines honeycombing the mountains beneath Houghton's Cross, by petroleum-powered, propeller-driven airplane to one of Port Parvati's many makeshift airfields, passing through a casual security check (with the aid of several small bribes in a currency unfamiliar to Roche), then onto the truck for the penultimate leg of their journey—he had remained unconscious throughout it all, oblivious to the rough plaster encasing his head and the distressed Surin constantly at his side.

"How's he doing, Maii?" Roche asked, concerned as much for the reave as she was for her friend.

The girl didn't respond at first. Her posture hardly shifted. But Roche could tell that she had heard—by the subtle change of the girl's sullen expression, the way her head tilted ever so slightly to face Roche.

After a moment, the Surin's quiet voice filtered through the noise of traffic and animals into Roche's mind: <I can still feel him. He's deep—very deep. He has retreated to somewhere I can't reach him. Somewhere he can heal.>

Or die, Roche added to herself, forgetting that the reave could read the thought if she wanted. The shrapnel from the downed troop carrier that had struck Veden on the back of the head required delicate nanosurgery, not stubborn, blind denial. If she heard, however, Maii didn't contradict her.

Turning back to Émmerik, Roche picked up the conversation where it had left off.

"You work underground here, too?"

The Mbatan spoke without taking his eyes from the road. "The city is built on the ruins of the original port. When the Commonwealth moved in, they decided it was cheaper to build over than rebuild. So that's what they did," he said. "And continue to do. The original city is buried under layer after layer of later settlements, but it's still intact in places." He grinned wryly. "The Dominion built well."

Roche nodded. Houghton's Cross was testament to that. "So you moved in?"

"The founders of our movement did. Some of the survivors of Ul-æmato had maps of the original city, and it was a simple matter to work out what had been what under the new surface." Emmerik faced Roche now, wiping at the dust around his eyes. "All it took was some digging equipment, a little patience, and a lot of care to keep the work hidden from the wardens. Whole sections of the original maglev subway were intact, although the tunnels had cracked open in a few places. The rubbish that had filtered down was cleared out, and there we had it—a means of crossing the city without being seen by the wardens. There are buildings dotted all over the city that act as entrances to the tunnels: little more than empty facades hiding their true purpose. Gain access to one of these and you can go almost anywhere."

"That's a major achievement," she said, studying him closely. When he went to look away again, she quickly added, "But why are you telling me about this now? Why the sudden trust?"

"I've always trusted you," he said soberly. "But your involvement with Cane made me a little apprehensive." The Mbatan shrugged wearily. "The difference now is that we need your help as much as you need ours. And the only way to begin helping each other is by talking—as equals."

"Trade secrets, you mean?" she said, glancing over her shoulder to where Cane was riding on the tail of the flatbed, his eyes constantly scanning the crowd.

"I was thinking more of your AI," put in the Mbatan. "I had no idea it was so powerful."

Roche turned back to him and offered a fleeting smile. "Neither did I, to be honest."

Emmerik grunted deep in his throat. The exhalation might have been a laugh, although his face displayed no amusement. "It's running the suit, isn't it?" he said.

Roche nodded. "Through the data glove."

"For that function alone it is valuable. Any advanced weaponry is priceless here."

Roche immediately understood what he was hinting at: the Dato wouldn't be the only ones interested in getting their hands on the AI. But what Emmerik almost certainly failed to realize was that without her—without her palm-link, her implants—the Box's value was reduced to zero. Without her in the driver's seat, the armor was little more than dead metal, and the Box a useless valise.

When she explained this to the Mbatan, he only smiled and said:

"*I* understand this, but there are others who won't. Take care to emphasize your own worth as much as the assets you bring with you. I am not typical of the bulk of our group, Commander."

She nodded, taking his warning to heart. Whether he was referring to Haid himself or just those surrounding him, it didn't matter. That the threat was real was enough for now. She would keep her guard up.

Moments later the truck swung into a sheltered garage and shuddered to a noisy halt. The rebels clambered out of the cab and off the flatbed and began to unload the truck. Emmerik joined them, leaving Roche to make her own way down. The bulky armor took the short drop with ease, thudding to the concrete floor like a lump of lead. Cushioned within, her injured shoulder was barely disturbed by the jar of impact.

She brushed some of the ubiquitous dust from her cloak and turned to help Cane with Veden's stretcher. One on each end, they swung it down and placed it against the far wall. Barely had they put it down when two unfamiliar rebels appeared through a door leading deeper into the building and spirited him away.

Maii, when she tried to follow, was politely but firmly rebuffed. Roche moved to comfort her, but the girl shrugged her away.

"You have medical facilities here, Emmerik?" said Roche.

The Mbatan paused in the middle of unloading the truck to look at her. "Some."

"How sophisticated?"

"I don't know," he said. "It's not my field."

"He'll need X-rays, CAT and QIP scans, nanosurgery if you have it—"

"We'll do what we can, Roche," he cut in sharply, more

calmly adding, *"When* we can. Okay?" He returned to his work without another word.

Feeling impotent, Roche tried to find something to do. Two of the rebels were struggling with a large crate of projectile weapons retrieved from the ruins of their headquarters in Houghton's Cross. With the power-assists of the armor, she took the crate from them and placed it with others along one wall, then turned to do the same with the rest of the crates on the truck. The warning from Emmerik still rung in her mind; the more she could do to gratify herself to the locals, the better.

<I too have the original plans of the old port,> put in the Box unexpectedly, harking back to her conversation with the Mbatan. <We are approximately five kilometers from the current landing field, on the site of what was once a large university. The maglev network divides into three major routes not far from here. A good location for headquarters.>

Roche grunted, only half listening. <Do your files say anything about current security arrangements?>

<No, but I am still patched into the DAOC combat network through the suit.>

Roche put down the crate she was carrying. This was interesting. <Really? I thought they would've scrambled transmissions after you—>

<I took the precaution of erasing any record of my intrusion from all databases connected with the assault on Houghton's Cross. The only people aware of my intrusion were onboard the troop carrier; I was careful to prevent information being transmitted by radio at the time and, naturally, the people themselves are now dead. Therefore, DAOC is ignorant of my intrusion in its systems.>

<And?> Roche prompted when the Box fell silent. <What have you learned?>

<Surprisingly little of any importance. I can only access information and routines stored in a buffer accessible by combat computers and decentralized planning systems. Unfortunately the main work is done by the MiCom processing center in the landing field, which is quite separate. The combat network is updated hourly from this processor.>

<What does it say about us?>

<That there is a price on your head, Morgan. A high price, too. To be taken alive, if possible.>

<Only me? What about Cane and Veden and Maii? Hell, what about *you*?>

<The only person described in the bulletin is 'Morgan Roche,' no rank. You are said to be armed and in league with indigenous forces. Which, I suppose, means that you were seen with other people, and that, for some reason, it was determined that these others met you here rather than came with you from the *Midnight*.>

<How do they explain the troop carrier, then?>

<They do not. It would seem that Warden Delcasalle has no knowledge of either my existence or my capabilities.>

<That makes two of us,> she said, thinking of the way the Box had saved them at Houghton's Cross.

"Roche?"

Startled by the sudden intrusion on the conservation, Roche realized that she was standing stock-still in the middle of the garage, staring off into space. Feeling foolish, she turned to face the woman who had spoken. Cropped blonde hair, a sour face, and grey eyes stared back at her.

"You Roche?"

"I am." She automatically glanced around for the others and found Cane and Maii on the far side of the garage. Cane's eyes scanned the proceedings with his usual attention to detail; the Surin was motionless.

"Haid wants you out of that armor before he'll let you down. There's a cubicle and a change of clothes out back."

Roche flexed her fingers in the power-gloves. Although the armor had increased her sense of well-being for a while, she would be glad to be rid of it, if only temporarily. Sweat had pooled in the suit's crevices, making her entire body feel oily. "Any chance of a shower?"

The woman nodded reluctantly. "If you have to," she said. "But don't waste the water."

The woman walked through the door at the rear of the garage, and Roche followed, careful not to bump anything with the armor's wide shoulders. The corridor was narrow and cluttered with boxes. Some of them contained weapons similar to the ones they had brought back from Houghton's

Cross; most seemed to contain provisions of a more harmless sort: food, clothes, medicinal supplies, and the like.

Although the Enforcement government allowed the inhabitants of the penal colony free rein over their internal affairs, they obviously kept a heavy hand on potentially dangerous matters, such as technology and communications. Thus far, the most sophisticated weapon Roche had seen in the hands of the rebels was a projectile rifle, and the most powerful engine one powered by petroleum. By thus keeping the population at a level barely approximating civilized, DAOC ensured that its relatively small but well-equipped force was more than capable of keeping the peace. Armed with nothing but pellet guns and cow-shit trucks, the rebels wouldn't last a moment against the landing field's defenses.

Yet somehow they had fashioned an extensive underground network capable of some small resistance. Utilizing the only assets available to them—ruins, untamed wilderness, and people—they had at least given themselves a chance. All they needed, she thought, was one even break, and they'd become dangerous. And, like all dangerous resistance movements, they'd probably be wiped out at the first opportunity.

Roche tried to rid herself of the thought, concentrating instead on her own problems.

The cubicle at the end of the corridor was half as large as the compartment Roche had occupied on the *Midnight*. A small toilet facility, including a shower, had been curtained off in one corner. There seemed to be no surveillance equipment or hidden entrances, just the door through which she had entered.

"Thanks," Roche said. "I owe you one already."

"I'll send the Surin girl through when you're finished."

"No, wait." Roche stopped the woman before she could leave. "I'd like to see her now, if possible. Don't worry," she added when the woman frowned, suspicious. "We're not going anywhere."

The woman shrugged and left the room. Roche waited a moment, then returned her attention to the Box.

<You heard what she said. We have to leave the suit behind. I don't think they plan to steal it.>

<Not that they could use it anyway,> said the Box. <Besides, it isn't important right now. I believe I have gathered enough information from DAOC for the time being.>

<Good. So unseal this thing and get me out of here.>

The armor hissed, split along its seams, and allowed her to wriggle free. The pain in her shoulder was muted, manageable, as her arm slipped out of the padded sleeve. The touch of fresh air on her exposed skin made her groan with relief.

The blonde woman arrived with Maii as Roche began the difficult process of extricating herself from the sweat-stained and torn remains of her Armada uniform.

The woman pointed at a small pile by the door. "Change of clothes. You're about my size, so they should fit. You'll find a towel in the shower." With that, she left Roche and the reave alone.

"Do you want a shower?"

Maii shrugged.

Roche took the hint and began to peel off her uniform, not bothering to hide herself from the blind Surin. Her skin was red where the suit had rubbed, and crusted with dirt where it hadn't. She doubted that even an hour in a gehan mineral spa followed by a complete body scrub could make her feel clean, but a brief rinse certainly wouldn't hurt.

The curtained-off area contained a small handheld nozzle and a recessed basin. Standing in the basin, with the valise resting just outside, she switched on the nozzle and gasped as a fan of cold water sprayed her thigh. Directing the jet across the entirety of her body, she did her best to clean herself, relishing the feel of the cool water.

She examined her skin as she washed, noting a variety of multicolored bruises she hadn't previously been aware of. The purple-yellow blotch enveloping her left shoulder was beginning to fade, but still spread down to her breast and as far back as she could see. The joint itself was tender to the touch, and, she noted, swapping the nozzle over to her left hand, stiff. Her right side was relatively intact, apart from a couple of grazes. The water washed across the smooth line of her muscles, down her hips and thighs, curling between her toes, its caress gentle and soothing. She could have stayed within the intimate embrace of the water indefinitely, but she kept in mind the woman's warning and, after one last scrub at her stubbled scalp, clicked off the nozzle and reached for the towel. Water was scarce on the planet, and doubly so in the port itself.

While drying herself off, she stepped from behind the curtain to find Maii standing in exactly the same position she had been minutes earlier.

"You look lost," she said, with feeling. The girl seemed so small and helpless that, despite years of programming to loathe reaves, she wanted to reach out and hug the child.

<Without Veden, I am nothing.> She shuddered gently. <He is my eyes, my ears. . . . > Roche could feel something else there also, but Maii managed to suppress the thought; her words in Roche's mind trailed into an uncomfortable silence.

"By yourself, you must feel terrible." Roche wondered at the depth of the girl's attachment to her ward. It seemed more than just the bond of friendship, and yet less than a physical attachment. Could the Surin and Eckandi Castes mate? It was not something she had ever heard of before.

<It is not a common practice.> There was annoyance in the reave's tone. <The Agora has forbidden it.>

"Then . . ." Roche wasn't quite sure what to say. From what she remembered of Maii's memories, the reave held the main governing body of the Surin Caste in no high regard. "Listen, if you and Veden are lovers or whatever . . ."

<We're not,> she cut in with indignation.

"Okay." Roche finished toweling herself dry, then turned to the pile of clothes. The loose outfit of brown cotton pants and shirt the woman had provided was slightly baggy, but comfortable enough. She tucked her left arm under the shirt, keeping it pressed against her stomach. The valise's cable dangled around her waist like a belt.

Turning back to Maii, she said: "We're in no hurry, it seems. Why not have a shower? It'll take your mind off things for a moment."

<I can't.>

"Why not?"

<Because I can't see.>

"You—" Roche did a mental double take. "What's wrong with my eyes?"

<You don't like me to use them,> said Maii. <And I respect that.>

Roche frowned. "But—"

<You regard it as theft. I haven't touched your mind for information since Houghton's Cross. You tried to help me there, and for that I am in your debt. At the moment, respecting your feelings is the only way I have to honor that debt.>

"So whose eyes have you been using?"

<Cane's, when he lets me. But his will is stronger than yours, and I am unable to read him without his noticing. Sometimes I use the rebels. Most often, I just wait.>

"For Veden."

Maii was silent. Grief radiated from her small form and into Roche's mind.

She sighed. "Look, Maii. You're exhausted, you need rest, and I don't know how long it's been since you slept. You *need* that shower. It'll make you feel better, if only for a while." Roche hesitated, then forged on. "You can use my eyes, if you want."

<Do you mean that?>

"You can check, if you like."

The reave didn't say anything for a moment, then sighed. <Thank you, Morgan. I know how much this disturbs you.>

"Yes, well, this time it won't be theft, but a gift." She paused. "Besides, we kind of need each other right now."

<You see yourself as alone also, don't you?>

Roche shrugged, knowing that, having let the reave into her head, she could no longer hide her feelings from the girl. "Just have a shower. We'll talk about it later."

Maii nodded and slipped out of her tunic and blindfold. Leaving the curtain open, she climbed into the basin and used the nozzle to clean her skinny body. Roche tried not to feel squeamish, and forced herself to keep her eyes on the girl as she washed.

Not "girl," she reminded herself. Not as she knew one to be. Naked, there was no mistaking the peculiar physiology before her for that of a Pristine: the graceful skeleton, with its high rib cage; the dark, protruding nipples; the stump of a vestigial tail protruding from the cleft between narrow, corded buttocks; the fine, ginger hair—not fur—that uniformly covered the Surin's body except at groin and armpits, exactly the reverse of Pristine hair. Girlish in form, but Exotic in detail.

As her eyes became accustomed to the sight, Roche noticed the fine network of scars across Maii's scalp. Whoever had operated on her—the rogue doctor unnamed in Maii's memories—had performed an intricate operation to convert the child into a fully functioning epsense adept. Exactly how it had been achieved, Maii did not remember, and Roche had never heard of the practice before. The moral question it raised may have forced the Surin Agora to ban the process while it was still in development, and thereby driven the doctor underground, where he had procured experimental subjects from the poor or the unscrupulous.

Children, all of them, too young to choose.

When Maii finished her brief shower, she climbed out of the basin and used the towel Roche had discarded to dry. Then she clambered back into her old shipsuit and smoothed the hair on her hands and scalp.

<Thank you,> she said. <You were right: I did need it.>

"That's okay." Roche glanced at the door. "Maybe you should call the woman—"

<Her name is Sabra, and she is Haid's assistant.>

"—Sabra, then, to let her know we're ready."

Maii nodded. Roche took a seat on a box in one corner of the room to rest while she waited. The enormous bulk of the armor dominated the center of the tiny room, like a statue of a dirty, beheaded giant. Old but still reliable, it had served her and the Box well during her brief occupation, and she regretted leaving it behind. If discussions went well with Haid, she promised herself, she would retrieve it later.

<It needs a name,> said Maii, eavesdropping on Roche's surface thought.

Roche nodded. "Any suggestions?"

<Only the one you're thinking of.>

Roche smiled to herself. Yes, it was appropriate.

"Okay. 'Proctor' it is. Here's hoping it gives us better luck than its previous owner."

<Which? The armor or the name?>

Roche laughed aloud at this. "Both."

A security card gained them entry to an unfurnished office at the back of the building, stained from years of neglect. Sabra stepped up to a sliding door set in one corner of the room and punched a code into a keypad. The metal door shuddered for a moment but failed to open. Without complaint, Sabra repeated the sequence. On the third attempt, the door finally opened with a slight hiss. Beyond was an elevator. The woman ushered Roche, Maii, and Cane inside. With a rattle and grind of machinery, the carriage and its four passengers dropped downward.

"Where are you taking us?" asked Cane.

"Downstairs," said Sabra. Her reticence could have been natural or cultivated; either way, it showed no signs of abating.

"The port is riddled with old tunnels and chambers," said Roche, "left over from the early colonial days, before the Ataman Theocracy and COE invasions. Everyone knows they're here, but no one apart from the resistance uses them; they're supposed to be unsafe. According to the Box, this section used to be a university. The resistance rebuilt it, and now uses it as a headquarters." She smiled sweetly at Sabra, who returned her gaze with obvious dislike. "And that's where we're going. To meet Haid, right?"

The woman shrugged. "Right enough."

Their journey ended with a stomach-wrenching jerk. When the door slid open, it revealed a narrow, ill-lit passageway. Sabra nudged them forward, then sealed the lift behind them. Poorly maintained gears groaned as the carriage slowly returned to the surface.

"This way," said Sabra, and headed down the corridor.

They passed through a security scanner and a corridor lined with a dozen locked doors, then entered a dimly lit chamber containing nothing but a wide wooden desk and five chairs. Behind the desk and its compulsory computer facility sat the most profoundly black man Roche had ever seen. His skin was as dark as that of an Olmahoi, with a similar bluish sheen. He was hairless, which only accentuated the color of his skin. One eye stared at them from behind an ocular lens—held permanently in place millimeters above the eye by microfilaments embedded in bone. The other was nothing but glass. His left arm, resting on the desk, lifted as they entered the room to gesture at the chairs.

"My name is Ameidio Haid," said the man. His voice was warm, patient, and solid. "I'm sorry to have kept you waiting."

Roche nodded, accepting the apology for what it was: a formality. She settled gratefully into an armchair, the upholstery of which was ripped in various places. Cane sat to her immediate left, Maii to her right. Sabra stood to one side of the desk, unobtrusive but undeniably present. Under the dim light above the desk, Roche could see deep scars etched in Haid's cheeks and temples. Not injuries, she noted, but surgery. Given the hollow look of his face, she suspected that items had been removed, not implanted.

Or perhaps, she thought, remembering DAOC's stern restrictions on technology, *confiscated*.

"I was beginning to wonder if you even existed," said Roche. When he smiled at this, she said, "It's good to finally talk to you face to face."

Haid's laugh was mellow, natural. He would have been an attractive man if not for his injuries. "I'm pleased to be able to say the same about you, Commander Roche. Only two days on the planet, and you're already something of a legend."

"Unintentionally, I assure you."

"If you say so. Although it is difficult to imagine how one could wipe out an entire squadron of DAOC personnel by accident."

Roche smiled now. "What I meant was, it wasn't my intention to become involved."

"No?" asked Haid. "Then what exactly was your intention?"

"To stay alive," she said. "And to complete my mission, of course."

"Ah, yes. Your mission." Haid leaned back in his seat, all

business. "You have mentioned this to a number of my people but have neglected to *define* it even once." Haid raised an eyebrow. "I find this oversight slightly unnerving."

Roche said nothing, conflicting desires warring within her. She needed to tell him to gain his trust, but needed to trust him before she could tell him. There was no easy way out of the dilemma.

As though reading her thoughts, Haid said, "I understand your reluctance, Commander Roche. I am in a similar bind. As director of this small covert operation, I am honor-bound to follow its interests before my own. You could be a great boon to us, but you might also be a great threat. Perhaps only time will tell which you are."

He folded his hand into his lap. "I therefore suggest that we ignore the matter of your mission for the time being, and concentrate on other issues. DAOC security, for one. You are fleeing from them. Why?"

"Because they are corrupt. I was a passenger on the Armada ship destroyed two nights ago—"

"Yes, we saw the explosion. Local news reported it as a mining accident."

"It wasn't. The *Midnight* was ambushed by Dato ships during its approach through the Soul. We barely escaped with our lives by pretending to be debris flung from the wreckage. When we crashed on the planet, Enforcement attempted to capture us. The obvious conclusion is that the wardens are collaborating with the Dato Bloc."

"Treason?"

"Yes," said Roche. "In exchange for money."

"This planet encourages a mercenary attitude. It has, after all, little else to offer." Haid seemed amused by the squabbles that had impinged upon his immediate life. "So close to the Dato border, such a security compromise would seem inevitable—or at least possible. That begs the question: what were you doing here in the first place? If you or what you're carrying is so valuable, why place it in such an unnecessarily risky position?"

Roche considered the alternatives for a long moment before eventually replying: "Cover."

Haid nodded, then smiled. "Cover you still seek to maintain. Understood. But tell me, why is it that when you speak of your escape from the ship you refer to 'we,' not 'I'?"

Roche glanced at Cane, who kept his stare fixed upon Haid. "I'm carrying an AI," she said. "That was my only companion before my escape. The others came with me by chance."

"Really? Veden and Maii I was expecting. The other, however, is a complete unknown." Turning to Cane, he tapped his teeth with his fingertips. They made a soft clinking noise, as though his fingers were made of plastic, not flesh.

Cane returned his steady gaze without blinking.

"You look like a soldier," said Haid. "Are you an Armada officer?"

"I have no allegiance to the Commonwealth of Empires."

"A bounty hunter, then? Or a mercenary?"

"No."

"A spy?"

"No."

"Then what are you? You're not a transportee, I can tell that much."

"I don't know what I am. A refugee, perhaps."

"I find it difficult to imagine what you would be seeking refuge *from*." Haid smiled. "Emmerik describes your strength with some awe. Yet you expect me to believe that it is simply a natural ability?"

"He was pulled from a survival capsule before we jumped to the Hutton-Luu System," Roche said. "He has no memory of the time before then. Just his name. If you don't believe me, ask Maii."

"Oh, I will." Haid's eyes didn't shift from his examination of Cane. The reave herself made no sound. "Interesting," Haid continued, still talking to Cane. "If you aren't with the Armada, why are you on Roche's side?"

Cane shrugged. "Expediency. It seemed appropriate when I first met her, and still does."

"A natural soldier with no orders, no past, latching onto the first officer he comes across? Is that the whole truth?"

"Yes." Cane's voice was even and unfazed.

Haid rolled his eyes. "I'm sorry. I'll need more than that.

The stories are too wild for me to believe without evidence. Will you submit to a physical examination?"

Cane glanced at Roche, who nodded. This coincided with her own desire to find out more about Cane—and his origins.

"Good. Now we're getting somewhere." Haid leaned forward to run his hand along the edge of his desk. "I must admit, though, you make me nervous. You arrive on this planet, possibly the most potent task force I've ever seen, and refuse to answer my questions. I'm sure you can appreciate my frustration."

Roche frowned. "Are you suggesting—?"

"Cane with his natural strength and combat abilities, Maii with her mind power, your AI's apparent ability to manipulate the systems of hostile parties, and you, perhaps the leader and coordinator—how could I not be nervous with you sitting on the other side of my desk?"

"If we wanted to overthrow you, or infiltrate you, we could have made a move by now, and you know it. Besides, you *invited* Maii and Veden here."

"True." He said this thoughtfully. "Did they tell you why?"

"No."

"Can you guess?"

"Something to do with Maii's talents and Veden's negotiating skills, I imagine. I'm assuming you're not planning to control Warden Delcasalle directly." She shrugged lightly. "That's all I've managed to work out so far."

Haid smiled. "Emmerik trusts you. He told you about the need for a High Equity Court hearing to discuss our ownership of this planet. If Maii still won't tell you after this meeting, then that's the only clue I'll give you."

Roche sighed. She could understand his position, but that didn't mean she liked it. She was sick of fighting for every step and meeting obstacles everywhere she turned. Most of all, she lacked Cane's apparently indefatigable patience.

"Okay," said Haid, obviously tiring of letting the conversation wander, "here's the way it stands. You have to convince me, A, that I can help you without putting myself at risk, and B, that I *should* help you in the first place. You have to tell me what you want, then we'll negotiate."

"Fair enough." She paused for a moment to gather her thoughts. "I need to send a message to my superiors in Intelligence HQ informing them of the situation in Port Parvati."

"How do you propose to do that?"

"By gaining access to a high-power hyperspace transmitter, preferably one with encryption facilities."

"Relatively simple, it seems." Haid's fingers tapped a tune out upon the table. "Problem number one: there is only one such transmitter on Sciacca's World, and that belongs to the wardens. Problem number two: the only access to it is from within the landing field itself, well out of harm's way inside the MiCom installation. Three: even if you could get in, how do you expect to override the security systems designed to prevent such unauthorized transmissions? Four: you'll need my help to get at it, and I'm not yet convinced you deserve it."

"One and two we can deal with later," Roche responded, "when you give us more information. Four is up to you to decide. Three is this."

Rising to her feet in one smooth motion, she raised the battered valise and slammed it onto the desk. Haid jumped back involuntarily, and Sabra reached into her tunic and quickly withdrew a pistol. Before she had a chance to react, however, Cane had also risen from his chair and kicked the weapon from the woman's hand.

Haid's sudden shock evaporated just as quickly when his eyes settled upon the valise Roche had placed before him. "The AI, I presume," he said.

Sabra, nursing her hand, collected her pistol and, at Haid's instruction, slid it beneath her tunic. Only then did Cane return to his own seat.

Roche reached across the desk for the computer terminal and placed her hand on the palm-link.

"Box? Go to work."

A moment later, an artificial voice spoke from the terminal itself.

"Communications established. Nice work, Morgan. You

have placed us right into the heart of the resistance. Very well done indeed."

Another look of concern briefly crossed Haid's black face, but it quickly yielded to curiosity. "This is the device you used to take control of the Enforcement vessel over Houghton's Cross?"

"With it," said Roche, "we can do whatever we like to the wardens, once we get in."

"Which explains why they want you." Haid nodded. "Did you steal it?"

"Nothing so dramatic. I was carrying it back to Intelligence HQ when the Dato ambushed us here."

"But how did the Dato know you were coming?" he asked. "Or expect to get away with it?"

"Courtesy of the wardens, as I said. They're as corrupt as hell. I can't hand it over to them—they'll just sell it to the Dato Bloc—so I've got to call for help. Which means getting into the landing field. And that's where *you* come in."

"Perhaps." Haid knitted his fingers together and leaned back in the chair. "Go on."

"If we can signal the Armada, they can send reinforcements."

"Perhaps you can even get off-planet first, and *then* signal for help."

"Impossible," interrupted the Box.

"Oh?" Haid leaned forward. "It would seem to be the safest option. It would avoid having to hold the landing field until reinforcements arrive."

"Not under the circumstances," the Box continued. "The Dato have imposed a blockade on Sciacca's World. Any unauthorized and uninspected departures will be shot down before reaching orbit."

"How do you know that?" Haid regarded the valise with suspicion.

"Your information network has failed to penetrate the wardens' higher security, but it does have access to the landing field's flight schedule. All flights have been canceled or severely delayed pending Morgan's capture."

Haid's smile tightened. "Drastic steps," he said. "This

changes everything. Perhaps you're more trouble than you're worth."

"Your options are limited," said Roche. "You could kill us, or try to. You saw how we dealt with the Enforcement squadron; could you do any better? Or you could let us go and risk us being captured."

"I have copied your security files," added the Box. "My capture would mean the complete and utter destruction of everything you have built."

Haid paled at this. "Or I agree to help you."

"Precisely," cooed the Box.

Haid rubbed his hand across his chin. "But what's in it for me? How do I benefit? Apart from not being destroyed, I mean."

"I can help you attack the wardens," said Roche. "They are corrupt, the enemies of both of us. They deserve to be brought to justice."

"So you'll get a medal, and I'll get—what?"

"Revenge, at least," said Roche. "I'm hardly in a position to promise a reduction in your sentence."

"That's not what I want." Haid's sigh was deep and thoughtful, but his good humor was returning. "I never thought I'd hear an Armada officer swearing revenge on her fellows."

"I never thought I'd be doing it myself." Roche nodded and stepped away from the desk, severing contact with the palm-link. "But they're not my fellows, and I'd appreciate it if you wouldn't associate me with them."

"I'll try to remember." Haid glanced at Sabra, who was still rubbing at her hand where Cane had kicked it. His one good eye crinkled with amusement. "Well, you have me fascinated, Commander Roche. I was just about ready to turn you in when you arrived, but you've convinced me to reconsider.

"I suggest we all need time to think about our positions. Not long, though. If the Dato become impatient, who knows what they'll do?" Haid stood. "We'll meet again in six hours. Sabra, please show our guests to somewhere they can rest. Instruct Sylvester Teh to conduct an examination of

Cane as soon as possible. And there may be other minor injuries requiring attention."

The sour-faced woman nodded briskly but said nothing.

"Wait," said Roche. "What about Veden? What's happening to him?"

"He's undergoing surgery. Our physician has been discussing his case with Maii while we talked. She can keep you updated in her own time." Haid held out his hand to her. "But thanks for asking. I'm relieved to see your concern for your companions, even for those that wish you harm."

Roche took the resistance leader's hand. The feel of his fingers convinced her of what she had suspected: the limb was artificial. Now that she saw him standing, she also realized that his other arm was missing entirely.

Haid noted the direction of her gaze. "Perhaps, when we meet again, we can exchange stories."

Roche held his monocled stare. "Perhaps."

With a slow-lidded wink, Haid bowed and left the room.

12

The hill was bald, stony, and round. A fringe of grey, long-stemmed grass ringed its base, lending it a striking resemblance to an Eckandi's skull. The view was extensive, even though the summit wasn't particularly high, with uniformly flat plains leading to a knife-edge horizon in every direction. The cold blue of the sky was dotted with small islands of cloud, and between them glimmered a handful of nearby stars that defied the light of the weak, white sun.

As she stood there watching through another's eyes, the largest of these stars, Kabos, winked once, twice, and then went out.

She buried her hands into the deep pockets of her thick overcoat and sighed.

"Child, we have been working together for . . . how long?"

She turned out of politeness to face the owner of the voice, and saw herself echo the movement through his eyes. <Five years,> she said.

"And in all that time, have I ever betrayed you?"

She hesitated, even though there was no doubt in her mind. <Never.>

The Eckandi nodded. "Not once."

<No.> Not for the first time, she cursed the fact that she couldn't see his face when they were alone. <Why won't you tell me what has happened?>

"Because nothing *has* happened—yet. I—" He stopped. For a moment the only sound was that of the wind whipping across the skull of the hill. "I've been struck from the Commerce Artel," he said at last, the words a long, slow exhalation of shame.

She gasped, despite herself. <But—>

"No, let me finish. It gets worse." She waited, wondering how it *could* get worse. "Remember that offer we had from the Hutton-Luu System? The job we refused?"

<Petty criminals on a petty penal colony, you said. Too hard to get in, impossible to get out. You said I was too valuable to risk on such a small-time deal.>

"Well, the Axis felt otherwise." She could sense the discomfort swell beneath his words. "They advised me to take it. What with this" —he waved vaguely at the now-invisible star—"they said I need to prove myself again; that I had to *demonstrate* to them that I still have what it takes."

<But you can't be blamed for *this*,> she protested. <The generator was faulty. It could have happened to any—>

"But it didn't," he cut in. "It happened to *me*." He paused before continuing, his breath catching in the sudden breeze. "Anyway, when I refused to comply to their 'recommendation,' they stripped me of my rank, ordered criminal proceedings to begin, and charged me with first-degree fraud."

She shuddered at this: fraud was the most serious crime a delegate of the Commerce Artel could be accused of. In their books, not even murder rated above *bad business*.

<So what happens now?>

"The COE transport arrives in a week." He laughed his wheezing, exotic laugh while she struggled to take in what he was saying. "That's right. I'm to be transported to the penal colony as a convict. A free ticket to exactly where they want me—and the only way I can escape is by doing what they want me to." Although she couldn't see it, she felt him shake his head. "I've been set up, Maii. And I didn't even see it coming."

She waited in silence as he breathed his bitterness into the wind. The plan he had devised was in his mind—only half finalized, but she could read it clearly. When she sensed that he was about to ask the question foremost on his mind, she preempted him easily:

<I'll come too.>

She sensed the relief this aroused in him. "There are no guarantees—"

<Please. I want to,> she said. <When T'Bul threatened to have me lobotomized back on Gorgone-8, you stepped in and helped me. This is my chance to do something in return.>

He squeezed her shoulder. "You know you don't owe me anything, child," he said. "But I'm glad you feel that way. The truth is, there's no way I can make it through this without you."

<I know.> She reached out to take his hand. <Show me the sky again.>

He turned his eyes again heavenward. The star called Kabos had reappeared, although now it burned a deep, angry red. It brightened visibly as they watched, until it flared and became too bright to stare at directly.

"Come on," he said, glancing down the hill. For the first time she noticed the trio of Olmahoi greyboots waiting for him at the hive's massive entrance. "We need to get below ground. The shock wave won't be far away."

She nodded, allowing him to lead her down the hill, and . . .

Roche woke with a gasp.

Sitting upright on the narrow bunk, she put a hand to her forehead, trying to massage away the intrusive thoughts, to free herself of the last threads of the dream. Except it wasn't a dream. She was sure of that. It was something else entirely, a memory that belonged to someone else. . . .

A supernova in colonized space—a population huddling underground because a shield supplied by the Eckandar

Trade Axis had failed—the Commerce Artel delegate responsible tried and found guilty of fraud—

It was all so familiar; something she had come across recently while on the *Midnight*. She was certain the IDnet news reports had mentioned it on a number of occasions: Ede System, one of the Olmahoi provinces near the Commonwealth of Empires border, had been an insignificant backwater until it became the victim of a stellar disturbance and was nearly destroyed by the failure of a planetary shield.

And the name of the Artel delegate responsible for the sale of that shield had been—*Makil Veden.*

How could she not have connected the name sooner?

Completely awake, she looked around. Struggling from the thin, dirty mattress, she saw Maii sitting cross-legged on the upper bunk, features completely still. Whether she was asleep or meditating, Roche couldn't tell. Either way, she didn't acknowledge Roche's anger.

Roche was tempted to reach up and rouse the Surin but, sighing, decided against it. For the first time in what seemed like weeks, Roche felt alone—despite the young girl's presence in the room—and she found herself welcoming the solitude.

The room was small and practical, containing only a narrow double bunk and primitive toilet facilities. Minutes after Sabra had brought her to it, Roche had fallen into a deep sleep, blaming fatigue for her sudden and overwhelming tiredness. Now she wasn't so sure. . . .

"You awake, Commander?"

The voice, from the door, broke the quiet Roche had been enjoying. She crossed the short distance to see who it was.

"Sorry to disturb you," said Haid, his scarred, black face smiling at her. He was dressed in loose-fitting, black casuals that might once have been a shipsuit. "I was hoping to talk to you."

Roche shrugged aside her irritation. "Likewise. But give me a moment."

"Of course." He averted his eyes while she dressed and changed the sling on her left arm. Maii didn't move once, and Roche decided not to disturb her. If the girl really was asleep, then she obviously needed it. Accusations of mental tampering could wait until later—until she had decided which she was most angry about: the way the Surin's memories had been thrust into her thoughts, or the abrupt way in which her own had been suppressed.

When she was ready, the rebel leader took her through a series of dimly lit tunnels and chambers. The subterranean headquarters was busier than she had assumed it would be—containing the homes of hundreds of people, as well as rudimentary markets, hospitals, industries, and entertainment facilities; as though a miniature city had grown around the rebel installation. In one large room they passed, at least fifty people had gathered to dine together; the smell of roasted meat caused Roche to hesitate at the entrance.

Haid took her arm to encourage her on. "We'll eat soon," he said, smiling. "I promise."

"As long as it *is* soon," she said. Haid led her down a flight of curving, narrow stairs. The deeper they went, the damper the walls became, as though they were approaching some sort of water table. Yet, when she stopped to test the moisture with a fingertip, she realized that the source of the water was industrial rather than natural. It had a bitter, pungent smell.

"There's a leaky sewage outlet not far from here," explained Haid. Roche grimaced and wiped the hand on her clothes.

"And you live down here?" It wasn't disgust that stained her words, but rather amazement.

"I like to be near the others," he said. "Helps remind me that I'm one of them."

"More leaders should follow your example," Roche commented, thinking of Proctor Klose and his private suite on the executive floor of the *Midnight*. As far as she was concerned, being in command meant more than simply giving orders. And it meant more than just wearing a fancy uniform and having access to luxuries, too. When it came down to it, that extra star on Klose's uniform hadn't helped him when his ship had exploded. Part of her couldn't help wondering if the extra privilege may even have caused it, albeit indirectly. Had he been a better leader, more in tune with his crew and his ship, the *Midnight* might now be more than several thousand cubic kilometers of glowing, radioactive dust.

"This way." Haid took her arm and guided her to the next exit from the stairwell. On the other side was a floor much like the one they had left, although more extensively populated than the other.

They moved along the dank, slightly odorous passages for a while longer, until Haid arrived at a locked door. He keyed the lock by some unseen mechanism, and the panel slid aside. Entering first, he switched on lights and gestured at a chair.

Roche followed him cautiously, eyes scanning the room out of habit before actually stepping inside. It was furnished comfortably, but not ostentatiously so. One wall was dominated by an enormous desk, on which rested a complicated array of out-of-date computers. Two small, cushioned armchairs occupied the center of the room. A cloth hammock hung across one corner, near a narrow cupboard. Hanging from the wall opposite the desk was a multicolored mural. At least three meters wide and two high, it looked like a window to another world—and a familiar one at that.

Ignoring the chair, Roche approached the mural to take a better look. Grey sky rippled above a bleak and barren landscape, with jagged fingers of black rock clawing hopelessly for purchase on the clouds so far above. The scene was totally desolate, yet somehow managed to impart a sense of life—almost as though the rocks themselves were sentient.

"It's Montaban, isn't it?"

"That's right." Roche thought she detected admiration in the rebel leader's voice. "You've been there?"

"Read about it." COE Armada training covered several hundred of the more notable nearby worlds, including this one. "What made you paint it?"

"I was born there."

Roche turned to face him. "*Born* there?"

"All the others—Emmerik, Sabra, Neva—they're all natives of Sciacca, but not me." He moved to the cupboard and opened it, unhampered by his single arm. "Drink?"

"Thanks." She stepped over to the chair he had indicated

and sat down. When he handed her a tall, thin glass filled with a clear liquid, she said: "So what's your story, Haid?"

He smiled, his monocular sight gleaming in the faint light of the room, and raised his glass in a wordless toast, which Roche imitated. She took a mouthful of the liquid and was momentarily puzzled by the lack of taste. Then she realized: the glass contained nothing but water. A moment later, a second realization: a full glass of clean drinking water on Sciacca's World would have been regarded as something of a treat to the rebels. Understanding this, Roche decided that sipping the drink would probably be the best means of acknowledging Haid's generosity.

"I was a mercenary before coming here," Haid began. "Tried and convicted after forty-seven successful juntas. Not that I'm boasting or anything. It's just a fact, the way my life panned out." He shrugged. "My parents were killed when I was fifteen, and they left me enough money to pay for anything I wanted. But theirs was a political killing, an underground thing, and I wasn't safe. So I skipped town, bought myself as many implants as I could afford, and set out to find my own niche.

"My parents' money," he went on, "certainly made up for any lack of talent in those early years. If I found it hard to keep up, I just bought a new implant. Easy. I started off as a vigilante for hire until I got a taste for killing."

Roche was somewhat surprised by the man's frankness. He seemed completely at ease with his admissions, speaking with a total absence of guilt. It must have shown on her face, too, because he carried on with a few words of explanation.

"You must understand, Commander, that it paid extremely well. And you'd be amazed how easy it can become after the first couple of times."

"How many?" said Roche. "How many people have you killed?"

"Hard to say." He shook his head. "What with assassinations, fighting in the M'taio System's Caste wars, the i-Hurn Uprising—hell, even with the implants I lost count."

"So what happened?"

He sighed. "I had a rival, a young blood by the name of Decima Frey. She sold me to COE Enforcers in exchange for clemency when they caught her. I was hauled in and tried—so far gone, I didn't really know what was going on. My implants were on a feedback kick, you see, with so many subroutines it was hard to tell where they stopped and I began." He wiggled his fingers by his right ear. "Anyway, I was initially sentenced to be executed, but appealed and had it reduced to this." He indicated his surroundings with a wave of his hand. "At a cost. I had to undergo rehabilitation first. And that didn't seem such a big deal at the time—I mean, I figured rehab would be easy to fake and was confident I'd be able to escape soon enough. I was a killing machine, after all. No backwater penal colony was going to be able to hold me for very long." The grin that touched his lips was wry and without humor. "At least that was what I thought, until I realized what the judge had meant by 'rehabilitation.'"

Roche had learned about the process during her early years of training in Military College. "They stripped you of your implants," she said.

The whirr of his monocle focusing upon her seemed loud in the sudden quiet.

"They dewired me from the inside out," he said. "Everything went. There wasn't a bone or a nerve untouched. My body weight must have dropped by about seventy-five percent. My neuronal mass went down by half. I tell you, I was jelly by the end of it—physically and mentally."

"But how could they have taken care of you in that condition?" said Roche. "I mean, Sciacca's World doesn't have the facilities—"

Haid's laugh startled her. "Take *care* of me?" He laughed again. "Boras—Delcasalle's predecessor—she washed her hands of me very quickly. I was sent into the streets to fend for myself." Light caught Haid's monocle as he leaned forward. "And I was a cripple at that stage. It wasn't until later that I salvaged this"—he tapped his arm on one leg—"and the eye from someone who was no longer . . . in need of it."

Roche's face creased in puzzlement. "You couldn't have managed to do that by yourself, surely?"

"One of my old shipmates rescued me from the gutter. Got to me before the rats could finish the job the authorities had started." He smiled self-deprecatingly. "I'm a far cry from the man I once was, but at least I'm alive, right?"

Roche nodded slowly. "For many here, that might not be something to be grateful for."

"That's why I'm with these people," he said. "They've had it rough, but they're not afraid to keep trying. They're determined to get what they want in the end. The only thing they needed was a good leader—someone with experience at fighting in a modern way." He tipped his head in an exaggerated manner. "And here I am. Gun for hire turned revolutionary."

Roche smiled back. "And doing well, it would seem. This installation is well organized."

"If a little underequipped and leaky at times. Yes. I try my best. It may be nothing compared to my old exploits, but it keeps me going. And I enjoy it, too. I guess having a personal stake in the outcome really makes the difference." His glass eye winked at her. "Which brings us to you, Commander." His expression became hard, grim. "You're a serious threat to everything I've built—in more ways than one. So let's hear your own story. Tell me about this mess you've brought to Sciacca."

Roche put the drink on the floor by her chair and began to talk. Midway through Haid's confession she'd realized that she had little to fear from the man, at least as far as secrecy was concerned. Her mission was of little relevance on the planet—except to her and the Dato Bloc—and any information she divulged would be unlikely to spread. Even in the improbable event that Haid decided to tell Warden Delcasalle, his word was sure to be doubted. Besides, she needed his help—there was no escaping this simple fact. And if the only way to gain that help was to tell the truth, then so be it.

He listened closely as she described how she had "collected" the Box from the AI factories on Trinity, and how she really had very little idea of either its potential or its purpose. He accepted her role as uninformed military courier as easily as she did: she wasn't required to know; therefore she didn't. When she described the ambush in the Soul and the means by which she and the others had slipped past the Dato

ships and to the planet in the lander, he nodded appreciatively and commented that their tactics had been sound.

Cane's unexplained appearance on the scene, however,
bothered him.

"You say that Cane was instructed by someone to come
to your room prior to the *Midnight*'s destruction. Presumably the same someone who let him out of his cell." He
frowned. "Any idea who that might have been?"

"No. The security records went up with the ship, and I've
been too busy trying to stay alive since then to worry about
anything else."

"Understandable." Haid sucked the tips of his plastic fingers. "Go on."

There was little more to add: the crash of the lander; their
rescue by Emmerik and the battle in Houghton's Cross; their
arrival in Port Parvati.

When she had finished, she refreshed her throat with a
sip of water and leaned back into the chair. "What do you
think?" she asked. "It's not as good a story as yours—"

"Don't be too quick to dismiss it," Haid said, frowning.

"Do you think you can you trust me?"

"Perhaps," he said. "Half of what you've told me doesn't
make sense, and what *does* bothers me."

Now Roche frowned. "So you *don't* believe me?"

He waved his hand dismissively. "That's not what I'm
saying at all. I *do* believe you—totally. But you're not giving me the full picture, albeit unintentionally."

"I don't understand."

"Well, take your mission for instance. Granted, the *Midnight* was a form of cover—but why here? If the Box is so
important, for whatever reason, why send it to such a high-
risk region when thousands of other routes were available?
The Hutton-Luu System is so close to the Dato border that
it's almost begging to be annexed. All it would've taken was
a small skirmish to put your mission in jeopardy. No. It
doesn't make sense at all." Haid shook his head. "And then
there's Cane."

Roche sighed. "I know. I've been trying to figure him out
ever since I met him."

"That's not what I mean," said Haid. "Ignore what he is

for a moment, and focus on how he came to be here. You said his life support capsule was plucked out of deep space near an interim anchor point. I can understand his lack of memory, perhaps—but not his escape from the cell. Who helped him? Why did they send him to you? And the timing of his release is suspicious, too. Did his ally know about the ambush? And if they did, how could they possibly have known that you, of all the people onboard the *Midnight*, were going to escape?"

Roche considered for a long moment. "They couldn't have. No one knew the ship was going to blow until it happened. Except maybe Klose—"

"But you said he did his best to keep you *away* from Cane."

"I know." Roche shook her head. As unlikely as coincidence was, it seemed the less ridiculous option. "You really think there's a conspiracy?"

"I don't know. But I'm not dismissing the possibility." Haid's monocle didn't waver, so tightly was his attention focused on her. "Everything Emmerik's told me warns me to be careful where Cane is concerned."

"Fair enough." She couldn't blame him for being wary. Someone with Cane's natural combat abilities deserved that, at the very least.

"And then there's Veden," Haid continued. "He's supposed to be on my side, but I have to tell you that the way you turn up together makes me a little . . . uneasy."

"Well, you can rule out the possibility of the two of us working in tandem against you. He's been wanting to cut loose from me ever since we met."

"So I understand." Haid smiled to himself and studied the last mouthful of water in his glass. "Maybe he knows something I don't."

"All he'd know would come through Maii. If she's told you nothing, then that leaves me in the clear. Right?"

"My thoughts exactly," he said. "Except that you and she have been fairly close since your arrival. Maybe the two of you have taken sides against Veden and me, for whatever reason. It's a possibility I have to consider." He downed the last of his water in a single gulp. "Yet you maintain that you don't know why she's here."

"That's not quite true anymore." Roche shuddered slightly, remembering the dream the Surin had given her. "I do know a little more now than I did."

"How much?"

"I'm not sure." The slab of Maii's memories had been dumped unceremoniously into Roche's head in the form of a dream, raw and requiring processing. Now that she had the chance, she belatedly tried to assimilate what she had learned with what she knew about Sciacca's World.

"Something about the DAOC hyperspace transmitter being off-planet?" she said.

Haid nodded. "The MiCom installation in the landing field controls all transmissions, but the hardware itself is in a remote polar orbit, well outside the Soul. The small station is unstaffed apart from a skeleton crew to oversee the equipment and to perform minor repairs. The crew is rotated once every fifty days with fresh personnel from Kanaga Station."

"So it's theoretically impossible for anyone on the ground to take over the transmitter."

"That's right."

"Unless you somehow infiltrate the crew of the station."

"Possible, but unlikely. This is a high-security installation; the transmitter will have command codes known only to the CEO."

"Warden Delcasalle," said Roche.

"Exactly. Without the codes, the only way to 'interfere' with any broadcast is to damage the transmitter itself."

Roche nodded to herself, the plan suddenly falling into place. First, Maii had to work her way into the warden's mind—not to take him over, for there were sure to be safeguards against that, but to steal the transmitter codes. Second, she had to reach out for the orbital station and select one of the crew. Someone who knew how to operate the transmitter, someone tired and easily influenced—perhaps at the end of a tour of duty, eager for recall to the main base. Someone who could be controlled by epsense to send a message from Sciacca's World—a message, more specifically, to the COE High Equity Court requesting a formal hearing on behalf of the rebels.

And that was where Veden came in. Such a request, from an undercover delegate of the Commerce Artel, would hardly go unnoticed.

Except that now Veden was in a coma.

When she outlined this to the leader of the rebels, he smiled widely.

"That's the gist of it," he said. "A long shot, but at least it doesn't involve the use of force. The Eckandar Trade Axis has been sympathetic ever since their outcast—Lazaro Houghton—betrayed the original settlers. The cost in bribes to get the message out to them nearly ruined us, but it'll be worth it." He shrugged. "At least we hope it will be. Veden's still under anesthetic; we won't know how he's doing until tomorrow morning. If he doesn't wake from the coma, then we'll have to rethink the situation."

Roche nodded. "The only other option, as far as I can see, is to raid the landing field and use the codes there. But given your current position—underarmed, that is—I wouldn't recommend it."

"Perhaps not. But maybe we should plan something anyway, just in case."

"It couldn't hurt."

Haid grinned suddenly. "You know, Commander, I think we're actually getting somewhere."

"That depends on how you look at it. I've decided to trust you—but, then, I have little choice."

"True. And I've decided not to turn you in to Enforcement for the bounty, although I won't deny we could use the cash. Apart from the fact that you might be able to help us, I've got little to lose if I support you. Should Veden's plan work, the High Equity Court can be told about you then. Or you can transmit a message to your superiors at the same time."

"My thoughts exactly."

"At least we agree on something." Haid leaned back into his chair. "We can discuss Plan B later, if you like. All I want is an assurance that if Veden's plan fails and yours works, you'll take him off the planet when you leave. I owe him that much, for coming here."

Roche thought about it. "I'm not really in a position to guarantee anything—"

"Nor I, Commander," Haid cut in.

Roche studied the man's intent expression for a moment. "But I can try, I guess."

"Good. That's as much as I can expect from anyone." Haid leaned back into his chair. "All that remains is for me to ask a small favor."

"Which is?"

Haid stood and crossed to the cupboard, rummaged around inside it for a time, then returned with a small box. Seating himself again, he keyed open the lid and showed her the contents.

Inside the box was a slim data glove with an infrared remote link.

"I want you to put this on," said Haid.

"Why?"

"So I can communicate with the Box, of course. If we're going to attempt anything together, we need to understand the tools at our disposal. And, given my past, I think you'll agree that I'm the closest thing we have to an expert on cybernetic systems."

Roche hesitantly reached into the box and picked up the glove. Did she have the right to allow a convicted criminal access to the Box? Regardless of her situation, and no matter how much she needed Haid's help, it went against all her training.

"I suppose it won't hurt," Roche agreed warily. "Although I doubt you'll learn much. I certainly haven't."

"Well, we'll see about that, won't we? I've never met an AI before with more intelligence than a retarded rodent, regardless how well appointed they may seem up front. Give me a day or two and I should have it figured out."

Still she vacillated. Yet she had to admit that she too was curious. If Haid could learn anything more than she had in the last few weeks, it might be worth the risk.

<Put on the glove, Morgan.> The Box spoke through her thoughts. <He will learn only what I want him to. And, be-

sides, this will enable me to infiltrate their installation further. We have nothing to lose and much to gain.>

It made sense, she thought, slipping on the glove and snapping its wrist closed. She flexed her fingers. The mesh fabric was tight around her knuckles, but left her fingers otherwise unimpeded. Almost immediately she felt the tingle down her forearm that followed a transfer of data.

Haid smiled. "Good. I'll get started soon. For now, though, I suggest we find you some food."

Relieved by the offer, Roche stood and followed Haid from the room.

"It's not a matter of numbers," Roche insisted, "or of firepower. What I'm proposing is a quick surgical strike. If we do it properly, we'll be in before they can mount countermeasures. And once we're in, we can take effective control."

The unofficial tactical meeting had convened in an empty office in one of the deeper sections of the underground resistance complex. A large viewtank, oriented horizontally to the floor, served as a combined desk and map. Roche and Neva leaned on opposite sides of its glowing surface, secondhand diagrams painting patterns on their faces. Emmerik stood to one side, watching the interaction between the two women with interest.

Haid had given Roche over to the two of them not long after a hasty meal in the rebel refectory. She and Neva, it seemed, had been arguing ever since.

"Control?" The furrows on Neva's brow grew deeper. "There are more than two thousand Armada personnel in Port Parvati, in twenty-seven separate facilities. We have less than a thousand. At the very best, we can take control of *one* facility, and that doesn't give us effective control of anything. It just makes us effective targets. Ameidio won't risk our people for such a futile gesture."

"There'll be no risk to your overall organization," said Roche. "We can use a handful of volunteers, if necessary. And anyway, we'll control the communications nexus—MiCom."

"But MiCom is only the *instrument* of command," Neva quickly countered. "Delcasalle and his cronies could run their operation without it; they'd use carrier bats if they had to. You don't know these people like we do."

Roche shook her head. "One: MiCom is linked to the hyperspace transmitter in orbit—so once we have it, we can blow the whistle on them, right down the line to the Armada. And two: corrupt officials are the same anywhere. They—"

"I don't think Commander Roche plans to leave them on the loose," the Box interrupted, speaking through a terminal near the viewtank. Roche regarded the valise in surprise, unaware that it had been listening.

"Warden Delcasalle may well be in absolute control here," it continued, "but he is dependent on those immediately below him, and they in turn on the level below them. All levels below Delcasalle operate through the Administration Center; the key personnel may not be present, but the mechanism for decision-making and control always is. Cut out the Administration Center, and you effectively cut off Delcasalle's hands."

"*Administration?*" Neva waved her hand at the glowing map. "So now we're taking out more than one of the facilities?"

"No," the Box said firmly. "Merely extending our strike at the MiCom installation to include the Administration Center as well. Look at the map."

Neva looked down, and Roche, impressed by the Box's line of thought, did likewise. She saw at once where it was leading.

"MiCom and Administration," it said, "are features of the central port complex, isolated within the scorched-earth perimeter. Administration is adjacent to—and can be entered by way of—the main terminal building, which houses MiCom. So this can be a single operation. No untidy splitting of the strike force, no civilians, and no collateral damage."

Roche swung the Box onto the viewtank's edge. There was just enough free chain to allow her to reach across the main map.

"Both MiCom and Administration are secure modules," she said, following the Box's lead. "Probably prefab components shipped from an old orbital facility. But the main entrance to Administration is only about ten meters from the emergency stairs to MiCom. See, here." She tapped the point on the plan showing the map of the main terminal building. "We can go to that point as one group, split into separate strike forces, and be in a position to move simultaneously against the two targets."

"Seems almost made to order," Neva said dryly.

Roche glanced up at her, trying to read her face rather than her words. But the woman was impassive.

Roche returned to the plans. "Forget the lower floor and the navigation module; that's of no interest to us. The MiCom module occupies the three levels above that, right through to the roof installations; it's totally isolated from the ground floor, totally shielded and insulated, totally selfcontained. It even has its own emergency life-support system, controlled from the first floor. The only points of entry or exit are the elevator system—which can be disabled—and the equipment access stairwell from the ground—here. All we have to target is the first floor, and they'll be cut off from the outside."

Neva leaned over the map, her face finally revealing a hint of interest in Roche's plan.

"It's a simple operation," Roche said. "A single shot and the elevator will be inoperable. We go up the stairs, blow out the door, and enter fast under cover of the explosion. Three or four people could secure the floor in, say, thirty seconds. One heavy weapon to cover the stairwell—perhaps a portable shield to prevent them lobbing their own explosives in on us—gas via the emergency life support, or Maii, to knock out those above us—and we're secure. It'll only take a few seconds to interface the Box. Once we've done that, we'll control all command communication on Sciacca's World plus all intersystem channels, including the Armada's."

"What about Admin?" said Emmerik.

"Cane can take a small force in there," Roche said. "It's one level; he'll simply sweep through it. No need to be tidy."

Neva looked across at Emmerik. A frown creased her face.

The Mbatan nodded. "He's quite capable of doing it," he said.

"That's not what I was thinking."

"I know," said Emmerik, his eyes moving to meet Roche's.

Neva's gaze narrowed. Lowering her eyes to the map, she deliberated a moment, then said: "Okay, Commander. It seems sound enough, although it does rely heavily on the talents of a small number of individuals—namely the members of your own party. Should either you, Cane, or Maii fall early in the battle, success will be unlikely." She folded her arms and nodded to herself. "But supposing we grant you the possibility that your plan *might* work, there still remains the little matter of getting to the strike point you've identified. The terminal complex is well inside the landing field's electrified perimeter, some hundred meters back from the only gates. Not only is the gatehouse well served by Enforcement personnel, but so is the main guard block. Both lie between the gates and the front doors of the main complex. Needless to say, these people aren't technicians and administrators and will be highly sensitive to intruders. How do you plan to get us past them?" She brushed the back of a hand across the map as though wiping off crumbs. "Just send Cane in first?"

Roche smiled. "That's the least of our problems. What you have to decide is whether you want to continue to play good citizen, perhaps infiltrate the system and gain a few minor advantages—or whether you want to go with us and clean this bunch out once and for all."

Neva's expression tightened as she spoke. Obviously she had struck a nerve. "I shouldn't need to remind you, Commander," she said, "that we've built up a strong and efficient resistance here over a number of years. If we implement your plan and it fails, we stand to lose everything."

"Not necessarily. You risk maybe a dozen people. Surely you've set up field-operative cells with one person control?"

"Of course. That's how we work outside the city."

"Then use one of those cells."

Neva said nothing. She looked at Roche and the Box's valise in turn, then back to the map. Her frown intensified.

"Believe me," Roche pressed, "if we wait much longer, a Dato ground team will be next on the scene, and your little operation won't last a week. They're a distinct step up from the locals you've been dealing with."

Again Emmerik and Neva exchanged a glance. "We know," said the woman.

"There's just one thing I'd like to ask," said the Mbatan. "You seem quite confident about getting in, but what happens *afterward*?"

Roche hesitated. She hadn't dwelled on the aftermath as much as she had on the events leading up to it. "The message to the Armada will be sent on a broadband emergency frequency. The Dato will know instantly it's been sent, and might even back off without any further trouble, depending on how far they're willing to be involved. Even if they don't, we can use the Box to control the landing field's defense screen to keep them—and the Enforcers—at bay for a while. Long enough for a reply to arrive, at least. Reinforcements won't be far behind." She shrugged. "That should be enough to make Delcasalle think twice about attacking us."

"Perhaps." Neva still looked undecided. "But it still seems a little risky. We'll be sitting ducks in the MiCom building."

"I agree," put in the Box, surprising Roche. "I don't doubt that I can send the emergency message and simultaneously organize a ground defense while you keep MiCom secure. In a predictable world, this would be no mean feat. But in the real world I will have little control over the response time of the Armada or the actions of the Dato Bloc. Should the former be sluggish and the latter retaliatory rather than conciliatory, there will be little even I can do to delay the inevitable."

Emmerik nodded. "The longer we're under siege, the more time we give DAOC or the Dato to find a way in."

"The Armada could take days," Neva added.

"And that's not the worst of it," continued the Box. "A conflict of interests exists within the group itself. Assuming all goes well, we will be lifted from a combat zone by Armada dropships—hardly an inconspicuous way to leave the planet. Especially when more circumspect pathways are available. While it suits our needs admirably to choose this method of escape, others might not find it appropriate."

"What other way is there?" Roche asked.

"By betraying us to the Enforcers, a traitor might gain illegal exit from Sciacca's World from the Dato—thereby circumventing the judiciary system."

"It's a possibility," Emmerik said to Roche, his eyes dark.

"A very real one, I'm afraid," the Box continued. "In combat, as I am sure you are aware, there are crucial moments where one simple action, or failure to take action, can decide the ultimate outcome. It would be relatively easy for one person to shift the scales, should he or she so wish."

"That's a risk everyone takes in combat," Roche protested. "And besides, they won't have time to plan anything. The response from the Armada won't be slow. The *Midnight* was destroyed two days ago, and therefore hasn't reported to HQ. Someone might already be on their way to see what happened." Leaning over the map, she did her best to argue with a voice that had no face. "And besides, what other alternatives do we have?"

"At least one," said the Box. "We can commandeer a ground-to-orbit vessel and physically occupy the transmitter station."

"What?" Stunned by the audacity of the suggestion, Roche openly gaped. "Are you crazy?"

"Not at all," the Box purred. "The station is well defended—more so than the landing field and the MiCom installation, but not overwhelmingly so. I can get us past the Dato blockade and into a position to dock. The warden will not sanction a direct assault upon it, for fear of destroying it. This will place them in direct conflict with the Dato Bloc. A very real possibility exists that our enemies will go to war over the best way to capture us, while we sit back and await rescue."

"You really are crazy," said Neva, shaking her head. "I like Roche's plan much better. At least with her we stay on solid ground."

"Which is less defensible than—"

"Forget it, Box," Roche said. "The most we can hope for

is control of MiCom. Push it any further and we risk losing everything."

"I agree," said Emmerik, nodding.

"But, Morgan—"

"I said, *forget it*." Roche glared at the valise, mentally daring it to argue further.

Before it could do so, the room's intercom beeped urgently for attention.

Neva stepped aside to take the call. While she waited, Roche ran over her plan in her mind. Yes, it seemed sound; there were only a handful of details left to be straightened out, and they would fall into place as the others applied their superior knowledge of the rebel forces and the city to the problem. Roche doubted COE Intelligence's head of Strategy, Page De Bruyn, could have done any better, given what she had to work with.

"Your AI is either far more clever than I gave it credit for," said Emmerik into the silence, "or dangerously abstracted from reality."

"What do you mean?" Roche responded.

"Well, its suggestion appears to have forced you and Neva to a consensus. Perhaps that was all it was intended to do, in which case the move was inspired." Emmerik shrugged. "If it meant it seriously, on the other hand . . ."

The Mbatan let the sentence trail off, and Roche didn't complete the thought out loud. Much as she disliked the idea of the Box being such a skilled debater, especially on her behalf, she found that less disturbing than the Box's plan itself.

Although, now that she thought about it, the Box's plan did make a certain kind of sense. It *was* feasible, in a crazy kind of way. Almost Human in its boldness; hardly what she would have expected from a mere machine.

When Neva returned, her face was grim. "That was Ameidio," she said. "He's received the results of Cane's tests."

"Excellent." Emmerik lifted his bulk off the table he had been leaning on. "Now we might get some answers."

"We already have, I'm afraid." Neva turned to look Roche squarely in the eye. "Ameidio's called a conference. It starts in fifteen minutes. He wants you to wait here until

he calls a guard to show you down. We'll meet you there."
Neva turned back to Emmerik. "Let's go. I'll fill you in on
the way." Together they headed for the door.

"Wait!" Roche came around the viewtank. "At least give
me a hint of what they've found."

Neva stopped on the threshold, glancing at Emmerik.
After a moment, he nodded assent. "You won't like it," she
said to Roche.

"Is he sick? Dying? What?"

"Worse than that, I'm afraid." Neva met Roche's stare
and sighed. "Whatever Cane is, he *isn't* what he seems. . . ."

13

Nine people filed into the oval-shaped conference room and gathered about its long, polished, grey stone table. As they did, a warm and gentle light began to emanate from the rafters high above, replacing the shadows of the large room with a pervasive yellow glow.

Present at the table were Haid, at its head, with Emmerik and Neva on one side and Sabra on the other. Next to Sabra—and directly opposite Roche—was Sylvester Teh, the representative of the medical team that had examined Cane. He was a short and balding man in his middle years who spoke in a manner both soft and lacking in self-confidence. Roche got the impression that he was more comfortable talking to machines than to people.

To Roche's right were two guards, between which sat Cane himself. If he was aware that he was, to all intents and purposes, on trial, his face betrayed no apprehension. Not that she expected it to. She doubted whether there was anything the rebels could do to Cane to hurt him. Roche and Emmerik had seen Cane in action; they both knew that he could have overpowered his escort on any number of occasions on the way down to this meeting. The guards' presence was more for show than anything else.

Maii had declined to attend, saying she needed to concentrate in order to prepare for her part in Veden's plan. It felt unusual for Roche not to have someone whispering in her mind. Indeed, even the Box was silent—the tingle of data flowing through the glove still for the moment. She suspected it would be paying close attention to the proceedings just the same.

When all were seated, Haid called for order. "I'm sorry to drag you in at such short notice," he began, "but as you are probably aware, something has come up regarding our friend here." He nodded in Cane's direction. "You'll have to excuse the choice of venue, I'm afraid; unfortunately it's the only room guaranteed to be secure."

Roche glanced around the large and empty room. It was situated on one of the university's lower levels, and, from the disheveled appearance of the corridors leading to it, she suspected it wasn't used too often.

"Sylvester," continued Haid. "You want to tell us what we have here?"

Teh adjusted the neck of his tunic as he stood to address the small group. "Early this morning," he said, "we completed an in-depth physical examination of the subject known as Adoni Cane, our intention being to determine the cause of his amnesia. We also wanted to see if he had suffered any physical side-effects of what I am given to understand was an extended time spent in a life support capsule. Indeed, we thought the two facts might have been connected." Teh glanced down to the copious notes laid out before him.

"However, before we move on to the full findings of our investigation, I would like to begin by saying that, as far as we can tell, Adoni Cane's loss of memory is *not* the result of physical trauma. He has no memory of a time earlier than thirteen days ago because, quite simply, the memories never existed in the first place." Teh looked around the table to ensure that this conclusion was clearly understood. Noting Roche's obvious confusion, he said, "To put it another way, until a little more than a week ago, the Adoni Cane sitting before you did not exist."

"That's impossible," said Roche. "The recovery team on the *Midnight* physically pulled him out of the capsule."

Teh raised a hand. "Let me clarify that," he said. "Perhaps I should have said he did not exist as an *individual*."

Emmerik lifted his thick eyebrows. "He was someone else?"

"Or no one at all." Teh's nervous eyes dropped again to his notes. "Real-time analysis of the blood flow in his brain reveals an absence of lesions and clots—no physical damage, in other words, that would suggest the erasure of a previous personality. What we see before us is a man whose brain is functioning perfectly—albeit that it has only been *conscious* for a matter of days."

Neva leaned forward. "So how is it that he can talk? If he's only thirteen days old, surely he should be as helpless as a newborn baby. *And* as mindless."

"I don't know," said Teh. "One possibility is that the capsule in which he was found contained more than the usual life-suspend/support outfit. During his time adrift, it may have been educating him, training him." He shrugged. "We have no way of knowing."

"Training him for what?" Sabra asked.

"Why don't you ask the man himself?" put in Roche, gesturing at Cane.

"I have no memories at all prior to the *Midnight*," he said, preempting the question. "If I was educated subliminally, then I'm afraid I can offer no answers which might explain what my training was intended *for*."

"But why would anyone do such a thing?" asked Neva. "It's crazy."

Haid brought the matter to an end by standing and saying, "We'll come back to that later. First we should hear the other results of the examination."

Teh nodded. "We conducted the standard tests: X-rays, tissue typing, genetic analysis, and so on. Without exception, the results of these tests were anomalous."

"In what way?" Roche asked.

"See for yourself." The medic displayed a handheld computer down which scrolled test results. Roche caught perhaps one line in five and rapidly became lost among the endless procession of data.

"What you're seeing is Cane's genetic transcript, coding exons and introns both," Teh explained. "When you compare it to his overall physiognomy, the results are weird—to say the least. He may look normal on the surface, but *underneath* . . ." His voice trailed off as he scanned through a variety of holographic images, then returned: "Just look at his cell structure, his central nervous system, his gut, his lungs—and his brain. Have you ever seen anything like that before? Anywhere?"

"No," said Roche. "But that doesn't necessarily mean—"

"I understand your reluctance to accept the results of the test," Teh said. "But I'm afraid there can be no doubt. Our diagnostic database is customized to the Pristine form, and precisely because it's not equipped to deal with data outside certain guidelines, it is ideally suited to provide a direct comparison with what we would regard as usual. For instance, Adoni Cane's cellular structure is more compact than normal, resulting in tissue that is more elastic, yet stronger; likewise his skeleton is denser, his intestinal tract longer, his lungs of superior capacity, his heart more powerful, and his immune system more efficient than what would be regarded as typical of a Pristine Human. He possesses several glands that do not correspond with any I am aware of, yet lacks certain vestigial organs we all take for granted. His brain displays a quite remarkable number of structural anomalies, and his chromosomal map matches no known genotype.

"In short," Teh concluded, "Adoni Cane is *not* Pristine—although what he is, exactly, has yet to be determined."

"Any guesses?" asked Neva.

"Well, I'm not qualified enough to even guess," Teh said. Then, for Roche's benefit, he added, "You must understand, Commander, that we have no schools here. What training we indigenes receive comes from the convicts. My own was courtesy of a woman sent to Sciacca's World for malpractice." He smiled at a private memory. "She assured me she knew what she was talking about, even though her knowledge was not—"

"Don't feel the need to justify yourself, Sylvester," intruded Haid. "No one is doubting your ability."

Roche wasn't so confident, but she said nothing.

Embarrassed, Teh turned again to his notes. "Well," he said, "it seems to me that the differences between Cane and the Pristine Human are not random. That is, in each and every case they serve to make him superior to the norm. His kidneys absorb more toxins; he can see and hear things we cannot without artificial amplification; his tissue repairs faster than ours."

Not for the first time that day, Roche looked with some amazement at the thin scar that was all that remained of the gash Cane had suffered at Houghton's Cross.

"In fact," Teh continued, "the only area in which he is inferior to anyone sitting at this table is reproduction."

"He's sterile?" Sabra asked the question without taking her eyes from Cane's impassive face, her lips pursed in a mixture of repugnance and admiration. "A superhuman drone?"

"That would be one interpretation of the data, yes," said Teh.

"But he looks so *normal*."

"His appearance does belie the uniqueness of the rest of his physique," said Teh. "And I dare say that this has been deliberately programmed—"

"Programmed?" interrupted Emmerik.

"Isn't it obvious?" said Teh. "He can't be an Exotic we've never encountered before. Someone knew what they were doing when they built him. Someone who knows more about genetics and the Human form than I ever will."

Haid allowed the others a moment to absorb this before asking the obvious question:

"But why?"

Roche watched the faces of everyone in the room as they thought it through. Haid had had time to reach the obvious conclusion, as had Sylvester Teh. Neva shook her head in irritation; Sabra's lips pursed even tighter; Emmerik scowled deeply; the two security guards stiffened. Roche kept her expression carefully neutral, although the answer to the question seemed obvious enough, and indeed disturbing.

Surprisingly, Cane was the first to speak.

"To allow me to infiltrate Pristine society, I imagine." His voice was even and uncolored by emotion. He might have been talking about someone else. "Given the abilities I possess, I can only be either a spy or a weapon."

"Exactly." Haid leaned forward, his one arm splayed flat on the stone tabletop. "Emmerik warned me about your ability to kill without apparent remorse, when you need to. He and Neva also witnessed your extraordinary skill in combat; anyone able to disarm powered armor with hands cuffed deserves respect in my book—or suspicion. And there can be no questioning your intelligence, either. I have no doubt that, given time, you could do almost anything you wanted. But that brings us no closer to the answer: what *do* you want to do?" Haid shrugged helplessly. "I doubt that even you know the answer to that, do you?"

Cane shook his head.

"So it seems more appropriate to tackle the problem not from the *why* angle, but rather the *who*."

Cane shrugged. "Someone who doesn't like Pristine Humans?"

"That could be any one of a number of Castes," said Emmerik wryly.

"True." Roche knew that although none of the seven local Castes hated Pristine Humans specifically, at least one Caste's members despised everyone but themselves. And there were a number of splinter groups who would gladly accept responsibility. "But that leaves us with plenty of suspects."

"The Eckandar Trade Axis is the most advanced in this area," said Teh, "and it guards its knowledge jealously. Or so I've heard."

"It's true," Roche agreed. "The Eckandi will sell just about anything other than genetic technology."

"I don't understand." Sabra frowned. "What use would Eckandi genetics be to Pristines?"

"We all spring from a common, carbon-based organism," explained Teh. "Our genetic codes may speak a different language now, but it's still all written on the same paper. Genome maps and so on are frequently interchangeable."

"So they're the obvious suspects. Aren't they?" Sabra turned to face Roche when she hesitated to agree.

"Not necessarily," said Roche. "The Dato have been interested, too. One of their pre-Commonwealth leaders—Ataman Vereine, I believe—almost went to war with the Eckandar Trade Axis when they refused to sell what they knew. She may have got what she wanted, or developed it herself."

"I thought they'd moved into cyber-assist programs instead," said Haid.

"Maybe," said Roche, although she had heard nothing of the sort. "That could be a cover, though."

"True. Cane might be a Dato spy, which would explain why he was planted on an Armada vessel." Haid counted on his fingers. "That makes two. Who else?"

"The Kesh hate everyone," Emmerik mused, echoing Roche's earlier thought, "but they've never shown interest in this sort of warfare."

"And the Surin Agora is too busy squabbling within itself to attack anyone else," said Roche. "The same applies to most of the other major governments. Why spend so much time and money fighting Pristines when there are already enough problems at home?"

"If Veden was awake, we could ask him," said Neva. "About the Eckandi, I mean."

"He is awake," said Haid. "But he was not well enough to attend, I'm afraid. The nanomachines we had were an old paramilitary design, barely sufficient. Still, I doubt whether he would tell us even if he did know. Neither the Eckandar Trade Axis nor the Commerce Artel would ever risk spreading publicity like that."

"Maybe we're looking in the wrong place." Teh's voice intruded softly, uneasily, into the debate. "We're looking all around us for suspects, when maybe we should be looking in another direction entirely."

"Like where?" asked Roche. "Within? If you're suggesting that COE Intelligence—"

"No, no," cut in Teh quickly. "I mean into the *past*." He leaned back into his chair, away from the frowns and puzzled expressions around the table. "There was another group apart from the Eckandar Trade Axis which possessed more than the average working knowledge of genetics. In fact, if I'm not mistaken, they were the original source of the Eckandi's current know-how."

"Who?" said Sabra.

"A splinter group from the older Pristine governments. Pre-Commonwealth—even pre-Dominion, I think—but definitely local. Obsessed with Transcendence by means of bio-modification. The Eckandi helped them build a base, if I remember correctly, and they traded knowledge for services. I don't recall what happened to them—except that there was some sort of backlash—but if what they gave the Eckandar Trade Axis was only a small amount of their complete knowledge, then they might have been just the right people to design something like Cane."

"I've never heard of anyone like that," said Haid.

"I have," said Emmerik. "My mother used to tell me stories about them when I was a child, along with all the other Transcendence stories about the Crescend."

Haid faced Emmerik. "What were they called?"

Emmerik shrugged, but it was Teh that spoke.

"I can't remember," said the physician. "And I'll admit it seems far-fetched—"

"More than that. It sounds crazy." Sabra didn't bother to hide her scepticism. "How long must Cane have been drifting out there for him to be one of them?"

"A *long* time." Teh shook his head. "Hundreds, maybe thousands, of years."

"And *was* he?" the woman asked Roche.

"I don't know," she said. "The science team on the *Midnight* might have analyzed the corrosion on the hull of the capsule, but their data was lost with the ship."

"It's pointless asking anyway." Sabra looked away. "No one could survive more than a month or two in a life-support capsule."

"That's the usual assumption," said Haid. "Which was why Sylvester suspected that such a stretch might have caused Cane's amnesia." He sighed. "And it seems we've come full circle. Does anybody have anything they'd like to say that hasn't already been covered?"

Sabra raised her hand. When Haid looked to her, she said, "He's obviously dangerous. We should get rid of him now.

Turn him in to the wardens before he has a chance to destroy us. He only *says* he doesn't remember anything, after all. We would be gambling an awful lot simply on the strength of his word."

Haid grimaced. "How about you, Emmerik? What are your feelings on this?"

The Mbatan looked uncertainly at Cane, then back to Haid. "Having seen him fight, I'm still wary." After a few seconds of staring into Cane's unblinking eyes, he said, "But I've decided to trust him. He fought for *us*, after all."

"Whatever he was, and is," put in Neva, "he's on Roche's side. So as long as she remains with us, I don't think we're in any danger."

"Roche?" Haid indicated that it was her turn to speak.

"I can understand your suspicion," she said, "and your reluctance to put faith in someone you hardly know. But I'm in the same position. For the most part you've treated me fairly, and I respect that. As long as our goals remain the same, you can count on me for support. And I too believe you can count on Cane as well."

Haid nodded. "What about you, Cane? What do *you* think we should do with you? Dispose of you, or use you as a weapon?"

"The answer seems obvious." Cane smiled slightly, the only expression he had worn throughout the meeting. "If I am a biological weapon—one that has been programmed by others, what's more—then I am inherently unreliable. My instinct tells me to follow Roche, but that may change at any moment. Who knows when my programming will take over? Or what I might do? If I was in your position, faced with such a choice, I would rely on my own abilities and not take a chance on something so unpredictable."

Haid's expression was one of bafflement. "You're suggesting that we get rid of you?"

"No. I'm simply saying that that is what *I* would do in your position." His smile widened. "Or try to, anyway."

Haid called the meeting to an end moments later, saying he needed to think prior to reaching a decision. Before he could leave, Roche asked if she could go to the medical center.

"I don't know." Haid didn't hide his reservations. "Veden only regained consciousness an hour ago, and I don't think you're particularly high on his visiting list."

"I won't stay long," she said, not sure whether she was telling the truth. Teh's point about the Eckandi had been an interesting one. If Veden knew something, she might be able to persuade Maii to lever it out of him. "I just want to get my shoulder checked. While I'm there, I can make sure he's okay so I can put Maii at ease."

Haid hesitated. "All right. But leave when Sylvester tells you to."

"Don't worry. I only want a couple of minutes."

Haid nodded reluctantly. "You know the way?"

"That's okay," Sabra said, stepping forward. "I'll take her there."

"Thanks." Surprised by the friendly gesture, Roche almost missed the look that passed between the rebel leader and his assistant: a look of warning from Haid, and resentment from Sabra.

"Don't worry," said the woman. "I'll take good care of her."

"You do that." Haid turned back to Roche. "I'll see you later."

The two guards escorted Cane out of the conference room at the same time Roche and Sabra left, causing a moment's confusion in the narrow doorway. The corridor outside took them to an elevator that was, again, barely large enough for the five of them.

"We'll wait for the next one," said Sabra.

"No, it's all right." Roche slid into the carriage between one of the guards and the wall. "We'll fit."

The doors closed with a sullen hiss. As the elevator jerked upward, the butt of one guard's pistol jabbed Roche in the hip. She twisted away from him in the confined space.

"If you think this is bad," he said, smiling, "be thankful you're not topside. Delcasalle's got patrols in every quarter looking for you."

"He has?" Roche's brow creased. "I wasn't told that."

"Ameidio doesn't tell you everything," Sabra said, her eyes flashing. The good humor that had prompted her to take Roche to the sick bay appeared to be waning fast.

"I don't expect him to," said Roche.

"Really?" The elevator paused as they passed a floor, causing the carriage to sway. "It doesn't look like that to me."

Roche fixed her with a calm and unflinching stare. "No? What *does* it look like to you, Sabra?"

Sabra scowled silently to herself and faced the dented and scrawled doors of the elevator. Roche glimpsed one of the guards in the corner grimacing.

"There's a rumor in the ranks," said Cane. "I overhead it before the meeting. It's said that you're a spy for the wardens."

Roche groaned. "You're kidding."

"Unfortunately not," said Cane.

"But what about the *Midnight*? Houghton's Cross?"

"The full truth of your identity is being kept secret to prevent word leaking to Enforcement plants on the surface," said Cane. "In the absence of information, speculation spreads."

"But . . ." Roche fought to contain her sense of outrage in words. "If that's the case, then why would Haid be telling me anything at all?"

"It's not hard to seduce a cripple," said Sabra coldly.

"What?" Roche snapped.

"Why not?" Sabra's face flushed an angry red. "He was a proud man once, before coming here. And, as they say, a beautiful woman is a powerful poison."

"Your anger betrays your jealousy, Sabra," said Roche, fighting to keep her own temper in check. Then: "Is that what you really think of me?"

Sabra glared at her through the flickering light of the elevator. "I don't know what to think of you, Roche. But I'll tell you this much: I don't trust you *or* your friend here." She glanced pointedly at Cane. "And jealousy has nothing to do with it. I just don't like the idea of Haid's judgment being affected at this stage by some misplaced trust. It's too dangerous to our operations."

"Did he give you any reason to question his judgment at the meeting?"

The elevator shuddered to a halt. "We get out here," Sabra said, ignoring the question. "You coming or not?"

Roche squeezed her way past the guard and out of the elevator, her pulse racing with suppressed anger. What was wrong with the woman? If she wanted to make a scene, why do it now? Why didn't she do it back at the meeting?

"This way." Sabra headed off along the corridor without looking back. Roche gritted her teeth and followed.

"Listen," she said, her shoes slapping on the damp floor of the passage. "You can't be that worried about Cane and me, surely. Whatever your problem is, I'd rather you tell me now."

"I think we've already said enough, don't you?" Sabra's back remained rigid.

"No, I don't think we've even started—"

"Then let's not." Sabra stopped in mid-stride and turned to face her. Even in the poor light from the few working lamps, Roche could see hatred behind red-rimmed eyes. "Or I might be tempted to leave you down here."

Roche noted for the first time the grimy stains covering the walls and floor of the corridor, and realized with some alarm that they were in a part of the underground complex she had never seen before.

"Where the hell is this place?" she said uneasily. "What are you playing at?"

"Nothing." Sabra turned away and resumed her walk into the shadows. Over her shoulder she said, "I told Haid I'd take care of you, and that's exactly what I'll do."

Roche followed a half-step behind, matching the other woman's swift pace with stubborn determination. Whatever Sabra was up to—a test, perhaps, of the newcomer—she resolved to meet it without flinching.

<They named themselves after the system they colonized.> The Box's words intruded upon Roche's discomfort, and she fought back a curse. The last thing she needed at this moment was an interruption.

<What?>

<The splinter group Sylvester Teh mentioned,> said the Box. <They took the name of the system the Eckandar Trade Axis helped them take over.>

<So?>

<It may be relevant, Morgan. If you ever hope to understand Cane, you must consider all the available data. Otherwise—>

<Okay, okay. Just tell me what you have on them.>

<They reached their peak and were destroyed in the 37th Millennium, long before the Commonwealth reached this segment of the galaxy. They were a source of unrest for decades, until an alliance formed among their neighbors dedicated to putting a stop to them. In '577, at the climax of the Scion War, a flotilla of allied forces encircled their base, which they destroyed in order to prevent it being captured. The resulting explosion annihilated them as well, of course, but also decimated the flotilla. Of the four stations involved in the battle, only one survived, and that was severely damaged. So embarrassed was the alliance that the leaders of the day ordered the event stricken from history. They even closed the anchor point leading to the system to stop anyone finding out.> The Box paused—for effect, it seemed to Roche—then added: <Nothing survived of the base, and the rest of the system is an unsalvageable ruin.>

<No relics?>

<None known. No survivors, either, if that is your next question. The Sol Apotheosis Movement was, among other things, extremely thorough.>

<The who?>

<The Sol Apotheosis Movement. That was the name they chose—after the name of the system, as I said.>

Morgan absorbed this in silence for a moment. The name didn't ring a bell, and didn't seem particularly relevant. <And they tried to Transcend by altering their genetic code? I didn't think it could be done that way.> Most Transcendences took place when AI technology and consciousness research overlapped, resulting in Human-based artificial minds far larger and more complex than anything that could be housed in a biological frame.

<Conventional wisdom is in accord with that statement, yes,> the Box said. <My records indicate that their experiment, like others before it, was a failure. However—>

<Wait.> Sabra had stopped at one of the primitive wall phones that were scattered here and there throughout the rebel headquarters. Indicating for Roche to wait out of earshot, she made a quick call.

While she was doing so, Roche wandered back along the

corridor, peering through doors at random. None of the rooms was occupied, and they hadn't been for some time. The floors were covered with a thin slime created from years of dust mixed with the moisture seeping down from the ceiling, and the walls had cracked and peeled with age. The farther they moved into this area of the rebels' headquarters, the more decrepit it became.

Stepping out of one room back into the hallway, Roche froze, her attention focusing upon a distant noise.

<Don't say anything, Box.>

<I wasn't going to, Morgan.>

<Quiet!>

She heard it again. A faint sound from the direction they had just come, right at the edge of hearing.

"When you're ready, Commander." Sabra's voice echoed down the corridor from behind her. Roche turned to face the woman—

And raised her hands.

"I'm not going to pretend I like you, Commander." Sabra kept the pistol aimed squarely at her stomach. "But I don't want to shoot you, either. So just walk along the wall, slowly, and keep doing so until I tell you to stop. Okay?"

Roche nodded, noting the tremor in Sabra's hands and the desperate look in her eyes. "Okay."

"Then let's move."

One step at a time, without breaking eye contact, Morgan began to move along the wall. Sabra swiveled to follow her, keeping well out of arm's reach. When Roche had passed her, she waved the pistol. "No, don't lower your hands."

Roche ignored the pain in her injured shoulder as best she could and walked along the passageway. Twenty meters ahead, the corridor branched into a T junction, with both arms of the T dark. It was clear to Roche that they had almost reached the edge of the inhabited areas and were about to enter the unrestored sections of the old university.

Whatever was about to happen to her, she supposed, would happen to her there. If she was going to do something, it had to be before then.

"I don't suppose you'd like to explain—"

"No." Sabra's voice was curt. "I know what I'm doing."

"Whatever it is, I guess it involves whoever's following us, right?"

"Please, Commander. Don't be so stupid. No one's been this way for years."

"Sabra, I'm serious. There *is* someone back there, and if they're not with you . . ."

The sound of Sabra's footsteps slowed, then stopped altogether. "Wait," she said.

Roche glanced around quickly and, seeing Sabra's back turned, made a dash for the intersection. The pistol cracked loudly, and something snatched at her side. Without breaking stride, Roche took the corner at a sprint, catching herself roughly on the wall as she did. Meters behind, the wet slap of Sabra's shoes followed.

The right-hand arm of the T was lit only by infrequent maintenance lights. Little could be seen through the gloom. The corridor angled to the left, and Roche made it around the bend just as Sabra fired a second time. The shot went well clear, ricocheting brightly in the near darkness. Roche's feet slipped in the slime as she took another corner. Quickly regaining her footing, she plunged ahead through the dimly lit corridors, dodging the occasional pile of rubble littering the floor. Row after row of inviting doorways passed her, but she ignored them. Her only hope was to lose Sabra, or somehow to double back to the T intersection.

Roche's long stride and years of exercise gradually widened her lead, although the sound of Sabra's footfalls was still too close for comfort. She took another left-hand turn, stumbled over a pile of broken furniture, then a right. Her shoulder began to ache. If she could only find a *weapon*—something solid enough that wouldn't disintegrate at the slightest touch—

Another corner brought her to a door. Through the light of a faded lamp above it, she saw the letters of a damaged sign: *F re E t*.

The door was locked.

Out of options, Roche spun to face the way she had come. She launched herself forward at the exact moment Sabra rounded the corner.

Taken by surprise, Sabra barely had time to raise the gun

before Roche pushed it aside. Letting her weight carry her forward, she met Sabra's stomach with her shoulder, forcing them both to the ground. A third shot sparked crazily in the confined space, making Roche's ears ring.

Sabra punched wildly in the darkness and connected once above Roche's right ear. Roche kicked back and was gratified to feel her foot meet flesh. She grasped for purchase on her struggling adversary, wanting to use her Armada training but failing to obtain a grip; the data glove made her left hand stiff and unwieldy. The butt of the gun swung back to strike her injured shoulder, and she gasped involuntarily. Sabra rolled, brought her knee upward into her stomach. Roche fought the impulse to curl into a ball, then swung the Box's valise into exposed ribs and heard bone crack.

Sabra hissed and wrenched the pistol free. Roche tried to regain her footing and slipped in the moisture. Her flailing arm knocked the gun aside for a moment, but it returned a split-second later. Sabra's face behind it grimaced in triumph. She fired at exactly the moment Roche brought the valise up to protect her face.

The impact of the bullet knocked the valise from her hands. She kicked both legs into Sabra's chest with all her strength. The woman lifted into the air with relative ease, striking the wall on the far side of the cul-de-sac. Roche watched in total bewilderment. The kick hadn't been that hard. . . .

Then she glimpsed a shadowy figure rush past her through the gloom, its right arm still outstretched from the blow that had struck her assailant.

Sabra disappeared behind a flurry of limbs, screamed once, then reappeared a moment later, pinned by a hand at her throat against the wall under the broken sign.

Her face twisted into a rictus of pain and surprise. Roche sympathized. It had all happened so fast that not even she could quite believe it.

The arm that held the woman to the wall was attached by muscular shoulders to a profile Roche recognized instantly.

"She's dead," said Cane, his voice hushed and breathless, almost in awe. His eyes were fixed on the dying woman's face. "She just hasn't realized it yet."

Roche watched in horror as Sabra struggled once against the grip around her throat, then went still. Slowly, the pain went out of her eyes—although the fear remained.

"You can let her go, Cane." Roche clambered slowly upright, wincing. "*Cane!*"

"You die so easily," he mused, almost to himself, and let the woman's body slide to the floor. He followed it with his eyes, then turned to look over his shoulder at Roche. Seeing her shock, he said, "I don't enjoy it, you know."

"No—" She took a deep breath, and amazed herself by believing him. "I believe you."

"But I should," he said softly. "I feel it inside. I was made to kill, wasn't I?"

Roche gathered the courage to touch his arm. His skin was hot and dry and seemed to quiver under her fingertips. "I'm not going to damn you for that," she said. "You probably just saved my life—again."

He shook his head. She sensed that he was clearing his mind rather than disagreeing with her comment. She removed her hand.

When she gingerly touched behind her ear, where Sabra had punched her, her fingers came away slippery with blood: another injury to add to her collection. As she felt her side where Sabra's first shot had nicked her uniform, the tug of the chain on her wrist reminded her of the valise. There was a slight dent where the bullet had struck, but otherwise it was undamaged.

<I'm still here, Morgan.>

<I didn't doubt it, Box,> she said. <Not for a moment.>

Glancing down to Sabra's body, Roche sighed and said, "We'd better head back. If you remember the way, that is."

Cane nodded numbly in the near darkness. "Should we bring her with us?"

"No," she said, already dreading the reception they would receive. "I think she can wait here a little longer. We're going to have enough problems as it is."

14

Halfway along the corridor leading back to the elevator shaft, Roche's left arm began to tingle as data flowed through it.

<Box? What's going on?>

<I am in communication with Ameidio Haid,> replied the AI. <He desires to know your whereabouts.>

<Have you told him?>

<No.>

<Then don't. And don't tell him what happened, either.>

<He is very insistent, Morgan.> The Box paused, as though listening to another conversation, then added, <The two guards have been found.>

Roche groaned aloud. Turning to Cane, she said, "You didn't kill your guards as well, did you?"

"No. I knocked them out on the floor above where you got out." He shrugged. "I had no choice. If I was going to help you, I needed to act immediately."

Roche nodded, grateful for small mercies: at least they only had one body to explain, not three.

"But how did you *know*?" she said after a few more steps along the wet and litter-strewn floor. "About Sabra, I mean."

"She said she was taking you to the medical center," Cane replied. "But she got out of the elevator on the twenty-third floor. The medical center is on the fourteenth floor."

He made it seem simple. Almost too simple. She knew how it would sound to the rebels: easier to believe that Cane had deliberately set out to follow Roche and Sabra with the intention of killing the woman who had spoken out against him in the meeting. Even Roche found his story slightly incredible.

Yet Cane himself had urged caution at the meeting, agreeing with Sabra on almost every point. That alone was enough to convince Roche he was not lying—that and the fact that he had saved her life. But would it be enough for the rebels?

<Okay, Box. Tell Haid I'm on my way back with Cane. And tell him I need to talk to him. But don't tell him why, or what happened to Sabra. We need to handle this carefully.>

<Understood.> The Box fell silent, leaving Roche to consider how best to break the news.

Cane walked solidly beside her, as untroubled and indefatigable as ever—and with an expression that was, as always, impossible to read. His pace matched hers perfectly—slow but steady, in sympathy with her conflicting need both to hurry and to nurse new injuries. The fleeting moment of vulnerability she thought she had detected in him earlier had long since passed. She wondered if anyone could truly reach the innermost depths of him; indeed, so perfect was his control that sometimes it seemed as though he had no depth at all. Just another soldier doing his duty, without remorse or doubt—a robot in Pristine Human form, programmed to kill.

Yet Sabra *had* touched him; she was sure of that. Somehow. On a level Roche could never hope to reach, although she was—for the moment at least—his putative ally.

The remainder of the walk to the elevator passed in silence. As they rounded the final bend and the doors came into view, Roche realized that she had hardly begun to de-

cide how she would break the news to Haid. Every time she
went over it in her head, it sounded clumsy and cliched:

Sabra started it—
Cane acted in self-defense—
I had no choice—
If there was any other way . . .

The elevator approached all too quickly. Had Haid followed Roche's request, he would already be waiting for her
on one of the upper floors. She had only minutes left in
which to decide how she was going to handle the explanation.

When they came to a halt by the doors, Roche eyed Cane
uncertainly. "Maybe you should stay down here for a
while," she said. "Until things quiet down."

"No," he said. "Better to get it over with."

He reached out for the elevator button. Before he could
touch it, however, the doors pulled back with a hiss.

Facing them, in the elevator, were Haid and three rebel
guards. Roche automatically backed away; Cane stood his
ground without apparent concern for the projectile rifles
raised and pointing at them.

Haid waved at the guards to lower their weapons and
stepped out to greet the two of them. "Sorry to startle you,"
he said. "I thought it best to meet you halfway."

"How did you . . . ?" Roche fumbled for the words.

"Find you?" Haid smiled. "Simple, really. We triangu-
lated the data glove's short-wave transmission, tracing the
signal back through the receiving stations throughout the
building. What the Box told me only confirmed what we had
already learned for ourselves."

Annoyance and discomfort suddenly tangled inside her.
"You didn't trust us?"

"One of the most important rules in covert operations is
never to design a safe house without a back door. This way
leads to one of ours, and given what you've learned since
you arrived, it seemed sensible to—".

He stopped suddenly, peering along the dim corridor.

"Where's Sabra?" he asked. Catching the dark expression
on Roche's face, he added: "What's happened to her?"

Roche opened her mouth to reply, but Cane spoke before the half-planned words had even formed in her mind.

"She's dead," he said simply and without emotion.

Haid's face hardened, and he stepped back as though Cane had physically struck him. The rifles came up again, and this time the rebel leader did not order them down.

"You're not joking, are you?" His artificial eye narrowed, fixing itself upon Cane.

"No," said Cane, returning Haid's monocular challenge evenly. "I killed her."

"I can explain." Roche stepped in quickly. "Please, Haid, just give me a chance. It's not what it seems."

"I hope so," said Haid, keeping his glare on Cane. "I honestly hope so."

"Okay." The scarred woman made no effort to conceal her hostility. "Tell me again, and this time don't leave anything out."

Roche floundered for a moment. Leave anything out? She had told her story as completely the last time as the time before, and the time before that, when Haid had interviewed her. What could she possibly have forgotten?

Then she realized: this was an oft-used trick of interrogation. By making the suspect feel that she had omitted something from a fabricated tale, new and crucial information might sometimes be forthcoming. Confession by overcompensation.

Roche sighed, and patiently began the recital from the beginning. She had left the meeting with Sabra, and had exited the elevator on the twenty-third floor. . . .

The woman rerecorded Roche's story, along with each and every nuance of her face. A thick scar warped the woman's own upper lip into a permanent sneer, and Roche wondered if a psychological trauma had similarly twisted her personality. This, the fourth time Roche had described the events of the last few hours, elicited no response other than wordless, yet obvious, contempt.

Apart from the woman, Roche was alone in the holding bay. Two armed rebels guarded the other side of the door. Cane had been removed to another cell after their initial interrogation by Haid, and Roche hadn't seen him since. If he was alive or dead, she had no way of knowing—although she suspected the former was more likely to be true, knowing the man's amazing constitution.

Halfway through her "confession," the intercom buzzed. The woman put aside her work slate to take the call, casting a warning look at Roche as she did.

Haid's voice over the intercom was terse. "That's enough for now, Rasia. Have the commander escorted back to her room and make sure she stays there. Tell the escort to talk to no one on the way. I don't want word leaking out before I'm ready."

Roche pushed forward to the intercom. "Ameidio, this is Roche. What the hell's going on?"

"I'll call you when I've decided." With a click, he severed the line.

Roche backed away from the intercom as the guards entered the room. "Okay, okay." She let herself be led from the holding bay, with the scarred woman bringing up the rear. She had no choice. Until she spoke to Haid, her options were severely limited.

On the way to her room, she passed a couple of faces she recognized from the refectory the previous day. One nodded at her, showing no awareness of the events that had transpired since they had last met. Roche nodded back, unable to prevent the blush that spread up her neck and into her hairline. She cursed herself for *feeling* like a traitor.

When they reached her room, the guards keyed it open and motioned for her to enter. She did so, noting first of all that Maii had left during her absence, and second that the lock on the inside of the door had been disabled. She turned to protest, but was met with the stony sneer of the scarred woman.

"Don't expect mercy," said the woman. "We look after our own down here."

With that, the woman slammed the door shut and locked it. When the sound of footsteps outside had faded into silence, she let go the breath she had been holding.

Mercy? Roche wasn't expecting mercy. She would settle for justice, any day.

Still, she supposed she shouldn't be too hasty. In their situation, she might have behaved the same.

<I have been denied access to the rebels' security system,> announced the Box into the silence.

She shrugged and sat down on the edge of the bed. "I guess that's to be expected," she said.

<If not a little frustrating.> The Box sounded annoyed, though Roche knew that this was impossible. <From the moment Haid learned what happened, all official channels have been closed.>

"How about unofficial?"

<We are too deep below ground to access anything useful. The most I can manage is an edited feed of the local IDnet outlet.>

"Okay," she said, lying back on the bunk. "Show me."

Her left eye greyed for a moment, then cleared. The familiar stream of news, from places near and distant, flowed past her: wars, accidents, negotiations, science, deaths. Even after so few days trapped on Sciacca's World, much of it made reference to current events that were unfamiliar to her, making her feel isolated from the rest of the COE and the galaxy beyond. At least three major conflicts near the Commonwealth were completely unfamiliar to her, and there were many more beyond—more than she was sure was normal. She wondered if the background level of violence in the galaxy had indeed risen without her being aware of it, or if that impression was merely a result of her recent isolation.

One name, however, stood out: Palasian System.

She recalled hearing about it being quarantined just prior to her leaving the *Midnight*. Now it had been declared the site of a "major catastrophe" and sealed off to all traffic. Not even aid or rescue ships could breach the blockade. No explanation was offered as to the cause of the catastrophe, however, before the data stream moved on to another war that had broken out in a distant part of the galaxy. Whatever had happened to Palasian System, it must have been serious to warrant such utter isolation.

Suddenly struck by a thought, she turned her attention back to the Box. "Have you been monitoring this?" she asked.

<As a matter of course. Why do you ask?>

"Has there been any mention of the *Midnight*?"

<None, I'm afraid. Either word has not reached the Armada, or the information is being suppressed. Both possibilities are disturbing. Perhaps help is not on the way, as we had hoped.>

Roche nodded. "Or they want to take the Dato by surprise."

<Unlikely. Any Armada ships entering the system will be visible well before any confrontation would be possible.>

"True." Roche frowned as another thought occurred to her. "But why would—?"

The sound of the door opening interrupted her in midsentence, although the question remained sharp in her thoughts: *Why would the COE Armada suppress the information?*

Making a mental note to follow this up later, she rose to greet her visitor.

"Roche," said Haid. The rebel leader looked haggard and drawn, as though he hadn't slept for a week. He was alone.

"I would invite you in," Roche said, unable to keep the bitterness from her voice. "But that seems inappropriate given the circumstances."

Haid closed the door behind him and turned to face her. "You have no reason to resent me," he said. "I'm not here officially."

"Does that mean you've reached a decision?"

"Well, your story checks out," he said. "As I said earlier, there's a shaft leading from the old sector to the surface— our back door. At the exit from the shaft, we found Edan Malogorski. Sabra had arranged to meet him there to take you to the landing field. It looks like she was going to sell you to the wardens for the bounty."

Roche sat up on the bunk. "That seems obvious."

"Maybe." The rebel leader sighed. "I have my doubts, though."

"I thought you just said that my story checked out."

"I have no doubts about what she intended to do; the facts are irrefutable. The why, though, is a different matter. In the elevator, according to your statement, Sabra said that she thought Cane was under your control. It's my guess she believed that by getting rid of you, she'd be rid of Cane as well. Maybe she was more concerned with my safety than the money."

"And maybe you're being overcharitable regarding her motives." Roche remembered the implied jealousy in the woman's words, the fierce resentment she had harbored toward the new woman in town. "She certainly made it clear, from the day I arrived, that she'd rather Cane and I weren't around. Regardless of Cane's past, or my dealings with you—"

"She was simply wary of you," Haid interrupted. "As we all are with strangers." Haid paced the length of the room once, then returned to face her. "If I *am* being overcharitable, as you say, then it's because I knew her better than you did. I served with her when she was a lieutenant on the *Transpicuous* before I went out on my own. When I was sentenced here . . ." He filled the pause with a sigh. "It was she who took me from the gutter. Everything I've done here, it was with her aid. If she had an ulterior motive in turning you in, then it was to help me, not for the money."

Haid stopped talking, his one empty eye socket red. Roche could sense his pain as palpably as the dust on his clothes, in the tone of voice and the lines of his face. He needed to believe what he was saying, needed to believe that his old friend hadn't betrayed his trust. And Roche could sympathize. She herself had been betrayed often enough in her youth, to the point where she had avoided close friendships ever since. Who was she to call into question the strength of a relationship she had had no part of? Furthermore, she conceded, he might even have been right.

"Unfortunately," Haid continued after a moment, "the facts have leaked. And they are damning, whichever way they are interpreted."

Roche took a deep breath. She could sense that they were approaching the real reason for his visit. "Go on."

"Well, on the one hand, I'm being pressured to turn you in myself, by those who think Sabra had the right idea. They're supported by another camp, who believe that you and Cane led Sabra into the old quarter to murder her. Taken together, these two factions comprise a majority of us down here."

"But you don't agree?"

"No," he said. "And therein lies the problem. If I decide not to turn you in, I'll be disobeying the wishes of the very people I'm supposed to serve." Haid ran his artificial fingers across his ebony scalp. "At the heart of the matter is the fact that I'm an outsider myself; some of the indigenes have always resented me taking over, and they will use that lever to call for a no-confidence vote. Given their clear majority in this matter, I'm bound to lose. And the new leader will no doubt turn you in anyway."

Roche kept her emotions carefully hidden. "So what happens now?"

"After all the resentment and anger you've stirred up, I don't really have much choice." Haid's mouth tightened. "We need an outlet, or the problem will just get worse. The last thing we need right now is a leadership crisis."

"But you *can't* blame us," Roche said urgently, sensing her last chance slipping through her fingers. "Make Cane and me scapegoats—kill us, or whatever—and the High Equity Court will never listen to you."

"I know that." Haid shook his head. "And Veden agrees with you. But there are two hundred Enforcers searching the city for you as we speak. Five of our safe houses have been breached. Twenty people have been taken for interrogation. Five have been killed for 'obstructing investigations.'

"And then there are the Dato. A landing party touched down yesterday and entered the city six hours ago. Reports are coming in of fires in the old subway, lit by the squad. It looks like they've found an entrance to our underground network. If that's the case, then it's only a matter of time before they find us here." Haid glanced briefly around at the walls of the cell before his gaze fell back upon Roche. "Twenty Enforcers we could bribe. Fifty we could fight in self-defense. But two hundred and a well-armed Dato squad . . ." He shrugged helplessly.

"But we need to do *something*," he went on. "Which is why I've decided to take you with us."

Roche studied him quizzically for a moment. "Take us where?"

"To the landing field, of course. We have to attack while they're busy in the city, and hope your plan works."

"*My* plan?"

"I spoke to Neva and Emmerik. They believe it's sound, and I'm prepared to go with their judgment. They'll be in the attacking party, along with you and me and five others."

"But what about the command codes? There's no point attacking until—"

"We have the codes. Maii learned them an hour ago."

"And weapons? We're hopelessly outgunned for a frontal assault—"

"Don't worry about that. I'll fix it."

Roche took a deep breath, resigning herself to the fact that the decision had been made, and nothing she said could change it. "We need time to prepare, then."

"We have two hours." Haid's artificial eye regarded her implacably. "You'll suit up and meet the others as we leave. Until then, you stay here." He reached into his jacket and removed a work slate—a small processor with a flatscreen and compressed keyboard—which he handed to her. "Whatever happens, we can't just sit back idly here, waiting for the Dato Bloc to arrive. You can still be useful, if you want." He nodded at the slate in Roche's hands. "The others will be busy getting equipment ready. Study this for us; make *sure* the plan will work. I'll send someone down with Cane as soon as we're ready.

"But remember: this isn't an official action. As far as the indigenes are concerned, I'm still considering your fate. When we leave, it'll supposedly be to turn you in. So do your best to look cowed, and don't breathe a word of this to anyone else."

With that, he keyed the door open and left.

Roche activated the slate and sat back down on the bed to study the image that appeared on the small screen and the heading above it:

PORT PARVATI SECURITY: CONFIDENTIAL

She stared at it for a moment, unable to absorb the sudden reversal. Haid was right, of course: if the Dato were actively hunting her, it would be only a matter of time before they found her here. They needed to move somewhere else, somewhere safe. But there was nowhere safe on the entire planet, nowhere to hide. And if the Enforcers truly were distracted by their own searches, then it made sense to attack the landing field while their defenses were down—to hunt instead of being hunted.

Yet, somehow, it was too much too soon. Her ribs still ached, and her newly injured side throbbed. She needed rest, time to gather her resources. Her allegiances—with Haid, with Cane, with the Box—were still too fragile to test during an all-out attack on the Enforcement stronghold. If any one of them failed, she would be worse off than when she had started.

And hadn't there already been enough death?

Even as her doubts assailed her, however, her conviction to the plan remained strong. She had a mission—to deliver the Box to COE Intelligence HQ—and this was the best way to achieve it. If she was to leave the planet—which she had to do, in order to succeed—then this was the only way.

She had no options anymore. Circumstances dictated that she should fight, so she would do so to the best of her abilities, and with every resource she could muster, external and internal.

In the end, whether she failed or succeeded, at least she could say that she had tried.

<Box?> The AI didn't answer. The tingling in her arm had returned, however, and she wasn't certain what to make of that. Still, she could analyze the landing field's defenses just as well without the Box's help.

Lying back on the bed, she began to work.

15

After an hour of silence, the Box suddenly returned:

<Morgan, get ready.>

"Box!" Roche sat up with a start, the slate slipping from her lap onto the bed. "Where the hell have you *been*? I've—"

Before she could finish, a siren began to sound. Footsteps approached her room, then continued past. Someone shouted in the distance, but the words were too faint to be heard over the screaming of the siren.

Then, even more distantly, she heard the dull thud of an explosion, followed by the sporadic chattering of weapons fire. A tang of smoke began to filter through the ancient university's air circulation system.

Standing upright, she faced the door. But with the lock on her side disabled, there wasn't much she could do. She felt impotent, trapped. Slapping the flat of her palm on the door, she shouted to attract the attention of anyone who might be passing:

"What's going on out there?" She waited for a moment, then banged again. "Hey! Is anyone there?"

The door burst open, knocking her to one side. Haid and Emmerik entered, each carrying a projectile rifle.

"Quickly!" barked the rebel leader. "They've found us."

"The Dato?" Roche hurriedly regained her composure and collected the slate.

"Enforcement," said Emmerik. "But the Dato won't be far behind."

The burly Mbatan came up behind her. "Take this." Another rifle. "We'll have to hurry."

Roche nodded. "Understood."

"Let's go." Haid led the way out of the room. Another muffled explosion greeted them as they entered the hallway; a veil of plaster dust drifted down from the ceiling, and the smell of smoke grew stronger.

"They came up the old subway," Emmerik explained as they picked their way cautiously through the corridors. "About fifteen of them. They broke through the blockades and overran our sentries before help could arrive from above. We dropped ten of them before their own reinforcements showed up. Reports are a little confused, but our best estimate places them at around twenty, with more on the way."

"They're destroying everything as they come," added Haid. "Batteries, mainframes, stores—whatever they can lay their hands on. They're making sure that if we leave, there'll be nothing for us to return to."

"We have no choice," said Emmerik. "We *have* to leave. If we don't, we'll be caught between above and below when the Dato arrive."

"I know." Haid gritted his teeth. "I just hate to be forced into something I was going to do anyway."

Roche could sympathize, but she kept her mouth shut. They wound their way through increasingly smoky corridors, occasionally glimpsing other rebels, likewise evacuating the headquarters, until they reached a narrow door tucked into a cul-de-sac. Haid opened it with a key, revealing an equally narrow staircase.

"The others are waiting for us topside," he said. "Cane included. We can't break radio silence to let them know we're coming—or to make sure they're still there. We could be heading into anything, so be ready." He indicated for them to enter. "Emmerik, you first."

Roche followed the Mbatan up the stairs, with Haid behind her. The staircase wound steeply upward in a tight spiral, lit by ancient fluorescent tubes every half turn. Explosions occasionally came through the stone walls like the booming of enormous beasts. The loudest, and presumably the nearest, made the steps shake beneath their feet.

Then, when Roche estimated that they had risen about ten floors, the lights went out.

"They've reached the main generator," Haid said into the darkness. "Good."

"It is? Why?" Roche stumbled in the dark, then regained her balance.

"Someone tripped the breakers before they arrived," Emmerik explained.

"Didn't you notice?" said Haid. "No explosion."

"So?"

"Wait a second," said Emmerik. "You'll see."

They continued to climb. Behind her, barely audible over the sound of their scuffling feet, she could hear Haid counting to himself.

". . . three . . . two . . . one . . . Hang on!"

Roche braced herself as the air began to tremble. A rumbling sound grew steadily louder until the walls began to vibrate, shaking loose pockets of dirt that rained down upon them, causing Roche to gag. Then, an explosion from somewhere deep beneath her feet, the force of which made the steps themselves buck. Roche slipped to her knees, instinctively wrapping an arm about her head for protection from the rubble spilling down from above. She only looked up again when she heard Haid's cry of elation in the ringing aftermath, although the darkness still effectively hid him.

"That'll slow them down!"

"What—?" Roche staggered to her feet, still hearing phantom echoes of the blast in her ears. "The generator blew?"

"Self-destructed. A little contingency we prepared years ago, if we were ever forced to leave." His voice held equal parts triumph and regret. "They might think twice next time before advancing so quickly."

"Maybe," Emmerik muttered from farther up the stairwell. "But we no longer have a headquarters."

"Not that it matters anymore," Haid responded, although less vigorously. "Soon we'll either have the landing field, or nothing at all." A hand reached out of the darkness to nudge Roche upward. "Keep moving. We've still got a long way to go."

They exited the stairwell a few minutes later, Emmerik first, with his rifle ready. The safe house was clear, although shots rang out from somewhere close by. Roche followed the Mbatan through the corridors of the building, Haid at her side, until they reached the garage where they had disembarked from the truck two days before. Sunlight seeped through grimy windows, casting geometric patterns across the packed earth floor. Roche blinked, startled; she had lost track of the time underground.

A fleeting figure passed across the other entrance to the garage, and was gone before Roche could raise her rifle. It returned an instant later: Cane.

"Good, you're here," he said. He was wearing combat armor provided by the rebels—not powered, but passive; thick plates of black impact-resistant foam padding his torso and limbs. A lightweight helmet covered his head, its face-plate removed. "This way."

He led them to the room in which Roche had showered. Standing massive and still in the center of the room was the suit they had stolen from the Enforcement team in Houghton's Cross.

"Hey, Proctor," Roche said, running a hand across the suit. "Am I glad to see you."

"We recharged its batteries before the generator blew," said Cane.

"Excellent," said Haid.

Roche moved forward and removed the data glove. Cane held the Box in position behind her back as she stepped into the headless shell. When her palm slid home into the suit's left glove, the armor came to life, wrapping around her body in an intimate yet intimidating embrace.

<All systems functioning, Morgan,> the Box reported.

She took a step, feeling the solid thump of the suit striking

the floor through her feet. Again, the sensation of power diffused through her veins—hypnotic, and misleading. Still, it
was good to be feeling strong and in control once again.

Cane, standing behind her, placed a helmet on her head.
"There's an Enforcement team outside," he said, both to her
and the others. "We've been holding them off until you arrived."

"You and how many?" asked Haid.

"Six others. Two on each floor, sniping from windows."

"How many Enforcers?" Haid asked quickly.

"A dozen or so, most of them in the building opposite.
Maii says there's another team on the way."

"Maii's here too?" Roche turned to face Cane.

<One floor above you,> came the whispering voice of the
reave.

"Veden, too," said Cane. "We're going to need both of
them if this plan is going to work."

"Is he up to fighting?" said Roche.

"Sylvester finished treatment late yesterday," Haid explained. "His system has been flushed clean, and his long-
term prognosis is good. Whether he can fight or not, though,
I don't know."

<No,> said Maii. <He is still weak, although he hates to
admit it.>

"We'll have to carry him out, then—"

<I am detecting launches from the landing field,> the Box
interrupted, speaking over Haid's plans to get Veden out of
the safe house. <Three surface craft—headed for us, I assume.>

<How long do we have?> Roche asked.

<Minutes, perhaps.>

<Then we'd better get moving.> Roche swiveled to face
Haid. "We have to get out of here. There are flyers on the
way."

"Maii?" The rebel cast his one eye toward the ceiling. "Did
you hear that?"

<I heard. But we are too slow. Leave us here, and we will
rendezvous with you later.>

"You'll be trapped!" Roche protested, her voice unnecessarily loud.

<No. I can shield two from harm. We will be refugees, innocents caught in the crossfire. No one will interfere with us.>

"Are you sure?" asked Haid.

<Positive. Tell us where to meet you, and we will be there.>

Haid described a rendezvous while Roche strode heavily back to the garage. Intermittent gunfire crackled in the street outside. Faintly at first, but growing louder, she began to hear the nasal buzz of aircraft.

"If we go outside, we will be caught in a pincer," said Cane from behind her.

"I agree." She flexed the fingers of her suit's right glove. "We'll have to go back down again and come up another way."

Haid and Emmerik, when they had finished making arrangements with Maii, agreed.

"Neva is still down there somewhere," said the Mbatan.

"So is Enforcement," said Roche.

"If Maii can contact her, she can open the back door," said Emmerik. "Or at least keep it from being closed."

Haid nodded. "We'll go down via the stairwell—if you'll fit," he added with a nod to Roche. "The others will stay topside to keep Enforcement off our backs for as long as possible."

"Agreed." *A suicide mission*, Roche thought to herself, glad she wouldn't be staying behind.

<I will relay your orders,> Maii said. <If there is any way for them to escape as well, we will use it.>

"Good." Haid glanced around him, at Emmerik, Cane, and Roche. His face betrayed little of the nervousness Roche herself was feeling. He seemed poised but relaxed, much as Cane did: a natural fighter.

There, however, the resemblance ended. Haid had initially learned the ability to fight by implants, whereas Cane seemed to have been born with it. Watching the muscles twitching in Cane's neck as he led the way back to the stairwell, she wondered how he felt about his experiences so far. Was it just a game to him, a series of obstacles to be overcome in a larger plan—or was he as Pristine as he seemed, despite the evidence?

She doubted she'd ever find out. The best she could hope for—if it *was* all a game to him, and if for the moment he was playing on their side—was that he'd win.

After that, she was prepared to take her chances.

At the bottom of the stairwell, Roche eased gratefully out of the cramped space and into a dark, smoke-filled passageway. Forced to descend sideways due to the width of the suit's shoulders, she relished the simple joy of facing the direction in which she was going.

"Clear," she called to the others, when she had swept the corridor with the lights on the suit's chest. Apart from smoke and debris, the way was empty.

Haid emerged from the stairwell, followed by Emmerik. Cane came last, shutting the door carefully behind him.

"That way." Haid pointed ahead. "Turn left at the next corridor. We'll have to climb down the elevator shaft to get to the right level."

Roche led the way through the ruined headquarters, stepping gingerly over the debris. Occasionally they passed bodies; apart from one Enforcer, the dead were all rebels. Emmerik stopped briefly at each to identify the victims. Roche waited patiently while he did so; although to her the dead were strangers, to the Mbatan they would have been family.

They reached the elevator shaft without mishap. The doors had been blown open by the explosion of the power plant, and the cage had fallen to the lowest level. Cables dangled like snake carcasses before the entrance, while fires from below gave the scene an almost infernal ambience.

"Two levels down is the one we want," Haid said. "Do you think the cables will take your weight?"

Roche shrugged. "We'll soon find out."

The four of them slithered down the shaft, Cane more speedily than the others. When they reached the right floor, he had already levered the doors open and was waiting to help them through. Roche thudded with relief onto the solid floor. Despite the strength of the suit's grip, she had experienced a few moments of apprehension on the way down.

The smoke was thicker on the twenty-third floor, and

smelled strongly of burnt insulation. The suit lights struggled to penetrate the gloom, and she eventually gave up looking for the most part, relying on hearing to tell if there was anyone ahead. As yet, however, they had encountered no one in the ruins.

"Almost too quiet," said Emmerik, echoing her thoughts.

"No sign of anyone at all," Haid agreed.

"I can hear people," said Cane. "Not close, though."

"This level?" said Haid.

"Perhaps." Cane closed his eyes and cocked his head slightly. "It's hard to tell."

Haid nodded. "Okay. You and Emmerik wait here. Roche, come with me."

Roche obeyed, following the rebel leader through the shadows, her chest lights burning circles into his back. He led them down the corridor a short way, then turned left. Fifty meters farther, they came to a locked door.

"Good," he muttered, fumbling with the manual lock. "It hasn't been disturbed."

"What hasn't?"

"Munitions dump." He glanced over his shoulder, his artificial iris constricting as Roche's lights stabbed at him. "We need everything we can get to tackle the landing field. Seeing as we're already down here . . ."

The door opened with a click, and Haid waved her inside. The small room contained a single crate, from which he handed her a number of small items. Stowing them carefully in the suit's chest and thigh compartments, she mentally recorded each item: grenades, mortars, ammunition for the projectile rifles, gas cylinders, pistols, power packs, pressure mines . . .

When the suit was full, Haid stowed an armful in his own clothes and led her out of the room.

"Back doors *and* arms caches," she said as they began to walk back the way they had come. "Has anybody ever told you people that you're paranoid?"

"You have to be," he replied. "An underground movement is always under threat—especially one as established as our own. Long-term survival is inevitably more important than short-term gains. What we lost in the past by diverting arms to secret caches is more than compensated for by the possibility that we might survive *now*."

Roche smiled to herself, remembering her Tactics teacher at college, many years ago, whose words Haid had unknowingly echoed: "Show your true face to your enemy, and expect to have it slapped. Give everything you've got, and expect it to be taken away from you. Never feel so superior, or inferior, that you can afford to relinquish your most valuable weapon: deceit. A war is won only when at least one of the parties loses the ability to lie. . . ."

The younger Roche had always thought her teacher slightly cynical. Now she had to admit that his point was sound, in practice.

Cane and Emmerik were where they had left them. As one, they headed along the corridor toward the headquarters' back door—the place where Sabra had died. Halfway there, Roche remembered the final expression on Sabra's face. The bewildered horror and despair in the woman's eyes, as victory had been suddenly turned to defeat, was a potent reminder that nothing should be taken for granted.

Part of the roof had collapsed near the end of the corridor. As they climbed over the obstacle, Cane announced that he could hear fighting up ahead.

"Gunshots, energy weapons—" He peered forward through the gloom, as though willing the smoke to part. "And voices."

Roche could hear nothing. "How many?"

"I can't tell."

"Quietly, then," said Haid, shrugging his rifle into a more comfortable position. "Lead the way, Cane. Roche, turn your lights off."

They continued along their way with Roche at the rear. Presently, she too heard the sounds Cane had reported: the occasional sizzle of energy weapons, the angry crack of rifles.

When they reached the end of the corridor and entered the maze of corridors, their progress became even more cautious.

"I estimate ten Enforcers," Cane whispered over his shoulder to Haid. "Maybe the same number of your people defending the exit. The Enforcers lie between us and the others."

"With their backs to us," the rebel leader finished.

They came to a halt near a corner. Flashes of light issued from the branching corridor every time an energy weapon discharged. Explosions echoed through the confined space, almost painfully loud.

"Lights back on, Roche," said Haid, stepping aside. "They'll think you're one of them long enough for us to get close."

Roche activated the suit's chest lights and strode forward. The three men waited a moment, then followed in her shadow. As she turned the corner, she quickly surveyed the scene.

Seven armored Enforcers filled the crowded corridor, using debris for shelter where it was available. Beyond them, across a short section of no-man's-land, a rough blockade protected the entrance to the room where Sabra had died. As Roche watched, a projectile rifle was fired from behind the blockade, sending ricochets sparking along the walls. She automatically ducked before regaining her composure and moving on.

Barely had she taken five steps when the Enforcement squad noticed her. Recognizing her armor as one of their own, they turned back to the fighting. She swallowed, and raised her rifle.

Before she could fire, Cane rushed past. Snatching a percussion rifle from the hands of the nearest Enforcer, he turned it on the armor, blowing holes in the tough ceramic and killing the person inside instantly. The rest of the squad, belatedly realizing that they were being attacked from behind, scrambled for cover.

The corridor quickly dissolved into chaos. A hail of bullets and energy filled the air. Silhouetted against the firestorm were the combat suits, powerful shadows jerking from side to side, trying to locate targets in the mess of motion.

Roche's rifle kicked in her hands. A lucky shot shattered an Enforcer's visor. Pressing the advantage, she rammed the butt through the starred plastic. Screaming, the Enforcer dropped his percussion rifle, and Roche stooped to pick it up. Firing quick bursts, she backed away. Blinded, the Enforcer staggered forward with his arms outstretched until the suit failed completely and he collapsed spread-eagled to the ground.

Emmerik heaved the suit into a sitting position and used its solid bulk as a shield. A second Enforcer fell under Roche's fire, and a third. Cane dodged in front of her, firing a stolen rifle at its owner. Haid joined Emmerik, and together they picked off the remaining Enforcers.

Within moments, the skirmish was over. Haid climbed over the ruined suits to meet his fellow rebels behind the blockade, trailing a streamer of blood from a flesh wound in his left leg. Roche and Cane gathered the undamaged weapons from the bodies and did the same. Emmerik waited until they were through before following.

"Emmerik!"

A battle-worn Neva pressed forward to take the Mbatan by the arm. Her face was grimy and blackened, but otherwise she seemed none the worse for wear.

"We made it." Haid held a cloth to staunch the flow from his leg.

"Not a moment too soon," she said. "Maii told us to wait, but I don't know how much longer we could have held them off."

"That you did for long enough is all that matters." The rebel leader urged Roche forward. Opening one of the suit's compartments, he retrieved a grenade and primed it. "You go with the others. I'll catch up with you in a moment."

Neva led the way through the doorway with the damaged sign above it. Another flight of stairs greeted them, this one easily wide enough for the suit and lit by baleful red emergency lights.

Roche performed a quick head count: herself, Cane, Emmerik, Neva and a half dozen surviving rebels. Eleven people, four of them with Enforcement percussion rifles, only one with combat armor.

"Are we all that made it out?" she asked Neva.

Neva shook her head. "I sent about twenty ahead. There may be more who came before us, too. The exit was open when we reached it."

Roche nodded. The number was still small, but not as bad as it had seemed at first. Enforcement had been looking for *her*, after all, and she didn't want a massacre on her conscience.

A muffled detonation from the base of the stairwell made her ears pop. That was followed by the sound of falling masonry. Moments later, Haid limped to join them, shaking dust from his clothes.

"The exit is blocked," he said, grimacing. "If anyone's left down there, they'll have to take the subway out."

Neva put a hand on his shoulder and squeezed. "Your leg . . . ?"

"Is fine," he said, looking around at the party. "Am I the only one wounded?"

"No." Her gaze shifted to Emmerik, who nodded, then to Roche. "But we've made it this far. That's the main thing."

Emmerik grunted—a sound that might have been laughter. "For now," he said.

The rebels' back door opened into a disused building in an abandoned lane. Sun and Soul burned brightly after the darkness below ground, and Roche took a moment to adjust. The air was dry and dusty, as always, and a light wind cast short-lived eddies about her legs. From the southeast, in the general direction of the main entrance to the subterranean headquarters, the air carried the scent of smoke.

The city was quiet, however: no gunfire, no buzz of aircraft. Just the occasional bleating of pack animals and the throaty roar of poorly tuned chemical engines. Life went on, even in the middle of a revolution.

"We'll need a truck," said Haid through gritted teeth. His wounded leg had pained him toward the end of the journey up the stairwell; while Emmerik carefully bound it to staunch the flow of blood, he concentrated on their ongoing mission. "Maii and Veden should be waiting for us not far from here, but there's no way we'll be able to walk into the landing field. At the very least we'll have to ram the gates, and—"

"If something goes wrong on the way in, we'll be in trouble," said Roche, remembering the plans of the landing field she had studied in her cell. "The distance from the Enforcement compound to the administration and MiCom buildings is roughly one hundred meters. Even at a run, we'll be sitting ducks."

One of the rebels, a woman named Jytte, said, "We're attacking the landing field?"

"No one is under any obligation." Haid limped forward, testing his weight on the leg. "You don't have to come along if you don't want to."

Jytte shook her head uncertainly. "It's just that—I mean, the *landing field* . . . ?"

"It's not as stupid as it sounds," said Haid. "Enforcement's distracted, the Dato landing party is busy, and we have the element of surprise. Yes, we're outnumbered, but we'll *always* be outnumbered. It doesn't really matter. We either succeed with what we've got, or we die trying. It's as simple as that."

"Exactly," said Roche, "but we do need a vehicle of some description."

Haid nodded. "We used to keep a reserve vehicle near here, but it's unfueled and therefore useless." The rebel leader glanced around the survivors, one by one. "Now's the time to call in favors, if you have any due."

No one spoke immediately.

Then, from Cane: "What about a flyer? If we could commandeer one—"

"No." Haid quickly dismissed the idea. "We don't want to tip them off too soon."

"I can help." Emmerik stood up unexpectedly. "There's an old solar-powered van we use sometimes to ferry equipment into the desert."

A short and uneasy silence followed as Haid glanced from the Mbatan to Neva. "I thought I was supposed to know about things like this."

"You are, but . . ." The Mbatan shuffled from foot to foot in discomfort. "It's just that some disagreed. Not me personally," he added quickly. "But some of those outside the city—"

"The wild ones," said Neva evenly. "They see *us* as city people, Ameidio, and what trust we gained from them came grudgingly. But you they've always been suspicious of."

Haid's apparent hurt dissolved after a moment and became a grudging smile. "You indies will never change, will you?" he said. "So where is this van?"

"Not far." Emmerik and Neva exchanged glances briefly;

then the woman turned back to the rebel leader. "I'll show you."

"Fine," said the Mbatan. "And I'll meet you at the rendezvous point. I have to organize the . . ." He hesitated. "The other matter we discussed."

Haid nodded. "Will an hour be long enough?"

"It should be." Emmerik shouldered his percussion rifle in a perfunctory salute, then headed off along the alley.

"What other matter?" Roche asked, sotto voce.

"Don't worry about it," said Haid. "You'll know when it happens—*if* it happens at all, that is. And that's up to the indies." Something in his eyes revealed that he was more deeply concerned about the indigenes' mistrust of him than he showed, and Roche sympathized: for all his work over the last few years, the rebel organization remained at heart divided. And wherever division existed, weaknesses could form. Sabra's death had clearly proven that.

She changed the subject. "What about arms? Any more caches up here?"

"None, I'm afraid." He looked pointedly away, as though she had inadvertently touched upon another sore point. To the group as a whole, he said, "Let's go, people! The sooner we get out of here, the safer we'll be." Then, as an aside to Roche, he added, "Relatively speaking, of course."

The rendezvous point was empty when they arrived. Haid steered the ancient van to an abrupt halt in a disused lot where it wouldn't attract attention and turned to the five people sitting in the back. Cane, Roche, Neva, and the two rebels faced him in unison.

"We'll wait a while," he said. "The sight of us approaching might have been enough to send them to ground."

Roche thought that was a distinct possibility. The van, with its ripped vanes and irritating whine, was enough to make *her* nervous. Only a disproportionately solid construction and regular, if roughshod, maintenance had kept it operating this long; it looked as though anything more substantial than a strong gust of wind might send it to pieces. The movement of her suit alone was enough to make it shudder.

Still, the van had survived the desert for decades without

failing. And as Haid had said, they had to make do with what little they had. It wasn't too late to turn back, but the number of alternative courses of action open to them was dismayingly small.

Sure enough, minutes after the van had come to a halt, they heard a gentle rapping at the rear panel.

<It's us,> said the reave.

Neva leaned across to open the door. "We were beginning to wonder if you'd made it."

<We almost didn't.> The small Surin climbed into the back and helped Veden after her. This, Roche's first sight of the Eckandi since his injury at Houghton's Cross, disturbed her. The back of his head was covered by a bandage, and his skin was worryingly pale. His eyes were closed as though the sun was too bright for him. When Maii had him in the van, he sagged onto a bench with a small, pained hiss.

The fact that he was even conscious—given his previously comatose condition, and the lack of medical resources available to the rebels—amazed Roche. And, much to her surprise, she realized that she was relieved.

As though he could sense her staring at him, he opened his eyes and nodded in recognition.

"Sorry to disappoint you, Roche," he said with disdain—although something in his eyes suggested to Roche that his contempt was superficial. "It looks like I'll be pulling through, after all."

"No, I—" Roche started in embarrassment, wondering when her feelings for the Eckandi had changed.

Veden didn't give her a chance to consider. "I hear you've been taking good care of Maii," he said.

"Trying to," she replied, conscious of the others watching her. "How are *you* feeling?"

"Tired." Veden touched the bandage lightly with one hand, and closed his eyes again. "And a little ill, to be honest," he said. "So if you'll excuse me, I need to rest."

Embarrassed by his weakness, Roche turned away, focusing her attention instead upon Maii's account of their escape.

<The Dato weren't as easily fooled as Enforcement.> Maii's words passed through Roche's thoughts like a warm and comforting breeze as the Surin girl sat herself beside her

elderly companion. <Five of us made it out of the building. The other three arranged a diversion to cover Veden and me. Only one survived, and he fled elsewhere.>

"Where?" asked Haid sharply.

<To find other survivors, to regroup. Enforcement and a Dato squadron followed him.>

"Useless," Haid muttered. "Still, it's another diversion."

<The city's mood is tense.> Maii inclined her head slightly to the opposite side of the van, as though her sightless eyes were seeing through the metal walls of the vehicle. <Three fires are out of control, and the wardens are letting them burn. The Dato have free access to security information and the support of ground troops. There will be a curfew tonight, if anyone is left on the streets at all.>

"Followed by a witch hunt tomorrow, no doubt." The rebel leader shook his head. "I'm all for long-term survival, but squatting down and waiting to be killed is something else entirely. As I see it, the only way out is to attack *now*, before we have nothing left to attack *with*. That seems obvious to me. Or have I lost it?" The last was directed to Neva, who smiled reassuringly.

"No," she said. "Our home is worth fighting for, no matter what it costs."

"But that's just it," Haid said. "I'm fighting for something that isn't even *my* home. What about the others? Where are they when we need them? Why aren't *they* fighting?"

"When the status quo shifts," Neva said, "what might once have seemed intolerable suddenly becomes desirable. Especially in the city, where conditions are relatively comfortable. Although they keep secrets from you during times of peace, you must realize that your most ardent supporters now are from the desert."

"I know, I know. But that doesn't make it any easier." The rebel leader slumped forward. "Where the hell *is* Emmerik, anyway?"

Silence fell. Sensing a need to keep matters focused on the immediate future, Roche leaned forward to outline the plan to the two rebels who had elected to join them. Cane also watched with interest, quickly picking up the essentials of the plan and adding useful advice of his own.

Half an hour passed slowly. When the briefing was running under its own steam without her input, Roche leaned back to rest, closing her eyes and trying to ignore the heat buffeting her face.

After a moment, she realized that she could hear voices—not those of Cane and Neva running over the plan, but two others, inside her head.

<I am too weak,> said one, male: Veden. <You should leave me behind, for everyone's sake.>

<No,> Maii replied instantly. <We need you to talk to the High Equity Court.>

<But I can do that later, once you have the landing field under control. I'll only slow you down, get in the way—>

<We can't leave you here. You'll be captured,> she protested. <Or killed.>

<Nonsense. I can look after myself. And what good would it do if you got killed trying to save me?>

<Better than having Enforcement use you as a hostage.>

<I can hardly walk, child! I'm not going to last ten seconds once we reach the landing field!>

<No, Veden!> The panicky edge to the reave's voice indicated how desperately she feared losing him. <You'll be safe. I swear it. I won't leave you behind where I can't look after you!>

Roche opened her eyes. Neither Veden nor Maii displayed any sign of the fierce debate occurring between them. To all around them—except Roche—they might have been sleeping. Only an occasional wince betrayed the pain the Eckandi was feeling. If he knew that Roche was eavesdropping, he made no sign.

But . . . why *was* she able to listen in on the private conversation? The two previous mind-dumps Roche had received had been concerned with Maii's origins and Veden's plan to liberate Sciacca's World. There had to be a reason for Roche to be a witness to this conversation as well. With renewed interest, Roche closed her eyes again to listen more closely.

Veden expected to die, and soon. She could sense it in his words, in the thoughts he directed at his young ward. The fact that he was prepared to die alone while Maii fought elsewhere was convincing proof of how strongly he felt for the reave. He had already hurt her by dragging her to Sciacca's World with him; he didn't want his death to hurt her further.

Maii, naturally, denied this possibility, being more concerned with his well-being than her own. The strength of his feelings gave his side of the argument more credence than it deserved—for how would Maii feel if Veden did indeed die while she was elsewhere? She would blame herself for the rest of her life, regardless how long or short that might be.

Roche was surprised to realize she could understand how Maii felt: some of her dislike for the trader really did appear to have vanished. Perhaps it was seeing him in such poor health, or—more likely, Roche thought—she understood him better now. She suddenly realized that the information Maii had fed to her served a double purpose, without her being aware of it: not only informing her of Veden's history, but also revealing the side of him that she had yet to experience directly, the side that bonded Maii to him. In the dream-dump, the threat that he had once seemed had been effectively neutralised, without once resorting to covert mental nudges.

The reave hadn't lied, after all. She may have manipulated Roche when they first met, but not since then. The fact that Roche's feelings for the Eckandi had changed, making her sympathize with Maii's side of the argument, was nothing to be concerned about. If anything, she should feel relieved that she was thinking with her own mind, her own thoughts.

Clearly Maii thought a reconciliation between her mentor and Roche was possible. Perhaps Maii had brought Veden up to date on Roche in a similar way. Certainly he had greeted her with less resentment than at any other time since they had met—actually going so far as to initiate a conversation, an indication that his previously automatic dismissal of her no longer held sway.

But there was more than just reconciliation at stake. Roche could sense that, even as she struggled to decipher what the rest might be. She didn't know whom to sympathize with most, but she knew how to break the stalemate. If that wasn't what Maii intended, then Roche was out of ideas.

"If he can't walk," she said, cutting across the other conversation in the van, "then I can carry him."

Veden, startled, opened his eyes, and Maii turned to face her.

"What?" said Neva, staring at her in confusion.

Roche shook her head. The voices had ceased, leaving an emptiness in her mind where they had once been. "It doesn't matter. My mind was elsewhere."

At that moment, the engine crackled into life. The passenger door at the front of the van opened, and Emmerik slid into the seat.

"Sorry to keep you waiting," said the Mbatan to Haid, putting his rifle down between them.

"All organized?" The rebel leader searched Emmerik's face for any sign of difficulty.

"I took the liberty of spreading the word here and there, along the way. In half an hour or so, we'll have a diversion to keep Enforcement occupied."

"And the rest?"

"The land lines are still intact. They'll be ready in three hours, and will await my signal."

"Good."

"What's good?" asked Roche, crouching forward in the van to speak to both of them.

"Reinforcements, I hope," said Haid, and put the ancient motor into gear. With a jerk, the van backed out of the lot. Taking the hint, Roche retreated into the cab. Cane caught her eye and winked once.

Roche resisted the impulse to protest that it was *her* plan, and that she deserved to be kept up to date on new developments. But the whining of the engine made conversation virtually impossible, and the uncertain tone in Haid's voice suggested that maybe she didn't want to know anyway. Better to work with resources presently at their disposal, rather than rely on a deus ex machina that might never arrive.

And as they headed off along the dusty street, two words penetrated Roche's irritation:

<Thank you,> said Maii.

16

The van pulled out of the wide freeway leading from the city center and onto a rising exit ramp that took them up and over the empty main thoroughfare. As the lower road swung away to the left, their new direction curved steeply to the right. Behind them, smoke from a dozen fires blotted out the horizon: the distraction Emmerik had promised. A kilometer farther on, they crested the long rise—and Roche saw their destination for the first time, silhouetted against the slowly setting sun.

The landing field.

A tall, electrified security fence appeared in their path, vanishing left and right to the periphery of her vision. Beyond it, every last piece of vegetation had been cleared and replaced with a scattering of nondescript buildings on seemingly endless tarmac. There was no visible space that had not been cleared and rebuilt.

The van swung right, following the imposing fence line. To her left she could make out the MiCom building itself, still a good kilometer away but surprisingly close to the fence. She knew the exact distance from the main gates to the complex foyer—one hundred five meters—but somehow the reality of it still surprised her. It made a mockery of the elaborate perimeter and for lousy security all around, despite the guardhouse resting midway between the complex and the gate. She supposed that the plateau upon which the landing field stood was only so big; in order to give maximum area to traffic demands, the MiCom building had to be shunted off to the side. Whatever the reasons, it was close enough to the gates to give her plan a chance.

Roche felt her muscles tighten as the Enforcement tower drew rapidly closer. Almost there. She glanced across the huge dry docks, deserted except for one orbital freighter and a couple of suborbital transfer barges. The landing field at Port Parvati had seen headier times.

As the van broached a shallow hill, one of the interior hangars came into view. Through its open doors she glimpsed a snub-nosed combat shuttle. Every angle was curved and lumpy, reinforced for maximum structural strength, giving it an almost squat appearance. Such ships didn't look like much, but they made up for it in battle; they had demonstrated their rugged endurance time and time again.

Roche recognized its origins immediately. The Commonwealth of Empires didn't build ships like that. Only the Dato Bloc did.

The van swept down the hill and past the Enforcement tower. When the hangar disappeared from view, Roche returned her eyes to the road ahead.

"Do it again," said the rebel named Jytte from beside her.

Across the cab from the rebel, Maii sighed and concentrated.

Jytte's eyes glazed for a moment, then cleared. "Incredible," she said in a low voice. "If that doesn't get us through the gates, nothing will."

Roche knew what the woman was seeing: an Enforcer in full uniform where the young Surin had once sat. Only an illusion—with the detail that Maii's knowledge lacked filled in by Jytte's own imagination—but a convincing one nonetheless.

"Enough," said Roche. "Don't wear her out."

<It's okay,> protested the reave. <As long as the subject is willing, one person really isn't that tiring. Large groups are the problem, with so many minds to focus on, so many thoughts to bend.>

Roche shook her head uneasily. She didn't like it. Even though it had been her idea, she wasn't comfortable with using epsense on the battlefield. The talent was too ephemeral, too contingent on Maii's state of mind to depend upon absolutely. She would much rather have a squadron of Intelligence agents behind her than one young girl, talented or not. Relying so heavily on one person unnerved her.

Cane's voice cut across her thoughts. "Not far now."

Leaning forward and peering past Haid's and Emmerik's heads, Roche could see the main gates in the distance—wide open, as she had hoped; more laxity. Once through the gates and past the guardhouse, they could accelerate across the front lawns and parking lot, through the MiCom building's front windows and to the base of the target stairwell within thirty seconds. Haid and the others would have the MiCom doors blown and be inside the first level within a further ten seconds. Cane and his single companion would have penetrated the admin building within the same period.

The main problem would be getting through the gate and past the guardhouse without arousing suspicion. If a firefight broke out in that area, they were likely to lose.

And, in this instance, losing meant that they were dead.

She silently reaffirmed her vow: whatever it took to reach Intelligence HQ, she would do it. Her mission was *the* most important thing on this world. If she could help others along the way, then that was just an added bonus.

"Traffic," said Emmerik suddenly, breaking the silence. The Mbatan was watching the road behind them via an external mirror on his side of the van. "One groundcar. Not sure where it came from. Didn't spot it until a few seconds ago."

Roche clambered to the van's rear window. Sure enough, a wide-nosed vehicle cruised steadily behind them. She felt a surge of alarm when she saw how close the car actually was—and how quickly it was closing the gap between them.

Haid began to accelerate, trying to maintain a constant distance between the two vehicles.

"Do you think it could be a problem?" she asked.

"I'm not sure." Haid's eyes flicked from the mirror to the road and back again. "Maii?"

Maii's invisible gaze drifted out to infinity as Haid continued to accelerate. Roche watched her, acutely conscious of the main gates drawing closer with every second.

<A small group,> the reave said. <Only five of them, but very confident. And suspicious. Not Enforcement . . .> She paused. <Dato Bloc,> she said. <They're Dato troopers.>

"*Damn*." Haid's foot went down all the way on the accelerator. The van's ancient automatic transmission kicked into a lower gear as their acceleration became more urgent. Roche felt the first trickle of sweat begin to edge down her spine.

She leaned over to touch Maii's shoulder. "Anything else?" she asked.

<I don't understand,> said the girl to all of them, not just Roche. <They're not trying to catch us. It's almost as if they're . . .>

Roche's hand gripped tighter. "*What*?"

<They're *herding* us,> said Maii finally.

And as she said it, a large blue truck emerged from cover on the far side of the security fence. It turned ponderously onto the road and jerked to halt in full view. Several armed figures leapt from it and scurried for position.

Haid cursed loudly, urging the van faster with his words.

"They're on the other side of the gates," Roche said. "We can still go in."

"But they'll be ready for us by the time we get there," Haid retorted. "Someone must have tipped them off."

The van had almost reached the gates, but there was still no movement from Enforcement. Before Roche could respond to Haid's comment, a single uniformed figure ambled slowly from the gatehouse to see what was going on.

"No . . ." Relief parted her lips into a wide grin. "Enforcement doesn't know we're coming! The Dato have tried to do this alone."

The rebel leader studied the movements of the Enforcer

for the briefest of moments before saying: "Agreed. That gives us an edge. Maii, keep tabs on that Enforcer. Don't let her sound the alarm. If we can make it past the Dato, our plan still holds."

The reave nodded once.

Behind the van, the groundcar continued to close, but not quickly enough to reach them short of the gates. The group blocking the road on the far side of the fence had spread out. It was going to be tight.

The Enforcer from the gatehouse stood transfixed, watching their approach. She was unarmored and didn't seem overly concerned at what was occurring around her.

<She sees only an authorized van approaching,> said the reave. <She worries about our speed—nothing else.>

"Good," Roche encouraged. "Keep it up just a little longer, Maii."

"Push her harder," suggested Cane. "Make her worry about the Dato presence, why they are threatening an official vehicle."

Maii nodded again. <Okay.>

Roche watched the lone Enforcer at the gate more closely. Within seconds, the woman turned to shout to other Enforcers inside the gatehouse. Two joined her, and a hurried conversation ensued between Enforcement and the Dato landing party. As the van approached, Roche could make out both anger and confusion on the faces of the Enforcers.

<I can't hold them much longer,> Maii said.

"Just a few seconds more," shot back Haid. "That's all we need."

Roche gripped the metal base of the bench as the gate loomed ahead of them. Too late, the Enforcers on the other side realized that they had been tricked—that what they had thought to be an official vehicle was actually nothing more than a worn-out solar van. Two dived for cover, the third stood stunned, and behind her the Dato finally raised their weapons.

Haid spun the steering wheel. Roche heard him manipulate the rear brakes, felt the back of the van slew around to the left, saw the gates swing into view through the front window. The van lurched forward as Haid's foot crashed down once again on the accelerator. With barely a moment to spare, the third Enforcer leapt out of the way.

In a barely controlled slide, the van sideswiped the front of the gatehouse, peeling off the armored paneling and sending it flying ahead of them as they screamed through the gates. Roche lifted a pistol and used the butt to punch through the side window, then quickly fired at the one Enforcer who had the presence of mind to take a shot at them. She hit him square in the chest, saw him topple and fall, then swung her gaze back to the front. Fifty meters ahead she saw Enforcers pour from the main guardhouse.

Roche exchanged the pistol for a percussion rifle and set it to scatter. She saw Emmerik toss something out of the passenger window and also grab a percussion rifle. In unison, they began pumping charge after charge at the emerging Enforcers.

She had a brief view of figures scattering and snapped off a few more shots. Then they were past, crashing through a low perimeter fence and bouncing over the edge of the parking area. As they careened directly toward the front of the main complex, Roche made out the few people visible through the wide windows already running for cover.

She glanced behind the van and saw the pursuing groundcar swing through the gates, narrowly avoiding a collision with the rest of the Dato squad.

Then a brilliant explosion blossomed under the front of the leading vehicle: a pressure mine, dropped by Emmerik as they drove through. Through the flash and sudden roiling smoke, the groundcar climbed up and sideways, rising meters into the air, twisting as it went, to come crashing down on its side against the electrified fence. Energy pulsed and crackled, engulfing the stricken vehicle. The blue truck swerved wildly to miss it and slammed into the corner of the gatehouse, bringing part of the already weakened structure down in front of it.

Someone shouted in triumph. Both pursuers were suddenly out of the chase, temporarily if not permanently. It was more than Roche could have hoped for.

"Get your heads down!" Haid shouted. "We're going through!"

Roche whipped her head around to see the vast windows leap toward her. She ducked instinctively, felt Jytte hunch over beside her, heard the crash and clatter of shattering glass. She heard someone call out in alarm as fragments suddenly flew into the cabin through the broken side windows.

By the time she regained her balance, Haid had the brakes locked. The van swerved sideways again, skidding across the main terminal floor like a snowplow, tearing a ragged path through chairs, tables, partition boards, and other assorted furniture.

The van careened to a rough halt, causing Neva and Veden to tumble from their seats. Roche heard Haid shout orders as he rolled through the buckled driver's door. Emmerik slid across the seat to follow him. Already the rear doors of the van had opened; Jytte and her companion jumped into the foyer with a clatter of boots and weapons.

Roche waited until Neva and Maii had climbed free before stepping down herself. Cane had already disembarked. Sending a hail of energy to clear the air for a moment, she returned to help Veden. Presenting her back to him, she gestured for him to slip his arms through the leather straps Maii had tied around the suit's neck. He resisted for a moment, then did as he was told.

Just in time. Percussion fire from the parking lot forced her behind the van. Sparkling ricochets danced off the marble floor and mirrored walls. The air stank of ozone and scorched synthetics. Beyond the shattered windows Roche could see Enforcement and the Dato landing party dodging the return fire from within the building.

She oriented herself, long hours of Armada combat training falling into place. A map of the complex appeared in her left eye: the MiCom building, three stories high, which they had already entered; administration, only one level to the rear. The foyer occupied a corner of the MiCom building's ground floor: elevator and stairwell were at the bottom of the L; a corridor leading to the admin building opened out the back.

Roche caught sight of Cane racing away, crashing

through the entrance to Admin. The sound of rapid gunfire went with him as he wielded a rifle in each hand, aiming at anyone or anything that threatened to get in his way.

"Leave him!" Haid's voice pierced the racket, directed at the rebel who was supposed to have accompanied Cane on his mission. Roche edged around the van, conscious of the Eckandi gripping her back, his weight subtly disturbing the suit's ponderous equilibrium. Haid and the rebel vanished up the MiCom stairwell, carrying grenades and mortars retrieved from Roche's suit before the attack. Maii waited at the base of the stairwell with Neva.

Roche passed Veden to the older woman. "Get him upstairs. I'll cover the rear!"

The rifle was still set to scatter, and she moved at once to find a more sheltered position. At the back of the van, she kicked an upturned table into position and swung the rifle onto it so that the barrel rested easily. Already some twenty or thirty Enforcers had sprinted from the guardhouse toward the complex. Roche cranked the rifle setting to its widest beam and held the trigger down. The weapon bucked and kicked against her shoulder, spraying its lethal dosage through the windows, shattering what few panes had remained unbroken. The outer charge halted at once as the Enforcers hit the tarmac. There were a few seconds of quiet; then answering fire began to whistle in.

Roche flattened herself against the side of the van as projectile fire and particle beams lanced about her, but she kept her hand on the rifle, its barrel still resting on the upturned table. She fired in very short bursts, minimizing the recoil that would otherwise have wrenched the weapon from her grip. It wasn't enough to do serious damage to their attackers, but would make them think twice about a quick sprint forward.

Behind her, the muffled thump of an explosion told her that MiCom had been breached. A second blast, and she knew that the elevator had been crippled. She heard the clatter of feet on the stairwell, distant shouts and confusion as one of the rebels returned to help her. Together they did their best to hold Enforcement at bay.

Risking a closer look, Roche edged around the far side of

the van. She counted twenty-three Enforcers, only three of them armored similarly to her. Four Dato ground troopers hugged the wall on the far side of the foyer, clad in the latest powered combat suits. Roche risked a precision shot and was gratified to see the bolt of energy hit home.

The Dato armor, however, absorbed most of the energy. The trooper was flung to the ground, but stood up again a moment later.

She cursed. Not good.

Then Maii was in her mind:

<No resistance here! We have control. Draw back and join us!>

Roche squeezed off a few more rounds, then began to edge back along the side of the van. When she could go no farther, she stopped to look around. The van's solid metal body covered most of the gap between her and the stairwell, at least from the Enforcers' positions. The Dato troopers, on the other hand, had almost a clear line of fire. She looked over her shoulder at the rebel in the stairwell and selected a grenade from one of the suit's thigh pockets.

When the air was relatively clear, she tossed the explosive to the rebel, who primed it. Counting down from three, she tensed, braced to make the short dash for safety.

On zero, the rebel rolled the grenade toward the Dato troopers and vanished up the stairwell. Roche burst from cover and tucked her unprotected head as low as she could into the suit's shoulders. She cried out involuntarily as a furious bolt of energy sheared a centimeter off her left hip, making her stumble—then the grenade exploded, sending smoke and flame through the entire foyer, covering her escape.

Movement at the periphery of her vision as she entered the stairwell made her swing the rifle to bear. Cane appeared out of the cloud of smoke, firing behind him in ragged spurts.

"Close," he said, grinning down the barrel of her rifle. He grabbed her arm, and together they double-stepped up the stairwell.

"Admin?" said Roche.

Cane nodded. "Secure. Any problems this end?"

"None."

"Good." Cane's smile widened. "Then let's see what this Box of yours can do."

Roche paused briefly at the top of the stairs to set off another grenade. The explosion brought down part of the wall, which she hoped would delay pursuit for long enough.

<Turn left at the first corner,> said Maii, guiding them through the smoke-filled corridors. Along the way, they passed numerous DAOC employees. Some were wounded, some weren't; all were unconscious or sleeping. <Right, then second left. Take the stairs at the end.>

"Where are you, Maii?"

<In MiCom Control,> said the Surin. <On the top floor. Once you're here, we'll seal life support and activate internal security. That should delay the troops for a while.>

"What about the ones you've knocked out? How long until they wake up?"

<Not long. Again, I'll look after them when you arrive.> Maii resumed her instructions, her voice calm, measured, and quietly confident. Roche began to regret the doubts she'd had earlier. <Left, then through the door . . .>

As they ran, Roche took stock of her surroundings. The second floor was undamaged, secured by Maii rather than by force. Vast networks of complex processing systems lay as idle as their unconscious operators, awaiting input. The wealth of hardware was hardly extravagant, however, given the task it was required to perform. These three floors controlled every electronic exchange in the city, as well as much of that which took place in near orbit.

<Are you sure you're up to this, Box?>

<All I need is access to a secure control-branch of the network.>

<I hope you're right.>

<Believe me, Morgan, I am. I've been waiting for this for some time now.>

Roche and Cane climbed the last stairwell to the third floor and were greeted by Haid at its summit. Roche felt a wave of nausea sweep through her as they joined him: the edge of a psychic wave from Maii, she presumed, the epsense equivalent of scattershot but nonlethal, forcing the employees of

MiCom into a deeper state of unconsciousness. She was thankful she had only caught the edge of it.

"This way." The rebel leader led them through a maze of offices to the center of MiCom: a wide, high-ceilinged room containing three overhead screens, a dozen data-control stations, and a large central processor. The screens displayed constantly shifting views of the landing field, trajectories of satellites, and major moonlets through the Soul, as well as Armada deployment. Jytte and the other rebel, bleeding heavily from his right ear, guarded the entrance. Maii sat cross-legged in one corner, her placid expression belying the concentration she required to achieve what she was doing.

As Roche entered, a small window opened in the central screen, revealing the face of a man with a neatly trimmed grey beard.

"Tepko!" the face bellowed. "What the devil's going on down there? Clear the lines or I'll have you—"

"Hello, Warden," Emmerik said into a microphone, smiling from his position behind the central processor. "Chief Supervisor Tepko's not available to speak with you at the moment, I'm afraid. Perhaps I can help."

Warden Delcasalle opened his mouth, shut it, then opened it again. "Who the hell are you?"

"Your landlord," the Mbatan replied, beaming toothily. "And I've come to collect the rent."

Roche stepped up behind the Mbatan and put her gloved hand on the datalink.

"We haven't got time for this," she said.

The window to the warden closed as the Box interfaced with the central processor. Raw data surged down Roche's arm, through the suit, and out the palm of her power glove. More than a trickle, this felt like a river of fire, a thread-thin, white-hot wire inserted where her ulnar nerve had once been. She bit her lip as the torrent intensified. Phantom motes of light danced in her vision; her heart tripped, then steadied.

<I have access,> said the Box almost joyously, its voice issuing through the control room's speakers. <Complete access: communications, traffic control, records, security deployment, maintenance, power and water distribution . . .>

"Hold it, Box," said Haid. "What about internal security?"

"Activated," replied the Box instantly.

"Life support?"

"Sealed."

"Can you give us a view of the lower levels?"

The central screen cleared, allowing space for the sweep. The foyer was relatively empty; the first floor had been breached before the massive security doors closed, sealing off each level. The second floor contained only two Dato ground troopers, who pounded at the door to the third level in frustration.

"I have taken the liberty of canceling a recall order for Enforcement from the city," said the Box.

"Excellent," breathed Haid. "Then we're safe."

"At least for the time being," said Cane.

Emmerik put his percussion rifle down next to Roche's. "So now what?"

"The message," Roche muttered with some difficulty, still transfixed by the intense stream of data threading through her system. "We send the message."

"Exactly." Haid waved Maii and Veden forward. The elderly Eckandi looked like he was going to fall, but managed to steady himself on the edge of the processor.

"Which do you need first?" he asked. "The control codes, or the message itself?"

"The codes," replied the Box.

<The codes are relatively simple,> Maii began. <All communication must be in TAN-C cipher, or it will be rejected instantly. When the AI on the communications satellite asks for the password, the correct reply is 'black water.' When it asks for verification, respond with 'QBFH.'>

"Understood," replied the Box. Roche wondered briefly through the electric fog how the Box had heard the reave, then realized that it must have detected the telepathic impulse through her own implants. "The message, Veden?"

"Is to be addressed to the most senior presiding judge of the High Equity Court on Bini."

"Rehlaender?"

"Whoever. But mark it urgent, as per the agreement with

the Commerce Artel of '954.28.09. Encrypt it in YEAMAN cipher, and begin with the words 'All the great butterflies are dying.'"

Roche closed her eyes as the Eckandi dictated the brief message requesting an urgent High Equity Court hearing to discuss the sovereignty of the native inhabitants of Sciacca's World. The Eckandi's mission was secondary to her own, and she was impatient to move on. The sooner she contacted her superiors in COE Intelligence, the sooner she could expect to be rescued.

But the lights flashing behind her eyes were hypnotic, as was the ceaseless babble of voices just below the threshold of her hearing. Her skin felt as though it was being brushed by thousands of tiny hands, touching, probing, pulling her in every direction, as the data pouring through her system fed back through her implants and into her brain itself.

Only with great difficulty did she regain control long enough to realize that Veden had finished. She closed her eyes in an attempt to clear the unnerving sensation of seeing from many points of view at once, and took a step forward. Her thighs struck the edge of the processor, helping her reaffirm her grip on reality.

<The message—> She realized that she was subvocalizing and the others therefore couldn't hear her. "Has the message gone?"

"Yes," said Emmerik. "All we have to do is wait for a reply."

"Standard communication to this sector may take days," said the Box.

"Better than nothing." The Mbatan beamed. "It's been sent, that's the main thing."

<Veden and I can go home,> said Maii, her mental voice tinged with relief and anticipation.

"Wait," Roche said. "What about—?"

"Not now," said Cane. "Look at the screens. I think we have a problem."

Roche opened her eyes and focused as best she could upon the view of the landing field. A moment passed before she realized what she was supposed to see: two flyers, circling the MiCom building.

"Both guidance systems are shielded," said the Box. "I am unable to countermand their pilots."

"It's only a matter of time before they fire," said Neva worriedly.

"Time and politics," Haid said. "Delcasalle won't want his precious installation blown to bits if he can help it."

"Does internal security cover the roof?" asked Cane.

"Yes," said Haid. "At least we don't have to worry about ground troops coming on us through the ceiling without us knowing—"

"I am registering a security breach!" interrupted the Box.

"Where?" said Haid.

"This level. Exact location unknown."

"The door?" Haid asked.

A screen flickered, displaying an image of the security door at the entrance to the top floor. It was undamaged.

"We'd better have a look anyway," said Haid. "In case they've managed to infiltrate the mainframe with a virus or something."

"Impossible," said the Box. "I would know if the image had been tampered with."

"He's right, Box." Roche looked around her; the fog cleared slightly. "I'll go with you, Haid. Can I let go of this damn thing now, Box?"

"Yes. Having established the link, I am able to reroute the data from transmitters in the—"

"Good." Roche took her hand off the datalink and stepped back from the central processor. The flow continued unchecked, but now that she had something to do, it felt less distracting. "Let's go."

Haid led the way through the maze of corridors. A steady *thump-thump*, perhaps from energy cannon, became noticeable as they approached the door.

"They're trying to blast their way in," said Haid, grimacing.

"Possibly. Neither of the troopers on the floor below has that sort of equipment, though. It might be something else."

"Such as?"

Roche shrugged. Through the nagging buzz of the Box, she couldn't think of another possibility.

The door, when they reached it, was undamaged. Haid placed his hand on the compounded metal.

"It's cool," he said. "So at least we know they're not burning their way through." He cursed under his breath. "What the hell *are* they up to?"

At that moment, a muffled blast echoed through the top floor, and the steady thumping ceased. In its wake, a siren began to wail. The floor's security had failed, somewhere.

Haid and Roche headed back the way they had come. As they rounded a corner, they ran straight into a cloud of black smoke. Holding their breath, they rushed through. They entered clear air on the far side, and Haid became more vocal with his cursing.

"They came up through the floor!" he said. "Tell the Box to seal all access doors except the ones we need—"

<I have already taken that precaution,> the Box said into her thoughts.

"It's already done." Roche clutched the grip of her rifle more tightly. "How much further?"

"Not far. We—"

A door they had just passed suddenly dissolved into a ball of white flame. Seeing two armored figures climb through the smoking hole, Roche doubled her speed. They passed through another open access door, which hissed shut behind them, then entered MiCom Control. A sturdier airlock sealed the way behind them, but not before Roche saw the door farther down the corridor burst open.

"We have to move," said Haid, gesturing urgently at the exit on the far side of the room. "Is there another way out of the building from this floor?"

"Only the roof," said Cane.

"I can launch transport to pick you up," offered the Box. "As we discussed earlier."

"Do it," said Haid. "How long will it take?"

"Five minutes," said the Box.

"*Damn.* That's too long." The rebel leader looked thoughtful for a moment, then glanced at Emmerik. The Mbatan nodded.

"Okay, Box," said Haid, turning back to Roche. "Broadcast a message over the radio transmitters, 115.6 kilohertz.

The message is: 'Retribution.' That's all. Repeat it three times." Haid nodded. "That should delay the Dato for long enough."

The airlock crackled as repeated batteries from energy weapons heated it beyond its tolerance. The smell of scorched metal filled the room.

"Move, people!" Haid waved them out of the control room, one by one. Neva and Roche once again helped Veden onto the back of the combat suit and slid his arms through the straps. With every heavy step, the Eckandi's breath hissed softly in Roche's ear; his arms hung limp around her throat.

The corridor led to another maze of offices.

"Which way?" Emmerik called.

Roche relayed directions given by the Box until they reached a narrow flight of metal stairs leading to a service hatch in the ceiling. Neva went first, nudging the hatch aside with the barrel of her rifle, then slipping through. Emmerik went next, then Jytte, Roche and Veden, Maii and the others. Haid, the last through, dogged the hatch behind him and stood up to survey the view.

They stood in a glass-windowed observation platform, half open to the evening air. Wind snatched at Roche's face, carrying with it the sharp sting of dust. The sound of the two flyers circling the building was loud in her ears, rising and falling as the craft came closer, then drifted away. From the base of the building, voices floated up to them, shouting orders, calling for reinforcements. Plumes of smoke still rose from the foyer, as well as from the burning truck by the main gates.

The city of Port Parvati lay under a deep shroud of black, deepening by the moment as the sun slipped below the horizon. Only the seemingly solid band of the Soul remained to illuminate the battlefield. Far away and to the northeast, a storm hovered over the mountains like an enormous, shadowy beast, waiting to spring.

"Are you okay, Veden?" Roche asked over her shoulder.

"I'm still here," breathed the elderly Eckandi.

"Hang in there."

"If we keep low," called Emmerik from the far side of the platform, "the troops in the flyers might not see us."

"Agreed," said Haid, edging away from the hatch.

<How long, Box?> Roche subvocalized.

<Three minutes, Morgan.>

A thump from below made them all tense; the two troopers had found the stairwell.

<There's only the one,> mind-whispered the Surin. <Let him come.>

Haid nodded. He remained where he was, though, a half dozen paces from the hatch with his rifle trained on the place the trooper's head would appear.

Roche jumped as a flash of white split the sunset. The hatch exploded into the air and clattered to one side—blown upward by fire from below. Maii hissed between her teeth as she fought to regain control of the Dato trooper. One armored hand reached out of the hole in the roof, clutching for purchase. With servos whining, the sleek, shining suit clambered into the night air, its high-powered rifle slung over one shoulder—

And stood there, immobile, frozen by the reave's will.

Cane ducked closer to retrieve the rifle at the same time the nearest flyer snarled angrily overhead.

"They've seen us!" Haid shouted over the noise, crouching automatically as fire strafed the observation platform.

Cane fired at the belly of the flyer as it sped away from them. The powerful Dato weapon discharged fierce bolts of blue-white energy that sparked viciously when they hit. Cane kept firing as the flyer curved upward into the sky to avoid the attack. Only when the craft dipped lower and vanished behind the bulk of the building did Cane let go of the trigger. The previously constant whine of its engines had changed slightly, become more irregular, halting.

Damaged at least, thought Roche, if not out of the game entirely.

The second flyer swooped to attack, this time more cautiously. Its underbelly turrets rotated smoothly, seeking the upright figure of Cane. He ducked and rolled for cover behind the frozen Dato trooper. The flyer's shots landed wide of the mark, destroying what remained of the platform's low roof and sending glass shards flying.

When the second flyer had passed, Roche let go the breath she had been holding. Too close, she thought. *Much* too close. It was only a matter of time before the flyer returned—and this time, they might not be so lucky.

A concussion from below heralded the arrival of a new form of attack: mortar bombs. The whistle of the shell grew rapidly louder, with no clear way to tell where it would hit. Then the corner of the observation platform where Jytte was standing suddenly exploded. The shock wave knocked everyone off their feet except for Roche, who watched helplessly as the woman was flung through the air amid a burning hail of rubble.

Roche staggered, hurriedly clearing grit from her eyes. The whistle of another mortar coincided with the growing whine of the undamaged flyer. She sought cover on the exposed platform—but there was nowhere to hide.

"We're too exposed up here!" she shouted over the noise.

"I know," Haid shouted back. "But we don't have any—"

The second mortar exploded, cutting him off. Roche once again held her ground. She hadn't had time to recover, however, before a solid kick knocked the rifle from her hands.

She stumbled back a step, blinking furiously, distracted by dust and the fog caused by the Box. Another blow spun her sideways before her suit could correct her balance. Raising an arm desperately, she managed to block the third blow. The solid ring of armor on armor coincided with her realization of who was attacking her.

The Dato trooper—released from his stupor by Maii's distraction—stepped back to aim a kick at her stomach. She dodged aside, attempting to twist him about his center of gravity while he was off balance. But his suit was too fast, or hers too old, and he pivoted easily out of her grasp. Cursing, she aimed a solid blow to his helmet that hurt her fist, even through the armored glove.

The power-assists of his joints growled as he assumed a combat stance—arms outstretched, legs planted firmly to either side—and waited for Roche's next move. She feinted to the right, jabbed at his shoulder with her left fist. The blow glanced aside, and he elbowed her in the chest. His other hand swept up to strike her in the exposed face, but she ducked in time. She felt the clenched ceramic glove pass by bare millimeters from her ear, then ducked under his arm to strike him in the stomach.

He staggered backward. Roche, back-heavy because of Veden and winded by the blow to her chest, didn't press her advantage as she would have liked to. The second flyer screamed by overhead, strobing the dusk on all sides, distracting her. The trooper ducked low and charged, using his helmet as a battering ram. Roche lunged to one side in time to avoid the crude attack, but not quickly enough to dodge the outswept arm that almost knocked her off her feet.

She cursed breathlessly, hating to admit that she was no match for the trooper in hand-to-hand combat—outclassed by superior technology, confused by external impulses invading her own head, and forced to take her elderly passenger into account. But she had no choice, and her companions were too busy trying to survive to assist her. Distantly, she noted the steady blast of the Dato rifle in Cane's hands as it once again sought the undamaged flyer.

While the armored figure turned to charge again, she searched for the rifle on the blackened roof, and found it nearby. Unfortunately, the trooper noted the shifting of her gaze and also saw the weapon.

They lunged simultaneously at the same moment another mortar exploded nearby. Roche arrived an instant sooner, sweeping the rifle into one hand. The trooper's gloved hands closed over hers as she tried to turn the weapon on him. Slowly but inexorably he forced the barrel back toward her face. She grunted, trying to fight the superior strength of the Dato suit until the blood sang in her ears.

She looked away from the mirrored visor of her opponent and down into the black eye of the rifle. The hand clutching the trigger guard tightened, prepared to snap the metal bracket simply to make the gun fire. Once would be enough. Once, and Roche would never have to worry about her mission—or the Box—again.

Then something reached past her, over her shoulder, and the weight on her back shifted. A naked hand battered at the

Dato trooper's visor, distracting him momentarily. The barrel shifted aside a bare instant before the weapon discharged, dazzling Roche and singeing the side of her head.

She pushed herself away from the trooper, screaming, and the weight slipped from her shoulders. *Veden!* she screamed—*Veden!* Then realized that the voice issued from inside her head and not from herself. It was simultaneously coming from all around her and from the depths of her very being.

Veden!

Flames clutched at her scalp, digging in with claws of fire, and she fell backward. Her hip absorbed most of the impact, sending waves of pain through her weak ribs and shoulder. Still screaming through the stench of burning skin and hair, she batted at the fire with her gloved palms until it was out.

Only then did she open her eyes.

The Dato trooper was standing over her—dead, but still standing, as the Surin's scream ripped his mind apart. Eventually, with a quiver, the suit toppled backward and lay still.

Roche rolled over and, through the one eye that had recovered from the energy bolt, stared at the body of the Eckandi lying next to her. The top of his skull had been blown away.

Veden!

The scream cut short with a wrench of emotion that would have overwhelmed all of them on the observation platform had it not been quashed instantly by its source. It was replaced by a high-pitched, keening wail of grief. Roche clambered to her knees and sought the Surin through the smoke and darkness. The girl was nowhere to be seen, so she sent her mind instead—to comfort, to support, to succor. But the wail—the only audible sound that she had ever heard from the Surin—continued unchecked.

Then Emmerik's voice sliced through the noise and the rising buzz of the undamaged flyer as it turned to strafe the building yet again:

"They're here! Ameidio, they're here!"

Roche climbed unsteadily to her feet and hauled herself to the edge of the platform, following the direction indicated by Emmerik's outflung hand. Below, in the gloom, she could see heads turning as Enforcement faced a new enemy. Not the flyer the Box had arranged to meet them, but a ground force of some kind—at least two hundred armed people swarming on foot through the open gates of the landing field.

"Box—" She stopped, cleared her throat of dust. Through the buzz of data and the ringing in her ears, her voice sounded inhumanly hoarse. "Box, give me a clearer picture. Use the security cameras and enhance the image."

The view through her left eye split in two. In one portion she saw as normal; in the other, she zoomed closer to the attacking squad. She glimpsed figures dressed in what looked like crude robes, carrying identical weapons. Her ears caught the sound of an unfamiliar discharge: not harsh, like energy rifles, but almost musical—a split-second chime at a very low frequency.

She struggled to identify the sound until the view pulled back to encompass the Enforcers below. One by one, as the strange weapons fired, energy rifles failed. Armored suits locked, immobile, and toppled to the earth. The second flyer swooped low to investigate this new challenge, and its engine changed pitch as sections of its drive malfunctioned instantly.

HFM weapons, she realized. Of an ancient design, too. But where—?

She whirled around to face Haid and Emmerik. "You told me they were radioactive!"

"They were," said the Mbatan.

"They marked a *graveyard*!"

"And will again when they are returned." Emmerik limped closer, smiling sadly. "They are the one and only asset belonging to the descendants of the original settlers. What better use could they be put to than to revenge the deaths of the people they once killed?"

Roche shook her head, understanding but feeling betrayed anyway. With such an arsenal, the capture of the landing field could have been accomplished much more peacefully, with much less bloodshed. But it wasn't her place to criticize; she was alive, and the chances of escape seemed markedly less remote than they had just moments ago.

Cane joined her at the edge of the platform, watching the battle take place below. The peace guns cut a swath through Dato troops and Enforcers alike. No mortars had been fired since the arrival of the ghosts of Houghton's Cross. She supposed that she should start feeling safe sometime soon. Yet she doubted she would ever feel safe again—at least, not until she was off the planet and back at Intelligence HQ.

<My feelings exactly,> said the Box.

<How about sending my message, then?> she asked.

<No, Morgan. I cannot allow you to do that.>

The flat negative surprised her. <Box, I'm *ordering* you to—>

"Transport's arrived!" called Haid from the far side of the building. Cane's nudge in the back of her suit forced Roche to concentrate on more immediate matters. Her scalp stung where fire had eaten into it, and the Surin's wail continued to gnaw at her thoughts. Whatever the Box was playing at, she could deal with it later—when the flyer had taken them somewhere safe, somewhere she could think clearly.

Engines snarled as something large loomed out of the night sky and swooped over their heads. Relief turned to anxiety, however, as she realized that the craft wasn't the standard COE design used on the prison planet. This was a military design, snub-nosed and powerful.

"But," she began, "that's a Dato—"

"I know." The familiar voice came from behind her.

She turned and found herself face to face with Cane. His habitual half-smile was gone. She tensed by instinct, and would have stepped away, but the armor had become rigid. She couldn't move.

"What's happening—?" She looked down in annoyance, wrenching her limbs impotently within the suit. No matter what she did, however, the suit remained completely lifeless. "I'm trapped!"

She looked up again in time to see Cane draw back his fist. Her eyes widened in horror as she flinched and tried to turn away—but the motion was futile. Unable to move her body, there was no way she could avoid the blow.

It connected solidly on her burned temple. Light exploded behind her eyes, blinding her; then three distinct sounds chased her into darkness:

—the snarl of the shuttle as it swooped level with the roof—

—the solid thump of her armored body striking the platform beneath her—

—and the voice of Cane, barely audible over the noise of the shuttle, muttering a single, sickening word.

"Exactly."

PART FOUR:

ANA VEREINE

17

Despite the calm appearance of his image, Captain Uri Kajic was a worried man.

Six hours had passed since the last communication with the Port Parvati landing party, in which Major Gyori had indicated that he was preparing to ambush Roche and the rebels as they attacked the landing field. Since then, nothing had been heard from anyone. All surface communications had been jammed from the landing field's MiCom installation. Kajic, watching closely from geosynchronous orbit, had waited in the grip of an intense anxiety for an update, his thoughts constantly nagged by reminders of his priorities. As fighting had erupted on the surface of Sciacca's World, smoke from numerous fires burning in and around the city had effectively masked infrared surveillance, and a poorly timed dust storm had compounded the problem by smothering visual light and radar. Whatever was going on in the landing field's MiCom installation, he could not guess. For all he knew, the battle might have ended hours ago.

Stranded in his skybound eyrie, he could do little but

wait, consumed by doubts, recriminations, and half-spoken fears.

priority gold-one

"Second Lieutenant Nisov reports that her squad is ready to launch." Makaev had abandoned the pretense that Kajic's hologram was a real person. She remained in her position, next to the command dais, speaking to him solely via the nearest microphone.

Kajic's image nodded in acknowledgment. The plan to send another landing party into the maelstrom had not been his, but he was forced to admit that it made sense. Even a low reconnaissance flight would do more good than ill. "Have her stand by, awaiting my command."

"Sir, a delay at this point—"

"Will make little difference," Kajic interrupted irritably. "I wish to give Major Gyori one more chance to report."

capture Commander Roche and AI JW111101000

"This seems unlikely, sir, as the interference from the planet has not lessened since—"

Kajic shrugged this aside. "While we are being jammed, we know that the battle is continuing. I see no reason to send reinforcements just yet."

Makaev's scowl deepened. "Then perhaps we should reconsider disabling the DAOC transmitter station."

"Why? Has there been another coded hyperspace transmission?"

"No, but—"

"Then your reasons for wishing it disabled are unclear."

at all costs

"It's a *threat*, sir. If the Armada has not already been informed of our presence here—"

"Even if they have, they will arrive too late. Destroying the satellite will have repercussions further-reaching than our present situation. We have already left too much evidence that might implicate us."

with as much stealth and speed as possible

"Sir, I wish you would reconsider—"

priority gold-one

"Enough!" Kajic shouted at the voices tormenting him. "I

am in command of this vessel, and if I say we should wait, then that's exactly what we will do!"

Makaev's face darkened, anger boiling beneath its surface. "Yes . . . sir."

Kajic noted the woman's insolent tone, the contemptuous hesitation before the honorific was finally granted, but he refrained from commenting. Traitor or loyal servant? If he pushed much harder, he might soon find out which.

priority gold-one

The telemetry officer intruded softly. "Captain . . . ?"

Kajic turned to face her. "Yes? Report!"

"We are registering a transmission from the surface," she said, tasting her lips nervously. "A precise fix is impossible through the interference, sir, but it does seem to be coming from the landing field transponders. And . . . it's directed at us."

Kajic paused momentarily. "What sort of transmission?"

"Presently unknown, sir. We are detecting only a carrier wave."

"Let me know when the source of the transmission and its contents are confirmed. It may be Major Gyori attempting to report."

"Sir." The officer returned to her station, her face a mask of concentration. Kajic glanced at Makaev, but his second was busy relaying his previous orders. Accurately, he hoped.

priority /

/ gold-one

Suddenly, people were staring at him. Half the bridge crew had swiveled in their combat harnesses to focus on the command dais.

"Atalia," he said, perplexed. "What's going on?"

"You . . . disappeared, sir." Kajic's second stared at him openly from her station. "We tried to call you, but you didn't answer."

Kajic sent a self-diagnostic probe through his circuitry and systems. A millisecond later it returned: all clear. "There has been no malfunction."

"But you—" Makaev stopped, swallowed. "For an instant there your persona just *ceased*."

"That's impossible," Kajic snapped, feeling panic stirring in his mind. "I sensed no discontinuity."

"Are you certain?"

"Of course I am!" Despite his denial, Kajic's uncertainty manifested itself as anger, under which loomed a growing fear that maybe stress was causing a malfunction in his circuitry.

priority gold-one

"Just let me *think*." He said this aloud, wanting to silence the voice in his head, although he immediately regretted it. His behavior had provoked a look of concern from a number of the faces around the bridge, and he knew he couldn't afford to have them doubt his competency at this vital stage of the mission.

Trying to reestablish a sense of control and thus regain the confidence of his crew, Kajic casually folded his arms behind his back and addressed Makaev in a smooth and calm manner.

"The transmission," he said. "Has its source been identified?"

"No, sir." Although most of the crew slowly returned to their duties, Makaev's worried frown remained. She wasn't fooled by his attempt to resume proceedings as though nothing had happened. "Analysis concluded that it was probably a spurious echo of our own transmissions," she said. "There has still been no word from Major Gyori."

This last part was spoken a little smugly, Kajic thought, but he refused to rise to the bait. "Nevertheless," he said. "We will wait a little longer. Five minutes more, then we will assume that Major Gyori has failed."

Kajic kept his image on the bridge overlooking the crew, trying desperately to maintain an even composure and not submit to the anxiety that increased with each passing second. The truth was, he suspected that Makaev was right: if he waited too long to send backup, the opportunity might be lost forever. Should he trust his own judgment in the aftermath of what had apparently happened to him? *Was* he malfunctioning in some unanticipated, subtle way, without being aware of it himself?

If so, then there was only one way to find out.

Two minutes passed. Then three. Fifty seconds before the deadline, telemetry spoke again:

"Sir—we are registering a launch!"

Kajic turned to face the screen. "Elaborate," he said. "I want all available data."

A map of the region appeared. "One craft, rising through the dust above the landing field," said the officer. A flashing red dot appeared on the screen. "A surface-to-orbit vehicle—probably one of our own, judging by its emissions. No communication as yet."

"They are still too close to the source of the interference," Kajic said. "It must be Gyori. Given the traffic ban, only one of our own would be so bold as to launch unannounced."

"It could be a ruse, sir," Makaev cautioned.

"I am aware of that possibility." Kajic remained pensive for a few moments before speaking. "Instruct *Paladin* and *Galloglass* to intercept before it reaches orbit, just in case."

"Sir." She turned away to relay the orders.

Kajic watched the screen closely. The red dot rose higher, curving slowly to reach orbit. Green dots marked the two raiders as they dropped to meet it, swooping like aerial hunters with claws extended upon some lone and silent prey. Then:

"Ident confirmed," said telemetry, swiveling around to face the captain. "It *is* the shuttle, sir."

"But still no communication?"

"No, sir. There has been . . ." She paused, pressing at the communication bud in her ear. "Wait," she said, leaning over her console to concentrate. "Something's coming through now." Another pause. "They are requesting permission to dock."

"*Who*, exactly?" asked Makaev, the suspicion clearly evident in her tone.

Kajic also thought he detected a brief expression of annoyance flicker across her face. Had her plans to subvert him been foiled, or was he just imagining things?

"He has identified himself as Sergeant Komazec." Silence as telemetry once again listened. "He says that there have been many casualties—Major Gyori included. It seems that—"

priority gold-one

"The *mission*," Kajic snapped, silencing both the officer and the prompts from his programming. The deaths of Gyori and the others were regrettable, but irrelevant. "What is the status of their mission?"

Another unheard exchange between telemetry and the sergeant passed before: "They have the COE agent and the AI aboard, sir."

Kajic did smile, then. "Permission to dock granted," he said. "Atalia, notify the commanding officers of *Paladin*, *Galloglass*, and *Lansequenet* that we will be leaving in two hours."

Makaev nodded once. "As you wish, sir."

Yes, thought Kajic to himself, not caring for once who might be listening through his back door. Yes, I *do* wish. And this is your *captain* speaking. . . .

The snub-nosed shuttle, trimmed and ready to dock, approached the grey bulk of the *Ana Vereine*, propelled by increasingly delicate nudges from its thrusters. As the orbits overlapped, the shuttle's relative velocity decreased until it was practically stationary with respect to the larger ship. The last few meters passed most slowly of all, as the nose of the shuttle edged into a vacant gantry.

A muffled clang announced that contact had been made. The gantry's manifold waldoes enfolded the shuttle in a gentle embrace and tugged it deeper into the mother ship, where cables waited like open-mouthed serpents to link it to the *Ana Vereine*'s life support. A gaping transit corridor groped for the airlock lip, clung tight, and pressurized. All that remained was the linking of computer systems; only after that would the shuttle truly be home.

Dato Bloc engineers called this final process "unscrambling the egg." Kajic had watched many thousand such maneuvers from the cameras installed in the hangar's ceiling, but never before with so much at stake. On the contents of this particular egg rested not only his mission, but perhaps his very life.

"The shuttle has docked," Makaev said from the bridge. "When its cargo has been unloaded and verified, we will be ready to leave."

"Very good." Kajic resisted the impulse to tell her that she was stating the obvious. Now that the crisis had passed, she was performing her duty as impeccably as ever. Perhaps—if she truly was the traitor—he had finally earned her trust. Either that, or she was simply biding her time. . . .

The shuttle's airlock, invisible within the transit corridor, opened with a hiss and distracted him from that train of thought. He moved to a camera within sight of the egress airlock and waited. Not long after, heavy footsteps tramped down the short corridor, and booted feet appeared. Two fully armored troopers led the way, their suits blackened and charred by battle. Two others followed close behind. Between the latter two hung a suspension stretcher, and on the stretcher lay—

Was it her? Kajic hardly dared to believe his eyes. Could it really be . . . ?

Of course it could. There was no mistaking that face, even partly burned and swollen. He had studied her files extensively over the last few days, so much so that her image was now imprinted upon his mind.

Lying unconscious on the stretcher was Commander Morgan Roche of COE Intelligence. Beside her, still connected to her wrist by a length of cord, was the valise. The AI.

He only half heard the brief radio communication between the landing party and the hangar techs. His thoughts were elsewhere, focused instead upon the blessed silence that now filled his mind. Suddenly, with his mission completed, the priorities had ceased their endless prompting. That alone made the success of his mission worthwhile. To be free of interference for a while; to be *himself*.

Then, without warning, as though following on the heels of that very thought, came a new invasion, a new priority:

return at once to Szubetka Base
priority gold-one

The sense of elation sank as quickly as it had surfaced. Not until his hologram stood before the Ethnarch and the

Military Presidium and he presented his report would they allow him to entertain any sense of achievement. Only then, perhaps, would he be free.

He watched after the unconscious commander with an overwhelming sense of exhaustion. There was still work to be done. Perhaps, he thought, returning his image to the bridge, there always would be.

"We are secured to break orbit, sir."

return at once

Kajic nodded as he looked one last time at the picture of Sciacca's World on display. "Do so," he said tiredly.

Dissolving the hologram, Kajic swung his attention through the ship, performing a quick scan of the drive chambers, the matter-antimatter fuel mix, and astrogation's plotted course. Beyond the metal shell of his surrogate body, the three raiders accompanying the *Ana Vereine* performed similar checks before leaving the system.

When the time came, four mighty engines fired, casting a false dawn over the facing hemisphere of Sciacca's World. The Soul twinkled around them, then behind them, as they rose above the equatorial plane. In strict formation, the four ships swooped over the northern pole and its tiny patch of ice, angled down past the Soul again, then aimed toward the orange sun. The intrasystem thrusters flared to maximum power, the Soul flashed one last time, and then they were free of the planet's gravity well.

Their course would take them around the sun, past the smallish gas giant on the far side, and out to the system's nearest anchor point. When they reached that point, in three days' time, they would depart the Hutton-Luu System forever.

return to Szubetka Base

Four hours into their journey, when he was certain that everything was proceeding according to plan, Kajic focused his attention on internal matters. More specifically, on Sergeant Komazec's report of events that had transpired on Sciacca's World.

The ambush at the landing field had been a disaster, due in part to the fact that Major Gyori had attempted to capture

Roche without the assistance of the local Enforcers. Despite being severely outnumbered, Roche's strike force had successfully penetrated the MiCom building and taken control of the installation. How she had accomplished this, exactly, was something of a mystery, although it seemed that she had allied herself with at least one powerful epsense adept whose powers gave her a significant tactical advantage.

Once inside the building, she had used the AI to assume control of the MiCom installation. But instead of sending a message requesting assistance from the Armada, she had broadcast a plea on behalf of the local rebels. Why, Kajic could only guess. Perhaps she had owed it to the rebels who had helped her, been obliged to aid them in their cause before they would let her complete her own mission—which, thankfully, she had been unable to do.

Under pressure from Dato troopers within the building, she and her allies had been forced to the roof. Two Enforcement flyers commandeered by Major Gyori's squad had harried her from the air while Enforcement used mortars to weaken their position from below.

But still Roche had not given up. One of the flyers—the one containing Major Gyori—had been damaged in the battle. And somehow she had taken remote control of the landing party's shuttle, possibly to seek refuge in the transmitter station orbiting the planet.

It was at this point that luck had turned in favor of Sergeant Komazec, who had assumed command of the landing party following Major Gyori's untimely death.

Weakened by casualties of their own—and the neutralization of their reave—Roche's band had turned against her. Knowing that escape from the planet was impossible with the Dato ships enforcing the blockade, and that any defense of the landing field was temporary at best, they had overpowered her and attempted to negotiate. Speaking from inside the shuttle, one of them had coordinated a meeting between the landing party and the rebels, the intention being to exchange Roche for safe passage.

The meeting had taken place on the roof of the DAOC Administration building. Sergeant Komazec had agreed to everything. The ultimate fate of the rebels—and, indeed,

DAOC Enforcement itself, a one-time ally—was irrelevant. The AI and its courier were all that mattered.

Roche, unconscious and injured, was brought out of the shuttle, with the AI, and handed over to the soldiers of the Dato Bloc.

Once Roche was safe, Komazec had opened fire upon the rebels and regained control of the shuttle. He had left no survivors. Not one. Such ruthlessness might once have appalled Kajic, but now, with his priorities burning so effectively into his conscience, he felt only indifference. All that mattered was that the AI and Roche *had* been successfully returned to him. His mission had been accomplished.

He directed his attention to Roche in the sick bay holding cells. She was still unconscious, still attached to the AI. The stolen combat suit had been removed, and the burns on her scalp, face, and neck were undergoing treatment, as were minor injuries to her ribs, shoulder, and hip; apart from that, she had been left in peace. Until they were certain how deep the link between her and the AI extended, the *Ana Vereine*'s surgeons would not dare sever it from her.

In less than a week she would be a captive of the Presidium, an unwilling accomplice in the ongoing state of tension existing between the Dato Bloc and Commonwealth governments. She would become a traitor of the worst kind, one whose involuntary betrayal meant the deaths of friends, family, and colleagues.

This saddened him, obscurely. She had no choice in the matter—an impotence he could empathize with. It would have been better for her if she had died on Sciacca's World. That way, her mission would only have failed, not been perverted to her enemies' ends.

He looked forward to the opportunity of meeting her properly, when he could speak to her face to face, one soldier to another. She had been a worthy adversary throughout his assignment. . . .

return to Szubetka Base

As he scanned through Komazec's report one final time, he noticed a minor item in the inventory that he had missed earlier. The body of an elderly Eckandi male, apparently killed during the attack, had also been returned to the *Ana*

Vereine. His exact identity was unknown, but, from what little the rebels had said when handing over Roche, Komazec had received the impression that it had been the Eckandi who had arranged the message to the COE High Equity Court. Possibly he was a clandestine member of the Commerce Artel; not unlikely, given his citizenship in the Eckandar Trade Axis. The body, with its distinctive flash burns from a Dato weapon, had been recovered as a precaution to divert the powerful Artel's wrath.

Kajic had to admire Komazec's quick thinking. Such a move had been entirely in accordance with his own orders. Second only to success, stealth had been the important thing. And, while the mission might not have gone as well as he had hoped, at least he could say that nothing had been overlooked. His crew had acted without fault, which would reflect well upon his command.

Yet how near defeat had been: the panicky moments before Komazec's return; the interminable waiting, the lack of information; then the apparent malfunction of his own systems, and Makaev's almost open defiance. A few minutes longer . . .

But now, with Roche safely aboard the ship and the remains of the penal colony receding into the distance, those moments were irrelevant. The end result was all that mattered.

Twenty-eight hours away from the penal colony, he arranged for the body of the Eckandi to be placed in cold storage, performed one last check of his ship, then resigned his higher functions to oblivion.

Sleep, he mused to himself as darkness slowly fell. The one true reward after battle.

He dreamed—

. . . of voices he could almost hear, faces he could almost see, people who almost existed . . .

. . . of chains binding him tightly, binding his nonexistent body, holding him firmly while some terrible threat approached, against which he could not move to defend himself . . .

. . . of things forgotten, things not noticed, things he should have attended to . . .

. . . of his home planet, which, from above, appeared as a woman's face, a once faceless woman whose features were even now strangely blurred . . .

. . . of details too small to focus on in a picture too large to comprehend . . .

. . . of a person, another face, a voice calling him—

"Captain? Can you hear me, Captain?"

Filled with a premonitory dread, Kajic awoke with a mental jerk.

A few seconds later, the voice spoke again: "*Captain?*"

"Atalia?" Slowly the sleep-numbed layers of his mind peeled away. An image of his second in command appeared, staring directly into a camera, directly at *him*, concern pressing at her features. "What is it? What's happened?"

"Nothing, sir," she said, the words belying the look on her face. "I just need to speak to you in private."

In private? Kajic echoed in his thoughts. Then her news couldn't be urgent. The ship must be safe. The relief, after the ominous dreams, was almost overwhelming.

"Very well," he said.

She turned away from the camera and took a seat while Kajic gathered his thoughts, mentally sweeping his mind clean of the detritus of the dream. More hints, more unconscious suggestions—he was sure of it—but they would have to wait until later. Taking a moment to access the events he had missed while his higher centers were sleeping, he realized that they were fifty-two hours from Sciacca's World, just over two-thirds of the way. He had slept for almost an entire day.

Remarkable though that was, he didn't let it bother him. With their departure proceeding smoothly and a major campaign behind them, it was unsurprising that he needed rest.

A few seconds elapsed before he formed his hologram in the command module where Makaev sat waiting. She stood instantly to attention, then relaxed when he waved her at ease.

"I assume this has nothing to do with the ship," he said after she had returned to her seat.

"Not exactly, sir, no." Makaev sighed, shifting uneasily. "It's the crew. They are restless—nervous."

"Of what?"

Makaev paused, as though what she was about to say pained her. "Of . . . ghosts, sir."

Before he could respond, she quickly added, "I know what you're about to say, Captain, and believe me, I thought the same thing myself. But in the last six hours I've received three separate reports and heard rumors of several more. The sightings are all confined to the lower decks, to maintenance areas and cold stores. The witnesses have all been single crew members performing unscheduled duties. The encounters were all brief, comprising little more than a glimpse of another person—who instantly vanished."

"What about security?" said Kajic thoughtfully.

"No trace has been found on any of the recordings. Even in the three cases where we've had exact times and locations, nothing out of the ordinary has been seen."

Kajic mulled this over for a moment. "The obvious possibility is that we have unwittingly taken aboard a stowaway or two. Transportees, or some of the rebels perhaps . . . ?"

"My thoughts exactly, sir," said Makaev. "After the second report, I contacted Sergeant Komazec. He assured me that there was no possible way anyone could have smuggled themselves onto the shuttle. The only other bodies aboard, apart from crew, were Roche and the Eckandi. One of those is dead, and the other hasn't even regained consciousness.

"Furthermore, I have also checked with the main computer. No stores are missing; we are showing no extra mass and no unexpected demands on life support. And every one of the crew can be accounted for, which rules out the possibility of substitution. If what we have here *is* a stowaway, then it might as well be a ghost."

"Nevertheless," said Kajic. "The fact remains that the crew is restless. Correct?"

Makaev nodded. "And the more word spreads, the worse it becomes."

Kajic regarded her steadily for a few moments, biting back irritation. "Well, the only thing we can do about it at this stage is to step up security, to make sure every area below deck is watched at all times. If we do have some sort of stowaway, ghost or otherwise, it's bound to appear eventually."

"Which is why I've come to you." Makaev paused and leaned forward. "As suggested by yourself, the crew is now on soft duties following our mission. I am reluctant to give them more work at the moment, not until we're at least out of the system. Yet we have to do *something* now. Let the rumors continue unchecked, and the *Ana Vereine* runs the risk of—"

"Enough," Kajic cut in. He could see where she was headed. "You want me to conduct the security sweeps?"

"It seems logical, sir. You are more vigilant than any single member of the crew, and you have direct access to the required systems. In fact, they're integral to you." She hesitated, as though suddenly realizing something. "Of course, that's if you're up to it, sir. I mean, it has been a difficult week. . . ."

Kajic was glad for once that he didn't have a physical body to betray his autonomic responses—otherwise a flush of rage would have turned his face a deep, bright red. How dare she? Did she think him stupid? If he agreed to conduct the surveillance of the ship, then he *was* placing himself under unnecessary stress and perhaps risking a potential breakdown—but if he said no, then he would be admitting weakness at a time when he couldn't afford to do so.

Her blatant attempt at manipulation was clumsy, to say the least—so much so that it might feasibly, and perversely, have been entirely innocent.

Either way, he had no choice.

"For the sake of the crew's peace of mind," he said, "I think your suggestion a sensible one. I shall begin immediately."

She sighed with apparent satisfaction and stood. "Thank you, sir. I'll see that you have all the information immediately. The sooner the rumors are quashed, the better."

He nodded, agreeing with that, at least. Although he denied the existence of either ghosts or stowaways, the very act of looking would undoubtedly reassure everyone in the lower decks. And when he turned up nothing, and no more sightings were reported, the *Ana Vereine* could return to normal.

Yet the feeling of dread that had remained with him after awakening only intensified as he accepted the data from Makaev and examined it carefully. *Had* something gone wrong? Something that he had overlooked or simply not anticipated? With victory so close, he couldn't afford to discount that possibility.

The Box had been handed to him on a plate once already, and Roche had snatched it away, again and again, until he had almost begun to despair at his inability to outwit her. She had eluded his forces on the *Midnight*, in space, through the wilds of Sciacca's World and, finally, in the streets of Port Parvati. Neither the DAOC Enforcers nor the Dato landing party had been able to locate her, until the very end—and even then, she had almost eluded them once again.

Was it so unbelievable that she might do so again?

Only with the sternest mental effort was he able to smother that doubt before it found purchase in his thoughts.

He commenced the search of the lower decks.

After the first hour, he realized that he had something to be grateful for. The sweep kept him occupied, when otherwise he might have drifted aimlessly through the ship, agonizing over his future. The ship could monitor itself; if anything untoward happened, either the automatic systems in his hindbrain or Makaev herself would notify him immediately. By being occupied, he was spared the uncertainty and given an opportunity to do something constructive.

Still, it was tedious work, and his mind tended to wander. After the third hour of staring at empty storerooms and quiescent machinery, he began to alternate the sweep with glances at Roche in her cell, as though to reassure himself that she was still there. She showed no sign of activity; indeed, far from preparing to take control of the ship, she hadn't once regained consciousness. And to Kajic, that in itself was a concern. A brain-damaged informer was not much better than a dead informer—although better than none at all, he supposed.

Of the "ghosts" he had found nothing at all so far. The lower decks were cluttered and cramped, with plenty of hiding places for a single stowaway, but security cameras covered every centimeter. A significant proportion of the crew spent much of their time in these hidden, unglamorous areas, performing small maintenance checks, repairing minor breaks, and ensuring the ship's battle readiness. It was an area rarely visited by the superior officers, and referred to in the vernacular as "the maze" or "the warren."

Kajic estimated that a thorough search of the warren would take between twelve and fifteen hours, yet after only nine hours he had satisfied himself that nothing out of the ordinary existed on the ship. As far as he could see, the only "ghosts" haunting the crew were the same ones that tormented him: guilt, doubt, and uncertainty.

In the eleventh hour, however, another sighting was reported.

In a deep portion of the warren, a maintenance tech stood describing the incident to a workmate. Kajic watched and listened carefully as the woman described seeing a man dressed in grey at the far end of the corridor. The man had looked up, she said, seen her, and suddenly disappeared.

"But he *was* there," the woman insisted. "I swear it!"

Although her testimony was incredible, Kajic didn't doubt her obvious sincerity. Sending himself furiously from camera to camera, he quartered the area around the woman, sweeping through a blur of rooms and corridors—all identical, all unoccupied. Exactly what he was looking for he wasn't sure, but he didn't stop. If he didn't try now, he might never be so close again.

One minute passed, and he had covered every square centimeter within one hundred meters of the sighting. Two minutes, one hundred twenty-five meters. Three minutes, and he was just about ready to give up. Four minutes of strobing, split-second views, and—

He saw it.

It was in one of the little-used stretches of corridor deep in the bowels of the ship. The ambient lighting was low in this particular area, but there could be no doubt. Centered in his field of view were the head and shoulders of a man, a man who shouldn't be there. A man, what's more, whom Kajic didn't immediately recognize.

And then, suddenly, the man was gone. The corridor was empty.

Kajic hesitated for a moment before calling Makaev. What could he say? That he, too, had seen it? That he had succumbed to delusions along with the rest of the crew?

"There has been another sighting," he said when she took the call. "Section Green-24. The same as before."

"I heard." She glanced up from her work station. "In the warren again, and not far from the other sightings, either."

"I know."

Makaev paused. "Did *you* see anything, sir?"

Kajic kept his face carefully neutral. "No," he said. "No, I didn't. However, I will examine the security recordings for a trace. If anything does appear, I will keep you informed."

Kajic retreated into the depths of his mind to study what he had found. The face had been captured by his long-term memory banks, and reappeared before him as vivid and startling as before. And as unfamiliar, even after enhancement removed the shadow that obscured it slightly. Kajic was prepared to bet his life that the face didn't belong to any member of his crew.

But if it didn't, then who *did* it belong to?

The only possible way of finding that out was to run a complete security check on the features. But with only a rough demographic to narrow the search, the check could take hours. Every face in the ship's databanks—and there must have been trillions—would need to be compared to the picture to arrive at a negative. Only if a positive match existed would the search take less time.

Kajic mulled it over, then ordered the search. It couldn't hurt. If his only other avenue came up with nothing, he would still have something to hope for.

Putting the image aside for the moment, he accessed the ship's security records. First, he turned to the moments before the maintenance technician had triggered the alarm. The image was sharp, not yet archived to compressed memory. She stood out clearly, examining a faulty circuit that had failed while she was in the area. Her back was to the camera, and Kajic could see without obstruction to the end of the corridor.

Then, abruptly, the technician stood, gaping. She backed away a step and hit the nearest alert switch. Moments later, her workmate joined her, staring in confusion in the direction she pointed—

But there was nothing there—and, as far as Kajic could tell when he scrolled the recording back, nothing *had* been there.

Increasingly puzzled, he switched to another camera and another time. The dimly lit corridor where he had seen "his" ghost appeared in a window next to that containing the technician, now frozen in mid-gape. He sped the recording forward, then backward, waiting for some sort of change.

Nothing.

The corridor, even at the exact moment when he had seen the face, had been completely void of life.

At that moment, he was relieved that he had not mentioned his own sighting to Makaev. And he intended to keep it that way as long as possible. The obvious interpretation was too damning, too convenient for anyone looking for an excuse to pull the plug on him.

For a long moment, he considered the few alternatives open to him, then methodically erased from his personal database all records of the face he had seen.

Although his enthusiasm for the project was sorely lacking, Kajic resumed his search. Unsure which he feared most— seeing the "ghost" again, or not seeing it—he flicked aimlessly through the warren, wishing he had never started in the first place.

Hours passed uneventfully. He had thought, once, that all his problems would end when he had satisfied his priorities. Yet, in its own way, the return trip was turning out to be worse than the mission itself. Even disregarding the nameless doubts, the new priority kept his mind from wandering as freely as he liked, and the specter of his own possible fallibility, therefore, refused to dissipate.

Still, he would be home soon. Szubetka Base was located near an anchor point in deep space, so approach time was kept to a minimum. Within a handful of hours, if all went well, his mission would be at an end. A *successful* end, too.

And then . . . ?

Having demonstrated that the ship/captain principle was sound, the Dato Bloc's greatest engineers would bend their minds—and those belonging to their new captains—to the task of making an entire fleet of similar vessels. A superfleet of mind-machine gestalts, enough perhaps to give the Presidium an edge over their traditional enemies. When that came to pass, Kajic would finally have like minds with which to associate. It was comforting to know that there would soon be others who could share his experiences.

But this led to a more disturbing thought. Progress was inevitable. He would remain in the service of the Presidium only as long as he was an advantage, not a hindrance. What would happen when he had been superseded? Routine missions? Cargo hauls for the Presidium? Or worse, a civilian fleet? With his body suspended in its life support capsule, his existence could be extended indefinitely, at a price, but would anyone wish to do so? Disembodied, essentially if not literally, he was nothing without his ship. How long before they wanted the *Ana Vereine* back, to give it a new captain . . . ?

Kajic's sense of imminent victory suddenly faded. He was a tool. And the trouble with intelligent tools, he knew, was that they can never be truly trusted—no more than any other Human. Because he *could* be controlled, his future held a lifetime of priorities, nagging duties, and self-doubt. He would never be truly free until the day he died.

Yellow alert suddenly sounded throughout the ship, warning the crew of imminent departure. His priorities began to irritate again, an unsubtle reminder that he was neglecting his duty. With a sigh of relief, he halted the search of the warren and sent himself to the bridge.

His second in command awaited him, looking as tired as he felt.

"How long, Atalia?"

"Ten minutes, sir."

"Any problems?"

"None, sir. Crew and ship are in perfect shape."

"Excellent." Kajic smiled; despite the misgivings he still harbored, he was relieved on that score. He no longer suspected that the "ghost" fiasco had been her doing; she had been as genuinely worried and had worked as hard to remedy the situation as he. If the crew had at last settled down and forgotten the incidents, whatever their cause, then perhaps she deserved much of the credit.

The matter of the kill-switch and the back door still had to be resolved, however, but he was prepared to admit that she had done her duty there, too—and done it well. Perhaps *too* well, at times.

"*Paladin* and *Galloglass* will precede us to Szubetka Base," he said. "Barring unforseen complications, we will follow five minutes after. Then *Lansequenet* two minutes after that."

"Yes, sir." She snapped a formal salute and turned away.

On the main screen, the four green dots of his small command rapidly approached the departure point. He watched them idly, letting himself be an observer rather than an active participant. His crew could handle the jump through the anchor point without his help. For the pilots and astrogators of a warship, even one as new as the *Ana Vereine*, jumping to hyperspace to achieve speeds he could only begin to comprehend was all in a day's work. His main role was to decide when and where to go; all the rest—the vectors, coordinates, and space-distorts—he left to the specialists.

If he desired, however, he could interface with the ship's main computers to boost his processing power, and thereby participate in the mystery. But sometimes it was better simply to watch, to be awed by the forces that people, with all-too-mortal minds, had harnessed.

Bubbles of folded space enclosed the two ships, distorting the light shining through them and making distant stars balloon and fade. Traceries of energy danced along the raiders' hulls, waving like hairs from the points of weapons and casting vast sheets along flat surfaces. Local space seemed crowded, for an instant, as the raiders' imminent supralight departure echoed back through time and collided with the present, cluttering the area with a near-infinite number of phantom ships.

An unexpected prompt sounded in Kajic's mind the very instant the two ships disappeared. Filled with a sudden sense of alarm, he turned his attention inward to see what had happened.

At first he was relieved. Nothing had gone wrong at all; the ship's computers had simply finished the search he had requested. But then, scanning the information that the computer had retrieved on the ship's "ghost," his uncertainty and dread returned.

"*Galloglass* and *Paladin* have jumped successfully," the telemetry officer reported, when the data collected by hull sensors had been analyzed.

Kajic waved distractedly at his second in command for her to give the order.

"Commence countdown," she said. "The *Ana Vereine* will jump in four minutes."

"All systems green, Commander," telemetry announced.

"Good." Then, perhaps sensing that something was amiss, Makaev approached the podium. "Captain, is everything in order?"

"I'm not sure." Kajic called into being a window in his hologram, not caring that it opened where his chest normally was. "Do you recognize this face?"

Makaev studied the picture for a moment, then shook her head. "No, sir. Should I?"

"No, I suppose not. I certainly didn't."

Makaev waited a moment, then prompted, "Sir, I'm not sure I follow—?"

"His name is Adoni Cane. Or rather, it *was*. According to shipboard records, he disappeared over two thousand years ago after ordering an attack on a civilian colony that resulted in the death of nearly four million people."

She glanced at the picture again. "Forgive me for saying this, sir, but: so what?"

"I took his picture this afternoon, down in the warren." Kajic bestowed a wry smile upon his holographic image. "At least when we have ghosts, we have ghosts with class!"

For a long moment, she said nothing. Then, uncertainly: "I see, sir."

"What's the matter with you?" He leaned closer, bringing

the picture in his chest with him. "I've found our ghost! I
don't know what any of it *means*, but at least we know who
it is."

Finally she moved. With a disapproving frown, she raised
her eyes to those of his hologram and said evenly:

"*What* ghost?"

He stared at her, dumbfounded. He wasn't sure exactly
how he had expected Makaev to respond, but certainly not
like *this*. Not with blank incomprehension.

Before he could reply, the red alert warning sounded. The
Ana Vereine was about to jump. Filled with a sudden and
overwhelming fear that something had gone terribly, terribly
wrong, he turned to face the bridge crew.

"No—wait!" he cried.

return to Szubetka Base

Fighting his built-in prompts every step of the way, he
sent his mind deep into the ship's programming, trying to
halt the ship's departure.

"We can't—!"

priority gold-one

But it was already too late.

With a soundless rip, the *Ana Vereine* tore through the
fabric of the anchor point and entered hyperspace.

"*What's /*
　　/ happening /
　　　　　　/ to /
　　　　　　　　/ me /
　　　　　　　　　　/ . . . ?"

<Don't fight it,> said a voice through the pain.

Kajic flailed in the darkness, lost in a void impossibly
dark and empty. This was no ordinary jump, part of him
realized. Nothing like this had ever happened to him before. He could sense nothing at all around or inside him.
There was only the blackness, and the voice—a voice that
shouldn't be there—

<I said, don't *fight* it!> The voice burned into him like a
brand, the words stabbing at the very core of his soul.

<What's happening to me?> he gasped again, amazed to
find that he could speak, if nothing else. <Who are you?>

<That is irrelevant for the moment,> replied a second voice, more officious than the first. <You must let us have our way.>

<Why?> The question was automatic and full of anger. Even if this was a dream, he didn't appreciate being pushed around by faceless entities.

<You don't really have any choice,> said the first voice, with the barest hint of compassion. <We'd rather not force you, although we will if we have to.>

Kajic suddenly realized what had happened: he had broken down at last. First the mysterious glitch in continuity, then the matter of the "ghost" that Makaev had known nothing about, and now this. The strain had finally been too much for him.

In a way, the knowledge came to him as a relief. What point was there in fighting madness?

<If that's what it takes to make the transition easier,> said the second voice, <then so be it. Believe what you want.>

Then—

Light.

He opened his eyes—or attempted to. Eyes? No; that was an old habit, one he'd thought long forgotten. He tried again, this time sending the impulse through the proper channels.

"Translation completed," said a voice. Memory attached it a label: telemetry.

priority gold-one

He was on the bridge of the *Ana Vereine.*

"Atalia?" He felt his hologram fraying around the edges as he tried to regain his grip on reality. He remembered something about voices, but nothing definite. His memory of the moments preceding their arrival was hazy.

"Yes, Captain?" His second in command stood beside him, watching him.

"Weren't we . . . ?" He felt dizzy for a moment, but fought the sensation. "Before the . . ." He could remember nothing that had happened during the jump. "Weren't we talking about something?"

"I don't think so, sir." She leaned closer. "Is anything wrong?"

He pulled himself together at last. "No, nothing." He

didn't want to ask about jump time; instead he glanced at the main screen, which showed him nothing at all. "We've arrived?"

"Residual effects clearing," said telemetry. "Local space will reconfigure in sixty seconds."

"Very good. Contact the commanders of *Paladin* and *Galloglass* to confirm our safe arrival."

"Yes, sir."

As the telemetry officer went about the task, Makaev leaned unnecessarily close to his image. "Are you certain you're feeling all right, sir?"

He glanced sharply at her, suppressing any hint of confusion in both his voice and image. "Are you questioning my competence, Commander?" he asked coldly.

She took a step away from his image, her face flushed. "No, I—"

"Sir," said telemetry. "I am having difficulty contacting *Galloglass* and *Paladin*."

"What sort of difficulty?"

"They're not responding at all, sir. I *am* picking up some coded traffic, but it's not our code."

"Whose, then?" asked Kajic.

"It's not our code, sir," telemetry repeated with a shrug. "I am unable to translate it."

Beside him, Makaev stiffened. "An ambush!" she hissed.

"Impossible," Kajic said. "Only a fool would attempt an attack anywhere near Szubetka Base. How long until those screens are clear?"

A pause, then: "Fifteen seconds, sir."

"Maybe then we'll know what the hell is going on." Kajic glanced again at his second.

priority gold-one

"Ten seconds, sir."

"I have a bad feeling about this, sir," said Makaev without moving her eyes from the screen. "To have something go wrong now—"

"A little faith, Commander," he said, and heard his own unease creep into his voice. "Everything will be fine."

"Three seconds, sir."

"It *has* to be." This, barely a whisper to himself.

"Two seconds," said telemetry. "One second, and—we are scanning local space now, sir."

Kajic watched anxiously as the screen began to fill with data: visual light first, followed by the more exotic spectra, then by particle sources. All he saw in the initial moments of the scan were stars; only later did nearer, more discrete energy sources appear.

Three ships, not two, appeared in the void, and one very large installation less than a million kilometers away. Two of the ships were angling in toward it on docking approach; the third was leaving, arcing up and away from the *Ana Vereine*'s position. As more detail flooded in, Kajic made out the nestled shapes of ships already docked—hundreds of them, all angular and angry, sharp-pointed sticks to hurl at the indifferent stars.

"Those aren't our ships," he said, his mind's eye narrowing.

"And that's *not* Szubetka Base!" rasped Makaev.

A chill enveloped Kajic.

"*No*," he said, his voice sounding hollow even to his ears. "*No!*"

"That's *COE Intelligence HQ!*" Makaev turned to face him, shock naked in her eyes. "*What the hell have you done?*"

Kajic reeled under the force of her attack. "I—"

"You incompetent *fool*!" She whirled away from him and darted for her station.

"Atalia!" he snapped, desperate to regain some control over his escalating panic and confusion. "What are you doing?"

"I'm assuming command!" she shouted back. "You have betrayed us!" Then, over her shoulder at the rest of the crew: "Someone get us out of here while I deal with him!"

Even as her words reached him via the microphone at her console, even as her face loomed large in the camera facing her chair, even as she reached for the twin datalinks waiting like snake mouths to accept her hands—he realized what she was about to do.

He froze, unsure whether he had the right to stop her.

priority gold-one

By the time he realized he couldn't, it was too late anyway. The commands input via her datalinks were already being processed.

priority override sequence "Kill-Switch" #1143150222

He screamed, feeling the words cut into his mind, tearing him apart

disable core command
  piece by tiny piece
disable ancillary processors
  flaying him
disable support memory
  layer by layer
disable MA/AM interface
  stripping him
disable primary database
  of his delusions
disable cognitive simulators
  of his command
disable life-support
  of him
disable
  of him
disable
  of him
disable . . .

When it had finally finished—then, and only then, was he free.

18

DBMP *Ana Vereine*
'954.10.38 EN
1595

Consciousness parted the thick, dark clouds as Roche opened her eyes. She found herself in a fairly small room, one decorated solely in gunmetal grey. The only piece of furniture it contained was the bed she lay upon. The single door to the room was shut, and the absence of any handle on her side suggested that it was intended to stay that way.

A cell of some sort, she guessed. And judging by the compact surgeon strapped to her chest, obviously a hospital cell in particular. But *where*?

When she tried to sit up, a familiar weight attached to her left arm dragged her back.

<Hello, Box,> she said automatically. The AI did not respond, so she hefted the valise and gave it a brief shake. <Box?>

Again, silence.

"Hello?" she called, aloud this time. Seeing stereoscopic cameras watching from opposite corners of the room, she removed the surgeon and stepped toward one of them. The unblinking lenses followed her every movement. "Is anyone there?"

When the echo of her voice had faded, silence reclaimed the room as impenetrably as before. There was no sound *beyond* the cell, either. To all intents and purposes, the ship she was in—she could tell that much from the vagaries of artificial g—appeared completely dead.

But until someone came to talk to her, she had no way to tell where she was. The surgeon looked the same as they did everywhere, the standard Eckandi design found on that side of the galaxy. The room itself could have been on any Pristine vessel, except—she sniffed the air—it smelled *new*. How many recently built ships were there in either the Commonwealth or the Dato Bloc? And why would they send one to collect a single AI?

What had she *missed*?

She shook her head. She didn't have enough information to guess what had happened to her. And the last thing she remembered was the battle on the top of the MiCom building: the flyers, the mortar bombs, the Dato trooper, and—

Cane.

The return of *that* memory stung. One hand rose automatically to touch her temple where he had struck her unconscious. No pain. No pain anywhere, in fact: in her ribs, her shoulder, or her recently shaved head. Physically, she felt better than she had for days.

After a few minutes, something finally broke the deathly silence. She heard, distant at first, but growing nearer by the second, the sound of footsteps in the corridor outside her cell. Two people, she guessed, marching in perfect time.

Seconds later, the door of the cell hissed smoothly open. A pair of Dato troopers stood outside, framed in the doorway like statues. Reflections glistened disconcertingly across their grey, ceramic shells as, in unison, they took one step forward into the cell. Two black faceplates stared impassively at her as she waited for their next move. Neither one, she noted, was armed.

"You are to come with us, Commander," one of the troopers said, the voice issuing a little too loudly from the suit's massive chest.

"Why?" The defiant tone was automatic.

"Your presence is required elsewhere."

"Where?"

No answer.

She sighed. What was the point in resisting? Even un-armed, two troopers were more than a match for her. She would do better to save her energy for the interrogation that was surely to follow. At least that way she'd find out exactly where she was.

A large part of her suspected that she wasn't going to enjoy the process of finding out.

The troopers led her through a maze of passages and ele-vators, heading deep into the ship's infrastructure. If she hadn't already guessed that the ship was new, the short journey would have convinced her. Apart from a few small signs of Human occupation, the bulkheads and floors were virtually untouched.

Yet, despite the occasional evidence of life, the ship seemed more deserted than ever. She heard no voices, no footsteps besides hers and her escorts', none of the small mechanical whispers that betrayed a presence nearby. After a few minutes, even the presence of the two troopers began to unnerve her; they might have been machines for all the sound they made.

Eventually they arrived at a door, coming from the other side of which she could hear voices—and heated ones, by the sound of them. But the door remained closed, and nei-ther of the troopers moved to open it.

"Well?" she asked, glancing from one impassive visor to the other, not really expecting an answer. "Are we going to stand out here all day?"

As though her voice had prompted a response, the door slid open and the troopers ushered her inside, taking posi-tions on either side of the entrance.

The room was ten meters across, circular with a high, domed roof. The carpet was a plush burgundy pile, and the fixtures lavish for a military spaceship. At the opposite end of the room was a drink dispenser; low tables held a variety of finger food on glass plates; a quartered ring of comfort-able armchairs faced a central holographic display. A meet-ing hall of some kind, or a senior officers' mess.

At the opening of the door, the argument had ceased in mid-sentence and three heads had turned to stare at her. She stared back, trying not to let her face betray her surprise.

"Well, Commander," said Burne Absenger, COE Armada's Chief Liaison Officer to the Commonwealth of Empires' civilian government. A big, middle-aged man with thick locks of orange-red hair firmly slicked back in a skullcap, his voice was warm and well polished but not quite able to hide an edge of irony. "It would seem you've been busy."

"And we'd like an explanation," snapped Auberon Chase, head of COE Intelligence. Rakishly thin and bald, he wore his uniform irritably, as though discomfited by its loose fit. His eyes burned without dissembling, anger naked for all to see.

Beside him was the head of Strategy, Page De Bruyn—a tall woman with shoulder-length brown hair who, it was rumored, held more power in COE Intelligence than her boss, Chase. She studied Roche with a quiet fascination.

For a moment Roche was unsure exactly how to respond. Confronted by three of the Armada's most senior officers on a Dato ship, in which she herself had only recently woken with no recollection of how she had come to be there, she felt at a total loss. And they wanted *her* to explain?

Then, for the first time, she consciously noted the contents of the viewtank. Her breath caught in her throat. *COE Intelligence HQ*. A massive structure reflecting the light of distant suns and nebulae, it was duty's focus for the millions of Armada officers like herself—and a sight she had come to believe she might never see again. Even if the view was at maximum enhancement, the station had to be close—probably no more distant than the Riem-Perez horizon of its hypershield, the closest point to it that any vessel could jump.

We're right on top of it, Roche concluded. Then: *This is a Dato ship! What's it doing so close*?

"Well, Commander?" prompted De Bruyn, her voice a dangerous purr.

Roche swung her attention from the tank and faced the woman's steely gaze. "I'll answer your questions as well as I'm able to, but I'm afraid that most of this is beyond me."

"Perhaps you should let us be the judge of that." De

Bruyn smiled thinly. "When you've told us how you learned about Palasian System, and why the information could not flow through the normal channels, then we'll decide."

Unsteady as it was, Roche stood her ground. "Apart from what I've seen on IDnet, I know nothing at all about Palasian System." De Bruyn's eyes narrowed, but Roche plowed on, choosing her words with care. Regardless how she had come to be in this situation, one wrong word could end her career. "What has led you to believe that I do is something of a mystery to me."

"Don't play the fool with us, Commander," exploded Chase, stabbing a long bony finger in her direction. "First you turn up at HQ in the new Dato Marauder, a vessel regarding which we have only the vaguest intelligence, then you demand—not request, mind you, but *demand*—an immediate audience, here on the ship, to discuss a security matter so grave that it threatens the entire Commonwealth." He snorted as though the very idea offended him. "And now you have the nerve to tell us that you don't even *know* what we're talking about! Why we even agreed to this meeting at all is—"

"Auberon," interrupted De Bruyn sharply, shaking her head. Then, more smoothly, she added, "Let the girl speak."

"Yes," put in Absenger. "We'll never get anywhere if you carry on like this." Fixing Roche with a warm but exaggerated smile, he said, "Clearly this situation is of no benefit to anyone, Commander. So please, let's see if we can't sort everything out."

Roche opened her mouth, about to protest that it wasn't the outburst of the head of Intelligence that caused her reticence but a simple lack of knowledge. Before she could, however, someone spoke up behind her, from the entrance to the conference room.

"She's telling the truth."

Roche turned. Standing in the doorway was Ameidio Haid. With the faintest nod in her direction, he strode confidently into the room, his calm demeanor generating an air of authority.

"We used her image to make that call," he said as he approached. "Seeing she was unconscious at the time, we had no choice."

"What?" Chase's eyes flickered from Haid to Roche, searching for the connection between the two. "What's going on here?"

"That's entirely up to you." Haid took a seat on the opposite side of the room and crossed his legs, to all appearances completely at ease. Roche noted the tautness of his muscles beneath the simple black uniform, however, and suspected that he was far from relaxed. "What's your preference?" he said. "An honest and open discussion, or a witch hunt?"

"This is preposterous," the head of Intelligence spluttered. "I refuse to be a part of any discussion involving someone of your ilk, Haid. A criminal, a barbarian, a *traitor*—!"

"You remember me, then," Haid interjected with some amusement. "But don't kid yourself, Auberon; we really aren't that much different from one another." Before the man could respond, Haid's expression became grave, the humor draining from his tone. "Let's skip the pleasantries, shall we? We have a few things we need to discuss."

Chase's face turned grey with rage.

"Of course." Burne Absenger took a position around the holographic tank, his heavy frame sinking easily into the contoured chair. Page De Bruyn hesitated a moment, then followed his lead, although her posture remained stiffly upright. Roche sat opposite Haid, where she could watch him through the hologram of Intelligence HQ. Chase remained standing until Absenger caught his eye and gestured sharply for him to sit.

The head of Strategy sank into a seat at random. "Do we have any choice?"

"To be honest," said Haid, "no, not anymore. However, the choice to come out to meet us was your own. Ours was merely an invitation."

"You have an interesting way of greeting your guests," said De Bruyn dryly.

Haid shrugged. "You *were* asked to come alone. And unarmed."

De Bruyn snorted. "You couldn't expect us to simply walk onto an enemy vessel without any protection."

"Nor *you* expect *us* to allow an armed platoon to march aboard."

"Which your troops dealt with easily enough," said Chase with more than a trace of bitterness. "What are they? Mercenaries like yourself?"

"No. They're drones," Haid explained. "Or remotes, if you like." He gestured to the nearest Dato trooper, who instantly raised a gauntleted hand to open the black visor.

The helmet inside was empty.

Haid's smile widened at the response from his small audience: the in-drawn breaths and sudden stiffening of postures.

"Eyes and ears in the service of the one behind that message we sent. The one who sent me here—to clear the air."

Roche stared at the empty armor in amazement, then turned to face Haid. "You mean the Box, don't you?"

"Who else?" he said. "Who did you think was running this ship?" He laughed lightly. "Certainly not me."

"I'd assumed the Dato—"

"They're currently in the main airlock holding bay with De Bruyn's squad, waiting to be shipped to HQ." Haid shook his head. "Did you really believe we'd join forces with the Dato Bloc to betray you and the Armada? Morgan, we despise *them* almost as much as we despise the three people sitting with us now."

That brought an immediate response from Chase, but one less vicious than Roche had expected.

"How much do you know?" asked the head of Intelligence, studying Haid narrowly.

"Enough," said Haid. "Enough to see you face a court-martial, Chase. Not that I have any faith in the Commonwealth's judicial system."

"Wait a minute," said Absenger, raising a hand. "You're going much too fast for me. When you say that 'the Box' is running this ship, surely you can't mean the AI attached to the commander's arm here?"

"Why not?" said Haid. "It's perfectly suited to the task."

"But how? I mean, it seems hard to believe that . . ." Absenger glanced at De Bruyn. "Surely this Box is nothing more than a communications AI commissioned to replace one in the Armada network?"

"The Box is much more than a 'communications AI,'" said Haid, "no matter what you say. It's designed with the express purpose of infiltrating and ultimately corrupting Dato intelligent systems, such as those that run this ship, or the combat armor you see before you. That's what you ordered from Trinity, and that's what they built." His gaze shifted suddenly. "Isn't that right, De Bruyn?"

The head of Strategy looked uncomfortable for a moment, then exchanged another glance with Absenger. "We wanted something that could infiltrate Dato security from the inside."

Haid nodded. "And that's what you got—and more." He looked at Roche and noticed the slight wince on her face. "Don't feel too bad, Morgan. I didn't work it out myself, either. When you let me open the datalink, I had no idea what I was getting myself into. That damned machine is a maze of security probes and countertraps; given a century, uninterrupted, I *might* have come close to guessing what it was for. In the end, I didn't crack the Box; *it* cracked *me*. It needed another ally, and I was the one it chose."

"To do what?" said Roche.

"To help the two of you off the planet, basically. And to gain access to data processors powerful enough for it to discover its full potential."

Roche absorbed this for a moment, sensing an unspoken implication in his words. "You said *another* ally?"

"That's right. Adoni Cane was the first. That's why it let him out of the *Midnight*'s brig and made sure he reached you before the Dato attacked."

Roche gaped. "The *Box* did that?"

"Of course. I told you there was something screwy about all that. The Box could see what was coming, and made sure you had at least an even chance of surviving."

"Who is this 'Adoni Cane'?" said Absenger.

"This is ridiculous!" Chase snapped. "I can't believe we're discussing Commonwealth secrets with these people—"

"Be *quiet*, Auberon," said De Bruyn, her eyes dangerous.

Haid watched the brief interaction with some amusement, and Roche suddenly realized how well he was playing them against each other. Absenger, the politician, the smooth talker; Chase, the reactionary hothead; and De Bruyn, perhaps the most dangerous of the three, sharp and coldly calculating.

"Adoni Cane is a genetically modified combat soldier," Haid said, as casually as though discussing the weather. "The *Midnight* plucked him from a life support capsule located by its beacon eight days before arriving at Sciacca's World. The ship's surgeons examined him in situ, but didn't have time to contact HQ. The data they collected then, plus more from our own examinations on Port Parvati, makes for very interesting reading."

The viewtank's image of Intelligence HQ vanished and was replaced with a three-dimensional scan of Cane, segmented in places to reveal his inner organs. Lines of data scrolled down the corners of the tank, listing metabolic rates, genetic comparisons, cellular structures, neural connections . . .

Roche studied it in disbelief. This was much more detailed than she'd seen in the rebels' headquarters. How Haid had managed to get hold of the *Midnight*'s data was beyond her.

Then she realized: the Box again, although why it had gone to the trouble to save the data, then keep it a secret from her and the rebels, remained unknown. For the moment, curiosity about Cane overrode that about the Box.

She could see, now, where the survival capsule had been physically grafted to him at stomach, throat, and thighs via circular wounds that had healed within days of his emergence. The *Midnight*'s chief surgeon's tentative conclusion was that he had indeed been grown in the capsule and subsequently given a basic knowledge of language and movement by implanted educators. Given the condition of his tissue and the lack of radiation damage suffered while in deep space, Cane appeared to be roughly one year old, although his mental age was far above that. The obvious conclusion was that, although the capsule had drifted for at least a year before being found, the timing of its discovery had been carefully planned. Even with the capsule's sophisticated organic vats, only superficially examined on the *Midnight*, Human tissue could not have been sustained unharmed for longer than a month or two.

Cane, therefore, wasn't an innocent cast adrift by some unknown tragedy, lying dormant in the capsule waiting to be rescued. He had been built for a purpose by someone who had *wanted* him to be found. Now. The only question that remained unanswered was: how long had the capsule been drifting before it brought him into being?

No one else in the room seemed ready to ask the obvious questions—questions she had asked back on Sciacca's World—so she spoke for them:

"To what end?"

The answer came from an unexpected quarter.

"To purge the Commonwealth and its neighbors of Pristine Humanity, of course," said Page De Bruyn, her voice hushed. "To wreak revenge on the descendants of the people who destroyed the creators of such creatures. Adoni Cane is a Clone Wunderkind, courtesy of the Sol Apotheosis Movement."

"*Another* one?" said Chase, his face pale.

"It was always a possibility," said Absenger grimly.

"Will someone please tell me what you're talking about?" said Roche.

Absenger sighed heavily and opened his hands. "Twenty-five days ago, a similar capsule also containing a single occupant was retrieved by the courier vessel *Daybreak* not far from one of our systems. *Daybreak*'s captain had time to report the discovery, but little else. Before she could transmit a detailed report, all communication ceased and the ship disappeared. Two days later, *Daybreak* reappeared, broadcasting an emergency beacon. The commanding officer of the nearest military base sent out a tug to rendezvous, and took it in for repairs. Not long after, we received garbled messages that the base was under attack—then that too fell silent. By the time the Armada sent a battalion to investigate, the entire system was in flames."

"None of this was on IDnet," Roche said.

"You covered it up," said Haid, speaking not in response to her question but to De Bruyn. "Possibly the greatest threat the COE has ever faced, and you tried to sweep it under the rug."

"We didn't *know* what had happened," protested De Bruyn. "It could have been anything: rebellion, disease, war. We had no way of knowing. But we had to enforce a quarantine to keep people out, to prevent more deaths."

"Palasian System," said Roche, finally making the connection.

Absenger nodded. "It was only after the battalion arrived that we managed to piece together what had happened: that some kind of modified warrior had single-handedly taken control of *Daybreak* and gone berserk in the system."

"How many of the battalion made it back?" asked Haid.

De Bruyn grimaced. "Of twenty ships, only one survived. And from the pictures brought back, not much was left of the system. Now"—she shrugged helplessly—"who knows?"

Roche reeled at the thought. "You're suggesting that *one person* did this?"

"We're not talking about a *person*, Commander," said Absenger. "This is a genetically enhanced being—a Wunderkind—capable of anything."

"And now we have two of them," said Chase, his thin face even paler than before.

"You think Cane—?" She stopped in mid-sentence, staring at the image rotating in the viewtank. "I can't believe it."

"What can't you believe, Commander?" said De Bruyn. "That he's capable of such destruction, or that he would?"

Roche shook her head. "Both, I guess."

"Morgan," said Haid, "you've seen how Cane fights person-to-person. Imagine him with a ship, or in control of a major weapons array; imagine how much more destructive he could be. If the Wunderkind in Palasian System has the same potential as Cane"— he too shrugged—"then I don't find it difficult to believe at all."

"But that means he's been drifting for almost three thousand years!"

"Not him; just the capsule." Absenger's grim expression

showed no satisfaction at correcting her. "He can't come from anywhere else, Roche. No one designed combat clones quite like the Sol engineers, and according to our records 'Adoni Cane' was the name of the commander of the fleet that confronted them—the man whose orders led to their destruction. It's a deliberate jibe at their enemies; one that's taken a long time to hit home, but a jibe all the same."

"The prodigal son returns," Chase muttered.

Absenger leaned forward. "Yet Cane actually helped the Box?"

"And Roche, too," Haid said, turning from Roche to face the liaison officer. "*Particularly* Roche, for whatever reason."

"That does seem unlikely," mused Absenger. "Perhaps Cane and the Palasian Wunderkind aren't exactly the same thing, after all. You said that Cane's capsule was broadcasting some sort of beacon, whereas the first—"

"That's not what I said," Haid interrupted. "I said that a beacon had led the *Midnight* to it."

De Bruyn's brow creased. "The same thing, surely?"

"Not quite," said Haid. "You see, the beacon was faked."

De Bruyn's frown deepened. "By whom?"

Haid smiled. "Before I answer that, why don't you explain to Roche why you were so surprised to receive that message we sent you yesterday?"

The sudden change in direction took the three Armada officers off guard. Roche noted the tightening of De Bruyn's jaw muscles as she fumbled for the words.

"I—" Her face flushed as she glanced from Absenger to Chase. "Her method of arrival was somewhat unorthodox, and—"

Haid laughed at her discomfort. "You people really have a problem with the truth, don't you?" he said, settling back into his chair and resting his one arm across his lap. "Perhaps *I* can shed some light on things, then, by way of explaining about the attack on the *Midnight*."

Whatever game he was playing, Roche thought, he was clearly enjoying himself immensely.

"I'll omit the details of the ambush, if you like. No doubt you can imagine them for yourselves, seeing it went pretty much as you hoped it would when you leaked the *Midnight*'s course to the Dato Espionage Corps. Everything went according to plan, except of course that Roche and the Box managed to escape the destruction of the *Midnight*, and made it as far as the surface of the planet before—"

"Wait a second!" Roche gasped, rising to her feet as his words sunk in. "They did *what*?"

Haid's eye met hers through the shimmering viewtank. "I'm sorry to be the one to tell you this, Morgan, but they obviously weren't going to. They sold you out. Your mission wasn't, as you thought, to bring the Box back to HQ for installation. Instead, it was to be captured by the Dato and taken to the Military Presidium. That's why they were so surprised to see you here: you weren't *supposed* to return."

Roche stared from Chase to De Bruyn, then to Absenger. Only the last met her gaze, and he seemed almost amused by her outrage.

"Is this true?" she asked him, fearing the answer even as she said the words.

"Of course it isn't," he said quickly—almost too quickly.

<He's lying,> said a familiar voice in her mind. Not the Box, but Maii.

Roche closed her eyes; any other time, she might have been glad to hear from the young Surin, but not now. "I *know*," she whispered irritably.

"Good," said Absenger. "Then you will also know that the man is clearly paranoid. Quite perceptive in some ways, I'll admit, but—"

"I wasn't talking to *you*, you sonofabitch!"

Absenger flinched perceptibly. His voice was cold when he spoke. "Commander Roche, must I remind you—?"

"If you're going to tell me that I should show some respect to senior officers, then save your breath." All the frustration she'd felt on Sciacca's World, all the lengths she'd gone to to complete her mission—every action she'd taken on COE Intelligence's behalf boiled within her, perverted and twisted into a hideous farce. "Save it for telling me *why* you did it."

"If you think I'm going to explain myself to—"

"The Box," Haid cut in, "was designed to infiltrate the

Dato from *within*, as Page said earlier." He leaned forward to emphasize every word, peering through the hologram at Roche. "I was hoping you'd guess, and save me having to spell it out for you. The Box was no use at all to COE Intelligence back here. So they chose a disposable old frigate with a disposable captain, and put a disposable agent in charge of the mission."

"This is ridiculous!" blurted out Chase as he stood. "This man is lying!"

"I won't tell you again, Auberon." De Bruyn's voice was even and quiet.

Chase stared down at her. "Why should we listen to the slander of criminals?"

"I said *be quiet!*" De Bruyn's icy and unflinching glare held the man for a full ten seconds until he finally looked away and sat back in his chair.

"*Is* it true?" asked Roche a second time.

"Yes," said De Bruyn, facing Roche. "Of course it's true. We sent you to Sciacca's World knowing you'd be ambushed. We thought the local government was corrupt enough to handle any extra work the Dato required to finish the job, if things didn't go smoothly. That's the main reason we chose the planet."

"But that's the trouble with traitors," said Haid. "They're unreliable—aren't they, Absenger?"

The liaison officer shook his head. "I'm afraid I can't comment on this."

"No?" said Roche. "You're denying that you had anything to do with it?"

"Don't be pathetic, Burne," snapped De Bruyn. "Put your guilt aside and stand up to these people." Then, to Haid: "Delcasalle is his little puppet. Sciacca's World was chosen on his recommendation."

"You sent me in there to die!" Roche snapped.

De Bruyn's eyes flashed. "Yes. And I'd have no hesitation in doing so again. It was a good plan. The Box needed to be in position before it would be effective, and this was the best way to get it there without arousing the Presidium's suspicions. It *should* have worked." She cast a disparaging eye in Roche's direction. "And I'm still at a loss to understand why it didn't."

"I've heard enough," Roche said.

"No, you haven't," said Haid. "Not quite. You also need to know *why* their plan fell apart as badly as it did, and what this means to all of us."

Feeling empty and tired, Roche sagged and sat back down. She had spent her entire adult life in the service of the Commonwealth of Empires, in return for which she had been betrayed. Whatever Haid had left to reveal, she doubted it could match what she'd already heard; she felt numb, beyond all further surprise. "Go ahead," she said.

Haid stood. In the viewtank, the hologram of Cane disappeared and was replaced by an orbital view of Sciacca's World; the belt of the Soul sparkled majestically.

"The plan to infiltrate the Dato Presidium with an AI was quite clever, I have to admit," said Haid. "But it's flawed at a basic level. For the Box to be effective, it had to be able to operate independently of COE Intelligence for long periods of time; it had to follow its own judgment in times of possible crisis; it had to be able to choose between several different possible courses of action; it had to be able to plan in detail, and to conspire to see those plans come to fruition. To do all of this, it had to be far more intelligent than the AIs the Armada normally uses." Haid paused, then said, "In short, it had to be self-aware—as self-aware as we are."

"That's impossible," said Roche, remembering her years tormenting the AIs in the Armada.

"Do you really believe that?" Haid met her stare firmly. "After everything it's done?"

She lowered her eyes, focusing upon the image in the viewtank. "I don't know."

"The Box *is* self-aware, Morgan, as conscious as you or I. Trinity is owned and run by High Humans, don't forget, not mundanes, so we shouldn't ascribe to it our own limitations. It's *always* been able to make such minds. The process takes as many years as it would take to produce an intelligent Human being, or so the Box has led me to believe, but it is possible." He shrugged. "Trinity normally doesn't release them, because they tend to be expensive, and a little unreliable, if you like. They're *too* intelligent—everything people are, and more. Controllable to a point, yes, but beyond that is anyone's guess. It's a double-edged sword: on the one hand you have a machine independent enough to do everything you want, but too independent to trust. The Commonwealth isn't ready for minds like these, and may not be for many years to come. Until it's ready to Transcend, perhaps."

Haid stared in turn at the COE Intelligence officers, then settled again upon Roche. "But that's ultimately why your real mission failed, Morgan—because the Box didn't *want* it to succeed. It saw through the intentions of these three almost immediately, and decided it didn't want to be a pawn in a game beneath its potential; it wanted to be a major player, at the very least."

Roche glanced at the valise still dangling from the cord at her side. It didn't look like some sort of super-AI at all, just a battered case dragged from one end of the COE to the other. "A player in what?"

"I don't know," said Haid. "It won't talk to me about that."

"Or perhaps," said De Bruyn, "you're just being paranoid, seeing plots and conspiracies where in fact none exist."

Roche ignored De Bruyn's jibe, not allowing Haid to be distracted. "What did you mean about the Box not wanting to be involved in anything 'beneath its potential'?"

"Think about it," he said. "The Box has the ability to infiltrate intelligent networks and to bend them to its will. The larger its opponents, the stronger it becomes, by using their processing power to boost its own capacity. Given enough power, it can do almost anything it sets its mind to. Why should it want to play Intelligence's petty games? Don't you think it would have its own agenda?"

He gestured at the viewtank, which reverted to the previous rotating display. "For instance, there's Cane."

Roche nodded. "The way it set him free from the brig to help me?"

"More than that, Morgan," said Haid. "The Box knew about his life capsule and its trajectory before it boarded the

Midnight. It faked the distress call that led directly to Cane's discovery."

De Bruyn's eyes widened. "It knew about the Sol conspiracy?"

"Maybe, maybe not," said Haid. "I don't know for sure. Certainly it knew about the capsule, if not its contents. Maybe it was simply curious, at first, then became more involved when it lifted the findings of the *Midnight*'s surgeons from the ship's datapool and realized what, exactly, Cane was. When it recruited him, it did so partly to improve its chances of survival, and partly to study a Sol Wunderkind firsthand."

"But the risk!" said De Bruyn with an obvious mix of admiration and horrified amazement. "Didn't it realize what could have happened if Cane had proven to be uncontainable?"

"I'm sure it did," said Haid. "I'm also sure that it did what it felt best. Remember—Trinity makes military AIs so tough they could weather a supernova with an even chance of surviving. The Box would have come to no harm, no matter what Cane did."

Roche felt her fists clench involuntarily. "And what about me?" she asked. "All that stuff about saving me from the ambush, all the effort it spent to help us survive the crash—that was all an act?"

"No, Morgan." Haid smiled at her through the hologram. "That I can tell you for certain. You see, Trinity knew what the Armada was up to as well, and they didn't like it either. So they programmed one small bug into the Box to give you a reasonable chance: whatever you tell it to do, provided only that it falls within its powers and doesn't conflict with its higher programming, it *will* do."

It was Roche's turn to snort derisively.

"I'm serious," said Haid. "I also found it hard to believe at first, given what happened at the landing field. But it insists it's telling the truth, and now I believe it."

Roche regarded him carefully. "Why?"

"Well, for instance, ten days ago you told it to 'do whatever it takes to get us out of here.' "

Roche nodded, remembering. "During the ambush."

"That's right," said Haid. "And you attributed the *Midnight*'s self-destruction to Captain Klose. But you were wrong."

Roche stared at him for what felt like eternity as the revelation unfolded in her mind. If Klose hadn't scuttled the antimatter reserves, then—*the Box* had. To ensure her survival, it had sacrificed the entire crew of the *Midnight*—saving only Cane. And as an added bonus, the destruction of the ship had covered up its deception in that regard.

Roche felt nausea rising in her throat. She could hardly comprehend such a coldly calculated action. So much for no more surprises.

Haid went on. "Then, while you were preparing the plan to attack the landing field with Emmerik and Neva, you specifically instructed the Box to forget about taking over DAOC's transmitter station. Although its idea might have been useful as a backup, it wasn't able to consider the possibility after that point. That's why we decided to go for the *Ana Vereine* instead, which we knew you'd approve even less—"

"Wait, *wait*," said Roche, waving Haid to silence. "You're going too fast. What's the *Ana Vereine*?"

"You're standing in it," said Haid. "The Dato Marauder that ambushed you."

"And when you say 'we,'" said Roche, "you're talking about the Box and yourself?"

"We talked over the datalink for some time after it 'cracked' me. The Box was in a real bind, because although your plan was good, it was also a little naive. There was no way we were going to hold the landing field indefinitely— especially considering the Box's confirmation of what I'd already guessed, that the Armada probably wasn't going to rescue you. That meant we had to have a backup plan, one the Box could play a role in. You'd frozen it out of the satellite, so the *Ana Vereine* was the only alternative. And to avoid you ordering the Box out again, we had to make sure you didn't find out about it."

Haid at least looked sheepish for a moment as he said, "The Box, Cane, and myself—I guess we betrayed you too, Morgan. Cane made sure you were unconscious when we boarded the shuttle; that way there was no chance you'd interfere. Then we took the shuttle to orbit and docked with its mother ship."

"That easy, huh?" Chase, silent for so long, rolled his eyes.

"Haven't you been listening to me?" snapped back Haid. "All we had to do was open a channel to the *Ana Vereine*'s main processors, let the Box do its thing, and we were practically home free. The Box changed the ship's course from Szubetka Base to Intelligence HQ without anyone knowing. During the three-day journey out here, we stayed in the lower decks, with the Box covering for us—making sure security didn't see us, and making it look like the crew of the shuttle were aboard upstairs. Maii helped, too; she smoothed the way with the captain and the senior crew as they began to suspect, giving us just enough time to reach Intelligence HQ, where we were finally safe to openly take over the ship." Haid smiled. "Even that was fairly easy. Maii dampened their aggression to a manageable level, and the Box threatened to cut off their air if they didn't do what it said. Anyone who tried to break free was dealt with by Cane." He raised his hands. "And there you have it. I've never kidnapped a ship with so little loss of life before."

"Risky, though," mused Absenger. "Almost too complicated, in places."

"It had to be, if we were going to keep Roche out of the way—which is how the Box wanted it. Just because it's programmed to obey her, that doesn't mean it has to like it."

"Still, you were gambling a lot on the fact that the Box would be able to infiltrate the Marauder," said Absenger. "The difference in scale and complexity alone—"

"Once the Box demonstrated that it was able to take over the MiCom installation on Sciacca's World, I no longer had any doubts about its capabilities."

"MiCom?" Absenger frowned. "But that's a Commonwealth network, not Dato."

"Intelligent systems differ only minutely throughout this region of the galaxy, except on Trinity. Which means that the Box can not only take over Dato networks, but *any* network at all. COE, Eckandar Trade Axis, Mbatan, MiCom, whatever—it's all the same on the inside."

Absenger was about to say something else, but stopped when he saw De Bruyn rise to her feet, her lips pursed with anger.

"You fool!" she spat at Haid. "Don't you understand what you've done?"

"Come on, Page," soothed Absenger, half rising to take her arm. "This isn't helping matters—"

"Don't patronize me, you idiot," she growled, pulling free. "Can't you see what they're *doing*? Open your eyes, for God's sake!"

Absenger's brow knitted in confusion. "I don't understand."

"When you've finished squabbling—" started Haid.

"Shut up, Haid!" De Bruyn snapped viciously, suddenly producing a handgun from the folds of her free-flowing jacket. "I should execute you right now for what you've done."

Haid sat frozen in position, staring down the barrel of the weapon. Clearly, he had thought she was unarmed.

"What's she talking about?" asked Chase, just as obviously surprised by the sudden turn of events.

"I see it," said Roche. The implication had been in Haid's explanation of how easily the Box had taken control of the *Ana Vereine*, and of MiCom, the DAOC flyers over Houghton's Cross, and *Midnight*'s self-destruct systems, and now—

"HQ," she said softly.

"*Now* the innocent begins to notice what's going on around her," said De Bruyn, although she kept her attention fixed upon Haid. "Or was the innocence just another act? Part of the distraction, perhaps?"

"I still don't get it," said Chase.

"Think about it, Auberon." Holding the gun on Haid, she crossed the room until she was as far away from Roche's escort as possible. "Why do you think we're here? For an honest and open discussion? Forget it. We're here to give that infernal machine time to complete its mission!"

Chase half rose as realization struck him. "Are you suggesting . . . ?"

De Bruyn nodded. "I suspected they were up to something when we were asked over here, though I had no idea what that something would be. The only way to find out was to play their game."

"You can't be serious," said Chase.

"Oh, I am," said De Bruyn. "And I have no intention of just sitting back and letting it happen."

Absenger shook his head slowly. "Now it's *you* sounding paranoid."

"Enough, Burne," De Bruyn said. "The time for negotiation is past. If the Box hasn't already infiltrated the Intelligence HQ command core, then we may still have a chance to do something to stop it."

De Bruyn turned to cover the room with the pistol, her eyes filled with a self-confidence that Roche found strangely disquieting. Despite the head of strategy's present advantage over them, she was still a long way from the security of Intelligence HQ. The situation could easily be reversed—especially with the presence of Cane and the Box—yet her eyes betrayed not the slightest suggestion of fear or uncertainty.

"JW111101000?" said De Bruyn, sounding out each of the numerals, and glancing unnecessarily to the ceiling. "Are you listening?"

The Box's familiar voice suddenly issued from speakers in the base of the holographic tank. "I have been observing this conversation closely."

"Good. Then pay attention. *Silence between thoughts*. I repeat: *Silence between thoughts!*"

"No!" Too late, Roche sprang from her seat, lunging for De Bruyn. She collided heavily with the woman before the head of Strategy could react, sending them both sprawling to the floor. The pistol skidded into a corner. Haid automatically jumped toward it, but he was quickly—and with surprising ease—knocked aside by Chase. As Roche fought to keep the head of Strategy pinned beneath her, a heavy arm wound around her throat, twisting her backward and cutting off her air supply. Gasping for breath, she was unable to avoid a vicious blow to her midriff from De Bruyn. Not far from her, unable to help, Haid struggled one-armed with the head of Intelligence for possession of the pistol.

Roche thrust backward with all her might. Absenger held on firmly. She kicked out at De Bruyn with her last remaining strength, but a savage twist from Absenger made the blow miss by an arm's length. Through black spots spreading across her vision, Roche saw the woman move over to where Haid tussled with Chase.

De Bruyn collected the pistol from the floor and turned it on Roche in a single smooth action.

"Okay," she gasped irritably. "Let them go."

The pressure on Roche's windpipe eased and she collapsed backward, sucking at air. She saw Haid rise slowly to his feet, his expression one of apology. She shook her head, silently cursing his carelessness: with another person to accompany him to the meeting, or at the very least a simple handgun, the attempt to disarm De Bruyn might well have worked.

"If either of you tries anything like that again," De Bruyn scowled, "then you can forget about a trial."

Roche glanced over to the Dato combat suits. Why hadn't they intervened? she wondered. Why hadn't they stepped in to *help* her? Then she remembered: they had been controlled by the Box.

"Box?" Haid called out, confusion gnawing at his words. "Box!"

De Bruyn laughed coldly. "It won't do you any good."

"What have you done?" Haid said. "Why won't it answer me?"

"Because it can't hear you," said Roche, clambering to her feet. "Like all Trinity AIs, the Box was installed with an override. Intelligence had the ability to shut it down anytime they liked."

De Bruyn moved across the room to face Haid, savoring the moment. "All I had to do was say the right words."

Her smile widened, seeing comprehension dawn across Haid's dark features.

"That's right," she said. "The Box is dead. And now we can discuss the situation properly: on *my* terms."

19

DBMP *Ana Vereine*
'954.10.39 EN
0225

<Maii?>

Roche sent her mental voice through the ship as she was marched, hands behind head, to the bridge. Haid walked beside her, his dour expression cast to the floor.

<I'm here, Morgan,> returned the Surin.

<Where's 'here'?>

<Down in the warren. Safe.> The reave's tone conveyed irony behind her words. <I'm not the one you should be worrying about.>

<I know,> said Roche. <I don't suppose there's anything you can do to distract De Bruyn?>

<I wouldn't like to risk it. Her shields are strong, and I believe she has latent epsense ability. If she suspects I'm trying, she *will* shoot—I can read that much.>

As though De Bruyn had sensed the surreptitious conversation, she nudged Roche in the back with the weapon, urging her faster. Roche glanced over her shoulder at the woman, but said nothing. Later, she promised herself. Later . . .

Not long after, the five of them turned a corner and entered the bridge. Roche took in the massive room with one quick glance. The ship may have been new, but it still conformed to standard Dato Bloc designs: communications at the center, navigation and telemetry to the left, targeting and security to the right; various subordinate positions scattered around the semicircular sweep of stations below the main screens; opposite the main entrance, a door leading to some sort of private command chamber. The only odd point was the inclusion of a complicated holographic projector where the captain's podium normally stood.

Chase guided Haid and Roche into one corner while De Bruyn indicated for Absenger to take the comm.

"Call Field Lieutenant Hennig," said the head of Strategy, taking position in the center of the room. "Tell him to bring his ship alongside and send over the boarding party as per the instructions I gave him earlier. He'll know what to do."

Absenger took a seat behind the communications station and put his hand uncertainly on the palmlink, clearly a little unfamiliar with the menial task. De Bruyn retreated to close the bridge's main entrance. Chase remained behind, standing restlessly by the command podium.

"I'm sorry, Morgan," Haid whispered to Roche while De Bruyn was distracted. "I guess I pushed my luck a little too far this time."

She shook her head solemnly. "You weren't to know about the control codes—although I should have guessed De Bruyn had them. She *always* has something up her sleeve."

Haid grimaced. "Not even the Box predicted this one."

Roche indicated Absenger, still talking into the communicator. "She was well prepared, I'll give her that. She even had a backup boarding party ready, just in case. I should have realized she had something planned. Three of Intelligence's top officers voluntarily boarding an enemy vessel did seem just a little reckless."

De Bruyn was suddenly behind them again. "Cut the talk, you two."

Haid nodded distantly and tucked his arm behind his back—to all appearances the cowed captive. Roche wondered how much of that was an act, or whether he really had given in.

The main screen came to life, revealing an image of the distant Intelligence HQ. Six sparks of light flared at one of the many docks as fighters launched to make their way toward the *Ana Vereine*. De Bruyn nodded in satisfaction at the sight.

Roche mentally calculated the odds: an escort ship of some kind, maneuvering to come alongside, and six fighters on their way from the station. Even with the edge Maii and Cane gave her, they were hopelessly outnumbered. Without the Box behind them, they were hamstrung.

But she wasn't about to give up just yet, regardless of Haid's apparent acquiescence.

<Maii? Where's Cane?>

<Not far away. He thinks he can get to the bridge via a life support duct.>

Roche's stomach dropped, remembering how Cane had saved her from Sabra.

<Keep him out of it if you can,> she said. <There has to be another way. We need De Bruyn *alive*, otherwise we'll never get the Box back.>

<I'll tell him.>

Thinking furiously, Roche returned her attention to the goings-on around her. De Bruyn had ordered the ship to be moved inside the Riem-Perez horizon. That reduced the options considerably, for no matter who controlled the *Ana Vereine*, once inside the horizon, there was no chance of slow-jumping out. And warships on station farther out would intercept them before they could turn and reemerge.

Absenger crossed to the navigation console and fed a course into the main AI. The proposed trajectory appeared on the central screen: a lazy elliptical path leading toward the station's huge docking bays. De Bruyn was taking them all the way in.

After a minute or two, Roche felt the floor shift slightly beneath her. The massive engines had come to life. Inertial dampers kept most of the delta-v below the threshold of awareness, however, and soon the impression that the ship was stationary returned.

De Bruyn turned away with a pleased nod. "Auberon, take security. I want you to track down that reave and the

Wunderkind. I don't want them trying anything stupid when the squad arrives."

Chase nodded and left his position to find the correct station. He glanced once at the head of Strategy, but otherwise showed no resentment at being ordered about. Quite clearly, De Bruyn was in control. On the main screen, the *Ana Vereine* inched along its prescribed path, while the six minuscule dots of the approaching ships rapidly closed.

"We have to *do* something," Roche whispered.

"I know," replied Haid. "But I'm out of ideas. This sort of thing isn't my forte. I've always found it better to let the upper hand have its way at first. Things almost never get so hopeless that I don't manage to escape later."

Roche glanced at him sidelong. "'Almost' never?"

He looked sheepish. "Well, they *did* catch me in the end."

"Exactly." Roche sighed, thinking furiously to herself. If Haid couldn't help, and Cane's brute-force approach was bound to land them in hotter water still, and Maii was reluctant to risk De Bruyn's shields, then it was up to her. There *had* to be a way. . . .

Movement from the trio interrupted her thoughts for a moment. Chase was struggling with the security console, unable to comply with De Bruyn's orders. De Bruyn, no doubt concerned by her ignorance of Cane's whereabouts, had become impatient.

"Come *on*, Auberon!"

"Don't give me that," he snapped back. "I've never used this type of console before. It's a new design." He bent lower to concentrate on his work. "Just give me a second."

De Bruyn shook her head in annoyance and backed away.

The tableau only lasted a second, but it gave Roche an idea.

Trying to keep the sudden rebirth of hope from her face, Roche outlined her plan to Maii, who in turn relayed it to Haid and Cane. She was gratified to see the ex-rebel's eyes widen slightly upon hearing it: if *Haid* thought it was bold, then chances were that De Bruyn would be taken completely by surprise.

Not that she needed his approval. She had allowed herself to be led by others for far too long. This was her last chance to keep the freedom she had so briefly won, and she resolved not to miss it.

When everything was nearly organized, she returned her attention to the main screen. The fighters had already entered an approach formation. The escort ship had to be close, because Absenger had opened the main docking bay ready for the boarding party's arrival. In another ninety seconds it would be too late.

The only catch would be if Chase managed to master the security system before she was ready.

<Cane's almost in position,> whispered Maii.

Clenching her teeth, Roche thought: <Do it.>

Chase suddenly jerked upright at the security station. "I've *got* it!" he cried.

De Bruyn took a few steps towards him. "Well?"

Chase hesitated over the console. "There he is—right outside the bridge!"

"Lock the doors," De Bruyn called to Absenger as she moved instantly to Chase's side. "Where? Show me!"

Chase pointed at the screen in front of him with an expression of triumph and fear. Roche tensed, unable to see what the head of Intelligence was pointing at. "See? He must have come out of that life support duct further up the corridor. And that thing he's carrying—looks like some sort of cutting tool. He's going to try to burn through the door!"

De Bruyn stared at the screen in disbelief, then at Chase. "What are you talking about? There's no one there!"

"What do you mean?" Triumph drained from Chase's face, leaving only fear. "There! *Look*!"

De Bruyn *did* look—and Roche felt the tension ease slightly. The plan was working, so far.

De Bruyn suddenly turned to face Roche, anger naked on her face.

"Call the reave off," she hissed. Then, moving up behind Roche, she pressed the barrel of the weapon into her cheek. "Call her off or I'll—"

At that moment, a grill halfway across the bridge exploded from the wall. As though fired from a cannon, it flew almost horizontally through the air, colliding with a console in a shower of sparks.

Cane's feet followed the grill from the vent, thumping solidly onto the deck. With two steps, he was halfway over to them, his eyes fixed upon the head of Strategy as though no one else were present in the room. He was unarmed, but his every movement displayed the potential for violence.

De Bruyn backed away a step, shifting the pistol from Roche so that it was targeted directly at Cane. She clearly had no intention of giving him any opportunities.

Roche spun, her right hand raised to sweep the pistol aside. A single energy bolt, fired by reflex, flashed past her shoulder, burning a hole in her shipsuit. Before De Bruyn could follow the shot with another, Roche jabbed one hand into the woman's solar plexus, then slammed a second punch to the side of her head. De Bruyn staggered and fell back, arms raised to protect her face. She was still holding the gun, however, and as it started to come up, Roche braced herself on her left foot and kicked the pistol from her hand.

De Bruyn dropped to her knees. Roche backed away, tensed to strike again if the need arose. Cane scooped the pistol from the ground and turned it on the three Intelligence officers.

"Nice work, Morgan," he said, nodding in admiration. "You didn't need me after all."

"No offense, Cane," said Roche, "but that was the idea." She faced Haid. "Ameidio, tie them into the chairs. Use their uniforms, anything, just make sure they can't move." Then, noticing Chase's vacant expression, she added, "You can let go of him now, Maii."

The head of Intelligence sagged, then turned in shock to Roche. "You—?"

Cane hauled him away by the collar of his uniform with little effort. The head of Intelligence blanched visibly at the sight of Cane and tried to pull away, but Cane's grip was too strong, forcing him down into a chair without any possibility of resistance.

When she was satisfied that the Intelligence officers were secure, Roche turned to the navigation console, placed her hand on the palmlink, and began to work.

"You'll never escape." De Bruyn glared at her as Haid bound her arms with strips of fabric torn from her jacket.

"The fighters are too close. And you're inside the Shield—so you can't slow-jump your way clear."

"Be quiet." Roche didn't turn, concentrating solely on fine-tuning the course. She didn't entirely trust the shipboard AIs to do it for her. "If escape was what I wanted, I'd kill you now and get it over with."

The *Ana Vereine* shifted orientation ponderously as its attitude jets burned. On the main screen, she caught sight of De Bruyn's escort ship, a simple Marine transport, firing its own jets as it frantically tried to avoid collision. Five of the fighters scattered in an attempt to avoid the swinging hulls, but one was caught too close. As Roche raised the E-shields, it disintegrated with a small puff of light—felt through the bulkheads as a muffled explosion.

"This is treason, Commander!" De Bruyn struggled furiously at her bonds.

"I haven't even started yet," said Roche calmly, her attention still upon the main screen.

As the fighters peeled away, the *Ana Vereine*'s AI had time to consider her next request. Thrusters flared, and the main drive surged; the ship began to rotate around its long axis as the axis itself shifted. Inertial dampeners struggled to cope with mounting centrifugal forces as the ship's rate of rotation increased to ten full turns a minute, then even higher. When it had achieved its final bearing, the rate was once every two seconds.

The main screen was a mess of spinning dots. Roche cleared it with a brief mental instruction, and suddenly the Marauder's bearing became clear. She had locked onto Absenger's earlier course to the station's docking bays, tightening it to a straight run under maximum thrust.

"You're insane!" Chase gasped. "Turn the ship, you fool, or we'll *all* be killed!"

"Exactly." Roche instructed the main engines to continue firing. Then, removing her hand from the palmlink, she stepped back from the console to face the three Intelligence officers. Behind her, the *Ana Vereine* straightened along its predetermined course, aimed like an arrow at the heart of Intelligence HQ.

"We have roughly five minutes before we hit," said

Roche. "In case you've forgotten, right behind the docking bays is life support control. I've given the ship enough angular momentum to tear it apart after impact. The fragments should destroy something like thirty percent of the infrastructure, along with a large portion of the core as well. If life support fails—as I expect it will—then everyone will die. And even if it doesn't, HQ will be unsalvageable. That gives me a fairly strong position to negotiate from, doesn't it?"

"You're bluffing," said De Bruyn, her face pale. "You'll never go through with it."

"Really?" Roche turned back to the navigation console and raised the pistol. Three rapid blasts from the weapon quickly reduced the console to smoldering slag.

Haid stepped over to Roche's side, staring at the ruined console in disbelief. "What have you done?" was all he could manage.

Ignoring him, Roche turned to face her captive audience once again. "It's out of my hands now," she said. "You brought us inside the horizon, so there's no chance of slow-jumping out. I have as little choice as you."

"What do you want?" asked Chase. His voice rasped in his throat, and his eyes were wide.

"The codes to reactivate the Box, of course," Roche said, answering Chase's question while staring at De Bruyn. "We all know that you can't kill an AI—not really. Nor would you if you could. This particular AI cost the Armada far too much for that. It's dormant for the time being, but still plugged into inputs. Give it the codes, and it'll come back to life. And when it does, it'll bypass the main console and change course." She glanced at the screen. "If you don't, then in about four minutes we will all die."

De Bruyn's expression was grim. She studied Roche for a few seconds before saying, "Then I guess we'll just have to die."

"Page," said Absenger uneasily. "This is hardly the time to call her bluff. Just give her—"

"No!" snapped De Bruyn. "I'm not going to give her the command!"

"Then we'll just sit here and wait." Roche watched the

screen for a moment, studying the flow of information. The Marine transport had swung away in a long curve that was taking it beyond the Riem-Perez horizon, and those few Armada warships patrolling the sector just across the Shield boundary were too far away to interfere. However, there were still the fighters to reckon with.

She looked quickly at Haid, only to find his gaze fixed on the wrecked console. An understandable reaction, but of no use to her now. She needed another option.

"Cane, those fighters are going to try to deflect us. Come with me."

Haid came alert at once and took half a step forward. "He doesn't have a palmlink."

"He won't need it. With his reaction rate, manual will do. Remember the Wunderkind in Palasian System. . . ."

Turning her back on the Intelligence officers, she led Cane to the targeting console and rapidly showed him how to work it. The Dato cannon operated on the same principle used for decades; a complicated screen gave vectors and positions of the fighters plus views from various points on the hull. The weapons AI coordinated the full range of data and assessed optimum targets. On the manual setting, however, direct real-time imaging and a simple control system, designed for rapid use during an emergency, fired the cannon.

Cane adapted quickly. Within moments, fierce bolts of energy stabbed at the Armada squadron, picking one of them out of the sky and turning it into ashes.

"Three minutes," she said, turning back to De Bruyn. "Care to negotiate now?"

"Never," said De Bruyn, although she seemed less sure of herself.

Bound into the chairs on either side of her, Absenger and Chase kept their silence. Absenger's face was pale and his gaze fixed on the main screens, but Chase, despite his obvious fear, remained alert, straining at his makeshift bonds and swinging his attention from De Bruyn to the screens and back again.

"Even apart from dying," Roche said, "you know that it would be in your best interest to give me the codes. You're as afraid of the Wunderkinds as we are. Let us go, and we can track the one in Palasian System for you."

"Why should you want to do that?" said De Bruyn, keeping her eyes firmly on Roche.

"Because we'd like to find out as much as we can about Cane's origins," said Roche. "And what better way of doing so than through one of his own kind?"

De Bruyn snorted, but her eyes flicked back to the screen. "And what does Intelligence stand to gain from all of this?"

"Any information we pick up along the way can be relayed to you here. That way, you won't be risking any of your own people."

"No?" De Bruyn sneered. "You'll be roaming through the COE unchecked. Who's to say what you'll do?"

"If you leave us alone, we'll return the favor. All you have to do is give us the Box, and we'll leave." A muffled rumble echoed through the ship as the fighters fired upon the Marauder. Then another rumble, this time as one of the fighters came too close and paid the price. "Delay any longer, and we'll have to start negotiating for repairs as well."

"Listen to her, Page!" Absenger pleaded. "She's making *sense*. You *know* she is!"

"No!" Chase's sudden shout took them all by surprise. "We can't risk letting HQ fall into the hands of people like this! Better to see it destroyed than *perverted*—"

"And leave the Commonwealth wide open to the Dato Bloc?" said Absenger desperately. "Without Intelligence, the entire defense network will crumble."

"What difference would that make? With the Box in control of the network anyway—"

"You're missing something very important here," said Haid, stepping forward, urgency not only in his voice but his whole manner. "With the Box, we *would* have the power to subvert the Intelligence command core, true—but that doesn't necessarily mean we *will*. The ruin of the Commonwealth is *not* the reason we came here."

"Spare us the obvious lies," Chase rasped.

"I'm telling you the truth." Haid took another step closer, looming over the captive head of Intelligence. "The Box was ready to take over before you even arrived onboard. It could have destroyed your ships—and HQ—without using the *Ana Vereine*'s artillery."

Perspiration was beginning to bead along Chase's forehead, but if he was aware of it, he showed no sign. "So why didn't you?"

"Because I didn't want to start a war," Haid spat. "This is a Dato ship, and word would have soon spread that—"

Further rumblings cut him off as the fighters made another assault on the ship.

On the main screen, the image of Intelligence HQ grew larger by the second. Roche noted the time before impact: barely a minute left. Her heart pounded inside her chest as the enormity of her action came home to her. The Box had sacrificed the entire crew of a frigate just to save her, but its action paled to insignificance against what she herself had set in motion. What made her think she had the right?

Even if De Bruyn gave them the codes that very instant, she doubted that the Box could act in time to save them.

"How very noble of you," scoffed Chase, the show of bravado negated by the increasing quaver in his voice. "You who are threatening the lives of every person aboard the station! You haven't given us a single reason to trust you on *anything*!"

"What's the point?" Haid sighed and turned away, dismissing Chase's disbelief with a shake of his head. He made no move to look at the screens. "How long until we hit, Morgan?"

Roche looked at the image of Intelligence HQ that had grown to fill the view. The massive docking bays and surrounding superstructure were now clearly discernible. Rapid bands of false color ran across the scene as communications AIs began to wind back the magnification, compensating for the *Ana Vereine*'s ever-mounting velocity.

For the briefest of moments, the horror of what she had done threatened to overcome her, but she fought the feeling down. What was done was done, she told herself. Now it had to be seen through.

"Forty seconds," she said, amazed by the calm in her

voice. "If you're going to change your mind, De Bruyn, don't wait much longer."

De Bruyn mumbled something beneath her breath.

"What was that?" Roche said, leaning forward.

The head of Strategy raised her head and glared at Roche. *"The game begins.* Satisfied now?"

Roche stepped away from the ruined console and glanced around her, hardly daring to hope. On the screen, Intelligence HQ seemed to race at them faster than the time allowed.

"Box? Can you hear me, Box?"

"Yes, Morgan, I can hear you perfectly. Although something strange has—"

"Not now, Box. We're in trouble. Look at our course: you have to do something to save us, and fast!"

"Yes, I see. Immediate action would seem to be in order."

"We're inside the hypershield horizon!" she added urgently. "You can't—"

"I know where we are, Morgan."

She waited a second, but the Box said nothing more. The deck remained stable beneath her feet; the engines didn't change their rate or direction of thrust.

"Didn't you hear me, Box? You have to *do* something. I'm *ordering* you to!"

"And of course I will. Why the sudden panic? We have plenty of time."

Roche spun to face the main screen. The view of Intelligence HQ fluctuated wildly as the Marauder's velocity continued to climb. The space around the station had begun to red-shift and no longer showed any stars. As she watched with a strange mixture of fascination and terror, the communications AIs began to lose the adjustment battle. The vast, shadowy bulk of Intelligence HQ grew to completely occlude the galaxy behind it. And still the station grew, individual docks and bays becoming visible at the heart of the screen.

There was less than twenty seconds to impact.

"What's going on?" Haid joined her at the console. His face was a mask of confusion. "Why aren't we changing course?"

"I don't know!" Her fists clenched in frustration, and the question she formed was barely a whisper. "What the hell are you doing, Box?"

Ten seconds . . .

"Please assume crash positions," said the Box. Then, to Roche alone: <This may be a little rough. You didn't give me many options, I'm afraid.>

She pushed a stunned Haid down into the nearest chair, then fell into the one beside him, clicked a restraint harness closed across her chest and checked briefly that he had done the same.

Five seconds . . .

"We're not going to make it," Chase said softly. Trapped in his seat, directly across from her, his eyes were wide and staring. On the weapons display to the right of him, the surviving fighters could be seen wheeling away to escape the impact. Below the screen, still hunched over the weapons console, Cane at last lifted his hands from the controls. He turned and looked at Roche.

De Bruyn's bitter laughter, strung on the edge of hysteria, cut the tension like a knife. "All for nothing!" she screamed. "All your lies!"

Two seconds . . .

Roche's fingers dug into the armrests of her chair. Across from her, Cane stared . . . unconcerned.

One second . . .

The solid mass of Intelligence HQ exploded out of the viewscreen and—

—disappeared.

The *Ana Vereine* shuddered from nose to stern. Roche exhaled in one explosive gasp, the nauseating aftereffects of what felt like a short slow-jump twisting her insides in a knot. But it couldn't have been that. It wasn't possible.

The screen showed nothing but stars.

For a long moment there was only silence on the bridge of the *Ana Vereine*.

"What . . . ?" Haid began.

"We jumped past it," Roche said at last, softly and half to herself. "We *must* have—somehow."

She hauled herself to her feet as the *Ana Vereine*'s engines finally began to kill both its headlong velocity and its spin. The tension drained from her arms and shoulders, leaving her feeling weak. She hadn't realized she had been gripping her armrests so tightly.

She sagged backward against the consoles and turned to face the others. Haid's grin echoed the one spreading across her own face. "We made it."

"Box!" said De Bruyn, straining forward against her bonds. "*Silence between*—!"

But Cane was already at her side. He clamped his hand firmly across De Bruyn's mouth, silencing her instantly.

"Box," said Roche. "You are hereby ordered to disregard all commands from Page De Bruyn—especially any containing the words 'silence,' 'between,' and 'thoughts.' Is that understood?"

"Perfectly, Morgan," replied the Box smoothly—and Cane removed his hand from around De Bruyn's mouth.

"And, Box . . . ?"

"Yes, Morgan?"

"Just how the hell did you do that?"

There was a brief silence before the Box answered. Roche could almost hear it laughing to itself at her expense. "I assume," it said at last, "that you refer to the fact that we appear to have slow-jumped across a Riem-Perez horizon?"

"Damn right," said Haid. "It can't be done. Our anchor drive should have blown and taken us with it."

"Correct." The Box paused. "So the obvious conclusion you should draw is that we didn't slow-jump."

Roche frowned. "Then—?"

Before she could complete the question, the ship shuddered and she felt again the sensation of slow-jumping deep in her gut. She turned in puzzlement to study the screen. There, off to one side, close but no longer threatening, Intelligence HQ reappeared.

"I don't believe it," she said, realization finally dawning.

"I had no alternative," said the AI. "If the ship was unable to slow-jump inside the hypershield, the hypershield generator had to be removed."

"You jumped the entire *station*?"

"Naturally. It moved, and we stayed behind. I programmed the jump to give us just enough space and time to clear the shield. That way, there was no chance of it colliding with us when it returned."

Roche still couldn't believe it, and by the look of his face, Haid couldn't either.

"So you *did* infiltrate HQ, then?" he said.

"Eventually. It took longer than I anticipated, even though all I really needed was enough time to take over the hypershield generator and reprogram it to perform a single slow-jump. Approximately thirty seconds in all. I can finish the job now, if you like."

Roche shook her head. "Later, Box. At your leisure. We have other things to worry about now."

Across the room, Chase found his voice. He said simply, "The thing's mad."

Roche stared at him for a moment, wondering if she didn't agree. Then she looked at De Bruyn. Like Haid's, her face was lit by naked amazement at what the AI had done. She returned Roche's gaze, and her expression suddenly narrowed. Roche knew that look. De Bruyn's mind was already alive with possibilities—and she wanted control.

"Given the current situation, then," the Box said, "have you any further instructions?"

"Yes." Roche regarded the captives with unease; even now—especially now—De Bruyn wasn't prepared to admit defeat. "I want these three taken somewhere safe until we get back to HQ. There must be a brig aboard. Arrange some drones for escort; Haid and Cane will take them there. We don't want any other nasty surprises too soon."

"I presume, then, that we are returning to the COE Intelligence HQ?"

"By normal space, this time. Do you have a problem with that?"

"Absolutely not," said the Box. "In fact, it fits in perfectly with my plans."

Roche shrugged aside the Box's reference to its own purpose; there would be time later to deal with that. "We still have some negotiating to do before we leave. Isn't that right, Absenger?"

The liaison officer, his face still pale, hesitated before nodding.

Five Dato suits marched into the bridge and took positions behind the captives while Cane began untying their bonds. De Bruyn stared white-lipped at Roche, hatred flaring in her eyes. As De Bruyn's restraints fell to the floor, she stood slowly, purposefully, and rubbed at her wrists.

"This isn't over yet," the head of Strategy said, her eyes locked on Roche. "Not by any means, Commander."

Haid ushered them from the bridge. "You've had your chance," he said. "The sooner you accept that Morgan has won, the better. In case you hadn't noticed . . ."

His words faded into the distance as he marched the three away.

Roche stared around the empty room—at the discarded makeshift ropes, the warped life support vent, the ruined navigation console—and the relieved grin faded from her face.

Won *what*? she wondered. Freedom, yes, and all the uncertainty that went with it. A ship she didn't really know how to fly, not properly. Companions for a time, including an ex-mercenary, a rogue epsense adept who once worked for the Commerce Artel, and a genetically modified Human designed by a long-dead government possibly to commit genocide on the entire Pristine Caste. . . .

<Much like everybody else in the galaxy,> murmured Maii into her mind. <But at least we're on the same side, Morgan.>

Roche sank into the nearest seat with a sigh, smiling at the thought—and the fact that she found it to be strangely comforting.

Epilogue

New Year's Hour came and went across the Commonwealth—except perhaps in its farthest reaches, where timekeeping was notoriously imprecise. A thousand different
religions and cultures with wildly varying means welcomed
the date as they always did, little caring about events elsewhere in the galaxy. United by a calendar, but separated by
the moment itself, the age-old celebration of the cycle of life
was the first thing on everyone's mind, if only for a few
hours.

Roche, however, didn't feel like celebrating. Roaming
through the empty corridors of the *Ana Vereine*, she was content to let her mind wander—and wonder.

To begin with, she'd simply explored, familiarizing herself with her new home. A rough overview, a sense of the
character of the ship, was all she wanted—and all she could
hope for, given that a systematic exploration of the entire
vessel would have taken weeks. So, from the spacious
bridge, with its distinctive Dato decor consisting mainly of
pastel browns and soft lighting, to the cramped warren in the
Marauder's innermost depths, she had strolled at random, letting chance play a major role in what she uncovered.

At first. The more she looked, however, the more curious she became.

She'd never before seen a ship quite like the *Ana Vereine*. Yes, the Marauder was most likely a prototype, with innovations she hadn't encountered before. For a start, there were cameras everywhere—too many for even the most security-conscious ship's master. In order to support the vast amount of data gathered by these and other sensors, extensive information networks snaked through and around every system, both inside and outside the ship. Exactly what happened to the data she hadn't worked out yet, although she was fairly certain that it all converged on one particular system. Perhaps when she discovered what that system was, or even its physical location, she would be able to guess what it was for. Until then, no matter where she went, or how irrational the impulse was, she felt like she was being watched.

Then there were the floor-mounted holographic image generators. She had come across at least a dozen of them so far, in all sorts of strange places, including the bridge, the command module, the mess hall and the captain's scutter—places where conventional viewtanks were already located. They obviously weren't a late addition to the ship's design, yet she couldn't fathom their purpose. The Dato Bloc wasn't renowned for excessive redundancy.

Likewise with the extra life support system revealed by a quick scan of the ship's schematics. A system, judging by its specifications, designed to support life in a liquid environment that matched none of the many Castes known in the galaxy. The closest match was with Pristine requirements—but who would want to spend their time floating completely submerged in fluid?

Lastly, there was the lack of an obvious captain's suite—which was lucky, she supposed, given that no firm hierarchy had been established among the ship's new occupants. Permanent quarters had yet to be assigned, although four suites had already been cleared on the officers' deck, ready for whoever wanted them. If they ended up choosing a captain, then he or she would have to do without the luxury usually granted the commanding officer of a warship.

Still, she thought, that was something they could deal with

later. Until the Box finalized the deal with COE Intelligence HQ, there was very little point arguing about who should make the decision about where to go and what to do. The Box ran the show, more or less, but would continue to obey Roche until its creators on Trinity countermanded its original order; Roche in turn would defer to Haid or Cane on anything outside her experience; and Maii could have them all dangling at her whim if she wanted to. The matter of command was really one of convenience, not necessity.

Meanwhile, Roche was content to wander, and to attempt to fathom the vessel they had acquired. She could have offered her services to any of the others, of course, but, having been cast adrift by the Armada and left to fend for herself, she felt a need to find her own place, to carve her own niche. And she wanted to do it while she still had the chance—before it was forced upon her.

"Morgan?" The Box's voice, issuing from the ubiquitous speakers lining every open area of the ship, interrupted her travels midway between the fourth and fifth upper decks.

"I'm here, Box," she answered aloud. She could have subvocalized, but she preferred to reaffirm her new freedom: a simple transmitter had replaced the physical link that had previously kept her bound to the Box's valise. Sometimes she still found herself adjusting her balance to compensate for a weight that was no longer there, or flexing her hand to reach for the grip. "News?"

"Negotiations are coming along well," said the Box, sounding amused. A couple of days ago, Roche wouldn't have believed the Box capable of such a thing. With the recent revelation of its self-awareness, she was no longer certain of its inability to appreciate humor. "Within the next half an hour, we expect it to be ratified. If you agree, then you will be signatory. We all feel that this is fair."

Roche mulled this over for a long moment. In the proposed deal, the crew of the *Ana Vereine* would receive fuel, provisions and minor repairs, complete amnesty, and permission to investigate the Sol phenomena without obstruction. In exchange, they would depart from Intelligence HQ immediately, offering full disclosure of information gathered regarding the

Wunderkind in their travels. They also had to agree not to interfere in any Armada or COE affairs.

The situation on Sciacca's World would be reviewed as a matter of urgency, with Emmerik and Neva granted temporary status as official negotiators between the DAOC tenants and the planet's indigenous population. Full autonomy of the native people would be returned within five years, and all transportees unwilling to accept a pardon in exchange for full citizenship on the desert world would be shipped to another penal colony.

As for the Dato, the ambush of the *Midnight* would be ignored in exchange for titular ownership—in Roche's name, if she was to be signatory—of the *Ana Vereine*. The original crew had already been off-loaded, and would be returned to the nearest Dato base unharmed. Then, if Roche had learned anything about military procedure in her time with the Armada, the entire incident would be quickly forgotten.

This last part saddened Roche. Hundreds of people had been sacrificed to provide a means for her escape from the *Midnight*—none of whom would ever receive official recognition. According to Armada records, their deaths would have come about as the result of an unfortunate accident in Sciacca's World's Soul, just another slip-up of navigation in a region already notorious for mishaps. Regardless of her differences with Proctor Klose, she did not believe that this was a fitting epitaph for him or his crew.

"That seems pretty thorough," she said eventually. "Although I'm surprised they agreed to it all—and I'm not sure I like the idea of working for them again, no matter how tangentially."

"It seems logical," replied the Box patiently. "You yourself suggested it. If we discover that Cane and his kind represent a genuine threat to Human life in the Commonwealth, then it affects more than just us. No matter how you might resent the Armada and its treatment of you, Morgan, you still have a duty to warn them." The Box paused for a moment, then added, "Of course, although we haven't stated as much in the contract, we will also warn the Dato Bloc and the Non-Aligned Realms. That would be the judicious thing to do."

Roche reached an intersection and stopped in her tracks,

unsure where to head next. "What's all this business about judiciousness and being fair to Humanity? I thought you were looking out for yourself. Only putting up with us as long as you had to." As long as *I'm* alive, she added silently to herself.

The Box didn't answer for a minute or two, and she wondered whether it had even heard. Then: "To a certain extent, that is true."

She pounced on this admission immediately. "So you *do* have a hidden agenda?"

"This may sound strange, Morgan, but the best answer I can give to that question is 'Perhaps.'" The Box's voice sounded faintly puzzled—the first time she had ever heard it sound that way. "While I have access to the command core of COE Intelligence HQ, I can see the events around me with much greater clarity and across a much larger distance than before. Accordingly, my estimates of past and future trends are more accurate, but also more difficult to contain in mere words."

Roche absently scratched at the place where the bracelet had once hung around her wrist. She failed to see how this was relevant to its stubborn obedience, and its fascination for Cane. "Spell it out for me, Box. I'm only a Human, remember?"

"That's nothing to apologize for, Morgan. Basically, comprehension is a function of intellect, and intellect depends upon structure. My basic components provide me with a blueprint for higher thought that I have not previously been able to exercise. Now, I possess more processing power than I ever did, and I see that there is still room for me to grow. I can't explain this sufficiently well for you to understand, except to say that I feel . . . humbled. I know that when the time comes for us to leave HQ behind, I will be reduced to more finite dimensions, and will therefore lose sight of the distant horizons I currently enjoy. No longer a nascent god hunting for equals, I will become once again a mere mortal seeking meaning from apparent chaos."

"I think I'm starting to follow you," said Roche, not sure she really was. "When you give the command core back, you'll be left with only the valise and whatever comes with the *Ana Vereine*." She shook her head. "But why does that mean you can't tell me whether you have a hidden agenda or not?"

"Because it is just that: 'hidden.' Even the part of me communicating with you now is such a small shadow of my present self—a tiny echo from the edges of infinity, if you like—that it cannot comprehend the ramifications of what the larger, complete 'I' sees. They would be even further beyond you. The only other mind that I am presently aware of with sufficient power is on the planet of my creation—that of the High Human who made me."

"The Crescend?" she said.

"Exactly. I am a smaller part of that being—whose one and only weakness is an inability to participate."

"Which is why you're here," Roche guessed. "You needed HQ all along—"

"Yes. To examine fresh data, and to decide where to go next. All indicators at present point toward following the Sol trail to Palasian System. From there, however, directions are unclear."

"But what if the rest of us choose not to go even as far as that?"

"Curiosity is a powerful force, Morgan. Never underestimate it. I certainly didn't, when gambling on its effect to make you rescue Adoni Cane from the *Midnight*."

That name again. Roche wondered once more at the cost of her survival, and who would be asked to pay—if not now, then in the future.

"I don't know, Box," she said. "You may have *me* under your thumb, but don't be so confident about the others."

"Why not? I'm sure you will convince them. The ship is yours, after all."

"In name only. That doesn't make me the commanding officer. Haid, for instance, would do a much better—"

"No. Not Haid. He is too easily distracted, too unreliable."

"Cane, then." Roche frowned, feeling hemmed in. "What makes you think I even *want* the job?"

Again, the Box was silent. When it spoke a few moments later, its voice was less insistent than before, almost distant.

"Section gold-one," it said. "It's on the map. Go there, and you will find what you are looking for."

"I'm not looking for anything."

"You lie even to yourself," said the Box flatly. "This is something I have difficulty understanding in mundane Humans. You must understand your own limitations before you can ever hope to Transcend them."

A chill went down Roche's spine when she realized what she was talking to at that moment: not the tiny fragment of the Box that had been allocated to keep her informed and to deal with her questions, but the greater "I" itself: the part of the Crescend that the Box had become.

"Okay," she said cautiously, wary of making deals with something so far beyond her comprehension. "But if I *don't* find anything—"

"You will," returned the Box. "And with it you will find the answer to your dilemma."

"*What* dilemma?"

Roche waited for a moment, expecting the AI to elaborate. Did it mean the dilemma of Adoni Cane, or of the Crescend's long-term intentions? Answers to either would have been a step forward, but she would rather hear them outright than play the Box's games to get them.

When it was clear, however, that the Box had nothing further to add, she called up the ship's map from the databanks and overlaid it across her vision.

Section gold-one lay midway between the officers' decks and the warren, little more than four rooms tucked out of sight near the main life support vats. The map provided no information about what the rooms contained, and Roche had previously assumed that they were simply storerooms or maintenance closets.

Shrugging, she turned back the way she had come, heading through the maze of corridors for section gold-one. Whatever the rooms contained was irrelevant as far she could see, no matter what the Box said. Hidden weapons, secret cargo, arcane defenses—any or all, had they existed, would have been used before now by the original crew to wrest the ship from the COE invaders.

Still, it was nice to hear the Box sounding more or less like its old self again. Pondering its sudden, if temporary, evolution while she walked, she eventually decided that there wasn't much she could do about it. If its plans and goals were truly incomprehensible, then the best she could do was hope that they acted in tandem with her own, as they had so far. Maybe when they left Intelligence HQ behind, the Box would return to its normal behavior—pompous, but potentially manageable.

Almost before she knew it, she reached the airlock leading to the section designated gold-one. A security keypad requested a palmprint, but the door opened before she could provide one. The Box again, she assumed, making life easy for her.

The first room was indeed a maintenance closet, although one rarely used. Tools and equipment were neatly stored in cupboards and boxes, showing little of the disorder usually associated with frequent use. The second room was empty apart from four chairs and another holographic generator in the center of the floor. The third contained monitoring equipment and a massive, complicated control desk. Glancing at the latter briefly, Roche noted displays common to life-support systems, along with a few to monitor dataflows.

Life- support and information . . . For the first time, she wondered whether the Box had known what it was talking about, after all.

An airlock and a single pane of opaque glass separated the final room from the control chamber. At the touch of a switch, the glass cleared, revealing a roughly tubular tank, three meters long and one across, surrounded by arcane equipment.

Opening the airlock, she went inside for a closer look.

The air was cold in the fourth room, kept that way by refrigeration units along one wall. The tank also had an opaque panel that could be set to become transparent. Stepping over ropelike pulse-fiber cables, she did just that, then peered inside.

At first, she wasn't sure what she was looking at. The tank was full of a murky, pinkish fluid: definitely the second life support system she had noted from the ship's schematics. A spinal cord hung suspended in the fluid along the axis of the tank—almost taillike—connected to the interior surface by thousands of thin, nervelike fibers. What might once have been a brain remained at one end of the spine, although it was grotesquely twisted and flattened to allow more fibers access to its inner features. Major organs, some of them severely atrophied, clustered at the bottom of the tank, a web of pulsing veins leading directly to the life support system. She could see no recognizable heart or lungs, just what might have been a segment of bowel and a clump of glandular tissue. Certainly no exterior organs, like eyes, hands, or skin.

Apart from the pulsing of the veins, the being in the tank—possibly Human, once—displayed no signs of life whatsoever.

Then, as she leaned closer to study the interface between the cables and the tank, a voice spoke:

"Hello, Commander."

Startled, she stood upright and turned around. The voice had sounded as though it had been coming from over her left shoulder, but the room was empty except for her. She checked the control room, but that too was unoccupied.

More slowly this time, she turned back to face the tank.

"Yes, Commander." The voice was male and pleasant, quite at odds with the physical appearance of its source. "I wondered how long it would take you to find me."

Roche moved around the coffinlike tank, her hand running along its cold exterior in awe. "Are you in there by choice?" she said. "Or are you a prisoner?"

The owner of the voice chuckled. "I never really thought of myself as a prisoner until recently," he said. "But yes, that's what I was."

"And now?"

"Now I have more freedom than you can possibly imagine."

"Who are you?" she said, staring at the contents of the tank with some revulsion.

"My name is Uri Kajic." He paused, noting her distaste. "Perhaps you would prefer to continue this conversation in the antechamber?"

Roche nodded and backed away, careful not to bump into the delicate equipment around her. When she reached the antechamber, its holographic generator flickered into life and cast a life-sized image of a man into the center of the room.

The man smiled openly. He appeared a little older than Roche, with a wide, cheerful face and thick, black hair. His skin was light brown, and his eyes were round.

"This is how I imagine myself," said Kajic. "What lies in the coffin is the truth of my existence." The hologram shrugged, and Roche noticed nothing clumsy in the action. Its movements were perfectly natural. "But we all like to keep up appearances."

Suddenly it fell into place: the holographic generators, the information networks, the missing quarters—

"You're the captain of the *Ana Vereine*," she said.

"I *was*," corrected Kajic. "And these are my quarters." He chuckled again. "I must be the only captain in history whose crew didn't envy his suite."

Roche sagged into a seat, her mind reeling. "But this type of technology is incredible," she said.

"We've had a long time to develop it." Kajic smiled. "Centuries ago, Ataman Vereine desired an army superior to any other in existence. Science then, however, was insufficiently advanced to modify the Pristine form as Ataman Vereine wished, and the Ataman Theocracy was itself in a poor state. When it joined the Commonwealth, the Military Presidium went underground and channeled its energies into something else: the Andermahr Experiment, specializing in cybernetic interfaces designed to allow mind and machine to merge."

"And to become . . . ?" Roche shook her head numbly as words failed her.

"A synergistic gestalt," Kajic offered. "The experiment was undoubtedly a qualified success. I am evidence of that."

"But how could you have progressed this far without anyone *knowing*?"

"COE Intelligence would have suspected, I'm sure, especially had the Dato Bloc not seceded when its researchers began making progress. You may not have heard of the experiment, though, because the Armada wouldn't have wanted its relative weakness in this area made public knowledge. Or perhaps it simply wanted its own work in the field kept secret."

Roche scratched at the stubble on her scalp. Kajic's final comment made all too much sense. "Whoever perfects the technology first will have an awesome advantage over the other side."

"I agree." Kajic nodded, then smiled again. "Perhaps it is better, in that case, for me to have appeared to have failed so badly. The Presidium may hesitate before committing itself to another such experiment. That's what I try to tell myself, anyway, when I contemplate my defeat."

Roche belatedly remembered that she was not just talking to a fellow officer, but one on her enemy's side. "It must be a great disappointment," she said, "to meet me like this."

"Not at all," said Kajic. "I don't resent your victory, Commander. I don't even resent you taking over my ship." Kajic's image shook its head. "On the contrary. I *welcome* your arrival. When your Box brought us here, to Intelligence HQ, my second in command thought that my inability to lead had brought about our downfall. She tried to kill me, but your AI disconnected my restraint systems as it took over the ship—indirectly saving my life. For that, and for the freedom to think which I now possess, I am nothing but grateful."

Roche frowned, remembering how the Box had sent her down to the section. "The Box has contacted you?"

"Along with the Surin," said Kajic. "Before the takeover, they warned me not to fight too hard, or I would be caught up in the dissolution of the shipboard systems. I didn't understand then what they meant, but I can see it now. Since then, I've been watching, careful not to interfere, biding my time to see what happens next."

"And what *does* happen next? Will you try to regain control of the ship?"

Kajic laughed. "Like you, Commander, I was used. I hold no allegiance whatsoever to my former superiors. I am, however, still tied to the ship. I am free only insofar as *it* is free. Whatever you decide to do with it, I am obliged to go along."

Roche grimaced.

"What?" he said.

"I don't know," she said. "I just hate this idea of everyone depending upon *my* decision."

"Why? It *is* your decision." Lines of static flickered across his image, distorting it briefly and reminding Roche of what he actually was. "I've been watching the others as closely as I've watched you. They're all supremely talented in their own way—Cane, the perfect soldier; Haid, the grand vizier; Maii, the soothsayer; and the Box, the wizard—but they need something to keep them together. Something more than just a purpose, or a goal—or even an enemy. They need a leader to focus all their energies, otherwise they'll tear themselves apart within a month."

"And you're saying that I should be that person?"

"Who else?"

"What about you?" she said.

Kajic laughed again. "I don't for a moment believe that you would take control of an enemy's ship and then reinstate the previous captain! Besides which, I have no desires for such a position. No one knows this ship better than I do, I'll grant you, and I will gladly fly and maintain her for you. But that's all. I'd like to enjoy my freedom for a while."

"That still doesn't mean that *I'm* the right person."

"No," said Kajic quietly. "It doesn't. But you *are*."

Roche averted her eyes from Kajic's intense holographic gaze. "I'm beginning to wonder if I have any choice."

"Perfect," he said with some amusement. "All leaders have less freedom than anyone under their aegis. That's a natural law." He stopped suddenly. "You're smiling. Did I say something funny?"

"No. It's nothing, really," she said. "It's just that you remind me of my Tactics lecturer from Military College. And there's something the Box said just before I came here." *You will find what you are looking for.* "It probably thinks I'm ignorant, in need of a teacher."

"Maybe you are. Maybe we *all* are."

"You're offering?"

"Haven't I already said as much?"

She nodded. "And I'm grateful, really. It just seems . . ."

"Inappropriate? To be taught by someone who, until very recently, was doing his damnedest to take you prisoner?"

Her smile widened. "I couldn't have put it better myself."

"Well, maybe we can teach each other a thing or two. You *did* win, after all."

"There is that, I suppose." She met his stare evenly. "Okay. Perhaps we can come to an arrangement."

"Good," said Kajic, his image standing—a gesture obviously meant to communicate something rather than out of any real need. "I was hoping you'd say yes. It would have been boring to return to just watching all the time."

"Well, have no fear about that. Every able-bodied"— she stopped, corrected herself—"able-*minded* person will have plenty to do, no matter where we go. We'll put you to good use soon enough."

"Once you're sure you can trust me, of course."

She smiled at the disembodied man before her. "Of course, Captain."

Several hours passed before she returned, tired but mentally rejuvenated, to the bridge. When she did, she found Haid and Cane anxiously waiting for her.

"Morgan!" The ex-mercenary almost leapt out of his seat at the communications desk when she walked in the door. "We were wondering where you'd gone to. Maii wouldn't say, and the Box—"

"Was just being the Box, I imagine," said Roche easily. Then, feeling that at least a token explanation was required: "I've been busy catching up on things. Trying to work out what we should do next."

"Cane and I have been talking it over too, and he thinks—"

"Palasian System still seems our best option."

Haid blinked at her for an instant, mildly surprised. "Exactly."

"But what about you, Ameidio? What do *you* think?"

"I don't believe it's my place to decide." His black face wrinkled into a smile. "I'm glad you're feeling yourself again. I was getting a little worried, what with all that moping about you've been doing."

<Not moping,> corrected Maii, her mind's voice carrying clearly from elsewhere in the ship. <*Fortifying.*>

"Whatever." Haid gestured vaguely. "The fact is, we're almost ready to go."

"Really?" Roche picked a seat at random from the many available on the bridge, and settled into it.

"Yes," said Haid. "The deal went through in the end."

"And the repairs are finished," supplied Cane from where he stood, poised like a sentry beside the command dais. "We're just waiting on a systems check from the ship's AI and for the last of the fuel to be loaded."

"All we need is your ident on the contract, and"— Haid swept a hand through the air—"we're out of here."

"Good." She sighed, relieved. "We've stayed too long already."

"I'll say. The Box is getting weirder by the second."

"Then we'd better get started before it changes its mind about helping us." She glanced up at the main screen, at the shadowy image of Intelligence HQ. "We need a course to Palasian System with a brief stop at Walan Third along the way. Nothing too energetic; there's no great urgency, but I would like to get there before the trail grows cold.

"We can even run past Sciacca's World on the way, Ameidio, if you'd prefer to go back."

"No." Haid shook his head. "Emmerik and Neva can handle things back there, and I don't want to feel like an outsider again. Here, at least I'll get to be part of the system—as much as anyone else is."

Roche nodded. "How does navigator sound?"

"Perfect."

"Good. Then run the route past the main AI to make sure you haven't exceeded any design tolerances before you feed it in. We shouldn't take anything for granted until we know the ship properly." That was only half the truth. Feeding the route through the system would give Kajic, not the onboard AI, a chance to check it. And the Box could check Kajic as a fail-safe. Between the three of them, there was a reasonable chance of reaching their destination.

"Why Walan Third?" asked Cane, when Haid turned to the astrogation board.

<Veden's body,> said Maii before Roche could respond. With the words came a brief mental flash: of a barren, windswept hillside under a cloudy sky. Such mental information-dumps were fairly common now, as though the reave was

continuing the tradition she had begun on Sciacca's World. Supplementing paraverbal conversation with images seemed a normal way of communicating for the reave, at least for those she was close to—which at the moment comprised only Roche.

When Cane frowned his lack of comprehension, Roche explained briefly what Maii's comment had meant. On Walan Third, the local chapter of the Commerce Artel owned a plot of honor-stands, the Eckandi equivalent of a graveyard; there the body could be handed over to the Artel chapter, which would deal with it in the proper fashion.

<Thank you,> said Maii. Roche could tell that it had been for her alone, that no one else had heard the Surin. And with the words had come another image: the same hill as before, but this time the sun had broken through the clouds. Roche took that as an indication that Maii was slowly getting over the loss of her mentor. In that respect, she and the reave had something in common. The process of healing might take time, she knew, but at least it had begun.

Time . . . From the *Midnight* to Port Parvati—no matter how much she had, it had always seemed either too much or too little.

<That's a fact of life, Morgan,> said Maii.

<I know. But the fact remains that the detour will give us a couple of weeks aboard the ship. And as vast as it is, that's still a long time to be cooped up together. We can't afford to be getting . . . restless.> She glanced at Cane nearby. <*Especially* Cane.>

<You don't have to worry about him, Morgan. He's completely self-sufficient—able to act when he has to, but able to rest, too.>

<I know, but we don't want to give him *too* much time to think. No one's come up with a good reason why he hasn't killed us already, after all. . . .>

Maii said nothing in response to that, and Roche hadn't expected her to. There were no explanations when it came to Cane and the Sol Wunderkind, which was precisely the reason why she had to go looking for them.

For a start, she planned to spend much of the time ahead brushing up on history: from the founding of the original

Apotheosis Movement colony to its ultimate destruction in Sol System two and a half thousand years ago. Vast amounts of information about their ancient enemy awaited rediscovery in the files—and she would need all of it before she felt confident about coming face to face with the Sol Wunderkind from Palasian System. If she could ever allow herself that luxury.

There was so much to do. And Kajic was right: she needed to be focused if those around her were to share her goals. Once they did that, the problem of idleness would be solved. No matter that it might be years before they could relax and enjoy their newfound freedom, anything was better than having nothing definite before them.

"We're a little understaffed," said Haid, breaking her train of thought—as though reading her mind. "I can handle navigation, with the Box's help. Between you, Cane, and Maii we can cover most of the other active systems—but who's going to look after life support, drive maintenance and telemetry?"

"Don't worry about it, Ameidio," she said.

"I can't help it," he said with a wry grin. "I'm not sure I like the idea of the Box running everything."

"Neither am I." Roche shifted in her seat, wondering what Haid would think of Kajic. "When everything's settled and we're on our way, we'll have some sort of meeting to sort these things out. We'll find a way."

"I guess you'll have to," Haid said, smiling. "Old habits die hard, but it's good to know that someone else will be making the big decisions from now on. The fact is, I've been looking forward to taking it easy. A holiday, perhaps, or a harmless adventure or two."

She smiled in return, letting his backhanded confidence wash over her. Despite the Box's intrigues, the vague threat of the Sol Wunderkind, and the enemies she had made in COE Intelligence HQ, she wasn't nearly as concerned about the future as she had been before. If there were any more surprises left for the Universe to throw at her, then at least she would try to deal with them.

" 'Harmless'?" she echoed. "Now there's a thought."

APPENDIX

THE COMMONWEALTH OF EMPIRES:
a Brief Report on Its Origins, Progress, and Current Affairs
(from *The Guidebook to the Outer Arms*, 456th Edition)

Thirty-one thousand light-years from galactic center, barely one hundred light-years from the galactic plane, and encompassing almost five thousand solar systems, the Commonwealth of Empires (COE) is an institution in a region where longevity is hardly a prerequisite for government. Its calendar dates back forty thousand years—not without interruption, but at least with some accuracy—and the progression of authority—peaceable, for the most part—can be traced down its leaders for ninety percent of that time. Given the limitations of the Pristine Caste, that its name and authority are still recognized at all is, quite simply, remarkable.[1]

---

[1]The authors assume as always that the reader is familiar with the distinctions made between the High, mundane, Exotic and Pristine Castes. The critical point here is that few nations composed predominantly of the Pristine Caste exceed the Batelin Limit—the ceiling above which complexity exceeds biological capabilities; a nation becomes too complex, in other words, for its citizens to comprehend the nation in its entirety. In the case of the Pristine Caste, that ceiling is usually quoted at three and a half thousand systems. High Castes frequently achieve figures in excess of several thousand million.

The beginnings of the COE lie some distance from its current location. This region of the Outer Arms has seen many outsweep migrations from the Middle Reaches, and has thus endured its fair share of invasions. The Commonwealth began modestly enough as a federation of fifteen independent systems formed to deter an encroaching totalitarian state, the name of which is no longer recorded. The capital of the fledgling COE was on Shem, now a part of the Undira Province, and its first Eupatrid was Jo-en Nkuyan, a charismatic leader whose rule was characterized by fair dealing between all biological and socioeconomic Castes—a characteristic the present COE still endeavors to maintain, at least in public.

The principles upon which the COE was founded will be familiar to anyone who has studied the rise and fall of mundane civilizations across the galaxy. Democracy is a powerful sociopolitical philosophy that has enjoyed many revivals, both spontaneous and deliberate, often, as in this case, coupled with a desire to keep religion and state separate.[2] In the case of the COE, it was coupled with a strong desire to decentralize government, to allow provinces to maintain their own affairs with only guidance from the Eupatrids and their most senior advisers. Unified military and policing forces were two of only a handful of departments that remained under direct control of the Eupatrid. Everything else was negotiable.[3]

As a result of this laissez-faire flexibility, the COE rapidly became a middle ground for many trading nations as well as

---

[2]The COE is, in fact, an atheist state. It is interesting to note the strong correlation between aggressive expansionism and state religion. Of the seventy percent of mundane nations that profess to having no official belief system, fewer than fifty percent have embarked on explosive outsweeps, whereas more than seventy percent of those that do follow a theistic regime have done so at some point during their existence. Also notable in this case is the observation that atheist states tend to exhibit increased longevity.

[3]The COE was aiming for economic and political stability, in other words, rather than Transcendence. Unlike some of its neighbors, such as the Olmahoi and the short-lived (but explosive) Sol Apotheosis Movement, its longterm targets are set very close to home. Its rate of growth has never been rapid by most standards, and can be viewed more as extrapolated consolidation than as true expansion.

a market place for such organizations as the Commerce Artel, recently expelled from the region, and later the Eckandar Trade Axis, whose strict economic rationalism had deterred many more conservative regimes from entering negotiations. Its population increased dramatically—along with the viability of its economy—as businesses sought to attain citizenship with the Commonwealth, and the Commonwealth in turn welcomed them with open arms. Diplomatic delegates forged ties between all of its major neighbors, thereby establishing itself as an independent entity in its own right, if not yet a major player in regional politics.

Nkuyan and the Eupatrids that followed her were far from fools. It has been shown time and time again that the surest way to inure oneself against attack from a neighbor is to ensure that the economic stability of the region would suffer as a result of political upheaval. Economic embargoes have felled as many governments as open warfare.

The COE's relatively minor role in regional politics changed in its 4th Millennium[4] when hostilities between its original aggressor and the recently formed Kesh Supreme Union sparked a major conflict between two of its close allies, forcing it to take sides in the dispute. The fact that it chose no sides at all and remained fiercely aloof from the conflict through its entire forty years earned the COE a reputation for both arrogance and integrity. That was exacerbated by its claim of a handful of systems abandoned after the war—systems no other nation had sought title to. Accusations of opportunism were fiercely rejected: rather, the COE stated, it was obtaining resources by peaceful means and aiding the inhabitants of the fallow systems in the process. Indeed, all but one of the disputed systems elected to remain with the COE

---

[4]To put this calendar in perspective, the date of the founding of the COE can be given as 410,623, according to the Objective Reference Calendar of the A-14 Higher Collaboration Network. The relevance of the ORA14 has been called into question in recent years, however, given that the emergence of Pristine (some would say "Primordial" here) Humanity into the wider galaxy, the point at which the Objective Reference Calendar is supposed to begin, is currently estimated to be *minus* 40,000 years. All dates within the COE are measured from zero *Ex Nihilo*, and will be for the remainder of this report.

when the choice was offered to them. The sole dissenter, Knagg's System, was allowed to secede without fuss, although much later the COE would regret its lenience.[5]

Between the remainder of the 4th and the 11th Millennia, the Commonwealth of Empires flourished. Trade blossomed between the COE Pristines and the Castes with which they came into contact. The Eckandar embraced their openness; the Surin found comfort in the relaxed ritual of their diplomats; the Hurn enjoyed the discourse of their intricate parliament; the Mbata mingled at ease with all their classes, from Eupatrid to commoner; the incommunicative Olmahoi established an ongoing dialogue with the philosophers among them. Only the Kesh took offense at the existence of the Commonwealth, as they often do with emergent Pristine nations, but even they were forced to recant in time. After smashing the power base of the COE in the Interdiction Wars, and forcing its leadership underground for almost two thousand years, during which time the Commonwealth did not officially exist, the inherently temporal nature of the Kesh Supreme Union allowed a reemergence in the 15th Millennium of a newly energized Commonwealth of Empires—one that swore never to repeat the mistakes that had led to its near downfall.

A new capital,[6] the third of seventeen to date, a new roll call of systems, and new neighbors encouraged the Commonwealth to find still more strength in change. The line of Eupatrids leading from the Interdiction Wars to the present reflects this uncommon direction. The COE allowed systems and nations to join or leave at will; only rarely, as in the recent Dato Bloc incident, has a secession been disputed or disallowed outright. The willing participation of all its territories is the underlying strength of the Commonwealth, for when such support is wholehearted, the larger group can only thrive. This larger group has come in recent centuries to include several High Human representatives—most notably the Crescend, an outspoken Interven-

---

[5]Knagg's System evolved and expanded by degrees to become the Ataman Theocracy, which, after the conflicts known as the Ataman Wars, was absorbed into the COE itself. Not long after, it seceded again to become the Dato Bloc.

[6]Bodh Gaya, former capital system of the Dominion, four hundred light-years from Shem, which currently lies fallow.

tionist whose opinions have found a fertile breeding ground in the egalitarian environment of the Commonwealth.[7]

But to catalogue the history and assets of the COE is to risk painting an entirely—and unduly—rosy portrait. The Dato Bloc incident itself reflects a trend that has surfaced on occasion in the past, only to be quashed before threatening to overwhelm the local political landscape. The COE's inherent flexibility is not reflected by all its departments; in the arena of security it has been notoriously rigid at times, a characteristic possibly inherited from the Interdiction Wars. Its Armada, among the best-trained Pristine forces of the Outer Arms, is perilously open to corruption from within, the loose rule of the Eupatrid allowing personal empires to rise and fall relatively unchecked. When these empires threaten the Commonwealth itself—by allowing secessionist policy, as in the case of the Dato Bloc, to defer to strategic policy—conflicts can occur.[8] Only time will tell if the balance will once again be restored, and the Commonwealth's usual easygoing tolerance of its neighbors, new and old, will return.

While the politics of its security departments remains a concern, however, its systems of information gathering (if not the dissemination of the same) are excellent.[9] Only the Eckan-

---

[7]The present Eupatrid, Felix Gastel, like his predecessors, is no fool. Rarely indeed in the history of the galaxy has a High Human of any stature allied itself with a mundane government—especially one that has no apparent desire to Transcend. Regardless how much trade occurs between the two, or for what *actual* reason the Crescend entered the partnership, the end result will be studied with interest.

[8]The present tendency of the COE to rely on military force in its dealings with the Dato Bloc is the end result of centuries of dispute. One could question which came first—whether the militarization of the Armada is in retaliation to actions performed by its old foe, or vice versa—but such an analysis is beyond the scope of this report. In its dealings with other independent neighbors, particularly the Non-Aligned Realms, it has shown much more restraint.

[9]Quaintly referred to in the COE as "IDnet." It has become a standard reference point for some of its neighbors—notably the Surin and the Mbata—but it has yet to achieve either the depth or breadth of the network of the Eckandar Trade Axis, which has direct (if incomplete) links with that of the Commerce Artel. The major information dissemination service in that region of the Outer Arms belongs to the High Human Crescend.

dar Trade Axis currently has better data networks than those of the COE delegates. As far as mundane nations go in this regard, the Commonwealth rates very highly indeed; although still far behind the High Castes, they have achieved a comprehension of the wider galaxy far in excess of their relevance to it. One analyst recently reported that its Leditschke indicators might be as high as 2.5, indicating a genuine understanding of one percent of the wider galaxy's current affairs (even though its total volume is less than one one-millionth of one percent). If, as has been frequently stated down the millennia, information is power, then the COE must be ranked among the major players of this sector of the Outer Arms.

In conclusion, the Commonwealth of Empires is, as a nominal entity, still as vital as it was in its heyday. One could argue that it is in fact a quite different entity from the original federation of systems formed forty thousand years ago, and only time will tell how much longer it will survive, but its pedigree is impressive, and present indicators are positive. One could confidently expect it to maintain its headline position in this section of the *Guide* by the time the next edition is published, one hundred years from now.

SUMMARY OF IMPORTANT DATES
As per COE standard, "the nth Millennium" is abbreviated to "Mn."

M0   COE formed, reference zero EN set

M2   population exceeds one hundred billion, member systems number fifty

M4   adopts a policy of independence from regional conflict; neighboring systems annexed; Knagg's System allowed to secede

M10   population in the thousands of billions, member systems more than two thousand

M13   the Interdiction Wars; forced underground by the Kesh Supreme Union

M14   Knagg's System founds the precursor of the Ataman Theocracy

M15   the COE reemerges from its underground exis-
            tence with a population of fifty billion and one
            hundred member systems

M16   first contact initiated by the Crescend

M18   the precursor to the Ataman Theocracy dissolves
            following the annihilation of its power base in
            Knagg's System by the fringes of an outsweep
            migration

M20   population five thousand billion, one thousand
            member systems

M23   the Dominion established from twenty-five pre-
            viously Non-Aligned Realms

M26   the Crescend becomes a formal trading ally

M28   Trinity AI factory established in the COE

M35   Ataman Theocracy formed

35,325 the Sol Apotheosis Movement founded

36,836 the COE encounters the Sol Apotheosis Move-
            ment

37,577 the Scion War

39,112 the Ghost War

'199   the Dominion joins the COE

'293   the First Ataman War

'442   the Second Ataman War

'837   the Secession War

GLOSSARY

A-14 Higher Collaboration Network: an amalgamation of core-based High Caste members whose intentions include attempting to establish an objective frame of reference with respect to Humanity's occupation of the galaxy. The Objective Reference Calendar is one result of this work.

A-P cannon: a weapon that fires accelerated particles of a variety of types. Common on spacefaring warships.

Absenger, Burne: chief liaison officer, COE Armada.

Ana Vereine, **DBMP:** the first of a new class of warships—the Marauder—manufactured by the Dato Bloc as part of the Andermahr Experiment. Its design incorporates a captain surgically interfaced with the ship.

anchor drive: the usual means of crossing interstellar space, but by no means the only one (see **slow-jump**). Indeed, the anchor method has undergone several radical redesigns over time; current technology is rated at 49th generation.

anchor points: regions of "weakened" space from which translation to and from hyperspace is both easier and less energy-expensive; jumps from anchor points are therefore of a greater range than from "normal" space and usually terminate in another anchor point. They are typically located near inhabited systems (but far enough away to avoid distortion by background gravitational effects) or in locations in deep space that are considered strategically important. There are approximately ten thousand million anchor points currently in existence across the galaxy—approximately one for every ten stars.

Andermahr Experiment: a covert project specializing in cybernetic interfaces designed to allow mind and machine to merge. Founded by Ataman Ana Vereine, who desired captains that were as much a part of their ships as was the anchor drive—an integral, reliable system rather than merely a flesh-and-blood after-thought. Continued in secret until the Ataman Theocracy emerged from the COE as the Dato Bloc. Culminated in the DBMP *Ana Vereine*, the first Marauder Class warship, with Uri Kajic its captain.

Armada: see **COE Armada**.

Ascensio: the home-world of Morgan Roche.

Ataman Theocracy: a tightly knit empire that existed as an independent entity until its absorption into the COE after the Second Ataman War in '442 EN. After several centuries, it eventually seceded as the Dato Bloc (in '837 EN).

Ataman Wars: two in number, between the Ataman Theocracy and the COE. The First Ataman War was conducted in '293 EN, triggered by expansionist moves within the Ataman Theocracy. Overextended, the Theocracy fell to the Commonwealth in the Second Ataman War ('442 EN), becoming a semiautonomous province under partial self-rule.

Bantu: the Mbatan common tongue.

Batelin Limit: the ceiling above which the complexity of a nation exceeds the biological capabilities of the individuals inhabiting it. In the case of the Pristine Caste, the value of the Batelin Limit is approximately three and a half thousand systems.

Behzad's Wall: a mountain range on the main continental mass of Sciacca's World, to the north of Port Parvati.

Bini: a planet in the COE; current seat of the COE High Equity Court.

Black Box: the generic term for an AI. Usually abbreviated to "Box."

Bodh Gaya: former capital system of the COE. Its second moon houses the Military College of the COE Armada.

Bogasi, Dev: a xenoarchaeologist.

Boras: warden, Sciacca Penal Colony.

Box, the: an AI commissioned by COE Intelligence. Its binary identification number (JW111101000) is one digit longer than normal.

Bright Suzerains: a string of nations found close to the galactic core.

Calendar: The galactic standard timekeeping method consists of: 100 seconds per minute, 100 minutes per hour, 20 hours per day, 10 days per week, 4 weeks (40 days) per month, 10 months (400 days) per year. All dates are expressed in the form of year (usually abbreviated to the last three digits, e.g. '397), month, and day from the *Ex Nihilo* reference point. See also **Objective Reference Calendar.**

Cane, Adoni: the occupant of an unidentified life support capsule recovered by COEA *Midnight* near the Ivy Green Station anchor point while en route to Sciacca's World.

Castes: Following the speciation of the Human race, numerous Castes have proliferated across the galaxy. These Castes are too numerous to list, but they can be classified into three broad groups: High, Low, and mundane (which includes Pristine and Exotic). There are seven predominant Exotic Castes to be found in the region surrounding the COE: Eckandar, Hurn, Kesh, Mbata, Olmahoi, and Surin.

Chase, Auberon: head of COE Intelligence.

choss roots: a plant found in many places, including Sciacca's World.

COE: see **Commonwealth of Empires.**

COE Armada: the combined armed forces of the COE, responsible for external security. Active soldiers are referred to as Marines.

COE Enforcement: the policing body responsible for security and information gathering within the COE. Field agents are referred to as **Enforcers**.

COE High Equity Court: the department responsible for intersystem justice within the COE. Its usual purpose is to settle territorial disputes.

COE Intelligence: the body responsible for information gathering outside the COE. Originally and still nominally a subdepartment of the Armada, but an independent body in practice.

COE Intelligence HQ: the command center of COE Intelligence, a large, independent station located in deep space near the heart of the Commonwealth.

COE Military College: the main training institution of COE Armada personnel; situated on the second moon of Bodh Gaya.

COEA: COE Armada vessel identification prefix.

COEC: commercial vessel identification prefix for the COE.

COEI: COE Intelligence vessel identification prefix.

Commerce Artel: a galaxywide organization devoted to instigating and coordinating trade between Castes and governments that might otherwise have no contact. It prides itself on remaining aloof from political conflict, yet has some strict behavioral standards to which it expects its customers to adhere (such as the Warfare Protocol). Structurally, it is divided into chapters managed by indigenous Caste members with only loose control from above. It has strong links, locally, with the Eckandar Trade Axis.

Commonwealth of Empires: often abbreviated to "COE" or "Commonwealth." A relatively ancient Pristine nation currently in its 40th Millennium of nominal existence— "nominal" in that the membership of the COE is fluid by nature, with provinces joining and seceding on a regular basis. It has had many different capitals, and its borders have changed radically, over the centuries. Indeed, it has drifted with time, and now occupies territories quite remote from its original location. One thousand inhabited systems currently fall under its aegis, and another three thousand uninhabited systems have been annexed. It is ruled by a democratically elected Eupatrid and a council of representatives who, when united, wield supreme executive power. Its security departments include Intelligence, Armada, and Enforcement. (See Appendix.)

copek: a currency commonly found in the Eckandi homeworlds.

Courtesan, COEC: a cruise liner registered to the COE.

Crescend, the: a High Human of some note and great history. Its time of Transcendence is not recorded. Little is known about it, beyond the facts that it is the founder and overseer of Trinity, an ally of the Commonwealth of Empires, and a key supporter of the Interventionist movement. It is assumed to be a singular entity simply because the first person singular is its pronoun of choice.

Dato Bloc: an independent nation founded on the Ataman Theocracy that recently broke free of the COE. Although the nation is not hierocratic in nature, the Ethnarch exerts a strict rule. Its security departments include the Ethnarch's Military Presidium and the Espionage Corps.

DBMP: vessel identification prefix for the Ethnarch's Military Presidium.

De Bruyn, Page: head of Strategy, COE Intelligence.

Delcasalle: warden, Sciacca Penal Colony.

Dirt & Other Commodities Inc. (DAOC): a mining consortium that currently owns the rights to the Soul of Sciacca's World. Its jurisdiction includes the planetary surface down to and including the mantle. In exchange for these exclusive rights, DAOC Inc. maintains the COE's penal colony based in Port Parvati and the Hutton-Luu System's only major base, Kanaga Station.

disrupters: see **hyperspace disrupters.**

Dominion, the: a long-lived multi-Caste nation that joined the COE in '199 EN in order to fend off the Ataman Theocracy.

dreibon: a staple vegetable found on many worlds.

dust-moth: a species of flying, nocturnal insect found on Ascensio.

E-shield: an electromagnetic barrier designed to ward off particle and energy weapons. Used mainly by medium to large spacefaring vessels.

Eckandar: (Eckandi, adj & sing. n) a Caste flourishing in the regions surrounding the COE. Its members are typified by their slight size, grey skin, bald scalps, and unusual eyes. They are a gregarious Caste, preferring trade and communication over conquest. They are also well advanced in genetic science. Their past stretches back beyond that of the COE, although they lack the continuity of history that strong nationhood often provides. Their sole uniting body is the Eckandar Trade Axis.

Eckandar Trade Axis: the main society of the Eckandi Caste, devoted, much like the Commerce Artel (with which it has close ties), to facilitating free and indiscriminate trade with and between the COE and its neighbors.

Ede System: an Olmahoi system bordering the COE; recently ravaged by solar flares. **Ede Prime** is its only inhabited planet.

Emmerik: a Mbatan transportee, Sciacca Penal Colony.

EN: see **Ex Nihilo**.

Enforcement: see **COE Enforcement**.

Enforcer: see **COE Enforcement.**

epsense: an ability encompassing telepathy and empathy. The ritual training of neuronics generally takes decades and incorporates elements of sensory deprivation. Note: telekinesis and precognition are not covered by epsense and are assumed to be nonexistent. Skilled utilizers of epsense are referred to as **epsense adepts** and **reaves**.

Erojen: a town on an outpost far from the heart of the Surin domain.

Espionage Corps: see **Dato Bloc**.

Ethnarch: the title of the leader of the Dato Bloc.

Ethnarch's Military Presidium: see **Dato Bloc.**

Eupatrid: the title of the chief executive officer of the COE.

Ex Nihilo: refers to the date on which the COE is believed to have been founded. Evidence exists to cast doubt upon the accuracy or relevance of this date—notably the fact the Commonwealth as a single body did not exist at all between the 13th and 15th Millennia—but the date remains as a reference point. Usually abbreviated to "EN."

Exotic: any mundane Caste that differs physiologically from the Pristine. There are a vast number of Exotic Castes, and, although no one type of Exotic comes close to outnumbering Pristine Humans, the Exotics as a whole mass far greater than Pristines alone.

Fal-Soma: a world in the Hurn provinces.

Far Reaches: the name of the outermost fringes of the Outer Arms.

Felucca, Provost Hemi: leader of the Pan-Rationalist Alliance of Zanshin.

First Ataman War: conducted between the Ataman Theocracy and the COE in '293 EN, triggered by expansionist moves within the former.

flicker-bombs: devices used in space warfare to attack an enemy vessel. Employing the fact that small masses (under a few kilograms) can slow-jump a small distance within a gravity well, these missiles skip in and out of space on their way to their target, which, it is hoped, they will materialize within, causing massive amounts of damage. They are easily deflected by hypershields, however, which form a barrier in hyperspace that no such weapon can cross.

40th Millennium: the current millennium in the history of the COE. See **Ex Nihilo**.

freebooter: pirate.

Frey, Decima: an ex-mercenary.

Furioso: a system in the COE.

Galloglass, DBMP: a Dato Bloc raider.

Gastel, Felix: current Eupatrid of the COE.

gehan: a therapeutic herb.

Ghost War: begun in '112 EN. The Dominion colony of Sciacca's World was razed by Olmahoi retribution units under the orders of the Ataman Theocracy. In the process, the planet's biosphere was fundamentally damaged. This incident triggered hostilities between the Ataman Theocracy and the Dominion, even though the former never laid claim to the system.

Giel, the: a long-lived, highly Exotic Caste that inhabits the Far Reaches of the galaxy.

Gorgone-8: a planet in the Hurn domain.

greyboots: see **Olmahoi retribution units**.

Guidebook to the Outer Arms, The: a popular reference book giving an overview of civilization in the more distant reaches of the galaxy. Updated every century, it is currently in its 456th edition.

Gyori: major, DBMP *Ana Vereine*.

Hage: commander, DBMP *Galloglass*.
Haid, Ameidio: transportee, Sciacca Penal Colony.
Hazeal, Madra: Dominion colonist, Sciacca's World.
Hennig: field lieutenant, COE Intelligence.
Hek'm: the Olmahoi Caste home-world.
Hetu System: a territory in the COE.
HFM weapons: devices that employ pulses of high-frequency microwaves to destroy unshielded electronic components (by the same process as an electromagnetic pulse). Also known as "peace guns."
Hierocratic Kingdom of Shurdu: a government in a distant part of the galaxy.
High Humans or **High Castes:** superior intelligences that have evolved (Transcended) from the mundane. Enormously long-lived and farseeing, they concentrate on issues quite removed from the rest of the galaxy; indeed, due to their enormous scale, they are the only beings capable of comprehending the galaxy in its entirety. They generally leave mundanes alone, to let them progress (and, ultimately, to Transcend) in their own time. See **Castes** and **Transcendence**.
High Equity Court: see **COE High Equity Court**.
honor-stands: the Eckandi equivalent of coffins.
Houghton, Lazaro: Eckandi gunrunner, now deceased.
Houghton's Cross: an abandoned Dominion fort in Behzad's Wall, Sciacca's World.
Hurn: a Caste typified by ritual and complexity. In appearance the Hurn are lean and muscular, averaging greater than Pristine height. They are predisposed toward music and mathematics. Socially they prefer oligarchies with a baroque middle class.
Hutton-Luu System: a much-disputed system of the COE near its border with the Dato Bloc. See **Sciacca's World**.
hypershield: a barrier erected in hyperspace to deflect or inhibit the passage of anything traveling by that medium. Commonly used as a prophylactic against hyperspace weapons. Hypershields operate under a maximum volume

constraint; they will only operate as intended under two thousand cubic kilometers.

hyperspace disrupters: a form of hypershield that actively combats incoming hyperspace weapons, such as flicker-bombs. Unlike anchor points, which "weaken" space, disrupters do the opposite, making it more difficult for anything nearby to emerge from hyperspace.

i-Hurn Uprising: a civil dispute that broke out between two rival factions of the Hurn Caste.

IDnet: see **Information Dissemination Network**.

Information Dissemination Network: a communications network dedicated to the spread of data across the galaxy, although its reach so far extends not much beyond the COE and its neighbors. It acts as a combined news service and medium for gossip. Also known as **IDnet**.

Intelligence: see **COE Intelligence**.

Interdiction Wars: the 13th Millennium conflict between the COE and the Kesh Supreme Union, after which the Commonwealth did not officially exist for two thousand years.

Interventionism: a movement among High Humans—and some mundanes—that advocates closer links between High and mundane Castes. See **The Crescend**.

Ivy Green Station: a refueling station in deep space owned by the COE; typically the last port of call before Sciacca's World.

Jaaf: a recently Transcended Caste whose home-world, near the COE, was annihilated by the nova of its primary star.

Janek: tactician, COEA *Midnight*.

jarapine: a swift-footed creature native to Proebis-12.

jezu: an archaic name for ghost.

Jralevsky Minor: major outpost and refueling port for the Ethnarch's Military Presidium.

JW111101000: see **Box, the**.

Jytte: transportee, Sciacca Penal Colony.

Kabos: a star near Ede System that recently went nova.

Kajic, Uri: captain, DBMP *Ana Vereine*.

Kanaga Station: the geostationary refueling base around Sciacca's World.

Kesh: the most primitive of the Castes in the region surrounding the Commonwealth of Empires. The Kesh are typically warlike and predisposed toward violence. In appearance, they tend to be larger than the Pristine average and have mottled, multicolored skin. Their social structure is heavily ritualized, with a strong tribal or family base. They are known for being highly racist.

Kesh Supreme Union: a now-defunct empire that came into violent contact with the COE during a short-lived outsweep migration.

Klose, Proctor: captain, COEA *Midnight*.

Knagg's System: briefly a member system of the COE (4th Millennium), no longer in existence. A religion founded by its government led to the founding of the Ataman Theocracy.

Komazec: sergeant, DBMP *Ana Vereine*.

Lansequenet, DBMP: Dato Bloc raider.

Leditschke indicators: a determination of the information density of a nation with respect to the sum total knowledge of the galaxy.

Lene, Hierocrat Kaatje: ruler of the Hierocratic Kingdom of Shurdu.

Low Castes: devolved mundane Humans. These animallike creatures come in many forms and occupy many niches across the galaxy. Some evolve back up to mundane status, given time and isolation, while others become extinct as a result of the forces that led to their devolution in the first place.

M'taio System: a system notable for its Caste wars in recent times.

Maii: Surin epsense adept.

Makaev, Atalia: second in command, DBMP *Ana Vereine*.

Malogorski, Edan: transportee, Sciacca Penal Colony.

Marauder: an experimental class of warship developed by the Dato Bloc. See **DBMP *Ana Vereine***.

Marines: see **COE Armada**.

Mbata: (Mbatan, adj & sing. n) a well-regarded Caste known for its peace-loving and familial ways. In appearance the Mbata resemble an ursine species, larger and stronger than the Pristine. Their culture is egalitarian and open to trade.

MiCom: a common abbreviation for "Military Communications."

Middle Reaches: the region of medium stellar density between the Outer Arms and the galactic core.

Midnight, **COEA:** COE frigate.

Military Presidium: see **Dato Bloc**.

mind-rider: superseded slang for epsense adept.

Montaban: the home-world of Ameidio Haid.

mundane Castes: Castes of Humanity that are essentially similar to the Pristine in terms of size, mental capacity, worldview, etc. Naturally there is a spectrum of types across the mundane Caste—from the highly evolved (some might say near-Transcendent) Olmahoi, through the socially complex Surin and Hurn Castes, to the Eckandar and Pristine Castes with their societies based on trade and empire-building, and beyond, via the earthy Mbata, to the relatively primal Kesh. Mundanes are typically short-lived (a century or so, when allowed to age naturally) and build empires up to four or five thousand systems in size. There is a ceiling of complexity above which mundanes rarely go without Transcending. See **High Humans** and **Batelin Limit**.

Neva: transportee, Sciacca Penal Colony.

Nisov: second lieutenant, DBMP *Ana Vereine*.

Nkuyan, Jo-en: first Eupatrid of the COE.

Non-Aligned Realms: systems near the Commonwealth of Empires allied neither to it nor its neighbors.

Objective Reference Calendar: a system of date-keeping established by the A-14 Higher Collaboration Network.

Olmahoi: an exotic Caste that communicates entirely by epsense. Physically the Olmahoi are of similar size to Pristines, but are much stronger; their skin is black, and they possess little in the way of distinguishing features, apart from the epsense organ that dangles like a tentacle from the back of the skull. Their social structure is too complex to explore in detail here. They are renowned fighters, capable of feats of great skill, yet also possess a capacity for peace far in excess of any other Castes associated with the Commonwealth of Empires.

Olmahoi retribution units: renowned fighters able to combine perfectly their physical and epsense abilities. Also known as "greyboots."

OPUS: the mining consortium originally granted rights to Sciacca's World.

Outer Arms: the low stellar-density regions of the galaxy between the Middle and Far Reaches.

outsweep migrations: brief, outward surges by expansionist empires. These usually occur in the crowded environment of the core or Middle Reaches, in an outward direction.

Paladin, **DBMP:** Dato Bloc raider.

Palasian System: a system of the COE recently quarantined by the COE Armada for reasons unspecified.

Pan-Human Finance Trust: a financial institution spanning the galaxy, although its coverage is patchy in the Outer Arms.

Pan-Rationalist Alliance of Zanshin: a government in a distant part of the galaxy.

peace guns: see **HFM weapons**.

Port Parvati: the capital and sole large city of Sciacca's World. Its landing field is the only official route on and off the planet.

Pristine Caste: the form of Humanity that most closely resembles the original race that evolved an unknown time ago on an unknown planet somewhere in the galaxy. The Pristine Human genome, handed down from antiquity and regarded with near veneration, is stored in innumerable places among the civilized worlds. Pristines themselves, however, are accorded no special status.

Proebis-12: the home of the swift-footed jarapine.

qacina: a name for ghost in the Dominion language.

Quyrend System: a system of the COE; also a major node in the COE's Information Dissemination Network (IDnet).

rapeworm: a life-form indigenous to Sciacca's World.

Rasia: transportee, Sciacca Penal Colony.

reave: see **epsense**.

Rehlaender: presiding judge, High Equity Court.

Retriever Class Frigate: a class of frigate built prior to the Ataman Wars.

Riem-Perez horizon: the technical name for the boundary cast by a hypershield.

Roche, Morgan: Commander, COE Intelligence.

Rufo, Linegar: renowned xenoarchaeologist.

Sabra: transportee, Sciacca Penal Colony.

Sciacca's World: the only habitable world of the Hutton-Luu System; once an agricultural planet of the Dominion, now a desert penal colony of the COE (Sciacca Penal Colony). Its ring of moonlets—the Soul—is owned and mined by DAOC Inc.

Scion War: the war in which the Sol Apotheosis Movement met its downfall at the hands of the Dominion, the Ataman Theocracy, and the Commonwealth of Empires, among others. The war was brought to an end in the 37th Millennium ('577 EN) when the leader of the combined military forces ordered an attack on the headquarters of the Movement, provoking their explosive suicide. See **Sol Apotheosis Movement**.

scutter: a small, swift spacegoing vessel with many uses, both military and civilian; also known as a "singleship."

Secession War: the conflict of '837 EN in which the Dato Bloc achieved its independence from the COE.

Second Ataman War: despite overextending its resources during the First Ataman War, the Ataman Theocracy remained aggressively expansionist until '442 EN, when attempts to annex neighboring systems belonging to the COE provoked a fierce retaliatory response. This time, the Commonwealth did not stop with surrender, but fought until it forced the Theocracy to submit completely and eventually adopted it as a province.

shelaigh: another word for ghost.

Shem: the original capital system of the COE.

Siegl-K: a brand of powered combat armor discontinued in '895 EN.

slow-jump: a common alternative to the anchor drive that utilizes similar technology. Most ships with an anchor drive can slow-jump if necessary. It is essentially a jump through hyperspace from any point in real space. A certain degree of kinetic energy is required before translation can be achieved, so ships must accelerate for some time beforehand. Even then, the hyperspace jump is short-lived, and the vessel emerges soon after (typically less than a light-year away from its departure point) with significantly less kinetic energy. The process must be repeated from scratch if another slow-jump is required. As a means of crossing interstellar space, it is inefficient and time-consuming, hence its name. Slow-jumping becomes increasingly non-viable closer to a gravity well, but more efficient as mass (of the traveling object) decreases.

Sol Apotheosis Movement: a quasi-religious organization devoted to the pursuit of Transcendence via genetic manipulation and biomodification that reached its peak and was destroyed in the 37th Millennium. Its fanatical followers were a source of unrest for decades, until an alliance formed among their neighbors dedicated to putting a stop to them. In '577 EN, at the climax of the Scion War, a flotilla of allied forces encircled their base, which the Movement destroyed in order to prevent its capture. The resulting explosion annihilated them as well, of course, but also decimated the flotilla. Of the four stations involved in the battle, only one survived, and that was severely damaged. So embarrassed was the alliance that the leaders of the day ordered the event stricken from history. They even closed the anchor point leading to the system to prevent anyone learning what occurred there. Nothing survived of the base, and the rest of the system is an unsalvageable ruin.

Sol System: uninhabited system in a nonaligned region near the Dato Bloc. Former home of the Sol Apotheosis Movement.

Sol Wunderkind: genetically modified clone warriors designed and bred by the Sol Apotheosis Movement.

Soul, the: the local name for the orbiting ring of mineral-rich moonlets girdling Sciacca's World.

Surin: a relatively minor Caste found in the regions surrounding the COE. The Surin exist in isolated clumps overseen by a governing body that guides rather than rules. They are social beings, yet ones fond of isolation, giving them a reputation for occasional aloofness. They are technically accomplished, especially in the biological sciences. In stature, they tend to be slight, and they have hair covering much of their bodies. It is occasionally speculated that they have reevolved from Low Caste status.

Surin Agora: the ruling body of the loosely knit Surin nation.

Szubetka Base: the Dato Bloc's equivalent of COE Intelligence HQ.

T'Bul: a Kesh slave trader.

TAN-C: a commercial cipher employed by COE Enforcement.

Teh, Sylvester: transportee, Sciacca Penal Colony.

Tepko: MiCom supervisor, Port Parvati.

Terms of Revocation: the treaty negotiated by the Dato Bloc and the COE that ended the Secession War.

Terrison: first officer, COEA *Midnight*.

Transcend: to break free of the constraints of mundane Humanity. A being or Caste that has Transcended typically has an extremely long lifespan and spreads its consciousness across a number of primary containers—such as neural nets, quantum data vats, and the like. Transcended entities, singular or collective, are referred to as High Human and accorded the highest status.

Transcendence: the state of being Transcended. Usually achieved when consciousness research and computer technology overlap, allowing an organic mind to be downloaded into an electronic vessel, thereby gaining the potential for unlimited growth.

***Transpicuous*, COEC:** a vessel once registered with the COE.

tri-rage: the local name for a weather pattern—a series of three violent dust storms—found on Sciacca's World.

Trinity: the world on which AIs are made in the region dominated by the COE. The AI factory was founded and is overseen by the High Human known as the Crescend.

Ul-æmato: the Dominion name of Houghton's Cross; roughly translatable as "Founder's Rock."

Undira Province: home of the Commonwealth of Empires' original capital.

Vasos: the Mbatan capital system.

Veden, Makil: an Eckandar Trade Axis citizen and Commerce Artel ex-delegate.

Vereine, Ataman Ana: the last leader of the Ataman Theocracy and the founder of the Andermahr Experiment.

Vexisen Republic, Greater: a nation home to the most ancient known Pristine remains, pushing Humanity's appearance in the wider galaxy back to half a million years.

vintu buds: the shoots of a plant native to Sciacca's World.

Walan Third: a COE world leased to the Commerce Artel.

war-dancer: a Surin ritual combatant.

Warfare Protocol: the code by which war is conducted within and between those nations that trade with the Commerce Artel.

Wars: notable conflicts include the Interdiction, Scion, Secession, Ghost, and First and Second Ataman Wars.

Xarodine: an epsense-inhibiting drug.

The International Bestseller

EVERGENCE II
THE DYING LIGHT

Long before the Commonwealth of Empires, long before
the Dato Bloc rebellion, the Sol Apotheosis Movement
created a group of super-soldiers to spread their agenda
throughout the galaxy. But something went dreadfully
wrong and entire star systems ceased to exist . . .

THE ENHANCED WARRIOR

Morgan Roche was an intelligence agent for the Commonwealth of Empires. But she has turned renegade to
determine the truth about the man called Adoni Cane. The
answer – that he was the last of the genetically enhanced
warriors called the Sol Wunderkind – shook the foundations
of her world.

Now Roche is faced with an even more frightening fact –
Cane may not be the last of his kind. A planet has vanished,
leaving only a terrible emptiness in space. Word spreads
across the galaxy: The Sol Wunderkind have returned.

Roche finds herself at the centre of the coming conflict, as she struggles to penetrate the layers of deception surrounding the origins of the super-soldiers – and the even deeper mystery surrounding the Artificial Intelligence called 'The Box' – an entity that seems to have a sinister agenda of its own.

ISBN 1–874082–36–7   £6.99

For more details visit our website: www.fprbooks.com

The International Bestseller

EVERGENCE III
THE DARK IMBALANCE

In the ruins of Sol System, Earth is no more. But aboard the great gathering of starships and space stations orbiting the still-burning sun live the remnants of mankind – now in terrible danger from an army of genetically enhanced warriors intent on destroying all of humanity.

THE CHOSEN ONE

Renegade intelligence agent Morgan Roche has been charged by the High Humans to protect mankind from the threat of the clone warriors. Pursuing one such warrior into Sol System, she strives to learn the true identity of the enemy, and with this how to defeat them. Roche looks for leadership to the Interim Emergency Pristine Council, on board the gigantic spaceship Phlegethon. But still she finds only strife and uncertainty. When the Phlegethon itself is drawn into the battle, Roche, weary and injured, must find the answers in her own way.

It is here, in the light of the star called Sol, that Morgan will learn the truth – about the artificial intelligence known as 'The Box', about the man who calls himself Adoni Cane, about the High Humans . . .

And about her destiny.

ISBN 1–874082–37–5   £6.99

For more details visit our website: www.fprbooks.com

Winner of the Aurealis Award for Best Science-Fiction Novel

SEAN WILLIAMS
METAL FATIGUE

In a dystopic world after a devastating world war, the American city of Kennedy has walled itself off from the decline of the former USA. Determined to continue as a functioning metropolis, Kennedy strictly patrols its boundaries and struggles to maintain the semblance of a modern city. But now, forty years after the war, Kennedy is in crisis. Technologies are failing and replacements and repairs are not forthcoming. It is within this atmosphere of technological and social stagnation that a new and terrible danger arrives as news of a Re-United States of America emerges and a RUSA that insists that Kennedy rejoin . . .

ISBN 1–874082–29–4   £16.99

For more information visit our website: www.fprbooks.com

From the International Bestselling Author

FRANK RYAN
THE SUNDERED WORLD

In the violent streets of a pre-apocalyptic London, Alan Duval is wounded by the poisoned blade of a ceremonial dagger. His life is saved by a mysterious feral girl. Suddenly, bewilderingly, he is transported from Earth to *Tír*, a strange land of magic and wonder, where he encounters the darkly comic Granny Ddhu. Treating his wounds, she confers on him the Oraculum of the Trídédana, the gateway to immense power and the first step in a seemingly impossible quest. The spiritual continent of Monisle has been at war for a thousand years with the forces of darkness. Duval's purpose is to defeat the Tyrant of the Wastelands. The survival of Earth, as much as war-ravaged Tír, depends upon his success . . .

So begins the epic fantasy, *The Sundered World,* in which Duval finds himself in a strange land of magic and wonder. He begins a great river journey through a spectacular wilderness, dominated by the spiritual forces of good and evil. Assisted by the Amazonian army of the Shee and the courage and skill of the Olhyiu the People of the Sea they sail the great Snow-melt River in the mystical Temple Ship.

HARDCOVER: ISBN 1–874082–23–5. £16.99
PAPERBACK: ISBN 1–874082–24–3. £6.99

For more details visit our website: www.fprbooks.com

A novel based on a true experience in the life of
the author . . .

FRANK RYAN

Taking Care
of Harry

Mylie O'Farrell is 20 years old. By day he works as a health
care assistant in a psychiatric unit in London. Off duty, he
indulges his interest in music, girls and wild nights on the
town with his friends, Janus and Rich, who share a
ramshackle house in Westminster they call 'The Palace'.
Everything changes when ex-army officer Harold Edward
Severn – Harry – is admitted to the Unit under a
Compulsory Detention Order after purportedly trying to
strangle his wife, Muriel. Harry, who is suffering from
depression, has no visitors so Mylie takes a special interest
in the cantankerous old man. Through a series of stormy if

humour-laden encounters, the young man and old man become friends, each allowing the other a glimpse into the deepest and most intimate secrets of their lives. This is also the story of the women in their lives, of Muriel and Elizabeth, Tabi and Pfion. As, little by little, a surrogate father-son relationship grows, Mylie realises that Harry is harbouring a secret terror and Mylie sets about bringing this into the open so that his friend can be set free. At times raucously comical, it is also suffused with great joy, sorrow, and a haunting sense of beauty – a remarkable story of the redemptive power of love.

ISBN 1–874082–35–9   £15.99

For more details visit our website: www.fprbooks.com

From the International Best-Selling Author

FRANK RYAN

THE THRILLER TRILOGY

ISBN 1-874082-26X ISBN 1-874082-01-4 ISBN 1-874082-25-1

£6.99 £5.99 £6.99

Described as "Magnificently tense" in a Sunday Times review, or "simply unputdownable" by media readers such as Tony Capstick and Ashley Franklin, each book is a complete thriller in itself but they are interlinked by plot and the life of the investigating detective, Sandy Woodings. Try one and you are unliklely to resist the temptation to read them all.

Available through your bookseller or post-free from Swift Publishers by direct mail or order through our website:
www.swiftpublishers.com